Harun smiled. **"Whatever mad**

a wishy-washy *

dear **kind of wife?"**

In all this time I've never seen him smile like that.

Right now, kidnapped and in this strange place, he was all she had—just as she was all he had—and the thought of losing this smiling man, now teasing her and caressing her hand, was unbearable.

"Well, maybe if you'd talked to me about what kind of wife you did want, I could answer that," she replied, in a light, fun tone. "But right now I'm rather clueless."

At that, he chuckled. "Yes, you're not the only one who's told me that I keep a little too much to myself."

Fascinated, she stared at his mouth. "In all this time, I've never heard you laugh."

She half expected him to make a cool retort—but instead, one end of his mouth quirked higher. "You think it took being abducted for me to show my true colors? Maybe, if you like it, we can arra

THE SHEIKH'S JEWEL

BY
MELISSA JAMES

First published in Great Britain 2012
by Mills & Boon, an imprint of Harlequin (UK) Limited,
Eton House, 18-24 Paradise Road, Richmond, Surrey TW9 1SR

© Lisa Chaplin 2012

ISBN: 978 0 263 89454 7
ebook ISBN: 978 1 408 97128 4

23-0812

Harlequin (UK) policy is to use papers that are natural, renewable and recyclable products and made from wood grown in sustainable forests. The logging and manufacturing processes conform to the legal environmental regulations of the country of origin.

Printed and bound in Spain
by Blackprint CPI, Barcelona

Melissa James is a born-and-bred Sydneysider. Wife and mother of three, and a former nurse, she fell into writing when her husband brought home an article about romance writers and suggested she try it—and she became hooked. Switching from romantic espionage to the family stories of the Mills & Boon® Cherish™ line was the best move she ever made.

Melissa loves to hear from readers—you can e-mail her at authormelissajames@yahoo.com.

To my editor, Bryony Green, with my deepest thanks
for all her help as I tried to make the deadline for
this book during an international move.

CHAPTER ONE

Sar Abbas, capital city of Abbas al-Din
Three years ago

'Is THIS a joke?'

Sitting straight-backed in an overstuffed chair, her body swathed in the black of deep mourning, Amber el-Qurib stared up at her father in disbelief. 'Please, Father, tell me you're trying to make me laugh.' But even as she pleaded she knew it was hopeless.

Her father, Sheikh Aziz of Araba Numara—Land of the Tiger—was also wearing mourning clothes, but his face was composed. He'd wept enough the first day, in the same shock as everyone else; but he hadn't cried since, apart from a few decorous tears at Fadi's funeral. 'Do you think I would make jokes about your future, Amber, or play with a decision that is so important to our nation?' His tone bordered on withering.

Yes, she ought to have known. Though he'd been a kind father, in all her life, she'd never heard her father make a joke about anything relating to the welfare of Araba Numara.

'My fiancé only died six weeks ago.' Amber forced the words out through a throat thick with weeks of tears. He'd been the co-driver for his younger brother Alim, in

just one rally. The Double Racing Sheikhs had caused a
great deal of mirth and media interest in Abbas al-Din,
as had the upcoming wedding.

Even now it seemed surreal. How could Fadi be
dead—and how could she marry his brother within
another month, as her father wanted? How could it
even be done while Alim was fighting for his life, with
second- and third-degree burns? 'It—it isn't decent,'
she said, trying to sound strong but, as ever when with
her father, she floundered under the weight of her own
opinion. Was she right?

And when her father sighed, giving her the long-
suffering look she'd always hated—it made her feel
selfish, or like a silly girl—she knew she'd missed
something, as usual. 'There are some things more important than how we appear to others. You understand
how it is, Amber.'

She did. Both their countries had fallen into uproar
after Sheikh Fadi's sudden death in a car wreck. The
beloved leader of Abbas al-Din had been lost before he
could marry and father a legitimate son, and Amber's
people had lost a union that was expected to bring closer
ties to a nation far stronger and wealthier than theirs.

It was vital at this point that both nations find stability. The people needed hope: for Araba Numara, that
they'd have that permanent connection to Abbas al-Din,
and Fadi's people needed to know the el-Kanar family
line would continue.

She swiped at her eyes again. Damn Fadi! He'd
risked his life a week before their wedding, knowing
he didn't want her and she didn't want him—but thousands of marriages had started with less than the respect
and liking they'd had for one another. They could have
worked it out—but now the whispers were circulating.

She'd endured some impertinent insinuations, from the maids to Ministers of State. That much she could bear, if only she didn't have doubts of her own, deep-held fears that woke her every night.

She'd known he wasn't happy—was deeply unhappy—at the arranged marriage; but *had* Fadi risked death to avoid marrying her?

Certainly neither of them had been in love, but that wasn't uncommon. Fadi had been deeply in love with his mistress, the sweet widow who'd borne his son. But with probably the only impulsive decision he'd ever made, he'd left his country leaderless in a minute. At the moment Alim, his brother and the remaining heir, was still fighting for his life.

'Amber?' her father asked, his tone caught between exasperation and uncertainty. 'The dynasty here must continue, and very quickly. We only gain from the mother of the dynasty being one of our daughters.'

'Then let it continue with someone else! Haven't I done enough?'

'Who do you suggest? Maya is not yet seventeen. Nafisah is but fourteen, and Amal twelve. Your cousins are of similar age to them.' Her father made a savage noise. 'You are the eldest, already here, and bound to the el-Kanar family. They are obligated by their ancient law on brides to care for you, and find you a husband within the family line. Everything—tradition, law, honour and the good of your family—demands that you accept this offer.'

Shamed but still furious, Amber kept her mouth tightly closed. Why must all this fall on her shoulders? She wanted to cry out, *I'm only nineteen!*

Why did some get responsibilities in life, and others all the fun? Alim had shrugged off his responsibilities to the nation for years, chasing fame and wealth on the racing circuit while Fadi and the youngest brother— what was his name again?—had done all the work. Yes, Alim was famous around the world, and had brought so much wealth to the nation with his career in geological surveys and excavation.

And then she realised what—or *who* it was she could be turning down. Even though a sudden marriage repulsed her sense of what felt right in her grief for the man she'd cared for deeply as a friend, the thought of *who* she must be marrying didn't repulse her at all.

Her father laid a hand on her shoulder. It was only with the long years of training that she managed not to shrug off the rare gesture of affection, knowing it was only given to make her stop arguing. For women of her status, any emotion was a luxury one only indulged in among the safety of other women, or not at all if one had the necessary pride. 'You know how it is, Amber. We *need* this marriage. One brother or another, what does it matter to you? You barely knew Fadi before your engagement was agreed upon. You only came to stay here two months before he died, and most of the time he was working or gone.'

Blushing, Amber turned her head, looking at the ground to the left of her feet. *Such a beautiful rug,* she thought inconsequentially; but no matter what she looked at, it didn't block out the memory of where Fadi had gone whenever he had spare time—to his mistress. And always he'd come back with Rafa's smell on his skin, some mumbled apologies and yet another promise he'd never see Rafa again when they were married: a promise given with heartbreak in his eyes.

Amber felt the shadows of the past envelop her. She alone knew where the fault lay with Fadi's death. Sweet, kind, gentle Fadi had always done the right thing, including agreeing to marry another ruler's daughter for political gain, when he was deeply in love with an unsuitable commoner, a former housemaid…and Amber, too, had feelings for another, if only from afar. And nobody knew it but the three people whose lives were being torn apart.

She knew Fadi would never wish her harm, but if it had been Amber who'd died suddenly, it would have set him free to be with Rafa—at least for a little while, until the next arranged political marriage.

She truly grieved for the loss of the gentle-hearted ruler, as she would grieve for any friend lost. Fadi had understood her feelings and sympathised with her, was like the moon's sweet light in her darkness. So—was it awful of her to feel this sudden little thrill that her wayward heart's feelings were no longer forbidden?

Fadi, I did care for you. I'm so sorry, but you're the only one who'd understand…

'I'm still in deep mourning, and you expect me to marry his brother while he's still in hospital with second- and third-degree burns? Won't that look—well, rather desperate on our part?' she mumbled, wishing she had something better to say, wishing she didn't feel quite so excited. Hoping to heaven her father wouldn't see it on her face. 'Can't you ask Alim if he'd be willing to wait a few months for the wedding—?'

'You will not be marrying Alim,' her father interrupted her bluntly.

Amber's head shot up. *'What?'*

'I'm sorry, my dear,' her father said quietly. 'Alim disappeared from the hospital last night, unequivocally refusing both Fadi's position and Fadi's bride. I doubt he'll return for a long time, if ever.'

Amber almost snarled—almost. Women of her station didn't snarl, not even when the man she—she *liked* had just run out on her; but she managed to hang onto her self-control. 'Where did he go? How did he manage it?'

'Within hours of waking, Alim used his private jet and his medical team from the racing circuit to help him transfer to a private facility—we think he went somewhere in Switzerland. He still needs a lot of graft work on his burns, but he made it obvious that he won't return here when it's done.'

'He must have been desperate to escape from me, leaving hospital when he's at death's door,' she muttered, fighting off a sudden jolt of queasiness in her stomach.

'I doubt it was a personal rejection, my dear. He hardly knew you. I think it was perhaps more of—ah, a matter of principle, or a reaction made in grief.' Her father slanted her a look of semi-apology; so he was capable of embarrassment, at least. 'I find it hard to blame him, after the part he played in Fadi's death… imagine him waking up to find Fadi's skin on his body. He must have felt he'd taken enough from his brother— life, skin…it must be horrifying enough, but wedding and bedding Fadi's bride on top of all that must have felt as if he'd done it all on purpose.'

'Indeed,' she agreed, but with a trace of bitterness. Surely this day couldn't get any worse?

'Since you won't ask, I'll tell you. The youngest brother Harun has taken up the position as Hereditary Sheikh, and has agreed also to become your husband.'

The swirling winds of change had come right from the sun, scorching her to her core. 'Of course he has!' Amber didn't know she spoke aloud, the fury of rejection boiling over. 'So having been rejected by brothers one and two, I'm expected to—to wed and bed brother number three with a smile? There are limits to the amount of humiliation I must accept, surely, Father?'

'You will accept whatever I arrange for you, Amber.' His voice now was pure ice. 'And you should be grateful that I have given such thought to your marriage.'

'Oh, such thought indeed, Father! Why not send me to the princess pound? Because that's what I've become to you, isn't it—a dog, a piece of property returned for you to find a good home and husband elsewhere? Find another owner for Amber because *we* don't want her back.'

'Stop it,' her father said sharply. 'You're a beautiful woman. Many men have wanted to marry you, but I chose the el-Kanar brothers because they are truly good men.'

'Oh, yes, I know that well,' she mocked, knowing Father would punish her for this unprecedented outburst later, but not caring. 'Unfortunately for me, it seems they're good men who'd do anything to avoid me.' She spoke as coldly as she could—anything to hide the tears stinging her eyes and the huge lump in her throat. Alim, the wild and dashing Racing Sheikh, had risked his recovery, his very life to get away from her. As far as insults went, it outranked Fadi's by a million miles. 'Am I so repulsive, Father? What's wrong with me?'

'I see you are in need of relieving your, ah, feelings,' her father said with a strong streak of cold disapproval that she had *feelings* to vent. 'But we are not home, Amber. Royal women do not scream or make emotional outbursts.'

'I can't believe the last remaining brother in the dynasty is willing to risk it,' she pushed in the stinging acid of grief and humiliation without relief. 'Perhaps you should offer him one of my sisters instead, because it seems the el-Kanar men are allergic to me.'

'The Lord Harun has expressed complete willingness to marry you, Amber,' her father said in quiet rebuke.

'Oh, how noble is Brother Number Three, to take the unwanted responsibilities of his older brothers, nation and wife alike, when the other just can't face it!'

'Amber,' her father said sharply. 'That's enough. Your future husband has a name. You will not shame him, or our family, in this manner. He's lost enough!'

She knew what was expected of her. 'I'm sorry, Father. I will behave,' she said dully. She dragged a breath in and out, willing calm, some form of decorum. 'That was uncalled for. I have nothing against the Lord—um, Harun, and I apologise, Father.'

'You should apologise.' Her father's voice was cold with disapproval. 'Harun was only eight when his father died in the plane crash, and his mother died three months later. For the past six weeks he's been grieving for a brother who had been more like a father to him, and he couldn't stop working long enough to stay at the hospital while the only brother he has left, his only close living relative, was fighting for his life. With so many high-ranking families wanting to take over the sudden wealth in Abbas al-Din, Harun had to assume the sheikh's position and run the country in Alim's name, not knowing if Alim would live or die. Now Harun's been left completely alone with the responsibility of running the nation and marrying you, and all this while he's in deepest mourning. He's lost his entire family. Is it so much to ask that you could stop mocking him, be a woman and help him in his time of greatest need?'

Amber felt the flush of shame cover her face.

Whatever she'd lost, Harun had by far the worst suffering of them all. 'No, it isn't. I'm truly sorry, Father. It's just that—well, he's so quiet,' she tried to explain, feeling the inadequacy of her words. 'He never says anything to me apart from good morning or goodnight. He barely even looks at me. He's a stranger, a complete stranger, and now I must marry him in a month's time? Can't we have a little time to know each other first—just a few months?'

'It must be now,' her father said, his voice sad, and she searched his face. He had a way of making her feel guilty without trying, but this time he seemed sincere. 'The sharks are circling Harun—you know how unstable the entire Gulf region has been the past two years. The el-Shabbat family ruled hundreds of years ago, until Muran's madness led to the coup that gave power to Aswan, the greatest of the el-Kanar clan, two hundred and fifty years ago. The el-Shabbat leaders believe the el-Kanar clan are interlopers, and if they ever had a chance to take control of the army and kill the remaining family members, it is now.'

Amber's hand lifted to her mouth. Lost in her own fog of grief, she'd had no idea things were so bad. 'They will kill Lord Harun?'

He nodded. 'And Alim, too, while he's still so weak. It's a good thing nobody knows exactly where he went. All it would take is one corrupt doctor or nurse and a dose of poison into his IV bag, and the el-Shabbats will rule Abbas al-Din once more—a nation with far greater wealth and stability than they ever knew while they were in power.'

'I see,' she said quietly.

'And we need this alliance, my dear daughter. You were but one of twenty well-born girls offered to Fadi—

and to Harun—in the past few years. We are the far poorer, less stable nation, and yet they chose alliance with our family and nation. It's a blessing to our nation I hardly expected; it's given our people hope. And I must say, in my dealings with all three brothers, Harun is the man I'd have chosen for you if I'd had the choice.'

His voice softened on the last sentence, but Amber barely noticed. 'So the contract has been signed,' she said dully. 'I have no choice in this at all.' Her only decision was to go down fighting, or accept her future with grace.

'No, my dear, you don't.' The words were gentle, but inflexible. 'It has been inevitable from the moment the Lord Harun was made aware of his duty towards you.'

She pressed her lips together hard, fighting unseemly tears. Perhaps she should be grateful that the Lord Harun wasn't leaving her to face her public shame— but another man willing to marry her from duty alone left her stomach churning. At least she'd known and liked Fadi. 'But he doesn't even look at me. He never talks to me. I never know what he's thinking or feeling about anything.' *Including me.* 'How am I to face this—this total stranger in the marriage bed, Father? Can you answer me that?'

'It's what many women have done for thousands of years, including your mother and my grandmother Kahlidah, the nation's heroine you've always admired so much. She was only seventeen when she wed my grandfather—another stranger—and within a year, eighteen, pregnant and a new widow, she stopped the invasion of Araba Numara, ruling the nation with strength and wisdom until my father was old enough to take over. Do as she had to, and grow a backbone, child! What is your fear for one night, compared to what Harun faces, and alone?' her father shot back.

Never had her father spoken to her with such contempt and coldness. She drew another breath and released it as she willed strength into her heart. 'I'll do my duty, of course, Father, and do my best to support Lord Harun in all he faces. Perhaps we can find mutual friendship in our loss and our need.'

Father smiled at her, and patted her hand. 'That's more like my strong Amber. Harun is a truly good man, for all his quiet ways. I know—' he clearly hesitated, and Amber writhed inside, waiting for what she'd give anything for him *not* to say '—I know you…admired Lord Alim. What young woman wouldn't admire the Racing Sheikh, with his dashing ways, his wins on the racing circuit worldwide, and the power and wealth he's brought to this region?'

'Please stop,' she murmured in anguish. 'Please, Father, no more.'

But he went on remorselessly. 'Amber, my child, you are so young—too young to understand that the men who change history are not always the Alexanders, or even the Alims,' he added, with a strained smile. 'The real heroes are usually unsung, making their contributions in silence. I believe Lord Harun is one of them. My advice is for you to look at the man I've chosen for you, and ask yourself why I brought this offer to him, not even wanting to wait for Alim's recovery. I think that, if you give Harun a chance, you'll find you and he are very well suited. You can have a good life together, if you will put your heart and soul behind your vows.'

'Yes, Father,' Amber said, feeling dull and spiritless at the thought of being *well suited* and having *a good life,* when she'd had a moment's dream of marrying the man she—well, she thought she could have loved, given time…

At that moment, a movement behind the door caught her eye. *Damn* the officious staffers and inquisitive servants, always listening in, looking for more gossip to spread far and wide! She lifted her chin and sent her most icy stare to the unknown entity at the door. She felt the presence move back a step, and another.

Good. She hoped they'd run far away. If she must deal with these intrusive servants, they'd best know the calibre of the woman who was to be their future mistress—and mistress she'd be.

'If you wouldn't mind, Father, I'd like to—to have a little time alone,' she said quietly.

'You still grieve for Fadi. You're a good girl.' Her father patted her hand, and left the room by the private exit between their rooms.

The moment the connecting door closed, Amber said coldly, 'If I discover any of you are listening in or I hear gossip repeated about this conversation, I will ensure the lot of you are dismissed without a reference. Is that clear?'

It was only when she heard the soft shuffling of feet moving away that Amber at last fell to her bed and cried. Cried again for the loss of a gentle-hearted friend, cried for the end of an unspoken dream—and she cried for the nightmare facing her.

Frozen two steps back from the partially open door to the rooms of state allotted to the Princess Amber, the man who was the subject of his guests' recent discussion had long since dropped the hand he'd held up to knock. Harun el-Kanar's upbringing hadn't included eavesdropping on intimate conversations—and had he not frozen in horror, he wouldn't have heard Amber so desperately trying to get out of marrying him. He wouldn't have seen that repellent look, like a shard of ice piercing his skin.

So now he knew his future wife's opinion of him… and it was little short of pure revulsion. Why did it even surprise him?

Turning sharply away, he strode towards the sanctuary of his rooms. He needed peace, a few minutes to think—

'Lord Harun, there is a call from the Prince al-Hassan of Saudi regarding the deal with Emirates Oil. He is most anxious to speak with you about the Lord Alim's recent find of oil.'

'Of course, I will come now,' he answered quietly, and walked with his personal assistant back to his office.

When the call was done, his minister of state came in. 'My Lord, in the absence of the Lord Alim, we need your immediate presence in the House for a swearing-in ceremony. For the stability of the country, this must be done as soon as possible. I know you will understand the anxiety of your people to have this reassurance that you are committed to the ongoing welfare of Abbas al-Din.'

His assistant raced in with his robes of state, helping Harun into them before he could make a reply.

During the next five hours, as he sat and stood and bowed and made a speech of acceptance of his new role, none of those hereditary leaders sensed how deeply their new sheikh grieved for a brother nine years older. Fadi had been more like a father to him.

Could any of them see how utterly alone he was now, since Alim's disappearance? He hid it behind the face of years of training, calm and regal. They needed the perfect sheikh, and they'd have one for as long as it was needed. Members of the ruling family were trained almost from birth—they must display no need beyond the privilege of serving their people. But during the ceremony, in moments when he didn't have complete control of his mind, Harun had unbidden visions: of eyes as warm as melted honey, and skin to match; a mouth with a smile she'd smother behind her hand when someone was being pompous or ridiculous, hiding her dimples; her flowing dark hair, and her walk, like a hidden dance.

Every time he pushed it—her—away. He had to be in command.

As darkness fell over the city he sat at his desk, eating a sandwich. He'd left the state dinner within minutes of the announcement of the royal engagement, pleading necessary business as a reason not to endure Amber's company. Or, more accurately, for her not to endure his company a moment longer than she needed to. He'd seen the look of surprise and slight confusion on her face, but again, he pushed it away.

His food slowly went stale as the mountain of papers slowly dwindled. He read each one carefully before signing, while dealing with necessary interruptions, the phone calls from various heads of state and security personnel.

In quiet moments, her face returned to his vision, but he always forced it out again.

Okay, so Amber was right; he hadn't looked at her much. What she didn't know was that he hadn't *dared* look at her. For weeks, months, he'd barely looked at her, never spoken beyond politeness, because he'd been too lost in shame that he hungered night and day for his brother's intended wife. Even her name had filled him with yearning: a precious jewel.

But never until yesterday had he dared think that she could ever become *his* jewel.

Lost and alone with his grief, unable to feel anything but pain, he'd been dazed when, out of nowhere, Sheikh Aziz wished him to become Amber's husband. He hadn't been able to say no. So close to breaking, he'd come to her today, touched by something he hadn't known in months, years…*hope*. Hope that even if she didn't feel the same, he wouldn't have to face this nightmare alone. Could it be possible that they might find comfort in one another, to stand together in this living death…?

And the overheard conversation was his reward for being so stupid. Of course Amber wanted Alim, his dashing brother, the nation's hero. As her father had said, what woman wouldn't want Alim?

A dream of twelve hours had now become his nightmare. There was no way out. She was stuck with him, the last option, the sheikh by default who didn't even want to be here.

What a fool. Hadn't he learned long ago that dreams were for other people? For Fadi, there had been his destiny as the next sheikh; for Alim, there was the next racing car, the next glamorous destination, the jets and the women and the adoration of his family and his nation. *Habib Abbas:* Alim was the country's beloved lion, their financial saviour since he'd found oil deep beneath the water of their part of the Gulf, and natural gas in the desert.

His parents would have been proud of him. They'd always known Alim was destined for greatness, as Fadi had said so many times. *We're all so proud of you, Alim.*

Alim, the golden child. Of course he had Amber's heart—and of course he didn't want it. He'd thrown her away without a thought, just as he'd thrown his brother into his role of sheikh. He'd left them both to their fate without even a farewell or reason.

And yet, he still loved Alim; like everyone else in the country, he'd do anything for his brother. Alim knew that well, which was why he'd just disappeared without a word. 'Harun will do it better than I could, anyway,' had always been his casually tossed words when Fadi had needed him for one duty or another. 'He's good at the duty thing.'

Harun supposed he was good at it—he'd been raised to think his duty was sacred.

I never know what he's thinking or feeling. To her, he was Brother Number Three, nothing but an obligation, a means to enrich her country. She was only willing to marry him after being bullied and brought to a sense of pity for his grief by her father.

No, he had no choice but to marry her now—but he had no taste for his brother's unwanted leftovers. He'd dealt with enough broken hearts of the women who'd been rejected by Alim over the years, calling the palace, even offering themselves to him in the faint hope that he had the power to change Alim's mind.

Not this time. Never again. I might have to marry her, but I'll be damned if I touch her.

'It's lust, just lust,' he muttered, hard. Lust he could both deal with, and live without. Anything but the thought of taking her while she stared at the ceiling, wishing he were Alim—

His stomach burning, he found he was no longer hungry, and threw the rest of the sandwich into the garbage.

It was long past midnight before Harun at last

reached his rooms. He sent his hovering servants away and sat on his richly canopied bed, ripping the thin mosquito curtain. With an impatient gesture he flung it away; but if he made a noise, the bodyguards watching him from one of the five vantage points designed to protect the sheikh would come running in. So he sat looking out into the night as if nothing were wrong, and grieved in dry-eyed silence.

Fadi, my brother, my father! Allah, I beg you to let Alim live and return to me.

Three days later, the armed rebel forces of the el-Shabbat family invaded Sar Abbas.

CHAPTER TWO

Eight weeks later

'HABIB Numara! Harun, our beloved tiger, our Habib Numara!'

Riding at the head of a makeshift float—two tanks joined by tent material and filled with flowers—Harun smiled and waved to the people lining the streets of Sar Abbas. Each cheering girl or woman in the front three rows of people threw another flower at him as he passed. The flowers landed on the float filling his nostrils until the sweet scent turned his stomach and the noise of the people's shouting left him deafened.

Still he smiled and waved; but what he wouldn't give to be in the quiet of his room reading a book. How had Alim ever endured this adulation, this attention for so many years? Fighting for his country, his men and repelling the el-Shabbat invasion—being wounded twice during battle, and having his shoulder put back in place after the dislocation—had been a positive relief in comparison to this.

You'll never be your brother.

Yet again his parents had been proven right. No, he'd never be like Alim.

As the float and the soldiers and the cheering throng

reached the palace he looked up. His future father-in-law stood beside his bride on the upper balcony, waving to him, looking proud and somehow smug. He supposed he'd find out why when he got some time.

Amber stood like a reed moving in the wind as she watched his triumphal entry. She had a small frown between her brows, a slight tilt to her head, as if trying to puzzle out something. As if she saw his discomfort and sympathised with him.

He almost laughed at the absurdity of the thought. She who loved Alim of racing fame and fortune, the real sheikh? *Right, Harun. She sees nothing in you but the replacement in her life and bed she'd do anything to avoid.*

She half lifted a hand. A smile trembled on her lips. Mindful of the people, he smiled and waved to his bride, giving her the public recognition and honour they expected.

It was all she wanted from him.

At last the wedding night she'd dreaded was upon her.

With a fast-beating heart, Amber stood in the middle of her bridal suite, with unbound hair, perfumed skin and a thin, creamy negligee over her nude body. So scared she could barely breathe, she awaited the arrival of her new husband.

The last of the fussing maids checked her hands and feet to be sure they were soft enough, perfumed to the right scent. Amber forced herself to stand still and not wave them off in irritation—or, worse, give in to her fears and ask someone, anyone what she must do to please a man she'd still barely spoken to. The way she felt right now, even the maid would do—for her mother had told her nothing. As she'd dressed her daughter for the marriage bed, the only words of advice to Amber had been, *Let your husband show you the way, and though it will hurt at first and you will bleed in proof of your virginity, smile and take joy in your woman's duty. For today, you become a woman.* And with a smile Amber didn't understand, she'd left the room.

In the Western world, girls apparently grew up knowing how to please a man, and themselves; but she'd been kept in almost total ignorance. In her world, it was a matter of pride for the husband to teach his wife what took place in the bed. No books were allowed on the subject, no conversation by the servants on the threat of expulsion, and the Internet was strictly patrolled.

She only wished she knew what to do…

More than that, she wished she knew him at all—that he could have taken an hour out of his busy schedule to get to know her.

In the end, she'd had the few months' wait she'd asked for, but it hadn't been for her sake, nor had they had any time to know each other better. The el-Shabbat family hadn't reckoned with Harun's swift action when they'd invaded the city. Handing the day-to-day work to his intended father-in-law, Harun had taken control of the army personally. Leading his men into battle using both the ancient and modern rules of warfare he'd learned since boyhood, Harun had gained the adoration of his people by being constantly in the thick of the fierce fighting, expecting and giving no quarter. The whispers in women's rooms were that he bore new scars on his body: badges of the highest honour. He'd spent no more than a night in the hastily erected Army hospital. Every time he'd been injured, come morning he'd returned to the battle without a word.

Within eight weeks he'd completely quelled the

bellion. By forgiving the followers of the el-Shabbat family and letting them return to their homes with little if any punishment and no public embarrassment, he'd earned their loyalty, his new title—and Amber's deep respect. By assuming control of the el-Shabbat fortune and yet caring for the women and children the dead enemy had left behind, he'd earned the love as well as the respect of his people.

If Alim was their beloved lion, Harun had become *Habib Numara,* their beloved tiger. 'It's a good omen for his marriage, with his bride coming from Araba Numara,' the servants said, smiling at her. 'It will be a fruitful union blessed by God.'

And in the weeks since then, as he'd put down the final shadows of the rebellion and with rare political skill brought together nation and people once more, Harun had had less time for her than Fadi had done. In fact he still barely spoke to her at all; but though he'd never said a word about his heroism on the field, he'd earned Amber's deep, reluctant admiration. If she still harboured regrets over Alim's disappearance, Harun's name now had the power to make her heart beat faster. He'd proved his worthiness without a word of bragging. She was ready to endure what she must tonight, and become the mother of his children.

As the main door opened the maid rushed to leave the room.

Sick to her stomach with nerves, she turned to where he stood—and her breath caught. It was strange, but it was only on the day she'd seen him returning to Sar Abbas as a national hero that she'd truly taken in his deep resemblance to Alim. A quiet, serious version, perhaps, but as, in his army uniform, he smiled and waved to the people cheering him in the streets, she'd seen his face as if for the first time.

Now, she struggled not to stare at him. So handsome and strong in his groom's finery, yet so dark and mysterious with those glittering forest-green eyes. She groped with one hand to the bedpost to gain balance suddenly lacking in her knees. He was the man who'd come home a hero. He was—magnificent. He was hers.

'None of you will listen or stand nearby,' he snapped at the walls, and she was filled with gratitude when she heard the shuffle of many feet moving away.

Lost in awe, she faltered in her traditional greeting, but bowed in the traditional show of deep respect. 'M-my husband, I...' She didn't know how to go on, but surely he'd understand how she felt?

Without a change of expression from the serious, cool appraisal, he closed the door behind him, and offered her a brief smile. 'Sit down, please, Amber.'

Grateful for his understanding, she dropped to the bed, wondering if he'd take it as a sign, or was she being too brazen? She only wished she knew how to go on.

He gave her a slow, thoughtful glance, taking in every inch of her, and she squirmed in embarrassment. Her heart beat like a bird trying to escape its cage as she waited for Harun to come to her, to kiss her or however it was this thing began. 'Well?' she demanded in a haughty tone, covering her rush of nerves with a show of pride, showing him she was worthy of him: a princess to the core. 'Do I pass your inspection, *Habib Numara?*'

For a moment, she thought Harun might actually smile as he hadn't done since the hero's return. There was a telltale glimmer in his eyes she'd noticed when he was in a rare, relaxed moment. Then, just as she was about to smile back, it vanished. 'You have to know you're a beautiful woman, Amber. Exquisite, in fact.'

'Thank you,' she whispered, her voice losing its power. He thought her exquisite? Something inside her melted—

He turned from her, and, drawing out a thin wreath of papers from a fold of his robe, sat at her desk. 'This should cover the necessary time. I forgot my pen, though. Do you happen to have one handy, my dear?'

Her mouth fell open as he began perusing whatever work he'd brought with him. He'd brought work to their wedding night? 'In the second drawer,' she responded, feeling incredibly stupid, but what else could she say?

'Thank you,' he replied, his tone absent. He pulled out one of her collection of pens and began reading, scrolling up and down the pages with his finger, and making notes in the margins.

She blinked, blinked again, unable to believe what she was seeing. 'Harun…' Then she faltered to a stop.

After at least ten seconds, he stopped writing. 'Hmm…? Did you say something, Amber?' His tone was the cold politeness of a man who didn't want to be disturbed.

'Yes, I did,' she retorted, furious. At least five different things leaped to her mouth. *What do you mean by covering the necessary time? What is it with the el-Kanar men? This is our wedding night!*

Don't you want me?

But at the thought of asking it, her confused outrage turned cold inside her, making her ache. *Why should this brother want me when the other two didn't?*

What's wrong with me?

But what came from her mouth, born of the stubborn pride that was her backbone in a world where she'd had

beautiful clothes and surroundings but as much control
over her destiny as a piece of furniture or a child's doll,
she stated coldly, 'If there's no blood on the sheet tomorrow, the servants will talk. It will be around both
our countries in hours. People will blame me, or worse,
assume I wasn't a virgin. Will you shame me that way,
when I've done nothing wrong?'

His back stiffened for a moment.

Amber felt the change in the air, words hovering on
his lips. How she knew that about him, when they'd still
barely spoken, she had no idea, but whatever he'd been
about to say vanished in an instant.

'I see,' he said slowly, with only a very slight weari-
ness in the inflection. 'Of course they will.'

He stood and stripped off his *kafta,* revealing his
nakedness, and Amber's heart took wings again.
Magnificent? Even with the scars across his back and
stomach he was breathtaking, a battle-hardened warrior sheathed in darkest gold, masculinely beautiful and
somehow terrifying. Involuntarily she shrank back on
the bed, wishing she'd found another place to sit. *I'm
not ready for this...please, Harun, be gentle with me...*

She couldn't breathe, watching him come to her.

But he walked around the bed as if she weren't there.
He didn't touch her, didn't even *look* at her. At the other
side of the bed, he put something down, and used both
his hands to sweep all the rose petals from the coverlet.
'I don't like the smell. Cloying.'

'I like it,' she said, halfway between defiance and
stupidity.

He shrugged and stopped brushing them away. 'It's
your bed.' Then he lifted the thing he'd put on the bed: a
ceremonial knife, beautifully scrolled in gold and silver.

'What's that...Harun...?' Her jaw dropped; she

watched in utter disbelief as he made a small cut deep in his armpit, and allowed a few drops of blood to fall into his cupped palm.

'What—what are you…?' Realising she was gaping, she slammed her mouth shut.

'Making a cut where it won't be seen and commented on,' he said in a voice filled with quiet irony. 'Thus I'm salvaging your pride in the eyes of others, my dear wife.'

'I don't understand.' Beyond pride now or remembering any of her instructions for tonight, she gazed at him in open pleading. 'What are you doing?'

He sighed. 'As you said, virgins bleed, Amber. It's my duty to ensure that your reputation isn't ruined. Pull the coverings down, please, and quickly, before the blood drops on the rug. Imagine what the servants would make of that.' His tone was filled with understated irony.

She closed her mouth and swallowed, and then swivelled around in the bed to pull the covers down.

She watched as he dripped blood into his other hand. 'It seems enough, I think,' he said after thirty seconds. Her husband of six hours looked at her. 'Which side of the bed do the servants know you prefer?'

Torn between shock and fury born of humiliation, she pointed.

'Thank you.' As casually as if he'd spilled water, he smeared his blood on the bed. Then he walked into the bathroom; she heard the sound of running water.

When he came out he returned to the desk, picked up his bridegroom's clothing, pulled it back over his head and let it fall to his feet. He sat down again, reading, scrolling and making notes.

Not knowing what else to do, she sat on the bed,

drawing her knees under her chin, her arms wrapped tight around them. And for the next hour, she watched him work in growing but helpless fury.

Why won't you touch me? she wanted to scream. *Why don't you want to touch me? What did I do wrong?*

But she'd made an innocent scene with Fadi when it was obvious he was running from her, and he'd told her about Rafa. *I can't marry her, but I love her, Amber.*

She'd made another scene before her father when Alim fled the country rather than marry her. *He has rejected both Fadi's position, and Fadi's bride.*

She was already the bad-luck bride in the eyes of the servants and the people—but if they found out about this, she'd never recover. Fadi had loved another; Alim fled the country—but neither of them had made the rejection this obvious.

Asking him why would only humiliate her further.

After a while, her husband said without looking at her, 'It would be best if you went to sleep, Amber. It's been a very long day for you.'

She lay back on the sheets, avoiding the smeared blood—but she kept watching him work out of a stubborn refusal to obey anything he asked of her. If he wasn't going to be a real husband, it relieved her of the necessity to be any kind of wife.

Suddenly she wondered how long a day it had been for him. How long had he been working—right up until he'd dressed for the wedding? During the ceremony and after he'd kissed her hand, touched her face with a smile, played the loving bridegroom—for the cameras and the people, no doubt. Now he was working again. Barely two months ago, Harun fought for his life, for the sake of a nation that didn't belong to him.

Did he ever stop, and just be a normal man?

Harun, just look at me, be kind to me for a minute.
I'm your bride, she wanted to say, but nothing emerged
from her mouth. She was lying on their marriage bed,
his for the taking in this shimmering piece of nothing,
and he was doing stupid paperwork.

He didn't even look at her, just as he never had before.

As a soldier, they said, he'd fought with a savagery
beyond anything they'd seen before. Like Fadi, had he
done it to escape her? What a shame for him that he'd
lived, forced into taking a wife he clearly didn't want
in the least.

She hated him. She hated this bed…and she couldn't
stand this ridiculous situation any more.

Pulling her hair into a messy knot, she got to her
feet, stalked into the bathroom, shredded the stupid
negligee in her haste to take it off, and scrubbed away
all traces of perfume and make-up under the stinging
heat of the shower.

Using the pumice stone she scrubbed at her skin
until it was raw, and took minimal comfort in the fact
that Harun would never know how he'd made her cry.

But as she scrubbed herself to bleeding point she
vowed she'd *never* make a fool of herself for an el-
Kanar man again. No, she'd show Harun nothing, no
emotion at all. She'd be a queen before him at all times,
damn it! And one day he'd come to her, on his knees,
begging for her…

If only she could make herself believe it.

CHAPTER THREE

Three Years Later

'MY LADY, the Lord Harun has requested entrance!'

Startled, Amber dropped the papers she was reading and stared at her personal maid, Halala. Barely able to believe the words she'd heard, she couldn't catch her breath. All the ladies were in a flutter of excitement… and hope, no doubt.

She could almost hear the whispers from mouth to ear, flying around the palace. *Will he come to her bed at last?*

Her cheeks burned with embarrassment at the common knowledge within the palace of the state of her marriage, the tag of bad-luck bride she couldn't overcome, but she answered calmly enough. 'Please show my husband in, and leave us. I need not remind you of what will happen if you listen in,' she added sternly, holding each of her ladies-in-waiting with her gaze until they nodded.

As the room emptied she smoothed down her dress, her hair, while her pulse beat hard in her throat. What could he want? And she had no time to change out of one of her oldest, most comfortable dresses—

Then Harun entered her rooms, tall and broad-shouldered, with skin like dark honey and a tiny cleft in his chin; she'd long ago become accustomed to the fact that her husband was a quiet, serious version of her dashing first crush. But today his normally withdrawn if handsome face was lit from within; his forest-at-dusk eyes were alive with shimmering emotion, highlighting his resemblance to Alim more than ever. 'Good morning, Amber,' he greeted her not quite formally, his intense eyes not quite looking at her.

He doesn't care what I'm wearing, Amber thought in sullen resentment. How foolish she'd been for wishing to look pretty for him, even for a minute. *I don't even know why I'm surprised. Or why it still hurts after all this time.*

Why had her father wanted her to wed this—this robot? He wasn't a man. He was barely human…at least not where she was concerned. But, oh, she'd heard the rumours that he was man enough for another.

She tamped down the weakness of anger, finding strength in her pride. 'You need something, My Lord?' she asked, keeping her tone meek, submissive, but just as formal and distant as his. 'It must be important for you to actually come inside my rooms. I believe this is the first time you've come here willingly in three years.'

He looked at her then—with a cold flash in his eyes that made her feel like a worm in dirt. 'Since you're taking the gloves off, my wife, we both know it's the first time I've been in here willingly at all, not merely since our wedding night.'

The burning returned in full measure to her cheeks, a stinging wave of embarrassment that came every time she thought of that awful night. Turning from him with insulting slowness, as if she didn't care, she drawled, 'You never did explain yourself.'

Yes, she'd said it well. As if it were a mere matter of curiosity for her, and not the obsession it had been for so long.

She marvelled that, in so long, there'd never been an opportunity to ask before—but Harun was a master at making certain they were never alone. His favourite place in the palace seemed to be his office, or the secret passageway between their bedrooms—going the other way, towards his room. Only once had she swallowed her pride, followed him out and asked him to come to her—

'I'm sure you've noticed that my life is rather busy, my wife. And really, there's no point in coming where you aren't welcome.'

The heat in her cheeks turned painful. 'Of—of course you're welcome,' she stammered. 'You're my husband.'

He shrugged. 'So says the imam who performed the service.'

Knowing what he'd left unsaid, Amber opened her mouth, and closed it. No, they weren't husband and wife, never had been. They hadn't even had one normal conversation, only cold accusation on her part, and stubborn silence on his.

Didn't he know how much it hurt that he only came to her rooms at night when the gossip became unbearable, and that he timed the hour and left, just as he had on their wedding night? Oh, she'd been cold and unwelcoming to him, mocking him with words and formal curtsies, but couldn't he see that it was only because she was unable to stand the constant and very public humiliation of her life? Every time he was forced to be near her she knew that soon, he'd leave without a word, giving her nothing but that cold, distant bow. And everyone in her world knew it, too.

'I didn't come here to start an argument.' He kept his gaze on her, and a faint thrill ran through her body, as delicious as it was unwelcome—yet Harun was finally looking at her, his eyes ablaze with life. 'Alim's shown up at last,' he said abruptly.

Amber gasped. Alim's disappearance from the clinic in Bern three years ago had been so complete that all Harun's efforts to find him had proven useless. 'He's alive?'

Harun nodded. 'He's in Africa, taken by a Sudanese warlord. He's being held hostage for a hundred million US dollars.'

Her hand fluttered to her cheek. 'Oh, no! Is he well? Have they hurt him?'

The silence went on too long, and, seeing the ice chips in his eyes, she realised that, without meaning to, she'd said something terribly wrong—but what?

Floundering for words when she couldn't know which ones were right or wrong, she tried again, wishing she knew something, anything about the man she'd married. 'Harun, what are you going to do about it?'

'Pay the ransom in full, of course. He's the true Sheikh of Abbas al-Din, and without the contracts from the oil he found we'd have very little of our current wealth.' He hesitated for a moment. 'I'm going to Africa. I have to be there when he's released, to find out if he's coming home. And—he's my brother.'

She'd expected him to say that, of course. From doing twelve hours of mind-numbing paperwork to meeting dignitaries and businessmen to taking up sword and gun, Harun always did what was right for the country, for his people, even for her, at least in public—but she hadn't expected the catch in his voice, or the shimmer of tears in those normally emotionless eyes. 'You love him,' she muttered, almost in wonder.

He frowned at her. 'Of course I do. He's my brother, the only family I have left, and he—might come home at last.'

The second catch in her stranger husband's voice made her search his face. She'd never seen him cry once since Fadi's death. He'd never seemed lonely or needy during the years of Alim's disappearance, at least not in her presence. But now his eyes were misty, his jaw working with emotion.

Amber felt a wave of shame. Harun had been missing his brother all this time, and she'd never suspected it. She'd even accused him once of enjoying his role too much as the replacement sheikh to care where Alim was, or if he was alive or dead. He'd bowed and left her without a word, seconds before she could regret her stupid words. She'd wanted to hurt him for always being so cold, so unfeeling with her—but during the past three years she'd been able to call or Skype with her family daily, or ask one sister or another to visit. She'd left him all alone, missing his brother, and she'd never even noticed until now.

The sudden longing to give him comfort when she knew he'd only push her away left her confused, even frightened. 'I'm sorry,' she said in the end—a compromise that was so weak, so wishy-washy she felt like an idiot. 'I hope he does come home, for your sake.'

'Thank you.' But it seemed she'd said the wrong thing again; the smile he gave her held the same shard of ice as his eyes. 'Will it make a difference to you?'

Taken aback, she stammered, 'W-what? How could Alim's return possibly make any difference to me?'

Harun shrugged, but there was something—a hint of fire beneath his customary ice with her. She didn't know why, but it fascinated her, held her gaze as if riveted to his face. 'He surrendered himself to the warlord in order to protect the woman who saved his life, a nurse working with Doctors for Africa. Very courageous of him, but of course one expects no less from the Racing Sheikh. Soon Alim will become the true, hereditary sheikh he should have been these three years, and I'll be back to being—Brother Number Three.'

By this point she wondered if any more blood could possibly pool in her face. Ridiculous that she could feel such envy for a woman she'd never met, but she'd always yearned to have a man care enough about her to make such a sacrifice. To know Alim, the man who'd run from *her,* could risk his life for another woman—

Then, without warning, Harun's deliberate wording slithered back into her mind like a silent snake, striking without warning. Frowning, she tilted her head, mystified. 'What did you mean by that—Brother Number Three?'

'It took you long enough to remember. Thinking of Alim, were you?' He lifted a brow, just a touch, in true understated irony, and, feeling somehow as if he'd caught her out in wrong behaviour, she blushed. Slowly, he nodded. 'I thought you might be.'

Her head was spinning now. 'You just told me he's alive and has been taken by a warlord. Who else should I be thinking about?' He merely shrugged again, and she wanted to hit him. 'So are you going to explain your cryptic comment?'

It took him a few moments to reply, but it wasn't truly an answer. 'You figure it out, Amber. If you think hard, you might remember…or maybe you won't. It probably was never very important to you.'

'I don't understand,' she said before she could stop herself.

His gaze searched hers for a few moments, but whatever he was looking for he obviously didn't find. For some reason she felt a sense of something lost she didn't know she'd had, the bittersweet wishing for what she never realised she could have had.

Before she could ask he shrugged and went on, 'By the way, you'll be needed for a telecast later today, of course, my dear. We're so glad Alim's alive, of course we're paying the ransom, et cetera.'

The momentary wistfulness vanished like a stone in a pond, only its ripples left behind in tiny circles of hurt. 'Of course,' she said mockingly, with a deep curtsy. 'Aren't I always the perfect wife for the cameras? I must be good for something, since you endure my continued barrenness.'

His mouth hardened, but he replied mildly enough, 'Yes, my dear, you're perfect—for the cameras.'

He'd left the room before the poison hidden deep inside the gently-spoken cryptic words hit her.

Brother Number Three.

Oh, no—had it been Harun standing behind the door when she'd discussed her unwanted marriage—no, her unwanted groom—with her father?

She struggled to remember what she'd said. The trouble was, she'd tried to bury it beneath a blanket of forgetfulness ever since she'd accepted her fate.

Brother Number Three…how am I to face this total stranger in the marriage bed?

Her father's words came back to haunt her. *He's been left completely alone…in deepest mourning…*

He'd heard everything, heard her fight with all her might against marrying him—

And he'd heard her father discuss her feelings for Alim.

She closed her eyes. Now, when it was far too late, she understood why her husband had barely spoken to her in all this time, had never tried to find friendship or comfort with her, had rarely if ever shown any emotion in front of her—and remembering how she'd reacted, then and just now…

For three years she'd constantly punished him for his reaction—one born of intense grief and suffering, a reaction she could readily understand…at least she could understand it now. During the most painful time of his life, he'd needed one person to be there for him. He'd needed someone not to abandon or betray him, and that was exactly what she'd done. He'd come to her that day, and she'd treated him with utter contempt, a most unwanted husband, when he'd been the one to salvage her pride and give her the honour she deserved.

No wonder he'd never tried to touch her, had never attempted to make love to her, even on the one occasion she'd gone to his room to ask him to come to her bed!

But had she asked? Even then she'd been so cold, so proud, not hesitating to let him know how he'd failed her over and over. *Give me a child and remove this shame you've forced on me all this time,* she'd said.

With a silent groan, she buried her face in her hands.

The question now was, what could she do to make him forgive her, when it was years too late to undo the damage?

* * *

Harun was climbing into the jet the next day when he heard his name being called in the soft, breathless feminine voice that still turned his guts inside-out.

She might be your wife, but she can't stand you. She wants Alim—even more, now she knows he's alive, and as heroic as ever.

The same old fight, the same stupid need. Nothing ever changed, including his hatred for his everlasting weakness in wanting her.

Lust, it's nothing more than lust. You can ignore that. You've done it for three years. After a few moments, struggling to wipe the hunger from his face, he turned to her. Afraid he'd give himself away somehow, he didn't speak, just lifted a brow.

With that limber, swaying walk, she moved along the carpet laid down for him to reach the jet from the limo, and climbed the stairs to him. Her eyes were enormous, filled with something he'd never seen from her since that wretched night a year ago when he could have had her, and he'd walked away. 'Harun, I want to come with you.'

A shard of ice pierced his heart. Amber hated to fly, yet here she was, ready to do what she hated most. For the sake of seeing Alim? 'No.'

She blinked and took an involuntary step back at his forceful tone. 'But I want to—'

He couldn't stand to hear her reasons. 'I said no.'

Her chin shot up then, and her eyes flashed. Ah, there was the same defiant wife he'd known and ached to have from three feet or three thousand miles of distance for so long. 'Damn you, Harun, it's all I'm asking of you.'

Harun turned his face away. Just looking at her right now hurt. For the first time she was showing him the impulsive, passionate side he'd believed slumbered deep inside her, and it was for Alim.

Of course it was for Alim; why should he expect anything else? In all these years, she'd only shown emotion once: when she'd asked—no, demanded—that he end her public shame, and give her a child. When he'd said no, she'd sworn at him for the first time.

But she'd just sworn at him again.

'You still care for him so much?' he asked, his voice low and throbbing with the white-hot betrayal he barely managed to hide.

She sighed. 'I'm not nineteen any more. I'm your wife. Please, just give me a chance. It's all I'm asking.'

A chance for what? he wanted to ask, but remained silent.

Something to the left of him caught his attention. Her bags were being stowed in the hold. With a sense of fatalism, he swept a hand before him. 'By all means, come and see him. I'm sure he'll appreciate your care.'

No part of her touched him as she pushed past him and into the jet. Her chin was high, her eyes as cold as they'd always been for him…except on that fateful night last year—and a moment ago, because she wanted to see Alim.

Damn her. Damn them both.

Yet something like regret trailed in the wake of the warm Gulf wind behind her. Harun breathed it in, refusing to yet again indulge in the wish that things could be different for them. It was far too late.

She was sitting upright and straight in the plush, wide seat, her belt already buckled. He sat beside her, and saw her hands gripping the armrests. He'd seen this on the times they'd had to go to another country for a state visit. She really hated flying.

His hand moved to hers, then stopped. It wasn't his comfort she wanted.

During the final safety check of the jet the silence stretched out. The awkwardness between them was never more evident than when they sat side by side and could find nothing to talk about: he because all he could think of was touching her and hating himself for it, and she presumably because all she wanted was to get away from him, as fast and as far as possible.

How she must hate this life, trapped in this submissive woman's role, tied to a man she despised.

'You are *not* Brother Number Three.'

Startled, he turned to face her, prompted by a tone of voice he'd never known from his cold, proud wife. The fierce words seemed to burst from her; the passion he'd always felt slumbering in her came to blazing life in a few restrained words. 'I'm sorry I ever said it, and sorrier still that you heard stupid words said in my own shock and grief, and took them so literally. I humiliated you before my father, and I'm sorry, Harun.'

Surprise and regret, remembered humiliation, yearning and a dozen other emotions flew around in him, their edges hitting him like the wings of a wild bird caged. He could only think of one thing to say, and he couldn't possibly say it to his stranger wife. *What am I to you now?* As ever, he resorted to his fall-back, the cool diplomacy that told her nothing about what he was thinking or feeling. 'It's all right.'

'No, it isn't. It's not all right between us. It never has been, and I never knew why. But we've been married for three years. In all this time, why didn't you try, even once, to talk to me?' Touching his cheek, she turned him to face her before he could school his stunned surprise that her hands were on his skin. 'I always wanted to know why you hated me. You were outside the door that day.'

Taken aback, he could only answer with truth. 'I don't hate you.'

An encyclopaedia could be written on the doubt in her eyes. 'Really? You don't?'

Reluctant understanding touched a heart shrouded in ice too long. 'No,' was all he said.

She sighed. 'But you don't trust me. You won't treat me even as a friend, let alone your wife.' She shook her head. 'I thought you were a servant when I heard your footsteps behind the door. I would never have done that to you—don't you know that?'

Her face was vivid with the force of her anger and her regret. She thought she wanted to know about his emotions—but she didn't have a clue. If he let out one iota of his feelings, it might break a dam of everything he'd repressed since he was eight years old.

I need you to be strong for me again, little akh, Fadi had said at his mother's funeral, only three months after their father died, and Alim had stormed off within minutes of the service beginning. *We have to stand together, and show the world what we're made of.*

I need you to stay home and help me, little akh, he'd said when Alim was seventeen, and his first race on the circuit gave him the nickname the Racing Sheikh. *What Alim's doing could change the nation for us, economically and socially. You can study by correspondence, right? It won't make a difference to you.*

I need you to come home, little akh. I feel like I'm drowning under the weight of all this, Fadi had said when Harun was nineteen, and had to go on a dig to pass his archaeology course. *I'll fix it with the univer-*

sity, don't worry. You'll pass, which is all you want, right?

'I suppose I should have known,' he answered Amber now. From the vague memories he had of his mother, he knew that it was dangerous not to answer an angry woman, but it was worse to answer with a truth she didn't want to hear.

'And—and you heard what my father said about—' her cheeks blazed, but her chin lifted again, and she said it '—about the—the feelings I had for Alim back then.'

As a passion-killer, hearing his wife say she had *feelings* for the brother who'd abandoned him to this half-life had to rank up there as number one. 'Yes,' he said, quiet. Dead inside.

'Harun, don't.' She gripped his chin in her hand, her eyes fairly blazing with emotion. 'Do you hate me for it?'

He closed his eyes against the passion always beneath the surface with her, but never for him. 'No.' So many times, he'd wished he could hate her, or just take her for the higher duty of making an heir, but he could do neither. Yes, he still desired her; he could live with that. But he'd shut off his heart years ago. There was no way he'd open it up, only to have her walk all over it again with her careless rejections and stinging rebukes.

'Stop it, Harun,' she burst out, startling him into opening his eyes again. 'Hate me if you want, but stop showing me this uncaring wall of ice! I don't know how to talk to you or what to do when you're so cold with me, always pushing me away!'

Cold? He felt as if he were bleeding agony whenever he looked at her, and she thought his feelings for her were cold? Harun stared at her, the wife he barely knew, and wondered if she was blind, or if it was because he really had covered his need too well. But wasn't that what he'd always done? How could he stop doing what had always been expected of him?

So he frowned again. 'I don't know what you want me to say.'

'Talk to me for once. Tell me how it hurt you.' Though she spoke softly, almost beneath her breath, it felt like a dam bursting, the release of a long-held pressure valve. 'I was *nineteen,* Harun, one of a legion of girls that dreamed of capturing the heart of the world-famous Racing Sheikh. I didn't know him any more than I could touch or talk to a literal star.'

She hadn't said so many words to him at one time since he'd rejected her one attempt at connection last year—and the bitter self-mockery in her voice and her eyes lashed even harder at him than herself.

So she thought of Alim as a star. Well, why not? Even now, years later, it was how the world saw him. The headlines were filled with adoring references to the missing sheikh, reinforcing his own aching emptiness. *He's my brother. Not one of you misses him like I do.*

When he didn't answer, she snapped, 'Do you feel nothing about it, Harun? Do you not care that I married you believing I was in love with your brother?'

The pain of it gripped him everywhere, like a vice inside him, squeezing the blood from his heart. Not care that she—

Believing she was in love with Alim? What did she mean?

Did he want to know? Could he stand to ask what she felt for his brother now?

This was too much. She'd changed so suddenly from the cold, imperious woman she'd always been with him; it left him wondering what the hell to say to her that wouldn't make her explode. After three years of icy disdain and silence, without warning she was demanding thoughts and feelings from him that threatened to take the only thing he had left; his pride.

'Of course I cared,' he said coolly. 'Quite humiliating, isn't it, to be the last brother in line in the eyes of your prospective bride—good old Brother Number Three. I didn't enjoy knowing that my wedding only took place because one brother died and the other brother ran away. Worse still to know she'd have done anything to have my runaway brother there instead of me.' He was quite proud of himself. Total truth in a few raw sentences, years of grief, loss and anguish— but told as if it were someone else's life, as if it didn't twist in his guts like a knife he couldn't pull out of him.

The fire in her eyes dimmed. 'I suppose it is,' she said dully. 'Thank you for your honesty, at least.'

And, too late, Harun knew he'd blown this last chance she'd given him to connect with her. She might have said and done it all wrong, but at least she was trying.

I never know what he's thinking or feeling.

For years the words had haunted him, leaving him locked deep inside what had always been his greatest strength—but with Amber, it felt like his deepest inadequacy. He'd grown up always aware that, hereditary sheikh though he was, he was the last in line, the spare tyre, the reliable son or brother. His parents had been busy running a nation, too busy to spend time with their children. The only memories he had of his mother was that she'd resented that the last child she could have wasn't the girl she'd longed for. His father, who wanted sons, contemptuously called him a sissy for his love of history and hiding in his room reading books instead of playing sports and inventing marvellous things as Alim could, or charming the people, as Fadi did. *He'll grow up to be a real man whether he likes it or not,* their father said with utter disdain when Harun was six. From that day, he'd been enrolled in all the action-man activities and ancient and modern knowledge of war-craft that made the family so popular with the people.

He'd learned to fight, all right…he'd had no choice, since his father had arranged constant martial-arts battles for him. But he'd also read books late at night, beneath the blanket with a tiny hand-torch, so the servants wouldn't see it and report to his father.

After their parents' deaths, Fadi had become the father he'd never known, raising both his brothers with greater love and acceptance than Harun had ever known from his parents, and yet he'd had to learn how to run the small, independent emirate. Harun adored Fadi, and Fadi had always loved him dearly, giving him the affection he'd craved for so long; but Fadi always comforted himself in the knowledge that, while Alim would travel the world, and put Abbas al-Din on the world and economic map, Harun would stay home and help.

Alim had always counted on it, too. *You've got Harun,* Alim would always say when Fadi asked him to come home for this duty or that. *He'll do it better than I can.*

So Harun supported Fadi's heavy load as Sheikh, kept learning war-craft and how to lead all the armed forces, continuing the studies that were his secret passion by reading books late at night. Since he'd been recalled home at nineteen from his one trip outside the palace, he'd never dreamed of asking to leave Sar Abbas, except on matters of military or state. His interests were unimportant beside the demands of nation, honour, family, and their people. Good old Harun, doing the right, the decent and honourable thing, always his brothers' support and mainstay.

The thing was, nobody ever asked him how he felt about it, or believed he had feelings at all. And so, as long as he could remember, he'd kept his thoughts to himself.

So how did he suddenly begin talking now, after all these years?

Amber sighed aloud, reiterating his failure with her. 'Say something, *anything,* Harun!'

What was he supposed to say? 'I'm sorry, Amber.' At this moment, he wished he'd realised how very young she'd been when they wed—as she'd said, only nineteen. He sat beside this wife who despised him, feeling the old chains of silence holding him in place, with a rusted padlock he could never seem to open.

'If it ruined everything we could have had, I wish I'd never thought of Alim,' she burst out, yet said it very quietly. She dropped his hand, and turned away. 'I never even knew him, but I was all alone here. Fadi loved Rafa, and you never looked at me or talked to me. And—and he smiled and was nice to me when he came. It was just a lonely girl's stupid crush on a superstar,' she mumbled, her cheeks aflame.

The finality in her words dropped him into a well of unexpected darkness. *Don't you understand, Amber? If he'd been anyone else, I could have ignored it.* 'What could we have had, Amber?' he asked, as quietly as she'd spoken.

Her left shoulder lifted in a delicate shrug. 'We married because you were a sheikh and I was a sheikh's daughter, for the sake of our nations. Harun, you've been so amazing the past three years. You've been a strong and loving leader for your people in their need, giving them everything they asked of you. But the only good part of our marriage was for the cameras and in front of the people. Now, if Alim comes back—well, what's left for us?'

Us. She'd said *us.* As if there were an *us*—or could have been. She'd admired him for the things he'd done? He couldn't get his head around it.

'I don't want a sham for the cameras any more. I don't want to live the rest of my life alone, tied to a man who never touches me, who doesn't want me.'

Harun had never cursed his habit of silence more than now. Strong, brave, lovely Amber had burst out with everything they'd kept locked in silence all these years, and his mind was totally blank. He'd been too busy keeping his nation intact and his heart from bearing any more scars to say a word to her about his wants and needs, and he'd presumed she didn't care what he wanted anyway, because she still loved Alim.

But if that wasn't the truth, why had she walled off from him so completely? He'd thought it was because she found him repulsive—but now?

But last year, she'd come to him. She'd asked him to make love to her...

'I never knew you wanted me to desire you,' he said, fighting the husky note of long-hated yearning with all he had. His pride had taken enough battering from this woman, and he'd been celibate far too long. *Say it, Amber, tell me if you want me—*

But with a jerky movement Amber unlocked her seat belt and got to her feet. Her eyes blazed down at him, thwarted passion burning bright. 'Can't you just talk to me like you're a normal man, and show me some human feeling? Can't you stop—stop fencing with words, asking questions instead of answering me honestly? Can't you stop being so cold all the time? I'm not your enemy, I'm your *wife!*'

Stop reading books, Harun! Stop saying yes and do it, be a real man like your brothers!

He rubbed at his forehead in frustration. 'Amber, stop talking in circles and tell me what you want,' he grated, knowing he sounded harsh but no longer caring. He felt as if he had enough to deal with right now without her baffling dramatics. Couldn't she see that she was expecting too much, too fast? 'Can we do this thing later? In a few hours I'll be facing my brother for the first time in years. Alim's my only family, all I have left.'

'It only needed that.' With a slow nod, those beautiful, liquid-honey eyes iced over, frozen in time like her namesake. 'We don't have to do this *thing* at all. Thank you, Harun. You've made my decision easy.' And she walked—that beautiful swaying dance she put into every effortless step—into the cockpit and asked in a voice as curt as her walk had been shimmering, 'I don't want to go now. Open the exit door, please.'

When it was open, she moved to the exit, her head high. At the opening, she turned—only her head—and glanced at him. She spoke with regal dignity, the deposed queen she was about to become. 'I hope your reunion with Alim is all you wish it to be. I hope he comes home to be your family.'

He opened his mouth, but she rushed on, as if unable to bear hearing his formal thank-you. 'When Alim becomes the sheikh again, I hope you find what you want out of your life. I hope you find a way to be happy,

Harun, because I'm going to find my own life from now on, without you or anyone else telling me what to do.'

Then, like a dream of beauty abruptly awakened, she was gone.

CHAPTER FOUR

Fifteen Days Later
The Sheikh's Palace, Sar Abbas

HARUN had asked Amber to be here at this private handover of the nation to the real Sheikh of Abbas al-Din, and so she'd come, from curiosity if nothing else—but it seemed as if nobody else would begin speaking, so she'd have to.

Maybe that was what Harun wanted from her, to break the ice?

Right now she felt as if she'd give anything to be able to do just that—to break the ice of Harun's withdrawn politeness. In the last fifteen days she'd come to regret her outburst. When would she learn to control her tongue and temper? Neither had got her anywhere with the el-Kanar brothers, least of all Harun.

'Welcome home, Alim,' she said, trying to smile, to repress the emotion boiling like a pot beneath the surface. 'It's good to have you back.'

Her long-lost brother-in-law looked older than the handsome, daring racing driver she remembered. The scars on his face and neck, the mementoes of the race that took Fadi's life, weren't as bad as she'd feared. He was still the kind of man who'd draw admiring looks

from women wherever he went, though, from the wariness in his stance when any woman was nearby, she
suspected he didn't know it.

Alim flicked a glance at Harun, but he stood impas-
sive, neither moving nor speaking. After a few moments
Alim bowed to her, a smile on his mouth as stressed as
the look in his eyes. 'Thank you, Amber.'

It seemed the charming daredevil who'd grabbed her
youthful fancy was gone—like her long-disappeared
crush. But this man was her brother-in-law, a stranger to
her—and this was not her reunion. So she waited, casting small glances about the room. The awkward tension
between the brothers was too hard to keep watching.

This beautiful, airy but neutral room was almost as
hard to look at. This had been Fadi's reception room
to meet foreign dignitaries, and it was where she'd met
all three el-Kanar brothers for the first time. The dear
friend who'd loved another woman, the glamorous racing hero who'd disappeared rather than wed her, and
the man of ice who'd done his duty by her in public, but
would do anything rather than talk to her or touch her.

Harun must have noticed that she and Alim were
both awaiting their cue from him. He spoke with an odd
note in his voice. 'I've moved out of your room, Alim.
It's ready for you, as is your office, as soon as you want
to resume your duties.'

Alim took a step towards his brother. 'Let's not pretend. Don't talk as if I've been sick for a few weeks. I
was gone for three years. I left all the grief and duty to
you. Harun, I wanted to say that...'

Harun shrugged, with all his eloquent understatement, and she realised he did it with Alim, not just with
her. It seemed he was skilled at cutting off more people
than her alone. He shut off anyone's attempts at emo-

tional connection, freezing them out with that hint of blue-blooded frost. *Come no further.* 'There's no need to say anything, Alim. It wasn't as if I had anywhere better to be at the time.'

But Alim wasn't having it. With a determined tone, he went on, 'I wanted to say, the choice is yours now. You've done a magnificent job of running the country, of picking up the pieces after Fadi's death and my disappearance. You're the nation's hero now, not me. If you want to remain the sheikh—'

'No.'

The snarl burst from her mouth, shaking her to the core, but it had a masculine note as well. Harun had echoed it even more forcefully than she had; he sounded almost savage.

Amber felt Alim staring at her, waiting. Maybe it was easier for him to hear her out first than to know what he'd done to Harun by his disappearance.

She flushed, and glanced at Harun—but as usual, he stood locked inside those walls of silence she couldn't knock down, even with catapults and cannons.

She fiddled with her hands, shuffled a foot. Did she want to hear Harun's reasons for wanting out before she'd spoken? Suddenly she couldn't bear to know, to hear all the reasons why she'd failed him, and heard words tumbling from her lips.

'I won't play sheikh's happy wife for anyone's sake any more. I'm tired of the pretence that everything's all right. I don't care what my father says. I want a divorce.'

She turned and walked out of the room, trying to contain the trembling in every part of her body. She reached her suite of rooms and closed the door behind her. It almost felt like a miracle to make it this far without being stopped, but she'd managed it by staring down anyone that approached her. She encountered more than twenty people, staffers or servants, all asking if they could serve her—all burning to know the answer to one question. Who was the sheikh now, Alim or Harun?

Sitting on the straight-backed chair at her desk, she counted in silence. If he didn't come this time—

In less than three minutes, the door swung wide open without announcement. 'Guard every possible listening place, but stay well away from it,' Harun snapped to someone outside, and several masculine voices lifted in assent. From behind the walls of her suite, she heard the soft shuffling of feminine feet moving away in haste, and smiled to herself.

'He comes to my rooms twice in a month of his own free will,' she murmured, as if to herself. 'Will the walls fall flat in shock?'

Harun's gaze narrowed. 'Is that really how you want to conduct this conversation, Amber, in sarcasm and anger?'

She lifted her chin. 'If it actually makes you feel something, I'll risk it.'

'You needn't worry about that,' he said grimly. 'I'm feeling quite a lot of things right about now.'

'Then I'm glad,' she said with sweet mockery. It seemed the only way to break through that invisible, impenetrable wall of concrete around him.

And it worked. With a few steps he was right in front of her, his chest rising and falling in abrupt motion, his normally forest-green eyes black with intensity. The emotion she'd hungered to see for so long had risen from his self-dug grave and the satisfaction hit her like a punch to the stomach. 'How dare you make an announcement like that with my brother there?'

'I had to,' she said with false calm, heart hammering.

'Without him there it would have done no good, because
it seems to me that you don't care what I say or what I
think. You've never once asked or cared what I want.
What's right for Abbas al-Din is all that matters to you.'

Ah, why did there have to be that little catch in her
voice, giving her away?

But it seemed he didn't even notice it. 'He wants to
marry the nurse that rescued him. He loves her, just so
you know,' he replied in a measured, even tone—but
the fire in his eyes showed the struggle he was having
in commanding his emotions.

Incensed, she jerked to her feet. 'Is that all you can
say? I tell you I want a divorce, and you only want to
remind me of a stupid crush I had when I was nineteen?
How long will you keep punishing me for words I said
and feelings I had when I was barely out of childhood?
I was grieving too, you know. I cared for Fadi. He was
like a big brother to me.' Afraid she'd burst into unseemly tears in front of him, she wheeled away, staring
hard out of that beautifully carved window, blinking
the stinging from her eyes. She'd rather *die* than cry in
front of him. 'I've always known I meant nothing to you
beyond the political gain to your country, but I hoped
you respected me a little more than that.'

The silence stretched out so long, she wondered if
he'd left. He had the knack of moving without sound.
Then he spoke. 'You're right. I apologise, Amber.' As
she whirled around he gave her a small smile. 'I had
my own stupid crush at nineteen—but I didn't marry
you while I was in love with your sister. Do you understand?'

They were the first words he'd ever spoken that felt
real to her, and she put a hand on the chair to feel something solid; the truth had hit her that hard. She'd thought

of it as a silly crush on a superstar all this time—but Alim was his brother. Though he'd said it simply, it sickened her. She'd married him with a crush on his *brother*—the brother that had publicly humiliated her. As far as deeply personal insults went, it probably couldn't get much worse.

'I understand,' she said, her voice croaky.

He nodded. 'We both know you can't divorce me, Amber. It would bring dishonour on the family and threaten the stability of the country, so I don't believe that was what you want most.'

Hating that he'd called her on her little power-game, she said wearily, 'I don't have to live here, Harun.' She rubbed her eyes, heedless of make-up. What did it matter what she looked like? He didn't want her, had never wanted her.

His jaw hardened. 'You'd make our problems public by leaving me?'

'I was never *with* you to leave you, My Lord. The little scar in your armpit is evidence enough of that.' But instead of feeling triumph at the taunt, she just wanted to cry. Why did she always have to attack? And why did it take attacking him to make him *talk?*

'So you're saying you'll drag us both through the mud by proving I didn't consummate the marriage?'

She lifted her face, staring at him in disbelief. 'Is that all you care about—if I embarrass you in public? When you've been humiliating me publicly for years!' she flung at him. 'Everyone in the palace knows you don't come to my bedroom! I'm known as the bad-luck bride, who's ruined the lives of all three el-Kanar brothers. Even my parents bemoan my inability to entice you—not to mention the lack of grandchildren—every time they visit or call me!' She was quite proud of

herself, laying her deepest, bleeding wound before him
with such flaming sarcasm instead of crying or wail-
ing like a weak woman. 'And of course everyone's very
well aware your lack of interest must be my fault, since
our wedding night was apparently consummated, and
you never came back.' She paused, and looked at him
reproachfully, before delivering the final blow. 'Oh,
and nobody in the palace has hesitated to tell me about
your lover and daughter. Do you know how it feels to
know that while you continue to leave me alone, you
gave another woman the only thing I've ever asked of
you—and even the servants know about it?'

Harun closed his eyes and rubbed his forehead,
shoulders bent. He looked unutterably weary, and part
of her ached to take the words back, to make this conversation any time but now. 'I would have thought you'd
know by now that servants only ever get things half-
right. The child's name is Naima. Her mother is Buhjah,
and she's a good woman.' His words were tight, lock-
ing her out again.

Amber stared in disbelief. She'd just bared her greatest shame to him, the very public and family humiliation she had to endure daily, and he could only speak
of his daughter and lover—the family he'd allowed her
to learn about from the servants?

Did he love Buhjah? Was that why he'd never cared
how she felt or what she needed? Just like Fadi, all over
again. Oh, these el-Kanar brothers were so faithful to
the women they loved. And so good at doing their public duty by her and then leaving her in no-man's-land,
stuck in a life she could no longer bear.

'Get out,' she said, her voice wobbling. She wheeled
away, her breast heaving with her choppy breathing.
'Just go. Oh, and you'd better lock me in, because it's

the only way your precious name won't be dragged through the mud you're so afraid of.'

'No, I won't leave it like this,' he said, hard and unbending. Oh, no, he wouldn't plead, not with her. Probably the mother of his child roused his gentleness and touch and had the man on his knees for her. For Amber, there was only an unending wall of ice. But then, why should she expect more? She was only the wife.

She buried her face in her hands. 'Oh, by all means, master, stay, and force me to keep humiliating myself before you. You're in control by law and religion. I can't stop you.' The words scraped across a throat as raw as the desert, but she no longer cared. It wasn't as if he gave a fig if she did weep or how she felt about anything—but the embarrassment at her less than regal behaviour might just get rid of him for a little while.

'Amber, I don't want to keep going like this. I can see you're hurting, but I don't know how to help you.'

Seconds later she heard the door close softly behind him, and heaved a sigh—whether in relief or from the greatest misery she'd ever known, she wasn't sure. Had she got her point across to him at last, or had she driven him away?

There would be no divorce. Her father would see her dead before he'd allow it, and she couldn't just disappear. Even if she weren't hemmed in by servants, she'd put her family through public shame, the scandal would leave her younger sisters unmarriageable and, worst of all, she'd have to leave her family behind for ever.

Unthinkable. Impossible. They were all she had, and, despite her ongoing conflicts with her father, she loved them all dearly.

So she was stuck here, for ever bound to this man—

'So why do I keep driving him away?' she muttered through her fingers. If she wanted any kind of amity in her life—and, most importantly, a child to fill the hole in her heart and end her public shame—she had to let Harun know the truth. That, far from hating him, she punished him for his neglect of her because she admired and desired him, and had since before their wedding day. Even now she pushed him in some desperate attempt to get him to really speak to her, to feel something, anything—

No. She'd die before she told him. He had to give her some sign first! But how to—?

The rag crossed her mouth with shocking suddenness. Panic clawed at her and she struggled, but within moments it was tied at the back of her head. Another bound her hands together behind her. She kept fighting, but then a sickly sweet stench filled her nostrils, and made her head spin before everything turned black.

Three steps from her door, Harun stopped and wheeled around. What was he doing?

Amber was crying, and he'd left her. He'd never believed he'd ever have the power to make her cry, but he had…talking of Naima and Buhjah—

'Idiot!' he muttered when at last a light went on in his brain and his heart after years of darkness. Was it possible? Could Amber be jealous? He struggled to think. Did she yearn for the child she'd demanded of him last year, the child he'd never given her—his children that were her right as his wife…or—dear God in heaven…he'd let her keep thinking Buhjah was Rafa's real name—that she was his lover, not Fadi's—

Amber was his wife. He owed her his first loyalty, not Buhjah and Naima, much as he cared for both of them. He owed Amber a lot more than the public presence he gave her. And—what if all her roundabout talking, her probing and proud demands for more than the child she'd asked him for a year ago were supposed to help him to work out that she wanted more? That she wanted him?

He stalked back through the door before he could change his mind. 'Amber, I'm not going anywhere—'

Then he jerked to a standstill, staring at the sliding door of the secret passage that joined the back of their bedrooms—the one that was never watched, at his strict order. It led to freedom through a tunnel below the palace, created during the seventeenth century, when many brides were taken by abduction. Amber's feet were all he saw as the door began to slide closed again, but they were sliding backwards.

Someone had her! If it was the el-Shabbats…or worse, the more virulent of the el-Kanar supportive factions who'd kept sending him messages to rid himself of her, that she was bad luck—dear God, the return of Alim might have spurred them to action. The faction of reactionary, old-fashioned autocrats hated Alim for his western ways, and wanted to keep Harun as Sheikh. If they'd taken Amber, they'd use her as leverage to make Alim disappear for good—and then they'd kill her to leave Harun free to wed a more fertile bride.

No!

'Amber!' he yelled, bolting for the door. He reached it before it slid shut, yanked it open and shouldered his way through.

Turning left, he ran down the passage—then a cloying scent filled his senses and mind; the world spun too fast, and he knew no more.

CHAPTER FIVE

THE screaming headache and general feeling of grogginess were the first indications that life wasn't normal when Harun opened his eyes…because when he tried to open them they were filled with sticky sand, and he had to blink and push his lids wide before they opened.

The second indication was when he saw the room he was in. Lying on a bed that—well, it *sagged,* he could feel his hip aching from the divot his body had made— he knew this was a room he'd never been in before. It wasn't quite filthy, but for a man who'd spent every day of his life in apartments in flawless condition, he could smell the dust, breathe it in.

The furnishings were strange. After a few moments of blinking and staring hard, he thought he hadn't been in a room so sparse since his tent during the war. The one cupboard looked as though it had been sanded with steel wool, the gouges were so messy, and it was old. Not antique, but worn out, like something sold at a bazaar in the poor quarter of the city. The one carpet on the wide-boarded wooden floor looked like an original eighteenth-century weave, but with moth-holes and ragged ends. The dining table and chairs had been hand-carved in a beautiful dark wood, but looked as if they hadn't been polished in years. The chairs by the windows were covered in tapestry that had long lost its plushness.

Thin, almost transparent curtains hung over the wide, ornately carved windows and around the bed, giving an illusion of privacy; but in a life filled with servants and politicians, foreign dignitaries and visiting relatives, he barely understood what the word meant.

He moved to rub his eyes, but both hands came together. His hands were tied with a double-stranded silken string. Could he break it if he struggled hard enough—?

The silk was stronger than it appeared. The bonds didn't budge, no matter how he struggled, and he swore.

A little murmur of protest behind him made him freeze halfway through pulling his wrists apart. A soft sigh followed, and then the soft breathing of a woman in deep sleep.

He flipped his body around to the other direction, his head screaming in protest at the movement, and looked at his companion. Pale-faced, deeply asleep, Amber was in bed with him for the first time, wearing only a peignoir of almost the same shimmering honey-gold as her skin.

For that matter, he wore only a pair of boxers in silk as thin as Amber's peignoir.

A memory as blurry as a photo of his grandparents' youth came to him—a vision of Amber's feet being dragged backwards down the secret passage. But, try as he might, nothing more came to him.

They'd obviously been kidnapped, but why? For money, or political clout? Why would anyone want to take them now, when it was too late? It made no sense, with Alim back and able to take his rightful place as Sheikh—

Unless…could this be part of an elaborate el-Shabbat plot to reduce the el-Kanar power base in Abbas al-Din? He'd just paid one hundred million US dollars for Alim's safe release. If Alim paid the same for his and Amber's safe return, it wouldn't bankrupt the nation, but it would be enough to create a negative media back-lash against the family. *Why do these people keep get-ting kidnapped?* Once was forgivable, but twice would be seen as a family weakness. If they'd taken Alim as well, it might destroy the—

An icy chill ran down his back. If it was the el-Shabbats, it would mean their deaths, all of them. Alim had just been taken hostage, beaten badly, and released only by ransom. How could he stand it again so soon? If Alim was taken or, God forbid, dead—his only brother, the only one he had left in the world—

He had to get out of here! When a guard came in, he'd be ready. He jerked to a sitting position, looking around the room for something, anything that could be used as a weapon.

Amber's tiny murmur of protest let him know he'd disturbed her. He dragged in a slow breath, taking a few moments to reorient himself. If anything had hap-pened to Alim, right now he couldn't do a thing about it. Getting Amber out safely had to be his first prior-ity—but even if they managed to escape, how could they reach home, almost completely undressed?

He'd wondered what kind of kidnapper would put him on a bed dressed in almost nothing, lying beside his scantily clad wife, but now he saw the point all too well. Without clothes, with no dignity, what could he do?

Find some clothes—and I will find a way out of here.

Slowly, gently, he got to his feet, making a face at the swishing slide of the shorts against his skin. He wore silk clothes only for ceremonial occasions, preferring cotton. Jeans and T-shirts had been his favoured fashion in his private time, until it had been made clear to him that, as replacement sheikh, he had to be seen to be the perfect Arabic man at all times.

With only two rooms, searching their cage didn't take long. Besides the bed, the dining set, the chairs by the windows, and the cupboard, there was only a prayer mat. He realised that was what had woken him, the call to prayer being made somewhere behind the building.

But even with his hands tied, he could look around.

The massive double door was locked. The only other doors, to the bathroom and the balcony, showed no chance of escape. The room they were in was five storeys up, without convenient roofs nearby to leap onto. Even if there were, he couldn't ask Amber to leap from one roof to another, and he couldn't leave her alone to face the consequences of his escape.

On the bedside tables were water glasses, and paper tissues. In the drawer on Amber's side there were about twenty hairpins.

They even knew how she preferred to do her hair, he thought grimly.

He crawled awkwardly under the bed, finding only dust. Using both hands together, he opened the cupboard—nothing at all but the hanging rail.

That had possibilities, if only he could get it out. But pulling and tugging at the rail made his head spin.

He checked through the bathroom, including the two small cupboards there. Even the most basic of bathroom goods could be used together to create something to help them escape.

'No floss, not even toilet paper in here,' he muttered moments later, resisting the urge to slam a cupboard, or throw one of the little bottles of oil at the wall. 'What kind of crazy kidnappers give their captives scented oils for their bath?'

Then his mind began racing. With the right oils, combined with the toothpaste and some water—he assumed they'd be fed and given water, at least—he might be able to make something...perhaps one of Alim's infamous stink-bombs from childhood, or some kind of fluid to throw in their kidnappers' eyes.

How he wished he'd paid more attention to Alim's scientific pranks when they were kids!

The bathroom held no more secrets. The bath was old and large, scrubbed clean. The toilet had a hose beside it. The towels were close to threadbare, useless for anything but basic drying. Their abductors weren't taking any chances.

He'd run out of options for now. With a clenched jaw, Harun let the pounding of his head and eyes dictate to him. He fell back on the bed, closed his eyes and breathed in the scent she wore. Intoxicating as an unfurled desert bud, soft and tender as a mid-spring night—was it perfume or the essence of Amber herself? He wished he knew. Drinking it in with each breath, savouring an intimacy so new and yet somehow familiar because of so many dreams, he returned to sleep.

Amber couldn't remember waking so peacefully since she was a child. In fact, had she ever woken feeling this warm and snuggly, secure and happy?

There was a sound beside her, a slow, rhythmic cadence she couldn't recognise. There was a scent she couldn't define, filling every breath she took. Where was she?

Opening her eyes, she saw the light sprinkling of

dark hair scattered across an unclad male chest lying right before her eyes. She took in a slow, deep breath, and it came again, the scent of belonging, as if she'd come home at last.

She barely dared lift her gaze—but she knew the scent, the feeling it gave her. She'd known it for so long from so far away. It was him. The perfectly sculpted statue of ice had become all warm, solid male. Her untouchable husband was within her reach at last.

They had so many problems to overcome. Their hopes and fears and most of their lives were unknown to each other—but at this moment, she didn't care. He was here. She was gripped by a long-familiar urge.

Could she do it?

It had started on their wedding night when he'd come to her, dressed as a groom ready to love his bride. It had persisted even after she'd emerged from the bathroom that night, clad only in a towel. With a glance, he'd gathered his blasted paperwork and bowed to her, the movement fairly dripping with irony, and, with a twist to his lips, he'd left the room without a word. She hadn't slept in weeks after that—and she'd endured three hundred and forty-four restless, hungry, angry nights after he'd refused her bed last year. Sometimes she thought she'd give anything to have this farce come to an end, and she could find a man who would actually desire her. But he didn't, and he wouldn't let her go, either.

The *thunk* came again, a sickening hit in the stomach at the remembered rejection. So why did the aching need to taste him with her lips and tongue still fill every pore of her? Why did she want him so badly when he was so cold and uncaring? She could never seem to break this stupid desire for the husband who despised her. The need to touch him was like the heat of a gold-refiner's furnace. There was no point in ignoring facts when just by her looking at him now, by her lying so close to him, her pulse was pounding so hard she wondered if it would wake him. Wondered and hungered, as she danced on a fine blade-point of need and pride and the soul-destroying fear of another rejection.

Do it. Just kiss him once, a little voice in her head whispered, soft and insistent. *Maybe it will cure you of all this wondering. Maybe it won't be as good as you think.*

Was she leaning into him, or was she dreaming again? His lips, parted in dreams were so close, closer than they'd ever been—

His eyes opened, looking right into hers.

Her breath caught, and she danced that razor-fine point again, aching and fearful as she scrambled to find her pride, the coldness that had been her salvation in all her dealings with him. Was the returning hunger she saw in his eyes merely a product of her overwrought imagination? If only she knew him well enough to find the courage, to ask.

If only every chance she'd ever taken hadn't left her alone with her humiliation.

Harun's gaze drifted lower. Torn between slight indignation and the spark heating her blood at the slow flame in his eyes, familiar pride rushed back to save her, won over the need for the unknown. She lifted a hand to tug at the neckline of her negligée, but the other hand jerked up with it. Looking down, she saw she was tied in silken bonds, as soft as the silken negligee that barely covered her nudity beneath.

As if she had never seen him before, Amber turned back to Harun. She let her gaze take him all in. He was almost naked…and he was fully aroused.

Blushing so hard it felt like fire on her cheeks, she saw his knowing, gentle smile. He knew she wanted him, and still he didn't say a word, didn't touch her. Wouldn't give her the one thing she craved, a child of her own. Someone all her own to love.

A beautiful, almost poetic revenge for my stupid words—isn't it, Harun?—always leaving me alone? When will you stop torturing me for the past?

Taking refuge in imperiousness, she demanded, 'Who dressed me this way? Who *undressed* me? Where are we?'

His gaze lifted to hers. For a moment she saw a flash of reluctance and regret; then it vanished, leaving that unreadable look she'd come to hate. 'I'm afraid I can't answer any of those questions. I can only tell you that I didn't undress you.' He lifted his hands, tied together in front of him, with silky white bonds that would only hurt if he struggled to free himself.

Her hands were tied with the same material—and she hated that some small part of her had been hoping that he'd been the one to undress her, see her naked, touch her skin. Foolish, pathetic woman, would she never stop these ridiculous hopes and dreams? She'd always be alone. The lesson had been hammered into her skull years ago, and still she kept aiming her darts at the moon.

Feeling her blush grow hotter, she retorted, 'Well, I think I can take it for granted that you wouldn't undress me after all these years.'

His gaze roamed her body, so slow she almost felt him touch her—tender, invisible fingers exploring her skin as she'd hoped only moments before, and she had to hold in the soft sound of imagined delight. It felt so *real*.

In a deep growling voice that heated her blood,

he murmured, 'I don't think you should take that for granted at all.' After another slow perusal, her body felt gripped by fever. 'We don't have the luxury of taking anything for granted in our situation.'

Even spoken with a gentle huskiness, the final words doused the edge of her anger and her desire, leaving her soul flooding with questions. 'What's going on here, Harun? Why would anyone—anyone…just leave us here, dressed like this?'

Say it, you coward. You've been abducted! But just thinking the word left her sick and shaking with impotent terror. *So much for being like Great-grandmother…*

'I don't pretend to know.' His gaze met hers, direct. 'We just paid one hundred million dollars for Alim's safe return. How much do you think Alim and your father between them can afford to pay for our ransom now?'

'I don't know about Abbas al-Din's treasury, but the recent troubles in the Gulf have drained Father's resources, paying the security forces.' Amber bit her lip. 'Do you think the el-Shabbats are behind this?'

'I certainly wouldn't rule them out, but this could be any of a dozen high-ranking families, not just the el-Shabbats. There are many families eager to take over rulership of our countries if they only had the funds,' he said quietly. 'Your father and Alim would have to take that into consideration before making any decision.'

'Do you even think either of them knows we're gone?' she asked, hating the piteous note in her voice, pleading for reassurance.

Harun sighed. 'I don't know. Alim's got so much on his mind at the moment. We walked out saying we weren't staying. I think he'll assume we left, possibly to talk out our troubles, patch up our marriage.'

I wish we had. Why didn't you want that? she almost blurted, but there were far greater necessities to talk about right now. She looked down again, frowning. 'Why are our hands tied, but not our feet? Why aren't we gagged?'

He moved his hands, and she felt a finger caress the back of hers. 'Maybe someone wants us to talk?' he suggested, his eyes glimmering.

Her mouth opened and closed. The surprise of his making a joke was too complete for her to quite believe in it. 'Oh, I wish,' she retorted at last, rolling her eyes. 'Perhaps they could make you talk to me if they repeatedly used an electric prod—you know, those things that shock animals?'

He grinned at her, and it relaxed his austere handsomeness, making her catch her breath. 'Do you think it's worth a try?'

Choking back a giggle, she fixed a stern expression in her eyes. 'Can you please be serious? How can we get out of here?' She bit her lip.

His eyes sobered. 'I don't think they need to gag us, Amber. We're at least five storeys up. The walls are thick, and the nearest buildings are a hundred metres or more away. There are guards posted outside the doors and at every building through the windows, and they'll be very hard of hearing. I doubt that any amount of screaming will bring help.'

Absurd to feel such warmth from the motion of one of his fingers when they'd been abducted and could be dead by nightfall, but right now she'd take whatever comfort she could get. 'You've already looked?'

He nodded, his face tight. 'There's no way out of here until they let us out. This abduction's been perfectly planned.'

'Do you think anyone's looking for us yet?' she asked almost piteously, hating to hear the word. *Abduction*. It made her feel so powerless.

He gave that tiny shrug she'd always hated, but this time she sensed it was less a brush-off than an attempt to reassure her. 'That depends on how clever our abductors have been, and what they heard us saying beforehand.'

She frowned. 'What could they have heard us say?'

He just looked at her, waiting for her to remember—and after a few moments, it struck her. In her need to push Harun into action of some kind, she'd stated her intention to divorce him, where a dozen servants or any palace or government servant could have heard. She'd shown her contempt for the existing laws and traditions. Any traditional man would have been shocked.

She closed her eyes. By coming to her room to discuss their problems instead of punishing her in front of Alim, Harun had treated her with the utmost respect. But she'd given him none. She'd ploughed ahead with her shocking announcement, thinking only of humiliating Harun in a public place to spur him into some kind of action. She'd thought only of herself, her needs—and now they both had to endure the consequences.

'I'm sorry, Harun,' she whispered. 'This is all my fault.'

'Let's not waste time pushing blame at each other or on ourselves, when we don't know what's going on.' Softly, almost hypnotically, his fingers caressed hers. 'Playing that kind of game won't help either of us now. We need to keep our minds clear, and work together.'

Her head was on his shoulder before she knew she'd moved. Or maybe he had, too. Either way she rested her head halfway between his shoulder and chest, hearing him breathe, drinking it in. 'Thank you.'

'For what?'

She smiled up at him. 'A more insecure man would have wasted an hour lecturing me on my unfeminine behaviour, on my presumption in challenging you in the first place, where others could hear. A less intelligent man would blame our situation totally on me. A man who felt his masculinity challenged might have beaten me into submission.'

He smiled—no, he grinned back. 'I never even thought of it. Whatever made you think I wanted a wishy-washy kind of wife?'

In all this time, I've never seen him smile like that.

Had she seen him smile at all, apart from the practised one for the cameras?

Maybe he knew she needed distraction from this intense situation, as weird as it was terrifying; but Harun was providing distraction and reassurance in a way she never would have expected—at least from him.

Was this why his men had followed him into battle with such blind ferocity? Had he made them feel they could survive anything, too?

Whether it was real or a trick, she had no desire to argue with him. Right now, he was all she had, just as she was all he had—and the thought of losing this smiling man, teasing and caressing her hand, was unbearable. 'Well, maybe if you'd talked to me about what kind of wife you did want, I could answer that,' she replied, but in a light, fun tone, 'but right now I'm rather clueless.'

At that, he chuckled. 'Yes, you're not the only one who's told me that I keep a little too much to myself.'

Fascinated, she stared at his mouth. 'In all this time, I've never heard you laugh.'

She half expected him to make a cool retort—but instead one end of his mouth quirked higher. 'You think it took being abducted for me to show my true colours? Maybe, if you like it, you can arrange for it to happen on a regular basis.'

She was in the middle of laughter before she realised it. The look, the self-deprecating humour, set off a strange feeling low in her belly, a cross between muted terror and an inexplicable, badly timed hunger. 'How can you be so serious all the time when everything is safe and normal, and be this…this *charming* man now, when we might—?' To her horror, she couldn't go on, as a lump burned its way up her throat and tears prickled behind her eyes.

'Well, you see, I'm trying to distract myself from a horrendous itch on my back that I can't scratch.' He lifted up his bound hands.

Even though it was delivered deadpan, it made her laugh again. If he'd spent all those years before being too serious, now it seemed she couldn't make him become so. And she knew he'd done it to distract her. His thoughtfulness in this terrifying situation touched her. 'I could do it for you,' she offered, gulping away the painful lump in her throat. 'Roll over.'

He did, and her breath caught in her throat as she realised anew that he was naked from the waist up. She looked at the wealth of revealed man, unseen in three years. He didn't have time for extensive workouts, but he was toned and a natural deep brown, with broad shoulders and a muscular chest and back.

'Where?' she asked, fighting to keep the huskiness

out of her voice. It was the first time she'd touch his body, and it was for a stupid itch.

'Beneath my left shoulder blade.' He sounded odd, as if his throat was constricted, but when she scratched the area for him, using both hands at once since they were both there, he moved so her fingers covered a wider amount of skin. 'I don't remember anything ever feeling so good,' he groaned. 'You have magic hands, Amber. How about you? Is there anywhere you can't reach that needs scratching?'

Yes, my curiosity as to why you never talked to me before now, why you never wanted anything but to hurt and humiliate me until now—when we could die at any moment. 'You scratch my back and I'll scratch yours?' she murmured, aiming for the light tone of moments before, but she was too busy fighting her fingers, aching to turn the scratch into a caress, to feel his body.

'Sounds good to me,' he said, and now he was the one that sounded husky. 'I'll scratch any itch you need me to. You only need to ask, Amber.'

Her breath snagged in her chest. Her rebel eyes lifted to his face as he rolled back to her, and his awkward, tied movements brought him far closer to her than he'd ever been. His thighs were against hers, and his eyes were nearly black as his gaze slowly roamed her silk-clad form, and lifted to her mouth. She'd never seen a man's desire before, and it felt like sunlight touching her after a long, black Arctic winter. 'Harun,' she whispered, but no sound emerged from her. Her body moved towards him, and her face lifted as his lowered…

Then Harun rolled away from her, hard and fast, and she felt sick with anger and disappointment.

CHAPTER SIX

AT LEAST Amber felt sick until she realised Harun was shielding her with his body. 'Who's there?' he demanded in a hard tone. 'I heard the door open. Show yourself!' He'd blocked her effectively from seeing the door, and whoever stood there couldn't see her, either.

She tugged fast at the peignoir, but realised that trying to cover herself with this thin bit of nothing was a useless exercise.

A man walked around the curtain, his bare feet swishing on the old woven rug. He was dressed in anonymous Arabic clothing the colour of sand, most of his face swathed in a scarf. Without a word he bowed to them both, an incongruous gesture, and ridiculous in their current setting. Then, covering Amber's scantily clad body with the sheet first, his eyes trained away, he used a thin knife to untie her, and then Harun. When Harun was free the man waved to the small dining table by the window, which had two trays filled with food and drink, and bowed again.

Harun leaped to his feet the second he was untied, but the man lifted a strong hand, in clear warning against trying anything. He clapped, and two guards came around the curtains, armed with machine guns. Both guards had the weapons aiming directly at Harun.

Amber balled her hands into fists at her sides, instead of holding them to her mouth. If they knew she wanted to be sick at the sight of the weapons trained on Harun, they'd know their power over her.

If Harun felt any fear he wasn't showing it. 'What is this?' he demanded, and his voice was hard with command. 'Where are we, and what do you want with us?'

The man only kept his hand up. His eyes were blank.

'So you're a minion, paid to look anonymous,' Harun taunted. 'You can stay silent so I don't know your dialect, but the money you're hoping for will never be of use to you or your families.'

In answer, the man moved around the room. He pointed to one possible escape route after another, opening doors, lifting curtains to show them what lay beyond.

Armed guards stood at the door, and at each flat building roof facing a window, holding assault weapons trained on them.

Amber scrambled to her feet and, clutching the sheet, shrank behind Harun, who suddenly seemed far bigger than before, far more solid and welcoming. 'Those men are snipers, Harun,' she whispered. Allah help them, they were surrounded by snipers.

'Don't think about it. They're probably not even loaded,' Harun whispered in her ear. He kept his gaze on the guard, hard and unforgiving as he said aloud, 'I promise you, Amber, we'll get out of this safely.' He flicked the man a glance. 'These men know who we are. They won't take any risks with us, because we mean money. The cowards hiding behind them are obviously too scared to risk dealing with us themselves.'

The guard's eyes seemed to smile, but they held something akin to real respect. He bowed one final

time, and left the room. A deep, hollow *boom* sound
followed moments later.

The door wasn't simply locked. They'd put a bar
across it.

Amber shivered. 'That was—unnerving.' Hardly
knowing it, she reached out to him with a hand that
shook slightly. Right now she was too terrified to remember it was weak to need anyone else's reassurance.

His hand found hers, and the warm clasp was filled
with strength. 'It was meant to paralyse us into instant
obedience,' he said, in equal quiet, but anger vibrating
through each syllable. 'Remember, we're their bankroll.
This is all a game to them. They won't hurt us, Amber.
They need us alive.'

'So why surround us with snipers?' She shivered,
drawing closer. 'Why put us in the middle of nowhere
like this? How can we be such a threat?'

After a short hesitation, he took her in his arms. 'The
Shabbat war,' he said quietly.

He said no more, made no reference to his heroic
acts three years ago—he never had spoken about it, or
referred to his title, *the beloved tiger*. But his acts were
the stuff of legend now, and the stories had grown to
Alexander-like proportions during the past few years.
The people of Abbas al-Din felt safe with Harun as their
sheikh. 'You mean they're afraid of what you'll do?'

'Thus far it seems there's nothing *to* do.' He made a
sound of disgust. 'They want us to believe they're prepared for every contingency, but even the guard's silence tells me something. They don't want us to know
where we are. They know if he'd spoken, I might have
known his nationality and sub-tribe through the local
dialect.'

She frowned, looking up at him, glad of the distraction. 'Why would you know his nationality or tribe or dialect?'

His voice darkened still further. 'Whoever took us knows that I have a background in linguistics, and that I know almost every Arabic sub-dialect.'

'Oh.' Another cold slither ran down her back, even as she wondered what he'd studied at university, and why she'd never thought to ask. 'I think I'd like to eat now.'

'Amber, wait.' He held her back by trapping her in his arms.

More unnerved by the events of the last hour than she wanted to admit, she glared at him. 'Why should I? I'm hungry.'

He said softly, 'You've been unconscious for hours, and you haven't eaten in a day. You came around the bed in fear, but your legs might not support you any further.'

So have you, she wanted to say but didn't. *I can stand alone,* her pride wanted her to state, but, again, she couldn't make herself say it, because more unexpected depths of the man she'd married were being revealed with every passing moment. And, to her chagrin, she found her legs weren't as steady as she'd believed; she swayed, and he lifted her in his arms.

'Thank you,' she whispered. It was another first for them, and the poignant irony of why he held her this way slammed into her with full force.

'Come, you should eat, and probably drink.' He seated her on one of the chairs. 'But let me go first.' This time she merely frowned at the impolite assertion. With a weary smile, he again spoke very softly. 'I don't think your body can take any more drugging, Amber. You slept hours longer than I did, and you're still shaking. Let me see if the food is all right.'

Touched again by this new display of caring for her,

Amber tried to smile at him, but no words came. Right now, she didn't know if the non-stop quivering of her body was because of the drugging, or because he was being so considerate…and so close to her, smiling at her at last. Or because—because—

'I've been abducted,' she said. She meant it to come out hard, but it was a shaky whisper. But at least she'd said it. The reality had been slammed into her with the guards' entrance. There was no point in any form of denial.

'Don't think about it.' His voice was gentle but strong. 'You need time to adjust.'

Grateful for his understanding, she nodded.

After making a small wince she didn't understand, he tried the water, swilling it around in his mouth. 'No odd taste, no reaction in my gums or stinging in the bite-cut I just made in my inner cheek. I think it's safe to drink.' He poured her a glass. 'Sip it slowly, Amber, in case it makes you nauseous.'

She stared at him, touched anew. He'd cut himself to protect her. He'd shielded her from the guard. He'd carried her to the table. The Habib Numara she'd heard so much of but had never seen was here with her, for her.

'How do you know about the effects of being drugged?' she asked after a sip, and her stomach churned. She put down the glass with a trembling hand. 'Were you a kidnapper before you were a sheikh?'

Her would-be teasing tone fell flat, but he didn't seem to care. He kept smiling and replied, 'Well, I know about dehydration, and you've been a long time without fluids. When I did a stint in the desert, it affected me far more than it should for a boy of nineteen. The next time, during the Shabbat war, I knew better.'

Curiosity overcame the nausea. She tilted her head.

'What were you doing in the desert at nineteen? Was it for the Armed Forces?'

'No.' He lifted the darker fluid out of the ice bucket and poured it in his glass. When he'd sipped at it, swilling it as he had the water before swallowing, he poured her a glass. 'I was in Yemen, at a dig for a month. There was a fantastic *tell* there that seemed as if it might hold another palace that might have dated back to the time of the Queen of Sheba. Sip the water again now, Amber. Taking a sip every thirty seconds or so will accustom your stomach to the fluid and raise your blood pressure slowly, and hopefully stop the feeling of disorientation. I'll give you some iced tea as soon as I know you can tolerate it.'

'Why were you at a dig?' she asked before she sipped at the water, just to show her determination and strength to him. She didn't want him to think she was weak because she needed his help now.

He looked surprised. 'You didn't know? I assumed your father would have told you. I studied Middle Eastern history with an emphasis on archaeology. That's why I minored in linguistics, especially ancient dialects—I wanted to be able to translate any cuneiform tablets I found, scrolls with intimate family details, or even the daily accounts.'

She blinked, taken aback. Her lips fell open as eager questions burst from her mouth. 'You can read cuneiform tablets? In what languages? Have you read any of the Gilgamesh epic in its original form, or any of the accounts of the Trojan wars?'

'Yes, I can.' His brows lifted. 'What do you know about the Gilgamesh epic?'

She lifted one shoulder in a little shrug. 'I learned a little from my tutors during my school years, and I read about it whenever it comes up in the *Gods and Graves* journal.'

It was his turn to do a double take. 'Where do you get the journals? Have you been in my room?'

She shrugged, feeling oddly shy about it. 'I'm a subscriber. I have been for years.' She hesitated before she added, 'I can't wait for it to arrive every month.'

'You know you can get it online now?' He looked oddly boyish as he asked it, his eyes alight with eagerness.

'Oh, yes, but I like to *feel* it in my hands, see the things again and again by flipping the pages—you know? And the magazine is shinier than printing it up myself. The pages last longer, through more re-reads.'

'Yes, that's why I still subscribe, too.'

They smiled at each other, like a boy and girl meeting at a party for the first time. Feeling their way on unfamiliar yet exciting ground.

'When do you find time to read them, with all you have to do?'

'Late at night, before I sleep,' he said, with the air of confession. 'I have a small night light beside the bed.'

'Me too—I don't want the servants coming in, asking if they can serve me. I just want to read in peace.'

'Exactly.' He looked years younger now, and just looking into that eager blaze of joy in his eyes sent a thrill through her. 'It's my time to be myself.'

'Me too,' she said again, amazed and so happy to find this thing in common. 'What's your favourite period of study?'

He chuckled. 'I'd love to know who the Amalekites were, where they lived, and why they disappeared.'

Mystified, she demanded, 'Who? I've never heard of them.'

'Few people have. They were a nomadic people, savage and yet leaving no records except through those
they attacked. *Gods and Graves* did a series on them
years ago—probably before you subscribed—and I used
to try to find references to them in my years of university. I have notes in my room at home, and the series,
if you'd like to read about them.'

'You'd really share your notes with me? I'd *love* to,'
she added quickly, in case he changed his mind. 'Did
you always want to be an archaeologist?'

He shrugged and nodded. 'I always loved learning
about history, in any part of the world. Fadi planned
for me to use it to help Abbas al-Din. He thought Alim
and I could use our knowledge in different ways. Alim,
the scientist and driver, would be the way of the future,
bringing needed funds to the nation, and exploring en-
vironmentally friendly ways to use our resources rather
than blindly handing contracts to oil companies. I would
delve into our past and uncover its secrets. Abbas al-Din
has had very little done in the way of archaeology because my great-great grandfather banned it after something was found that seemed to shame our ancestors.'
He grinned then. 'When I told Fadi what I wanted to
do, he gave me carte blanche on our country's past.
He thought it would be good for one of the royal family to be the one to make the discoveries, and not hide
any, shall we say, inconvenient finds. After the dig at
Yemen, I organised one in the Mumadi Desert to the
west of Sar Abbas, since Fadi didn't want me to leave
the country again—but it turned out that I couldn't go.'

As he bowed his head in brief thanks for the food,
and picked up a knife and fork to try the salad, she
watched him with unwilling fascination. She didn't
want to ruin the mood by asking why he hadn't gone

that time, or why he hadn't taken it up as a career. She knew the answer: Alim's public life had chained Harun to home, helping Fadi for years. Then Fadi's death and Alim's desertion had foisted upon him more than just an unwanted wife.

He nodded at the salad, and served her a small helping. 'I think everything is okay to eat. The most likely source for drugging is in the fluids.'

After she'd given her own thanks, she couldn't help asking, 'So you keep up with it?'

'Apart from subscribing to all the magazines, I have a collection of books in my room, which I read whenever I have time. I keep up with the latest finds posted on the Net. I fund what digs I can from my private account.'

'It must be hard to love something so much, to fund all those digs you fund, and not be able to be there,' she said softly.

His face closed off for long moments, and she thought he might give her that shrug she hated. Then, slowly, he did—but it didn't feel like a brush-off. 'There's no point in wanting what you can't have, is there?'

But he did. The look of self-denial in those amazing eyes was more poignant than any complaint. She ached for him, this stranger husband who'd had to live for others for so many years. Would he ever be able to find his own life, to have time to just *be?*

As if sensing her pain and pity for him, he asked abruptly, 'So, do you have any thoughts on who might have taken us, and why?'

Wishing he hadn't diverted her yet, she bit her lip and shook her head. 'I've been thinking and thinking. This feels like the wrong time. If the el-Shabbats were going to do it, it should have been a year or more ago— and they would have paid for the African warlord to kill

Alim while they were at it. What's the point of taking us now? Alim's back, he'll probably marry the nurse… the dynasty continues.'

'I know.' He frowned hard. 'There doesn't seem to be a point—except…'

Amber found herself shivering in some weird prescience. 'Except?'

He looked up, into her eyes. 'We didn't continue the dynasty, Amber. Too many people know we've never shared a bedroom. The most traditional followers of the el-Kanar clan think you've brought me bad luck, and hate Alim's Western ways. They probably think we've already poisoned any future union, given who and what the woman is who Alim intends to marry.'

She frowned deeper. 'What do you mean, who and what she is? How could we affect his chances with this woman?'

He shrugged. 'You might as well know now. Hana, the woman Alim loves, is a nurse, and, yes, she saved his life—but though she was born in Abbas al-Din, she was raised in Western Australia, and isn't quite a traditional woman. Not only that, but Hana's not the required highborn virgin—she's a commoner, an engineer and miner's daughter. And that's not the worst.'

'There's more?' she asked, as fascinated as she was taken aback. This was sounding more and more like one of the many 'perils of Lutfiyah' films she'd enjoyed as a child.

'Believe it…or not,' he joked, in an imitation of the 'Ripley's' show she'd seen once or twice, and she laughed. 'Though Alim's arranged for her illegal proxy marriage to a drug runner to be annulled, the man's still in prison. You know how the press will use that—"our sheikh marries a drug runner's ex-wife". What's left of the Shabbat dynasty will make excellent mileage of it, perhaps start another insurrection.'

Amber gasped. 'How can Alim possibly think he'll get away with it? The hereditary sheikhs will never allow such a marriage!'

He gave another, too-careless shrug. 'Alim has brought our country much of its current wealth. And Hana's become a national heroine by saving his life at the risk of her own—without her, he'd be dead now, or he might never have come home. That belief is likely to start a backlash against the worst of the scandalmongers. And, given our lack of an heir in three years, the sheikhs that profit most from the el-Kanar family, and are desperate for the dynasty to continue, will vote for the marriage. By now Alim's probably made his planned public announcement that he either marries Hana or I remain his heir for life. To Alim, it's her or no one. He's determined to have her. He loves her.'

The bleakness of his eyes warned her not to touch the subject, but a cold finger of jealousy ran up her spine and refused to be silenced. 'She's a lucky woman. Is that how you feel about—about—what was her name?'

'Buhjah, you mean,' he supplied, with an ironic look that told her he knew she'd deliberately forgotten the woman's name. 'You really don't know me at all, Amber.'

She felt her chin lift and jut as she faced him, willing her cheeks not to blush at being caught out. 'And if I don't, whose fault is that?'

'Too many people's faults to mention, really.' He turned his face, staring out into the afternoon sky. 'And yes, the blame is mine, too—but blaming each other for anything gets us nowhere in our current position.'

'All right,' she said quietly, shamed by his honesty.

'So I'm thinking perhaps this abduction could be a reactionary thing—those who love Alim most are taking us out of the equation, or some relations of Hana's are doing this to force the media and hereditary sheikhs to accept the marriage, which means we'd be safely returned once the marriage is accepted and the wedding arrangements begun.'

She frowned at him. 'That's a very pretty story, and very reassuring, but what is it you're not saying? Who do you really think it is?'

His shoulders, which had been held tense, slumped just a little. 'Amber...'

'I'm not a child,' she said sharply. 'This is my life, Harun. I need to know what I'm facing if I'm going to be of any help to you.'

After a few moments, he came around the table and stood right over her. A quick, hard little thrill filled her at the closeness she'd so rarely known from him. 'Those who hate Alim's Western ways might have taken him, too,' he said so quietly she had to strain her ears to hear him, 'and they've put us here, in these clothes, this enforced intimacy, to create the outcome they want.'

'Which is?' she asked in a similar whisper, unwillingly fascinated. He was speaking so low she had to stand and crowd against him to hear.

'The obvious,' he murmured, moving against her as if they were playing a love-game. 'They want a legal el-Kanar heir from a suitable woman—and who could be more suitable than you?'

She felt her cheeks burning at the unprecedented intimacy. 'Oh.' She couldn't think of anything to say. But the stark look in his eyes told her something else lay deeper. 'There's something wrong with that happening, isn't there?' she mouthed against his ear. Again he didn't answer straight away, and she said, soft but fast, before she lost her courage, 'Whatever it is you fear most, just say it. It's my life, too. I deserve to know.'

The silence stretched out too long, and she wondered if she'd have to prompt him again, or make him angry enough to blurt it out, when he whispered right in her ear, 'But if we make love and you get pregnant, Amber, they'll have no reason to keep my brother alive.'

CHAPTER SEVEN

WHO was constantly conspiring against them? Even half naked and moving against each other as if they'd fall to the bed at any moment, it wasn't going to happen.

Would they ever enjoy a normal marriage, or was it Amber's pipe dream?

Then she looked into Harun's eyes, and saw the depth of his fear. *Alim is all I have left.*

An icy finger ran down her spine as she understood the nightmare he was locked in. How could she find it in her to blame him for putting his brother's life first?

Slowly, she nodded, trying to force a calm into her voice she was far from feeling—for his sake. 'Then we won't make love,' she said softly.

The intensity of his gratitude shone in the look he flashed at her. 'Thank you, Amber. I know how much you want a child. This is a sacrifice for you.'

'If it was one of my family in danger, I'd be saying the exact same thing to you.' Her voice was a touch shaky despite her best efforts. 'So tell me what's next?'

With a brief glance she didn't quite understand, he moved back to his side of the table. 'I checked the room pretty thoroughly while you slept. There's no window that isn't watched, no door or way out that isn't fully

guarded, including the roof. And as you saw, there are
snipers everywhere.'

'So that's it?' she asked in disbelief. 'We're stuck
in this golden cage until someone pays our ransom?'

Slowly he nodded. 'Yes,' was all he said, and her
stomach gave a sick lurch. Then he gave her a knowing look. It clicked into place—of course, the guards
were listening in. They had to be careful what they said
aloud. 'We're stuck here—and if you don't like it, remember you agreed to marry me.'

Not knowing what he wanted from her, she made
herself give a delicate shrug, as if being abducted were
something she was used to. 'Well, at least they're treating us better than Alim was treated in Africa.'

'And that's just as well, since Alim was always the
action man in the family.'

The look in his eyes said he'd almost rather be treated
badly. She frowned.

'You feel shamed by this abduction?'

He didn't look at her as he said, 'I can't get you out
of this danger we're in, Amber. I searched out every
possible way, but there's none that gets us both out, and
in safety. I don't know what they want, but we have no
choice but to comply.'

'And that makes you feel incompetent? Harun, you
were drugged and brought here against your will—'

'But that didn't happen to Alim, did it? He sacrificed
himself. He was even a hero in being abducted.' His jaw
tightened. 'What sort of man am I if I can't even fight,
or find a way for us to escape? If Alim couldn't rescue
himself, what hope does someone like me have of getting us both out of here?'

The unspoken words shimmered in the air. *Even
when he was taken, Alim had sacrificed himself, risked*

his life to save the woman he loved. I am less than a man in comparison to my brother.

His voice rang with conviction—the kind that came from intimate knowledge of truth of feeling. And she wondered how many times he'd felt that way before he'd become a hero in his own right. How hard had it been to be the younger, quieter brother of the nation's hero, to live in the shadow of a world superstar?

'Someone like you?' As she repeated the words an unexpected surge of hot anger filled her, at what she wasn't yet sure, but its very ferocity demanded she find out. 'How did they take you?' she shot at him.

He shrugged again. It was another cool, careless thing, a barrier in itself, and, three years too late, she realised that this was what he did, how he pushed people away before he'd say something he might regret. 'Tell me, Harun!'

'Fine,' he growled. 'I came into the room, and saw you being dragged away. I had no time, I just ran after you, and they took me, too. Because I didn't stop to think it through, I failed you. And yes, before you say it, I know Alim would have done better!'

'*How* would he have done that?' she snapped, even angrier now.

He shook his head. 'If I'd stopped to think—if I'd called the guard—'

'Then they might have got away, and I'd be here alone, terrified out of my mind.' She slammed her hand down on the table. 'I don't *care* what Alim would have done. He isn't here. *You're* here, because you tried to save me. You didn't have to do that!'

'And what a wonderful job I did of it, getting drugged myself, and ending up with us both in this prison,' he retorted, self-mockingly.

As if incensed, she grabbed his shoulders. 'You're here with me, Harun. You think you're nothing like Alim? You're just like him! You're more of a hero to me than he can ever be. Do you think he'd have sacrificed his freedom for me the way you have? Don't you know what you did—how much it means to me?'

He looked up at her, a look she couldn't decipher in his eyes. 'You've never willingly touched me before,' he said slowly.

Lost in an odd wonder, she looked down, to where his fingers curled around her arms. 'Nor you me, before today,' she whispered. Suddenly she found it hard to breathe.

Too quickly, they both released the other, and she felt as bereft as he looked, for a bare moment in time, both breathing hard, as if from running an unseen race. It felt so real. Was it real? She only wished she knew.

'I—I'm so glad you're here with me, Harun,' she said, very quietly. 'No matter how it happened. Without you, I...' She shook her head, not sure what it was she was going to say. 'I'm glad it's *you*,' she whispered, so soft he probably couldn't hear it.

'Amber.'

So quietly spoken, that word, her name, and yet... She was torn between so many remembered humiliations and unfamiliar, almost frightening hope, her lips parted. She looked into his eyes, and saw—

The door rattled and opened.

Just as she'd looked up into his eyes like that—with a softened, almost hopeful expression, the real woman, not the part she was playing, he knew, could *feel* it— the noise of the rattling handle broke the moment. At the entry of the man swathed in his sand-hued outfit and headscarf, Amber had started, flushed scarlet and looked back down at her plate as if nothing else existed.

Harun couldn't stand up until he had control of his body—and that was a task of near-impossible proportions, given what she was almost wearing. Thus he'd desperately thought of this farce of play-acting for those watching them. If they'd known he was hurtling down the invisible highway of a man condemned to fulfilling the prophecy they'd put in place for him, they'd leave him totally alone with Amber—*your wife, she's your wife*—and she looked like the gates to paradise…

Stop it! Just don't look at her.

She wasn't looking at him like that now. In fact she wasn't looking at him at all. She waited until their guard had cleared away their food trays and left the room, before murmuring, 'Are you sure there's no way out of here? I think we should check the rooms together. There might be something…'

Pride reared its useless head for a moment, but with a struggle he subdued it. Even if he could easily take offence, he chose not to start another fight. Besides that, they both needed something to distract them right now—at least he did, and desperately.

'Good idea,' was all he could manage to say. 'I was drugged still when I looked. I might have missed something.' He knew he hadn't, but he had to get away from her.

She must have seen him stiffen. She peered at him, anxiety clear to read in her eyes. 'I just want to be sure—and, really, what else is there for us to do right now?'

He could think of something else incredible, amazing, and dangerous to do—but he nodded, trying not to look at the sweet delight before him. 'You need to know for yourself. I would have, too.'

Her voice was filled with warmth and relief. 'Thank you.'

Why wasn't it a cold evening? Then he could cover her with the bed sheet—a towel—anything. Not that it would help; the image of her unfettered loveliness had been burned in his brain since their wedding night. 'You try out here, while I do the bathroom.'

After shoving her chair back, she froze. 'I—I don't… I think I'd prefer if we stayed together. That is, if you don't mind,' she said in a very small voice. She still wasn't looking at him, but, from the fiery blush before, she was far too pale.

Harun cursed himself in silence for thinking only of himself, his needs. Amber was frightened, and he was all she had. Who else could she turn to for strength and reassurance? 'Of course I'll stay with you,' he said gently. 'Where would you prefer to begin?'

Without warning she scraped the chair back and bolted to him. 'I c-can't think. I don't know what to do.' She pushed at his shoulders in obvious intent.

Forcing compassion and tenderness to overcome every other need right now, he pushed his chair back, and pulled her onto his lap. He held her close, caressing those shining waves of dark-honey hair. 'I'm here, Amber. Whatever happens, I won't leave you.'

'Thank you,' she whispered in a shaky voice, burrowing her face into his neck. 'I'll be better in a minute. It's just that man—his silence terrifies me. And those guns…I can't stop seeing them in my mind.'

'It would scare anyone senseless,' he agreed, resting his chin on her hair. *Don't think of anything else. She needs you.*

'Were you scared? In the war, I mean?' she whispered into his neck. Her warm breath caressed his skin, and sent hot shivers of need through him. Every moment the struggle grew harder to not touch her. Just by being so close against him, she made his whole body ache with even hotter desire.

Could she feel what she was doing to him? He'd been permanently aroused since waking up the first time; his dreams had been filled with fevered visions of them that he couldn't dismiss, no matter how he tried.

For Amber's sake, control yourself. She doesn't want you, she needs reassurance.

'Of course I was scared,' he said quietly, forcing the safe rhythm, palm smoothing her hair. 'Everyone was, no matter what they say.'

'They said you showed no sign of fear.' She looked up, her eyes as bright as they'd been before, when they'd made a connection over their shared love of archaeology. It seemed his bride wanted to know about him at last. 'Everyone says you fought like a man possessed.'

Everyone says... Did that mean she'd been asking about him, or drinking in every story? What had she been thinking and hoping in those years he'd ignored her?

'I had to lead my men.' He wondered what she'd think if he told her the truth: he'd fought his own demons on that battlefield, and every man had Alim's face. Where his brother was concerned, the love and the resentment had always been so closely entwined he didn't know how to separate them—and never more so than when he discovered his bride wanted Alim. And he was paying for that ambivalence now, in spades. If Alim had been taken, or God forbid, was dead…

'Everyone said you took the lead wherever you were.'
She sounded sweet, breathless.

But though something deep inside felt more than
gratified that she wanted to know about him, had been
thinking of him, he sobered. 'Even killing a man you
perceive as your enemy has its cost for every soldier,
Amber. The el-Shabbats had reason for what they did.
I knew that—and Alim had left the country leaderless;
he clearly wasn't interested in coming home. I wondered
what I was doing when I took the mantle.'

'So why did you fight?' she murmured, her head on
his shoulder now.

He wanted to shrug off the question, to freeze her
out—but his personal need for space and silence had to
come second now. Amber's and Alim's lives were on
the line because he'd put his *feelings* before the needs
of the nation. 'When the el-Shabbats chose Mahmud el-
Shabbat for their leader, a man with no conscience, who
was neither stable nor interested in what was best for
anyone but his own family, they forced the war on me.'

'You became a hero,' she murmured, and he heard
the frown in her voice. Wondering why he wasn't happy
about it.

Harun felt the air in his lungs stick there. He wanted
to breathe, but he had to say it first. 'I can still see the
faces of the men whose lives I took, Amber,' he said
jerkily. 'War isn't glorious when you live it. That's a
pretty story for old men to tell to young boys. War's an
undignified, angry, bloody mess.'

'I saw you coming in on the float,' she said quietly.
'I thought you looked as if you wanted to be anywhere
but there.'

He almost started at her perception. 'All the glory I
received on coming back felt wrong. I'd taken fathers

from children, sons from parents, made widows and orphans, all to retain power that was never mine to keep.'

At that she looked up. 'That's why you gave it back to Alim without a qualm?'

Slowly, he nodded. 'That, and the fact that the power wasn't mine to give. I was only the custodian until his return.'

'You related to the people you fought against.' It wasn't a question; her eyes shimmered with understanding. Her arms were still tightly locked around his neck, and he ached to lean down an inch, to kiss her. His yearning was erotic, yes, but beneath that some small, stupid part of him still ached to know he wasn't alone. Where Amber was concerned, he was still fighting inevitability after all these years.

'To their families,' he replied, struggling against giving the uncaring shrug that always seemed to annoy her. 'I became an orphan at eight years old. I lost both my brothers almost at once.' He held back the final words, unwilling to break this tentative trust budding between them.

'And you lost your wife even before the wedding day.' She filled in the words, her voice dark with shame even as she kept her head on his shoulder. 'You were forced to fight for your family, your country while you were still grieving. You gave everything to your country and your family—then you were abandoned by Fadi, by Alim, and, last, by me. I'm sorry, Harun. You were alone. I could have, should have tried to help you more.'

How could she say those things? It was as if she stared through him to see what even he didn't. She seemed to think he was something far more special than he was. 'No, Amber. I never told you. I shut you out.' Tipping her face up to his, he tried to smile at her, to keep the connection going. 'All of it was my fault.'

'No, it wasn't, and we both know that—but blame won't help us in our current situation,' she retorted, quoting his words back to him with a cheeky light in her eyes, and her dimples quivering.

He grinned. 'Someone's feeling feisty.'

She winked. 'I told you I'd feel better in a minute. Or maybe five,' she amended, laughing.

'Then let's begin the search,' he suggested, not sure if he was relieved or resentful for the intervention. Her lips glistened like ripe pomegranates in the rose-hued rays of the falling sun through the window, and he was dying to taste them. And when she wriggled off his lap, he couldn't move for a few moments—so blinded by white-hot need for her, all he could see was the vision of them together in bed as they could have been for years now.

What sort of fool had he been? Within a day of giving her some attention her eyes were alight with desire when she looked at him, or when he was close. If he took her to bed right now, he doubted she'd even want to argue.

'Wrong time, wrong place—and Alim could die,' he muttered fiercely beneath his breath, feeling the frozen nails of fear put the coffin lid on his selfish wants.

Keeping Alim's face in his mind, Harun fell to his knees, looking for loose boards in the floor with ferocious determination. He wouldn't look at her again until his blood began to cool; but whenever he heard her husky voice announcing she still hadn't found anything, he looked up, and with every sight of her wiggling along the floor in that shimmering satin the fight began over. Hot and cold, fire and ice—Amber and Alim…

MELISSA JAMES

101

The suite of rooms was small. Amber unconsciously followed the path he'd taken while she slept, knocking softly on walls, checking bricks for secret passages. But then she hung so far out of the window he grabbed her by the waist to anchor her, and had to twist his body so she wouldn't know how much she affected him. Fighting also against the burning fury that those men with assault rifles would be looking at her luscious body, he pulled her back inside with a mumbled half-lie about her safety.

She sighed as she came back into the room. 'We're so far up, even if we tied the sheets and bedcover together, we'd have a two-storey drop or more.' She glanced at him. 'You could probably make it to the ground, but I'd probably break my legs, and then they'd just take us again.' Biting her lip, she mumbled, 'I wish I'd had the same kind of war training as you—dropping out of planes, martial arts and the like. I wish I could say I was a heroine like my great-grandmother, but the thought of breaking my legs makes me sick with fear.' She looked him in the eyes as she said, 'You should go without me. You have to save Alim.'

Hearing the self-sacrifice in her voice, remembering how she'd been so furious when he'd run himself down earlier, even if it was an act, he felt something warm spread across him. After all these years where he'd ignored her, did she really think so much of him?

Or so little, that she could even suggest he'd go without her, put his brother first, and abandon her to her captors?

Quietly, he said, 'I dropped out of planes with a parachute and spare. And even if I could use a sheet as a makeshift parachute, and jump in the darkest part of the night, I'd still have to outrun the guards, and find a place of safety or a phone, and all without water or food—and wearing only these stupid things.' And there was no way he'd leave Amber alone to face the consequences of his escape.

He was taken aback by the success of his diversion when Amber giggled. 'Oh, the visions I'm having now—the oh-so-serious Sheikh Harun el-Kanar escaping abduction, but found only in his boxer shorts!'

Though he laughed with her—because it was a funny thought—right now he wasn't in the mood to laugh. 'I would never leave you, Amber. That probably seems hard to believe—'

Her eyes, glowing with life and joy, a smile filled with gratitude, stopped him. She did believe him, though he'd done nothing to earn her trust. That smile pierced him in places he didn't want to remember existed. The places he'd thought had died years ago...trust, faith, and that blasted, unconquerable hope.

Trust had died even before his parents, and, though he still prayed, a lot of his faith had eroded through the years. And hope—the last shards of it had smashed to bits when he'd heard her agree to marry him, despite loving his brother.

Or so he'd thought, until today.

'Let's check the bathroom again,' she suggested. 'Sometimes there's a loose tile on the floor that is the way out—or even in the bath itself. My great-grandmother had one egress made through the base of the tap in the bath, after the war ended. We should check it out thoroughly.'

Grateful for the reprieve from his dark thoughts, he followed her in and got down on hands and knees beside her, but turned to search in the opposite direction.

Anything rather than endure the torture of memory—
or of watching her lovely body wiggling with every
movement.

This time he forced his eyes to stay away. If she held
a shadow of desire for him now, it was just through enforced proximity and her need for human closeness.
She'd never shown a single sign of wanting him, or
even wanting to know him better, until now. He'd never
seen anything from her but cold duty and contemptuous
anger until the day she'd heard Alim was back.

That was the way his life would be. How many times
did he have to convince himself over and over that
duty and supporting family was his only destiny? How
many times had his parents told him that he'd be useless for anything else? How many times in the twenty-
two years since they'd died had Fadi enforced his belief
that duty was first, last and everything for him, that
he was born to be the supportive brother? Yet here
he was, no wiser. At thirty years old, he still hadn't
learned the lesson.

Was it the after-effects of the drugs that had weakened his resolve, or was it just a case of too many years
of denial? But the desire in her eyes, the curve of her
smile, the music of her laughter—and everything that
was almost clear to see beneath that peignoir—were
killing him to resist. Even the sight of her bare feet was
a temptation beyond him right now.

This was the exact reason he'd avoided her so long
before. But now he couldn't make himself avoid her,
even if he could parachute out of here with that stupid
sheet. He couldn't leave her alone…and so here they
were, only the two of them and that delicious bed…
and with every moment that passed, it became more

impossible to resist her. How long could he last before he made a fool of himself?

But that was exactly what the kidnappers wanted, and damned if he'd give it to them.

CHAPTER EIGHT

BY NIGHTFALL, they had covered almost every inch of both rooms, and found no way out. All her hopes dashed, she sat on the ground, slumping against the cool bath tiles in despair. 'We're not getting out of here, are we?'

'Not until they let us out.' There was a strange inflection in his voice.

Arrested, she turned to look at him. 'What is it?'

Harun didn't reply.

'I'm not a child, Harun, or an idiot. I'm in this with you, like it or not, and there's nowhere for you to conveniently disappear to here, no excuse or official or quiet room for you to get away from me. So you might as well share what you're thinking with me.'

After a moment that seemed to last a full minute, he said, 'I think your father may be our abductor.'

'What?' They were the last words she'd expected. Gasping, she choked on her breath and got lost in a coughing fit to be able to breathe again. Harun began using the heel of his hand in rhythmic upward motions, and the choking feeling subsided. Then she pushed him away, glaring at him. 'Why would he do that? What would be the benefit to him, and to Araba Numara?

How could you even think that? How dare you accuse my father of this?'

Harun was on his haunches in front of her, his face had that cold, withdrawn look she hated.

'For a daughter who doesn't share my suspicions, a daughter who believes implicitly in her father's innocence, I notice you put the two most natural questions last. Instead, you asked the most important questions first—why, and what benefit to him in abducting his own child. You believe it's possible at the very least, Amber. Everything makes sense with that one answer. Why there have been no demands or threats as yet, why we were left in this kind of room dressed this way, and why we're alone most of the time. Your father has probably endured some ridicule and speculation over our not producing an heir, and he wants it to end.' He gave her a hard look. 'He has no son, and you're the eldest daughter. He hasn't named his brother, or his nephews or male cousins as his heir. Any son we have will be qualified to become the hereditary sheikh for Araba Numara, so long as he takes his grandfather's name...and I assume that keeping the line going is important to him.'

Every suspicion he'd voiced could be exactly right. And it all fitted her father too well. Though he came from a very small state in the Emirates—or maybe because of that—he enjoyed manipulating people until they bent to his will. And yes, he'd want a grandson to take his name and the rule of Araba Numara.

'If you're right, and I'm not saying you are, I will never, never forgive him for this.' Then she shot to her feet, and cried, 'Hasn't he done enough to me? Three years of being his pawn, left in a foreign country and shuffled from one man to another, none of whom wanted me! Can't he just leave me be?'

The echoes of her voice in the tiled bathroom were her only answer. The silence was complete, just as it had always been when she'd tried to defy her father's will, and she slid back down the tiles. 'I hate this, I hate it. Why can't he let me have my life?'

Harun's eyes gleamed with sadness. 'I don't know, Amber. I'm no expert on family life. I barely remember my father, or mother.' As he slid down beside her, the feeling of abandonment fled along with her outrage—and, as natural as if she'd done it for years, she laid her head on his shoulder. 'It's probably best not to think about it,' he said quietly, wrapping his arm over her shoulder, drawing her closer. 'And remember I could be wrong.'

'We both know you're not. It makes too much sense.'

'There is the other solution I told you before,' he said very quietly.

She nodded.

'If they won't let us out until you're pregnant, we may have little choice but to comply.'

A tiny frisson of shock ran through her. 'B-but what if we are wrong—wouldn't that risk Alim's life?' she stammered.

'Only if he has been taken. We just don't know.' His eyes hardened. 'I can't keep living my life for honour alone, Amber. Alim's the one who left his family and his nation too many times to count—and why did he finally return? For the sake of a woman he can't even marry. I've done everything for him for ten years, and it's time I did something I want to do.'

Softly, she murmured, 'And now you want me?'

'Yes,' he replied, just as soft.

His mouth curved; his eyes softened. And he brushed his mouth against hers.

With the first touch, it was as if he'd pulled a string inside her, releasing warmth and joy and need and—and yes, a power she hadn't known existed, the power of being a woman with her man, *the* man for her. She made a smothered sound and moved into him as her lips moved of their own will, craving more. She turned into him, her hands seeking his skin, pulling him against her. Eager fingers wound into his hair, splayed across his back, explored his shoulders and arms, and the kiss grew deeper and deeper. They slowly fell back until they lay entangled on the floor. Amber barely noticed its cold hard surface. Harun was touching her at last, he was fully aroused, and she moaned in joy.

'As far as first kisses go, that was fairly sensational,' he said in a shaky voice. 'But we're only a few hours out of the drugs. Today hasn't been the easiest for either of us. Maybe we should rest. If we feel the same tomorrow…'

Bewildered by the constant changes in his conversation, she sighed. 'Yes, I think I need to sleep again. But I really should have a bath.'

After a short silence, Harun said quietly, 'No, sleep first. Come, I'll help you to bed.' He swept her up again, as though she weighed nothing, and carried her back out to the main room. He could have taken her to bed and made love to her all night and she'd have loved it.

Reaching the bed, he laid her down. 'Rest now, Amber. I swear I won't leave you,' he whispered, his voice tender, so protective. Had the *habib numara* become her very own tiger—at least for now?

She ought to know better than to think this way. They barely knew each other, and he'd never shown any interest in touching her until today.

She ought to feel grateful to their abductors. For

the first time Harun was looking at her as a person. For a captive, she felt happier than she had in a very long time.

Too tired to work through the confusion, she allowed her heavy eyes and hurting heart to dictate to her. She needed temporary oblivion from the events of the past day, to blank it all out. But even as she slid towards sleep, she felt Harun's presence in the chair he'd drawn up beside the bed. Touched that he was standing guard over her, keeping her safe without presuming to share the bed, she wanted to take his hand in hers and cradle it against her face, to thank him for all he'd done today. But he'd done so much for her; she couldn't demand more than he'd already given. She sighed again, and drifted into dreams.

And shaken far beyond anything she knew, too aroused to sleep, Harun sat beside her the whole night. He didn't get on the bed—he didn't dare—but he remained on guard, ready to protect her if there should be a need.

She's a stubborn, rebellious daughter, with no regard for law or tradition. I wouldn't pay a single dinar for her return. Let Sheikh el-Kanar pay it, if he's worried about her at all, but I doubt it. He ran from her in the first place, didn't he?

Shivering in the night suddenly turned cold, the echoes of her father's uncaring tone still ringing in her ears, Amber jerked to a sitting position in the bed. Praise Allah, it had only been a nightmare—

But this bed, sagging slightly, definitely wasn't hers, and choppy breathing came from a few feet away. Adjusting to the darkness and unfamiliar room, she gradually took in the form of her husband sleeping in a chair beside the bed.

Although the sight of him made her ache somehow—he looked like a bronze statue of male perfection in the pale moonlight, even half crumpled in the chair—reality returned to her in seconds, the reasons why they were here. And what they'd done to convince their abductors that they were cooperating...

A hot shiver ran down her spine.

She looked again at her sleeping husband, realising anew the masculine beauty of him. His face was gentle in repose, seeming so much younger.

She reached out, touching him very softly. His skin was cool to the touch. He was shivering as she'd been; there were goosebumps on his arms. His sheet must have slipped to the floor long ago, and he was still half naked, only clad in those silky boxers. Obviously he'd left her the blanket, but she'd kicked it off some time in the night.

During the search earlier, neither of them had found a second covering of any kind, so she could do nothing but share the blanket they had. The modesty he'd given her in sleeping on the chair was touching, but it was ridiculous when they were married. If either of them took sick, they had no way to care for the other.

'Harun,' she whispered, but he didn't move. Taking him by the shoulder, she shook it, feeling the flex and ripple of muscles beneath her fingers. 'Harun, come—' she stopped herself from saying *come to bed* only just in time '—under the blanket. You're cold.'

An indistinct mumble was his only response.

Impatient, getting sleepy again, she grabbed his shoulders with both hands, pulling him towards her.

MELISSA JAMES   111

'Come on, Harun. You'll be in agony in the morning, sleeping like that. I can't afford for you to get sick.'

Something must have penetrated, for he fell onto the bed, landing almost right on top of her, his leg and arm falling over her body, trapping her. 'Mmm, Amber, lovely Amber,' he mumbled, moving his aroused body against hers, his lips nuzzling her throat. 'Taste so good…knew you would. Like sandalwood honey.' And before she could gather her wits or move, he kept right on going, lower, until he was kissing her shoulder, and she had no idea if he was awake or seducing her in his dreams.

She couldn't think enough to care…her neck and shoulder arched with a volition of their own as he nibbled the juncture between both, and the bliss was *exquisite.* And when his hand covered her breast, caressing her taut nipple, the joy was sharp as a blade, a beautiful piercing of her entire being. 'Harun, oh,' she cried aloud, craving more—

His eyes opened, and even in the moonlit night she saw the lust and sleepy confusion. Gazing down, he saw his hand covering her breast. 'I'm sorry…I was dreaming. I didn't mean to take advantage of you.' He shook his head. 'How did I get on the bed?'

A dull ache smothered the lovely desire like a fire-retardant blanket. 'I woke up—you were shivering, and I pulled you over. The sheet wasn't warm enough for you,' she replied drearily. Who had he been dreaming of when he'd said her name? 'It's all right. Take the blanket and go back to sleep.'

'Amber…'

'Don't,' she said sharply. *Don't be kind to me, or I*

might just break down. She rolled away from him so he wouldn't see her humiliation. 'Goodnight.'

The next afternoon

Any moment now, he'd pick her up and throw her on the bed, and make love to her until they both died of exhaustion.

He'd been going crazy since last night. Pretending to sleep for her sake, he'd lain still on the bed until his entire body had throbbed and hurt; he knew she was doing the same. Then, just as his burning body talked him into rolling over and making love to her, her soft, even breathing told him she slept.

That he'd made Amber cry simply by not continuing to make love to her was a revelation to him. In three long, dreary years, all he'd known was her contempt and anger, even the night she'd asked him to come to her bed. But within the space of a day, he'd seen her show him regret, budding friendship, trust, need and—for that blazing second when he'd awoken with his hand on her breast—pure desire for him. He'd come so close to giving in, giving them what they both wanted—only a tiny sound from outside the room, a shuffle of feet, a little cough, had reminded him of their watchers, had held him back.

And how could he risk his brother's life?

It kept going back to that choice: their personal happiness, or Alim's life. If there was a way to know Alim was safe, if they could escape and have some privacy, he'd give their abductors what they wanted, over and over. Now he knew Amber wanted him...

But without meaning to, he'd hurt and humiliated

her. His apology had wounded her pride in a way she was going to find extremely hard to forgive.

After hours of silence between them and no touching, he spoke with gentle deliberation. 'I'm sorry about last night.'

Her lips parted as her head turned. 'You already apologised. Anyway why should you apologise? You were dreaming, right?' Oh, so cold, so imperious, her tone—but his deepest male instincts told him it was the exact opposite of what she felt inside.

He looked into her eyes. 'I heard a cough outside the room. The first time I make love to you will not be by accident, with an audience of strangers through holes in the wall.'

A surprised blink covered a moment's softness in her eyes. 'That's a fairly big assumption to make.'

Despite the cold fury in her voice, he wanted to smile. 'That we'll make love? Or that you can forgive me for neglecting you all these years, and welcome me in your bed?'

'Either. Both,' she said quietly, 'especially considering the neglect was of epic proportions, and publicly humiliating.'

At that, he offered her a wry smile. 'I had no wish for a martyr bride, Amber. I'm fairly sure you didn't want a dutiful, reluctant husband, either. I believed you had no desire for me; you believed that I never desired you. All this time we both wanted the same thing, if only we'd tried to talk.'

She looked right into his face, her chin lifted. 'Did you really just say that—if *we'd* tried to talk?'

He had to concede that point if he wanted to get anywhere with her. 'You're right, I'm the one that didn't try—but ask yourself how hard you'd have tried, if you'd thought I was in love with your sister.'

Another slow blink as she thought about it. 'Maybe—'

But just as the frost covering her hidden passion finally began to soften he heard the door open, and he cursed the constant interferences between them—but then, with a smothered gasp, Amber bolted off the window seat and cannoned into him. 'He's pointing that rifle at me,' she whispered, shaking, as his arms came around her. 'And…and he's looking at me, and I'm only wearing this thing.'

Like a whip he flung around to face the guard, putting Amber behind him. 'What is this?' he demanded four times over, in different dialects. 'Answer me, why do you terrify my wife this way?' Again he said it in another few dialects—all of Amber's home region.

The man never so much as glanced their way; he answered only by moving the rifle inward, towards the dining table.

Amber's chest heaved against his back as she tried to control her fear.

Three men followed him into the room, bearing a more substantial meal than they'd eaten yesterday, or at breakfast, three full choices of meal plus teas, juice or water. The men set the table with exquisite care, as if he and Amber were honoured guests at a six-star hotel. Then they held out the seats, playing the perfect waiters—only the maître d' was holding an assault rifle on them.

Harun stood his ground, shielding Amber with his body. 'Move away from the chairs. Don't come near my wife. Stop looking at her or I will find who you are after this and kill you with my bare hands.'

After a moment, with a look of deep respect the head

guard bowed, and waved the others back. When they were out, he took several steps back himself before he stopped, staring at the furthest wall from their captives.

Harun led Amber to her chair and seated her himself, blocking her from their view so they could see no part of her semi-exposed body. 'Now get out,' he barked.

He bowed again, and left the room.

'Thank you,' she whispered, hanging onto his hand when he would have moved.

'There's nothing to thank me for.' Some emotion he couldn't define was coursing through him, as if he were flying with his own wings. He didn't trust it.

'I can't take much more of this—this terrifying silence,' she muttered, her free hand clenching and unclenching. 'Why did he point the rifle at me? What did I do?'

Harun had his own ideas, but he doubted saying, *Their objective is achieved, Amber, you ran straight to me,* would help now, or bring her any comfort. She might even begin to suspect him.

Instead of sitting, he released her hand, and wrapped his arms around her from behind. 'I know I may not seem like much help to you in this situation, Amber, but I swear I'll protect you with my life if need be.'

She twisted around so her face tilted up to his. 'You know that's not true. Last night, I told you how glad I am you're here…and you saw, you must have seen that…' Her lips pushed hard together.

It was time; he knew it, could feel it; but still he would give her a gift first. 'Yes, I saw that you desire me, how you loved my touch.' With a gentle smile, he touched her burning face. 'And you had to see how much I desire you, Amber. If it hadn't been for the guards, we'd have made love last night.'

She said nothing, but her eyes spoke encyclopaedic volumes of doubt. 'You said my name. I wasn't sure if you meant it.'

In the half-question, and the deep shadows in her eyes, he saw the depth of the damage he'd done to her by his neglect. She had no idea at all; she'd never once seen his desire until last night, and she even doubted it had been for her.

It seemed he'd hidden his feelings too well—and at this point he doubted just showing her would be enough. He had to open up, starting now.

'I did mean it, Amber. My dreams were of you. My dreams have been of you for a long time.' Taking her hand again, he lifted it to his mouth and pressed a lingering kiss to her palm. When she didn't snatch her hand away, but drew in a quick, slightly trembling breath, he let his lips roam to her wrist. 'Sandalwood honey,' he murmured against her skin. 'The most exquisite taste I've known.'

She didn't answer him, except in the tips of her fingers that caressed his face, then retreated. So tentative still, she was afraid to give anything away. Unsure if, even now, he'd walk away again and leave her humiliated. He'd damaged her that much through the years, which meant he had the *power* to hurt her—and that meant more than any clumsy words of reassurance she could give.

It was time to give back, to be the one to reach out and risk rejection.

So hard to start, but he'd already done that; and now, to his surprise, the words flowed more easily. 'You need to know now. I haven't been with any woman since we married. I kept my vows, as difficult as that's been at times.'

Her look of doubt grew, but she said nothing.

He smiled at her. 'It's true, Amber. I didn't want a replacement. I wanted you.'

The little frown between her brows deepened. 'Then why…?'

Walking around to face her, he took both hands in his and lifted her to her feet. 'I refused to continue last night because our audience made it clear they were there watching us. I'm not a man who likes applause and cheering on, and I didn't think you'd want your first time to be here, where any of them could see us.'

'No, I wouldn't. Thank you for thinking of it,' she murmured, her gaze dropping to his mouth, and his whole body heated with a burst of flame at the look in her eyes. 'But I don't understand why you didn't come to me before—oh.' She nodded slowly. 'Because of what I said to my father.'

'I'm not Alim. I'll never be like Alim.' She had to know that now. He'd rather burn like this the rest of his life than be his brother's replacement in her eyes, or in her bed.

'I know who you are.' And still she stared at his mouth with open yearning that made him define the alien, flying feeling—he was so *glad* to be alive, to be the man she desired.

Then her head tilted, and he mentally prepared himself: she did that when she wanted to know something he wouldn't want to answer. 'Why do you think you can never compare to Alim? I barely knew him. You must have known that; he left for the racing circuit days after I met him, and then ran from the country as soon as he could leave the hopspital. He never wanted me, and you say you did. So why didn't you try for me?'

As far as hard questions went, that was number one.

He felt himself tensing, ready to give the shrug that was his defence mechanism, to walk away—

Trouble was, there was nowhere to go, no place of escape. And he knew what she was going to say before she said, very softly, 'You promised to talk to me.'

At that moment he almost loathed her. He'd never broken a promise in his life, never walked away in dishonour; but trying to put his disjointed thoughts together was like trying to catch grains of sand in a desert storm. What did she want him to say?

'Just tell me the truth,' she said, just as quietly as before, smiling at him. As if she'd seen his inner turbulence and wanted to calm it.

Nothing would do that. There was no way out this time. So he said it, hard and fast. 'I don't compare to him. I never have. What was the point in trying for you when you wanted a man that wasn't me? I was never anything but a replacement for him, with Fadi and with you. I always knew that.'

CHAPTER NINE

IF THERE was anything she'd expected Harun to say, it
wasn't that. She'd hoped to hear a complaint about his
family, or about how he'd lived in the shadow of a famous, heroic brother—but never that calmly spoken
announcement, like a fact long accepted. *I don't compare to him. I never have.*

A sense of foreboding touched Amber's heart, a pre-
monition of the hardships facing her if she chose to
spend her life with this man. *How would I have ended
up, had Alim been my brother, if I'd lived in the shadow
of a famous sibling and ended up taking on all the responsibilities he didn't want?*

The thought came from deep inside her, from the
girl who'd never really felt like a princess, but a com-
modity for sale to the highest bidder. And she spoke
before she knew what she wanted to say. 'That's another big assumption to make, considering my total
acquaintance with Alim has been five days, and I've
known you three years.'

He flicked her another resentful glance, but she
wouldn't back down. He had nowhere to go, and his
honour meant more than anything. He'd answer her, if
she waited long enough.

Lucky she wasn't holding her breath; she'd be dead

by the time he finally said, 'I know what I am in your eyes, Amber. And I know what Alim is.'

She frowned. 'One sentence made in grief and not even knowing you, and that's it? You just write me off your things to do list? *Marry her and ignore her because she insulted me once when she didn't know I was listening? I don't care if she apologised.*'

Another look, fuming and filled with frustration; how he hated to talk. But finally he said, 'I'm not Alim.'

By now she felt almost as angry as him, but some instinct told her he was deliberately pushing her there to make her stop talking to him. So she'd keep control if it killed her. 'That sounds like a statement someone else told you that you're repeating. And don't tell me Fadi ever said it to you. He adored you.' After a long stretch of silence, she said it for him. 'How old were you the first time your parents told you that Alim was better than you?'

The one-shoulder shrug came, but she didn't let herself care. So he said it, again with that quiet acceptance. 'I don't remember a time when they didn't say it.'

He wasn't angry, fighting or drowning in self-pity. He believed it, and that was all.

Bam. Like that she felt the whack of a hammer, snatching her breath, thickening her throat and making her eyes sting. His own parents had done that to him? No wonder he couldn't believe in her; he didn't know how to believe in himself. And the truth that she'd pushed away for years whispered to her inside her mind, why she'd fought to push him out of his isolation and to notice her. *I love him.*

Every messed-up, silent, heroic, inch of him. He'd crept into her soul from the time he'd marched away with his men, and returned a hero, hating the adulation.

She'd been amazed when he'd handed everything back to Alim without wanting a thing. She'd thought him so humble. Now she knew the truth: he didn't think he deserved the adoration of the nation; that was Alim's portion. He'd been in the shadows so long he found the limelight terrifying.

Don't you see, Amber, I'm doing everything I can do?

The words he'd given her in rejection of creating a child with her finally made horrible sense…and she knew if she pushed him to tell her everything, he'd never forgive her.

'Before our wedding, my father told me that the lion draws obvious admiration, but you need to look deeper to see the tiger's quiet strength. I've known that was true for a long time now,' she said softly, and touched his face. Warm and soft, not the unyielding granite she'd found repellent and fascinating at once; he was a man, just a damaged, honourable, limping, beloved hero, and she loved him.

He stared at her, looked hard and dazed at once. He shook his head, and her hand fell—but she refused to leave it like that. She touched him again. *'Habib numara,'* she whispered. 'I've wanted you for so long.'

He kept staring at her as if she were a spirit come to torture him—yes, she could see that was exactly what he was thinking. He needed time to believe even in this small miracle. So she smiled at him, letting her desire show without shame or regret.

After a long time, he took her by the hands. *'Mee johara,'* he said huskily. *My jewel.*

Her heart almost burst with the words, pounding with a joy she'd never known.

Don't hesitate, or he'll think the worst. So she wound her arms around his neck. 'I've been alone so long, waiting for you,' she whispered so softly only he would hear it. 'Kiss me and call me your jewel again.'

But instead, the hard bewilderment filled his eyes again. 'You've waited for me?'

'So long,' she murmured against his ear, and let her lips move against his skin. She felt him shudder, and rejoiced in it. 'You fascinate me with the way you can make me hate you and want you and love you—'

He stilled. Completely. And though she waited, he didn't ask her if she meant it. She felt his pain radiating from him, the complete denial of what she'd said because he didn't dare believe, not yet. Lost in a life of expectation and self-denial, in a world where his own parents didn't seem to love him, at least in comparison to Alim, how could he believe?

In a life where both of them had hidden their true selves from self-protection, one of them had to step into the light…and at least she'd known her family loved her. For once, she was the strong one; she had to lead the way.

'I love you, Harun. I have for a long time.' She pulled back, her hands framing his face as she smiled with all the love she felt. 'It began when I saw you march away to war, and I kept wondering if I'd see you again. I heard all the stories of your courage, leadership and self-sacrifice, and was so proud to be your woman. And when you came back and refused to talk about it, but just kept working to help your people, I began to believe I'd found my mate for life.'

His frown grew deeper with every word she said. 'Before we married.' The question was hidden inside the incredulous statement. He didn't believe her.

With difficulty, Amber reined in her temper and said, 'I never looked at you before we were engaged—

but once we were, I couldn't stop looking at you. But on our wedding night, I thought you didn't want me at all. I thought you hated me. I was only nineteen, I was told nothing but to follow your lead…I didn't know what to do.'

At last his features softened a little. 'So you followed my lead, all these years.'

She murmured, 'Pretending to despise you when all I wanted was to be in your life, in your bed. I cried myself to sleep that night.' Inwardly her pride was rebelling more with every word she spoke, but the relief at finally getting the words out was greater. Besides, pride wouldn't help either of them in this situation. Neither would useless worry over who heard their conversation—given the people they were, that would happen no matter their location. 'If I'd known why you avoided me…'

He moved an inch closer, his features taut with expectation, and she exulted in the evidence that he wanted her. 'What would you have done?'

'This,' she whispered, and kissed him.

It was a clumsy attempt, a bare fastening of her lips on his, and she made a frustrated sound. She felt his lips curve in a little smile as he put his hands to her hips and drew her closer, and took over, deepening the kiss, arousing her with lips and hands until she forgot everything but him.

Let your husband show you the way. For years she'd felt nothing but contempt for her mother's advice—it had only led her to utter loneliness and self-hate. But now Harun showed her the way, and the joy spread through her like quicksilver. He had one hand in her hair, another caressing her waist while he kissed her, and she found her body taking over her will. She moaned and kissed him even deeper, moving against him and the fire grew. Oh, she loved his touch, the feel of his body sliding on hers—

Were they in bed? She didn't remember moving her feet, or landing on the mattress; his hand was on her breast again and it was that knife-blade touch of exquisite perfection...

Then there was only the soft swish of air on her skin, and she made a mewing sound of protest before she could stop it. 'Harun?' she faltered, seeing him standing beside the bed. 'Did I do something wrong...?'

'No...something very right.' He finished pulling the curtains around the bed, and turned to smile at her. 'It will only be wrong if you tell me you want to stop.'

The black blankness was gone from his eyes; the ugly memory had been chased away, and by her. She felt her mouth curving; her eyes must be alight with the happiness and desire consuming her. 'After waiting three years for you, do you think I could?' No matter who was there, or why they'd come to this place, or what happened in the past, they were here now. He was all hers at last. 'Now, Harun. Please.'

And she held out her arms to him.

CHAPTER TEN

The next morning

So THIS was what she'd waited so long to know...

Through the cracks in the curtains he'd pulled around the bed last night, the rising sun touched Harun's sleeping face; his breathing was soft and even. Slowly Amber stretched, feeling a slight soreness inside her, but what they'd shared had been worth every discomfort.

He'd been right. With each touch, each kiss and intimate caress, the feeling went from wonderful to exquisite to an almost unbearable white light of beauty, until the ache inside her, the waiting and the wanting was intolerable, and she thrashed against him in wordless demand. And still he kept going, teasing her in kiss and touch until she'd pleaded with him to stop the sweet torture, and take her.

She was so ready for him that the pain was brief, a cry and a moment's stiffening, and it was done; soon the ache was to know the joy again. She kissed him and moved her body so he moved inside her. He smiled and called her his jewel again, and the familiar endearment, one her parents had given her years ago, was so much more beautiful from his lips, with his body on hers, inside her.

They made love slowly, Harun giving her infinite tenderness and patience. The beauty built higher as she became ready for the next step, and he took her there. The joy became bliss, and then something like being scorched by the sun, and yet she couldn't care, couldn't fear it or want to stop. And just before she cried out with joyful completion, he whispered, 'I can't wait any more—Amber, Amber…'

He shuddered in climax almost at the same time she did. As he held her afterwards, he caressed her hair and whispered, *'Mee habiba `arusa.' My beloved bride.*

She smiled and refused to give in to the temptation to ask if he meant it. The whispers in the women's rooms the past few years told her that men could become tender, poetic even at these times, but could forget it in minutes.

They made love twice more in the night, once at her instigation. If she was awake, she couldn't stop herself from touching him or kissing him.

Looking at him laying beside her now, his face almost boyish in sleep, his brown skin aglow in the light of sunrise, she felt her body begin the slow, heady tingling of arousal. Leaning into him, she kissed his chest, loving the taste of his skin. Unbearable to think of stopping now—she kissed him over and over, in warm, moist trails across his body.

His eyes were open now, and he was smiling at her. Her insides did that little flip at the relaxed, happy man who was finally her lover, and she was lost in wanting him. 'Come here,' he growled, and pulled her on top of him.

Laughing breathlessly, she whispered, 'I'm sorry I woke you.'

Now the smile was a grin. 'No, you're not.'

She bit her lip over a smile. Was she a fool to feel so happy? Did she care? 'No, I suppose I'm not sorry at all.'

'So this is how it's going to be, is it? I'll be worn out by your constant demands?' His twinkling eyes told her how much he hated the thought.

'I'm sure you knew I was a little on the demanding side when you married me,' she retorted, mock-haughty, but she moaned as his lips found better uses than teasing.

This time he taught her new things that pleased him, and she let him know what she loved, and it was beyond beauty, more than physical bliss. It was joy and peace. It was deep connection, communication without words. It was happiness so complete she couldn't think of anything to match it.

She'd heard about the endless pleasure of making love, but never had she dreamed this act of creation could be so life-changing. It was far from just her body's gratification; it was giving a part of herself, her trust, her inner self to Harun, and he gave himself to her.

She wondered if he felt the same, or whether it was this way every time he—

No, she wouldn't think of his former lovers now. She couldn't bear to think of him in this intimate position with another woman. She was his lover now, and he was hers. And she'd make sure it stayed that way.

'Are you in pain at all?' he asked as he held her afterwards.

'A little,' she admitted.

'Stay there a minute.' He got out of bed, and walked into the bathroom, wonderfully naked, and she couldn't help staring at his body. Unable to believe that, because of an abduction of all things, she finally had him all to herself. And within two days, they'd become lovers.

Had the passion been there all along, simmering beneath the surface? What might have happened long ago had he not overheard her silly girl's romantic dream of marrying a superstar? If she hadn't overreacted to his coldness on their wedding night—a decision she knew now he'd made in a mixture of intense grief and betrayal—would they always have had this joy together?

The sound of running water was soon followed by a lovely scent, and she smiled when he came back into the room. Then the mere sight of him, unclad and open to her in a way he'd never been, made her insides go all mushy with longing. 'Come.' He lifted her into his arms with ease. How had she been so blind, never realising until now just how big and strong he was?

He placed her in the bath, which was hotter than she normally liked it, and she squealed, and squirmed.

'The heat will help with the discomfort,' he said, his voice filled with tenderness. 'The bath oils can be good for that, too, I've heard. Just wait a few minutes.'

Deciding to trust him in this, she settled into the water with a luxurious wriggle, and soon she discovered he was right; the soreness lessened. 'Thank you, this is really helping,' she said as he came back into the room with the bed sheet. 'What are you—?' She stopped as he began washing it at the sink. 'Oh…thank you.' She blushed that he'd do something so intimate for her, and not think it beneath his masculine dignity.

He turned his face and smiled at her. 'What happened is nobody's business but ours. It's a hot day, so it should be dry by tonight. Besides, you need time to recover.'

She'd wondered what their kidnappers would make of the bloodstain on the sheets—or even the sheet hanging out of the window to dry; but his thoughtfulness touched her anew, even as his unashamed nakedness, and just his smile, made her insides melt. 'Are you sure about that?' she murmured huskily.

He made a sound halfway between laughter and a groan. 'You're going to kill me, woman. I need time to recover.'

'Oh. I didn't know men had to recover,' she said, rather forlornly. 'I just thought you might like to share my bath…there's plenty of room, and it's so lovely and warm…'

The sheet was abandoned before she finished the thought, and he was in the enormous, two-person bath with her, hauling her onto his lap. 'Recovery be damned. You're definitely going to kill me, Amber el-Kanar my wife,' he muttered between kisses growing hotter by the moment, 'but at this moment, I can't think of a better way to go.'

As she dissolved under his touch neither could she.

The next day

It was only as they finished breakfast that the conversation of the first night began working its way up Harun's consciousness from the dazed mist of contentment and arousal he'd been happily wandering in. The guards no longer intruded on them, but knocked on the door and left food there. They waited in silence at either end of the corridor, not moving or speaking. The assault rifles were no longer trained on them from the windows.

'How much longer do you think they'll keep us here?' Amber asked, as lazily content as he.

He didn't want to break their bubble by saying *when they know you're pregnant*. And then Alim was in real danger. 'So you're tired of my company already?' he teased.

Predictably, she blushed but smiled, too. 'Not quite yet.' As if to negate the words, the underlying fear they'd both been ignoring—that if their abduction wasn't the work of her father, the danger was still real and terrifying—she came around the table and snuggled into his lap, winding her arms around his neck. After a long, drugging kiss, she whispered, 'No, not quite yet—but this has got to be the strangest honeymoon two people ever had.'

He smiled up into her face, so vivid with life, flushed with passion. 'That's a bad assertion to make to a historian, my bride.'

'I love stories about history,' she murmured, nibbling his lips.

Between kisses, he mumbled, 'In the Middle Ages, a honeymoon was a very different thing from what it is now. A man who wanted a woman—or if he needed her wealth, dowry or the political connections she brought, but couldn't have her by conventional means—drugged her, kidnapped her and constantly seduced her. He did so by keeping her half drunk on mead—that's a honey-based wine—for a month, until the next full moon, so her father would know she'd been very properly deflowered. Then he'd bring her back to her family, with the woman hopefully pregnant, and present the father with the fait accompli. If the father didn't kill him, but accepted the marriage, he'd then ask for the dowry, or the hereditary title and lands, or whatever it was he'd wanted.'

'So what's different from this situation?' she demanded, smiling, with more nibbling kisses. 'Okay, we didn't have the wine, but we had the political marriage, the drugs, the abduction, and the deflowering.'

'True,' he conceded the point, deepening the kiss before saying, 'but I assure you I didn't organise this, I didn't drug you, and I have no further demands for your father. I'm perfectly happy with what I have right now.' *Apart from not knowing whether my brother is alive or dead...*

Her eyes seemed to be always alight now, either with teasing or with passion. 'I'm enough for you, then?'

More than enough—you're everything I've ever wanted, he thought but didn't say. They were lovers now, but he had no idea where they'd go from here. She wanted him, she'd even said she loved him; but he couldn't begin to believe she wanted more from him than this time. Proximity, passion, fear, curiosity—to end her three-year shame, or to have the baby she'd demanded from him a year ago. Whatever the reason she'd given herself to him, he didn't know. Since they'd made love, neither of them had spoken beyond the here and now.

The only thing he knew for certain was that they must get out of here, and soon. Their private time here was running out, and the only emotion he could bring up was regret. Could they keep up their amity, their passion, when the world intruded on them once again?

'I should have thought of this plan myself, years ago,' he said, grinning and kissed her to distract himself from his dark thoughts. 'We could have been doing this for years.'

'Who says it would have worked on me then?' she demanded, mock-haughty but with twinkling eyes, and he laughed and showed her how easily it would have worked with a touch that made her moan in pleasure.

'Tell me more historical titbits,' she muttered between kisses growing more frantic by the moment. 'I love the way you teach me about history.'

He didn't know if she meant it or not, but he began telling her of ancient marriage rituals in their region, while she kept murmuring, 'Mmm, that's so fascinating, tell me more,' between explorations of his body with her hands, fingers and lips.

They soon returned to bed, whispering historical facts to each other in a way they'd never been intended.

'I want to please you, *mee numara,*' she whispered as she caressed his body with eager innocence. 'Show me how your—how to make you happy.'

How your other women touched you. He heard what she'd left unspoken, but again he barely believed she could be jealous. 'You please me constantly already.' Surely she could see that in the way he couldn't stop touching her?

A fierce look was his answer. 'So you won't return to her.' It wasn't a question or a plea, but a demand. She wanted him all to herself—she did care—and some deep core of ice he'd never known existed inside him began to melt.

Caring for him made this her business now; it was time to tell her the truth.

'You have nothing to fear, Amber. You never did,' he said in a jerking voice because telling anyone someone else's secret wasn't in his nature. 'You know Buhjah means joy. It was Fadi's nickname for Rafa, the woman he loved, and she loved to hear it again when Fadi was gone, from the other person closest to him. Naima is Fadi's daughter, my niece. I've never touched Buhjah; I see her as my sister-in-law. In fact I arranged a very advantageous marriage for her a few months ago, and, though part of her still loves Fadi, she's very happy.'

Amber's mouth fell open, and her eyes came alight. 'Do you mean that? There is no other woman?'

The ice inside him was melting so quickly it unnerved him, but she'd been open with him, and deserved the whole truth. 'There never has been. I've never knowingly broken a promise in my life. I wasn't going to start with our marriage vows.' He saw the look in her eyes; he had to stop her, because she was about the say the words he couldn't yet believe in, and he wasn't sure he wanted to hear them. So he grinned and said, 'So long as you're in my bed, I'm content. Even if there were fifty other women in the room right now, you leave me too exhausted to think of looking at them.' Exhausted, sated and so incredibly joyous: how could she be worried? She was a demanding and giving lover beyond any he'd known.

Her face, her whole body glowed with a furious kind of intent he'd never seen until he touched her, his warrior woman. 'No other woman but me.' Again, it wasn't a question; she was demanding her rights with him. No other woman had ever demanded so much of him, but her fierce, unashamed possessiveness made him come as vividly alive as she. In making love, Amber had none of that cold, queenly pride, but a ferocious need for him, an attitude of *'you're mine'* that translated in every touch, throbbed in every word, and made him feel so glad to be her lover. 'While you're in my bed, I don't want to look at another woman,' he vowed solemnly.

With an inarticulate little cry she leaped at him, and with a kiss he took them both beyond thought.

They spent the afternoon in bed. Not that there was much else to do, but he thought now it wouldn't matter

if there was a choice; their need for each other was almost blinding. Once in a while he wondered who was
listening or watching, but then she'd touch or kiss him,
and they were gone again.

Later that night, contented once more, Amber
wrapped herself in the sheet to use the bathroom, and
trod on the bed curtain, pulling it down. Scrambling
behind the ones still hanging in place, and making sure
she was covered by the sheet, she whispered, 'Fix it,
Harun, quickly!'

Loving that she could be so demanding and unin-
hibited with him and yet was so modest otherwise, he
rolled off the bed. Then he felt himself being jerked
back down to the bed with a thump. Half indignant, half
laughing, he was about to kiss her when she shook her
head, and her mouth moved to his ear. 'Harun, I think
I know how we can escape.' She laid her hand across
his lips. 'Put the curtains back in place, but leave the
end with me.'

The imperative command spoken beneath her breath
put his brain back in order. He hung the cheesecloth
back in its place. He'd just turned to her when she put
a finger to her lips. He nodded, and crawled across
the bed to reach her. 'Make sounds as if we're making
love,' she mouthed.

Puzzled but willing to indulge her, he made a soft
groaning sound, and another, and bounced, making the
old bed squeak, and he heard the soft swishing of feet
moving from the holes in the wall. The guards had obviously been ordered to give them privacy.

She nodded and waved her hand. *Do it again.*

As he continued she folded the end of the curtain
over, and looked closely. She probed it with her fingers.
Pulling something from the bedside table, he couldn't

make out what in the darkness, she moved it into the material. Then she whispered in his ear, 'This is one of the hairpins they gave me. If we twist them a bit, we can use them like clothing pins. We can use a curtain each, doubled over, and weave the pins through to hold the edges together.'

'You're going to make us wear togas?' he whispered back, trying hard not to laugh, but intrigued nevertheless. He made another necessary noise.

She nodded, her face adorably naughty in response to his groan. 'We girls played dress-ups enough as children. I destroyed sheets and curtains regularly until the servants complained, and Father made materials available to me. I made my sisters be my emperors or slaves. I was always Agrippina or Claudia, of course.' And then her grin faded. 'And the rest of the curtains we can tie together with the sheets.'

The simple brilliance of the plan caught him by surprise, as did her knowledge of Roman empresses' names. *She really does love history.* 'In the middle of the night, I take it?'

She nodded again. 'You go first, since you have the greatest chance of making it safely down, while I make, ah, appropriate sounds.' She nudged him, and he groaned again, while she sighed and moaned his name. 'Then I follow.'

He shook his head. 'No, you'll go first.' The slowest person had to go first. Then if anyone saw them, or the light came early or a check, he could jump down and—

'No,' she whispered urgently. 'You weigh more than me, and these curtains might not last long. I'm not athletic, and I might panic if the curtains begin to give. If you're already down...'

'I could catch you,' he whispered back, seeing the sense in that.

'You can get away,' she finished at the same time. 'You're the important one—you have to live. I couldn't bear it if you were hurt, or caught because I let you down.' Then she moaned again. 'Oh, my love, yes…'

Words she'd said while making love, but he'd taken them with a grain of salt in his experience, women became very affectionate during the act when he pleased them, and he'd never had a more compatible lover than Amber.

But she'd said it now: *My love*…and it disturbed him somehow, left him with that restless, needing to get out of here feeling. Yet she was willing to sacrifice herself—she saw him as the important one—and it caught him like a jab to the solar plexus. He'd always been the replacement, with the disposable life. Until now. Until Amber.

Did she really mean it? The doubts were insidious, but part of him now, a part so intrinsic he wouldn't know how to get them out of his system.

'Amber,' he groaned, and then whispered, 'I'll go first, but only because I can catch you—and because you're more vocal than me, during, ah…'

With a grin, she jabbed him in the side with her elbow, and he chuckled low. *Objective achieved,* he thought with a wry twist to his lips. She was distracted—and more, she was laughing. It was stupid, but he wanted her to stay happy for what would probably be their last day together. He could see her plan working. Already he was adding to her plan, with his commander's training—and planning what to do when he had Amber safe somewhere. If his brother had been taken, or, Allah forbid, killed, he knew what he had to do. If Alim was safe, the plan barely changed.

Though he had no choice but to go ahead with finding their abductors, he could no longer conjure up anger, humiliation or regret. In this abduction, he'd been given a gift beyond price. He could barely believe Amber had been in front of him for years and he'd been too angry, too betrayed or just too plain stupid to look for the passion beneath her ice when she looked at him, and her courage under this extreme test.

But for now, he had to go forward. If she was still willing when he'd found their traitors… 'So we do this tonight. We can go home.'

A few seconds too long passed before she answered. 'Yes. Um, wonderful.'

He looked at her, frowning, and saw the uncertainty he heard in her voice mirrored in her forlorn expression. 'This is your plan, Amber. Why are you hesitating?'

Still wrapped only in the sheet, she wiggled her toes, and shook her head. 'It's silly.'

'I can't agree or disagree with that statement until I know what "it" is,' he said, concerned. Though it was hard to see her expression clearly in the waxing moonlight to the east, he thought she looked lost. After a while, she gave a little half-shrug—and with a small start, he realised it was an unconscious emulation of his own act when he wanted to hide his emotions. 'Tell me, Amber.'

'You'll think I'm stupid,' she muttered. 'You'll laugh at me.'

So Amber really cared what he thought about her. Touched, he took her hands in his. 'No, I won't, no matter what. I promise. Now tell me.'

She couldn't look at him; her hands pulled out of

his as she looked anywhere but at him. Frowning, he watched her, and waited.

After a few moments she spoke, her voice low, but clearly fumbling for words. 'Out there—' her arm shot out, her finger pointing towards the window '—everything will change; we won't be able to control what happens. You'll have duty—your responsibilities, or your work, or maybe at last you can do whatever you want to do with your life. I don't know what I'll have.' She lifted her face, and she was so beautiful and so sad he wanted to haul her close, kiss her and tell her it would be all right; the world, their families and life wouldn't come between them. But he couldn't guarantee anything at this point, and she knew it.

'I ruined your plans, didn't I? I never thought beyond here and now, or what you wanted.' He tipped her face up to his. 'Did you want your freedom so badly?'

An almost violent shake of her head answered him. 'I regret nothing. You—you've made me so happy, if only for a few days.' Her hair fell over her face. She seemed very small and fragile. 'I don't know what to do now. I don't know what's in my future. It's different for you, the whole world's there for you, anything you want, but what do I do, Harun? Where do I go from here?'

An ache filled him, not for his sake but hers. Raised only to be a sheikh's wife, to be a political helpmate and child-bearer, Amber had now lost her chance to be another man's wife, to bear children. From what Aziz had told him, the only career she'd been trained for was that of a powerful man's virgin bride, his consort and mother of his children. If she'd been taught to believe it was her only use, no wonder she was lost now. 'I can't answer those questions. Only you can do that.'

Her head shook almost violently. 'I can't. I'm not—I'm not ready.'

'You're not ready for what?'

'To leave, to give up, to go back to—to the life I had before. I don't want to go back to that…that emptiness. I've been so happy here.' She looked up again, and in the time between sunset and moonrise he still saw a look of sadness so profound, the ache grew and spread through his body.

The irony didn't escape him. It had only taken being abducted to show him how little palace life meant to Amber. He felt awful, having left her alone in it so long; but how could he have dreamed the imperious princess who'd cried at the thought of marrying him could be so happy here, in a place with few creature comforts, and being alone with him? With just a small amount of his attention she'd become the most giving, ferocious, amazing lover he'd ever known.

He was happy now with what they had, so happy, but she was lost. He wanted to help her, but at this moment he didn't know what she needed most—his reassurance or her freedom. 'What can I do to help?'

She leaned forward and whispered harshly, 'We could die tonight.'

'Yes,' he agreed quietly, wondering where she was going.

She shuffled her feet on the bed, twisting her hands around each other for a few more moments, and finally whispered, 'I'm not ready to let you go, Harun. I need you one more time before the world comes between us.'

He almost let out a shout of laughter, an exclamation of amazement and the pure joy of it, but, remembering his promise, he held it in. 'That's all you want?'

She gave a tiny headshake. 'It's all I'm asking for

now…no decisions to make, no family to please, no duty to perform, no anger or pride or servants' gossip. Just give me tonight.' Dropping the sheet, she burrowed her body against his, burying her face in his neck. 'Just give me you, one more time.'

Shaking, his arms held her tight against him. How had he ever been so stupid as to believe he'd married a cold wife? By heaven, this woman was a warm-hearted, generous miracle, a gift from God who'd given him chance after chance every time he'd screwed it up or hurt her again. But this time he wasn't going to leave her crying, alone with her pain, leaving her to hide behind her only solace, her pride.

He laid her tenderly back on the bed, and closed all the window shutters and the bed curtains before returning to her. 'Just you and me.'

Her lips fell apart, and her eyes glowed. 'Thank you,' she breathed, as if he'd offered her a treasure beyond price.

'You're welcome.' Was his voice as unsteady as it sounded to him? After three long, lonely years, he realised what he could have had with Amber all along: a willing wife and lover as generous as he could have dreamed, a woman who didn't care in the least about his family name or position; all she wanted was him.

Give me a chance. It's all I'm asking.

It was all she'd ever asked of him: to give her a chance to show him the woman she really was inside. But he'd just kept pushing her away until he'd been given no choice in the matter. The chance she'd asked for had been forced on him, and he'd only given her grudging trust. Their alliance had been years too late, forged from desperation. And still, when he thought of what Amber had given him in return…

Praise God for their abductors, and this ruthless method of bringing them together.

How could he let her go after this? Was this the last night he'd ever have with her?

'You can have whatever you want. Just ask and it's yours, I swear it,' he said, even now only half believing she'd take him up on it.

Her eyes shimmered at his words. 'Do you think, when we go back, we could maybe go on a honeymoon? Just us, you and me?'

Something inside him felt as if it burst open, something tightly locked away too long. 'Of course we can. I'll have a few things to do first, but as soon as they're done...'

She nodded, and kissed him. 'Of course. I can wait.'

She'll wait for me. He smiled, and wondered if he'd ever stop smiling again. 'We know we don't need to take the honey-wine with us.'

'No, and you don't need to drug me.' Her returned smile was a thing of pure beauty. 'You'll ravish me day and night, and I'll let you.'

'I'll do my poor best.' He bowed as he laughed. 'Let me? I doubt you'd let me stop, my jewel. And you'll ravish me.'

'Of course I will,' she replied earnestly, as if he'd asked her for reassurance.

In all his life, he'd never remembered feeling like this—as if he could fly. The hope he'd believed dead was back, the terrible, treacherous thing he hardly dared to believe in was whispering to him that, this time, he wouldn't be hurt or left alone; he'd finally found the one who would want to stay with him. 'I have a yacht off Kusadasi on the Adriatic Sea. I haven't used her in years. We could cruise through the Greek Islands, or we can head to the east if you prefer. It'll be just you and me, for however long you want.'

'Oh, Harun…' She wound her arms around his neck, and buried her face in his shoulder. He heard her mumble some words, but, though he couldn't make them out, he felt the warmth of her tears against his skin, and then her lips roaming him in eager need.

Squelching that traitor's voice inside him, knowing he had to leave her first, he lifted her face and kissed her.

CHAPTER ELEVEN

How long do I want with you? I want for ever.

Had he heard her say it? She didn't know. All she knew was that in the last few days, she'd truly become a woman—and the frustrated desire she'd known for so long, the admiration and longing for her husband had become total and utter love without her even noticing. Harun had ignored her, but he'd never intentionally hurt her; he'd left her alone, but he'd fought for peace in Abbas al-Din, and worked himself half to death to hand his brother a country in good economic and political shape when Alim returned.

Had Alim ever really been a champion in her eyes? Perhaps in a public way, but it was nothing in comparison with the way she saw Harun.

During the past three years, Harun had shown her the real meaning of the word *hero*. Being a hero didn't have to come in flashy shows or trophies or spilling champagne in front of cameras; it wasn't in finding wealth, writing songs or poetry or giving flowers; it was in wordless self-sacrifice, doing the right thing even when it hurt, giving protection and—and just giving, expecting nothing in return.

She loved the man he was, and she no longer needed or even wanted fancy words or riotous acclaim. She just needed him, her quiet, beloved tiger, her lover and her man, and now she had him to herself, she never wanted to let him go again.

But she knew there was little choice in that. She'd lose him again; but for now, she'd take what she could with him.

'What do you want most to get from your job?' she asked while they waited for the deepest part of the night.

He didn't ask her to explain; he knew what she wanted: to connect with him, to know him. 'It's the really ancient history that fascinates me—our early ancestors. The Moabites during the Ishmaelite period, and Canaan, with the Philistines to the west. I want to know who they were beyond the child sacrifices and the multiplicity of gods.'

She held in the shudder. 'They sacrificed children?'

'Yes, they sacrificed their firstborn to the god Malcam, believing it brought his blessing to their crops. Archaeologists have found the sites of newborn cemeteries all over modern-day Israel and Lebanon, Jordan and Syria.'

This time she couldn't hold it in. 'That's disgusting.'

'Our ancestors weren't the most civilised people.' He grinned. 'But what I want most of all is to discover traces of the real people called the Amalekites. It's still hotly contested by historians as to who they were, because they just seemed to disappear from the human record about three thousand years ago.'

'How can that be?' she asked, wide-eyed. 'How can a whole nation of people just vanish without trace?'

'They didn't—there are records, but none belonging to them. It seems they were a warrior-nation that didn't keep their own records. Other contemporary nations speak of them as the most terrifying warriors of

their time…oh, sorry, I must be boring you to sleep,' he
teased as she tried valiantly to hold in her third yawn.

'No, no, I want to know,' she mumbled, snuggling
deeper against his chest. 'I'm listening, I promise—
just sleepy.'

Harun smiled down at her, and stroked her hair as
she fell into a deep sleep. He could give her an hour; it
was just past midnight.

It was heading for two a.m. when he woke her.

Instinctively Amber reacted to the gentle shaking
by rolling into him, seeking his mouth. It was amazing
how quickly she'd become accustomed to needing him
there. 'I'm sorry, I let you sleep as long as I could,' he
whispered, after they'd shared a brief, sweet kiss. 'We
have to start on the plan.'

With difficulty, she reoriented herself. 'Of course, I
have the pins ready. We'll need to be as silent as possible.'

'If we make any noise, I'll make some lover-noises to
cover it, and you do that laughing thing you do.'

She felt her cheeks heating, but smiled. 'I can do that.
Now help me pull the curtains down. We'll just take one
down at a time—and while I'm making one toga, check
the windows to see how many guards are stationed.'

The curtains proved no hardship in pulling off the
rail, except in the slight swish and slide of falling off
the rail, once it was loosened. She pulled him to her and
deftly wound the doubled fabric over his shoulder and
around his waist. 'What I wouldn't give to be able to
rip the towels into strips,' she murmured as she had to
push the pin-head through the fabric every time. 'Then
we could have a waist-sash.'

He groaned her name softly, and pushed the bed

down with his hand. If they got quiet for any length
of time, the guards would return. 'Here, let me.' He
twisted the ends of the pushed-through pin so each end
bent back on itself. 'No chance of its undoing now. Put
one at my waist and it should be fine.'

'Two is better.' She worked two pins into the waist,
at the rib and hip level. 'Now if one goes the other will
hold.'

They both made appropriate noises while he got
down another curtain and she made her toga; he helped
her twist the pins, and the cheesecloth felt surprisingly
strong under his hands. Amber felt breakable in comparison, or maybe it was the fear in her eyes.

They continued making sounds of love as he twisted
the remaining curtains and sheets together in sailing
knots.

It was time. It was nearly three a.m. and they couldn't
keep up the noises much longer, or the guards would
become suspicious. Seeing the fear growing in her eyes,
he held her hands, smiled and whispered, 'You know
what to do. I'll pull the rope three times when I reach
the bottom. Be strong, my Kahlidah, my Agrippina.'

She gulped at the reference to her great-grandmother.
'I'm trying, but right now I don't think I take after her.'

She was falling apart at the worst possible time, and
he had only seconds to pull her back together. 'I'm rely-
ing on you, *mee numara,* my courageous tigress. This
is your plan. You can fulfil it. You *will* do this.' And he
kissed her, quick and fierce.

'I think I'll leave any roaring until later,' she whispered with a wavering smile.

Harun winked at her. 'I'll be waiting for you.'

With one swift, serious look he kissed her a final
time; with a little frown and eyes enormous with fear

and strangely uncertain determination, she waved him off.

He crept to the window, and checked as best he could. If guards were posted around he couldn't see them—but then, he thought the numbers of guards had thinned out in the past day. They'd achieved their first objective, he supposed, and would let them enjoy their faux honeymoon.

At first, he had thought that with every piece of furniture but the chairs being nailed to the floor, he could use a bigger piece as a ballast. The closest to a window least likely to attract attention was the dining table—but now it looked too old, fragile; it might break under his weight. After scanning the room again, he saw the only real choice was the bed, since the wardrobe was too wide, taking rope length they couldn't afford.

The bed was the furthest from any window. This was going to be tight.

He looked at her again, and pulled at each corner of the bed, testing its strength, while Amber covered the noises as best she could with cries of passion, but her eyes were wide and caught between taut fear and held-in laughter.

The sturdiest part of the bed was the corner furthest from the window, but he estimated that would leave their rope at least eight feet short. Having jumped from walls in his army training, he knew they couldn't afford the noise he'd make in landing, or in catching her. If she'd come that far, seeing the gap.

This was Hobson's choice. A swift prayer thrown to heaven, and he made his decision, tying the rope with a triple winding around the nearest bed leg and through the corner where the mattress rested.

Then, slowly and with the utmost care, he let the

makeshift rope out of the window closest to the bed, and in the middle of the room, an inch at a time. It was frustrating, wasting time they didn't have, but throwing the rope could lead to its hitting something and causing attention.

At last the rope could go no further. He leaned out, and saw the rope was only short by about three feet, and he breathed a quiet sigh of relief, giving Amber a thumbs-up.

Her smile in the moonlight was radiant with the same relief he felt. With a short, jaunty wave and another wink he hoped she could see, he climbed over the sill, gripped the cheesecloth in both hands and began the drop.

The hardest part was not being able to bounce off the building, but just use his hands to slide down. By the time he'd reached the smoother sheet part of the rope, his hands were raw and starting to bleed. He and Amber had discussed this even as they'd loved each other the final time; she knew what to expect.

He only hoped her courage saw her through. But she was only twenty-two—what had he done with life by then? Yes, he'd passed all his training exercises with the armed forces, but that was at the insistence first of his parents and then Fadi. He'd replaced Alim and Fadi at necessary functions, but again, he'd been trained for it all his life. He'd told Amber how to rappel down the rope, but if she panicked—

In his worry over her, he'd rappelled automatically down the final fifty feet. His toga was askew, but his pins held. Running even by night in their bare feet would be hard, harder on Amber; would they make it?

Stop thinking. He looked around and again saw no guards. Vaguely uneasy, he checked out their surroundings, and tugged on the rope slowly three times. Within moments he saw her looking out of the window. Beckoning to her lest she back out, he hoped he'd done enough.

It was long moments before she moved—time they didn't have; the eastern sky was beginning to lighten. Then she slipped over the edge and, using only her hands, began dropping towards him. His heart torn between melting at her bravery and pounding with fear that she'd fall, he braced himself to catch her.

She stopped at the point where the sheets took over from the curtains, and he almost felt the raw pain her hands were in. He did feel it; his hands took fire again, as if in sympathy.

Come on, Amber. I'm waiting for you...

A few moments later, she began sliding down—literally sliding—and his heart jack-knifed straight into his mouth.

Allah help me!

A slight thump, and a madly grinning Amber was beside him, looking intensely proud of herself. 'You thought I was falling, didn't you?'

He wanted to growl so badly the need clawed around his belly, but instead he found himself kissing her, ferocious and in terrified relief. 'Let's go.'

'Which way?'

He pointed. 'I can't believe I didn't recognise where we were before, but from above the perspective changes, I suppose. This was one of the first battle areas during the el-Shabbat war. We're only about fourteen miles from Sar Abbas.'

Her face changed, losing some confidence. 'Fourteen miles. I can do that,' she whispered, frowning like a child facing a wall. 'Let's run.'

His uneasiness growing—why wasn't anyone trying
to stop them?—he took her hand and ran southwest.
Towards the dimly lit road only a mile away where he
hadn't been able to see it before, behind the part of the
building without windows. The brighter lights of Sar
Abbas glinted in the distance like a welcoming beacon.

CHAPTER TWELVE

The Sheikh's Palace, Sar Abbas, a few hours later

IN THE opulent office that had been Harun's but was now his, Alim stared at Harun when he walked in the door unannounced, and then ran headlong for him. 'Praise Allah, you're back, you're alive! *Akh, mee habib akh!*'

Brother, my beloved brother. Harun had the strangest sense of déjà vu with Alim's outburst, the echo of words he himself had spoken only a few weeks ago in Africa. But Alim sounded so overwhelmingly relieved, and Alim's arms were gripping his shoulders hard enough to hurt. He didn't know what to make of it. 'So you were given demands?'

'No.' His brother's face was dark with stress and exhaustion as they all sat down on respective chairs around his—*Alim's* desk. 'This never went public, but two guards were found drugged in the palace the night you disappeared, and another almost died saving me from an abduction attempt. I came to check on you and you were gone—and Amber too. We sent all our usual guards away, and filled the palace with elite marine guards. Under the guise of army exercises I've had the best in the country looking for you, and hunting down your abductors. How did you get away? What happened?'

'I wish I knew.' Harun frowned. 'It was like they wanted us to get away. The guards disappeared, and we rappelled down a rope of sheets and curtains. We ran to the highway into the city and I called in a favour from an army captain who drove us the rest of the way.' He grinned. 'We only stopped to change, since our attire wasn't quite up to palace standards.' He flicked the grin over to Amber, who was watching him with a look of mingled pride and exasperation—at his cut-down version of events, he supposed.

'Maybe their plan was contingent on us all being taken,' Alim said quietly. 'Any thoughts on that, *akh?* You're the tactician in the family.'

'He's more than that,' Amber interjected sharply, the first words she'd spoken.

'Alim didn't mean anything by it, Amber.' He reached over, touched her hand to quiet the protest he felt wasn't yet done.

'I meant it as a compliment, actually, Amber.' Alim was frowning. 'Harun's the one that saved the country while I was lying in a bed in Switzerland, and he ran the country while I drove a truck.' He met Harun's eyes with an odd mix of admiration and resentment. 'I've only been here a few days and I've got no idea how you did it all so well.'

Harun felt Amber gearing up for another comment born of exhaustion and—it made him want to smile— the urge to protect him, and he pressed her hand this time. 'We think it might have been some el-Kanar supporters who wanted an heir.'

'You mean they wanted an heir from you and Amber?' At his nod, he earned a sharp look from Alim.

'And who don't support my, shall we say, less than traditional ways, and my choice of bride.' When Harun
didn't answer, he was forced to go on. 'Then I can assume the rumours about the state of your marriage were
correct?'

Neither moved nor spoke in answer.

After a flicked glance at them both, Alim avoided
the obvious question. Amber's face was rosy, her eyes
downcast. It was obvious she was no longer the ice
maiden she'd seemed to be the week before…and Harun
could almost swear Alim's left eye drooped in a wink.
He certainly seemed a little brighter than before.

'So I'd guess you think the plan was to kill me and
install you as permanent ruler.'

It wasn't a question, but still Harun nodded and
shrugged. 'That's what they planned, but they left one
thing out of the equation.' He met his brother's enquir-
ing look with a hard expression. 'I never wanted the
position in the first place. I still don't want it. Stepping
into Fadi's dead shoes was the last thing I wanted three
years ago. Less still do I want to be in your shoes now.'

Alim stilled, staring at him. 'You don't want to be
here at all, do you.'

Again, it was a statement of fact.

'He never did.' Amber spoke with the quiet venom
of stored anger. 'Tell him, Harun. Tell him the truth
about what you've sacrificed the last thirteen years so
he could do whatever he wanted.'

Alim only said, almost pleading, *'Akh?'*

'Amber, please,' Harun said quietly, turning only his
head. 'I appreciate what you're trying to do, but this is
not the time.'

'If not now, when…?' Then Amber's eyes swivelled
to meet his, and she paled beyond her state of exhaus-

tion. 'You're going to sacrifice yourself again—you'll sacrifice us, even—to fulfil your sacred duty. And for *him*.' She jerked her head in Alim's direction. 'Is he *still* all you've got?'

'Harun?' Alim's voice sounded uncertain.

Harun couldn't answer either of them. He was lost in the humbling knowledge that she could read him so easily now—that he had no time to formulate an explanation; she knew it all. And she wasn't going to support him.

When he didn't speak Amber made a choking sound, and turned on Alim. There was no trace of her old crush as she snarled at his brother, 'You'll let him do it for you again, won't you? Just as you let him do everything *you* were supposed to do, all these years. He gave up *everything* for you, while you were off playing the superstar, or feeling sorry for yourself in Africa, playing the hero again. Did you ever *care* about what he wanted? Did you think to ask him, even once?'

In the aftermath of Amber's outburst, all that was audible in this soundproof room was her harsh breathing. She stared at Alim in cold accusation; Alim's gaze was on Harun, tortured by guilt. Then Amber turned to him, her eyes challenging. She wasn't backing down, wasn't going to let him smooth this over with pretty half-truths.

The trouble was, his mind had gone totally blank. It had been so long since anyone asked him for unvarnished truth or stripped his feelings bare as she'd just done, she'd left him with nothing to say.

At length she turned back on Alim. 'Harun never told me any of it, just so you know. Fadi did. I hope you've appreciated your life, because Harun gave it to you! And he's going to do it again. For once, Alim, be a real man instead of a shiny image!'

Then, pulling her hand from Harun's, she turned and ran from the room.

Harun watched her go, completely beyond words. Devastated and betrayed, she was still loyal to him to the end. Why was it only now that he realised how loyal she'd always been to him?

Loyalty, courage and duty…Amber epitomised all of them, and he'd never deserved it.

'Have you hated me all these years?' asked Alim.

The low question made him turn back. Alim's eyes were black, tortured with guilt. 'Don't,' he said wearily when Harun was about to deny it. 'Don't be polite, don't be the perfect sheikh or the perfect brother, just this once. Answer me honestly. Have you hated me for having the life I wanted at your expense?'

For years he'd waited for Alim to see what he'd done, to ask. For years he'd borne the chains that should have been his brother's—and yet, now the question was finally asked, he couldn't feel the weight any more. 'I hated that you never asked me what I wanted.' Then he frowned. 'What do you mean, the perfect brother?'

Alim pulled a face of obvious pain, and rubbed at the scars on his neck and cheek. 'I need some of Hana's balsam,' he muttered. 'Don't pretend you don't know what I mean. It was always you with Fadi—Harun this and that, you did such a wonderful job of something I should have done or been there to do. Even if I'd come home, I'd have done a second-rate job. I was always well aware you were the one Fadi wanted, and I was second-best.'

It was funny how the old adage about walking in another's shoes always seemed so fresh and new when you were the ones in the shoes. 'I never knew he did that.'

Alim shrugged, retreating into silence, and it looked

like a mirror of his own actions. So it meant that much to Alim. It had hurt him that much.

He'd just never realised they were so alike.

'It must have hurt,' he said eventually, when it was obvious Alim wasn't going to speak. This was new to him, being forced to reach out.

Another shrug as his brother's face hardened and he rubbed at the scarring. Though it wasn't quite the same, it was a defence mechanism he recognised. He thought Amber would, too…and she'd have tried again from a different position. Poking and prodding at the wound until he was forced to lance it.

Suddenly Harun wanted to smile. All the things he'd been blind to for so long… Amber knew him so well. How, he didn't know. She must have studied him at a distance—or maybe it was just destiny. Or love.

That the word even came to him with such clarity shocked him. What did it mean?

'Do you know what it's like to be inadequate beside your little brother at your mother's funeral?' Alim suddenly burst out. 'Fadi never let me forget it. No matter what I achieved or did, I never measured up to you.'

Harun stared at him. '*Fadi* said that?'

'All the time,' Alim snarled.

It was hard to get his head around it: the brother he'd always adored and looked up to had played favourites, just as their mother and father had. The insight turned all his lifelong beliefs on their heads—and the indestructible Racing Sheikh became a man like any other, his big brother who was lost and hurting.

The trouble was he didn't have a clue what to do with the knowledge that the brother he'd resented so long was the only one who could understand how it felt to be him. 'Did you hate me for that?' he faltered.

A weary half-shake, half-nod was his only answer, yet he understood. 'I'm sorry, Alim,' he said awkwardly in the end, but he wasn't sure what he was apologising for.

Alim gave another careless shrug, but he saw straight through it. Some scars bled only when pulled open. Others just kept bleeding.

'So, what did you want to do with your life that you didn't get to do, while I was off being rich and famous?' Alim tried to snap, but it came out with a humorous bent somehow.

Willing them both to get past what had only hurt them all these years, Harun grinned. 'Come on, *akh*. I don't change. Think. Remember.'

Alim frowned, looking at him with quizzical eyes... and slowly they lit. 'The books, the history you always had your nose stuck in as a kid? Do you want to be a professor?'

'Close.' The grin grew. 'Archaeologist.'

'Really?' Alim laughed. 'You want to spend your life digging up old bones and bits of pottery?'

'Hey, big kid, you played with cars for years,' he retorted, laughing.

Alim chuckled. 'Well, if you put it that way...okay, I'm growing up and you're getting to go make mud pies.'

The laughter relaxed them both. 'So you have no objections?'

'I have no right to object to anything you want to do, even if I have the power.' Alim came around the desk, and gave Harun a cocky grin. 'I promise to get the job right, and not bother you or force you home for at least the next thirteen years.'

Harun looked up, his expression hardening. 'Thanks, but I'm not applying for digs just yet. I have something I need to do first.'

Alim tilted his head.

'You just said you wouldn't object to anything I wanted.' Harun shook off Alim's hands as they landed on his shoulders, and stood. 'First, I have to renounce my position formally, publicly state I don't want the job.' He met his brother's eyes. 'I have to disappear until everyone in the nation accepts you in the position, or our friends will try again…and this time they might get it right.'

'I guess I'd better let you do it…but you're all I have left, Harun.' Alim's face seemed to take on a few more lines, or maybe the scars were more pronounced. 'Take care with your life, little *akh*. Don't leave me alone to grieve at your funeral.'

The words were raw, but still Alim squared up to him, looking him in the eye. And Harun realised he was the taller brother—something he'd never noticed before. 'I'm doing this *for* you. I'm the soldier in the family. I have to hunt them down.' He spoke through a throat hurting with unspoken emotion. 'Until the group's disabled, you'll never be safe—and neither will the woman you love.'

'And if I don't want you to do this? If I say that without you, I have nothing?'

Too late, he heard the choked emotion, and understood what Alim wasn't saying. 'What about Hana?'

His brother's jaw hardened still more. 'That's no more open to discussion than your private life with Amber. But let me say this now, while I can, because I know you're going to disappear, no matter what I say. Are you leaving because you hate me for Fadi's death— or can I hope one day you'll forgive me?'

The words sliced Harun when he'd least expected it.

He wheeled away, just trying to breathe for a minute, but his chest felt constricted.

'I have to know, Harun.' The hand that landed on his shoulder was shaking. 'Despite the fact that you were his favourite, I loved him. He was more father than brother to us both from the time we were little.'

All he could do was nod once.

After a stretch of quiet, Alim asked, 'Do you blame me for his death?'

'Stop,' he croaked, feeling as if Alim had torn him in half.

'I need to know, Harun.'

There were so many replies he could make to that assertion, but he'd been where Alim was now. He knew better than Alim did that staffers and servants and all the personal and national wealth that oil and gas could bring, even the adoration of a nation, the whole world, didn't halt the simple loneliness of not having the woman you wanted love you for who you really were inside.

It seemed this was a week of unburdening, whether he wanted to or not.

'Fadi made his own decision,' he said eventually, staring out of the window. 'I always knew that. He was so unhappy at the political marriage he had to make— not just with Amber, but any suitable woman. He loved Rafa with all his heart. I don't think he wanted to die, just to escape from inevitability for a few days.'

After a long time, Alim answered, sounding constricted. 'Thank you.'

He shrugged again. 'You saw how unhappy he was, didn't you? I saw it too, but I didn't know what to do; I had nothing to offer him. You gave him escape for a little while, because you loved him. His death was

a terrible accident, one that scars you more than me.
I never blamed you for it.' *Only for running off when
I needed someone the most,* he thought but didn't say.
Alim had more burdens on his shoulders than he'd ever
dreamed. He found himself hoping Hana would come
back to him, and make him happy.

'Thanks, *akh.*'

Two words straight from the heart, the word *brother*
filled with choked emotion, bringing them both a measure of healing—and yet Harun wondered when it was
that he'd last heard someone speak to him that way. Fadi
had never been one for pretty words, just a clasp on the
shoulder in thanks for a job well done.

*Do you think…we could maybe go on a honeymoon?
Just us, you and me?*

Amber had spoken to him from the heart, probably as
much as she'd dared when he'd never once told her what
he wanted with her—and he realised what he'd done by
making his decision without involving her.

He turned back to Alim. 'I need to find Amber.'

Alim nodded. 'That you do, brother. I think it's
time—or way past time, actually—that you told her
how you feel about her.' Startled, Harun stared at him,
and Alim gave a small smile. 'I saw it on your face the
day you first saw her, and even in the way you looked
at her today. I knew then, but I understand it now. It's
how I felt when I first saw Hana. It's how I still feel
even though she's gone.'

'You…knew how I felt about Amber?' he asked
slowly, taken aback by his brother's insight. Alim saw
more about him than he'd ever realised.

Alim shrugged. 'Why do you think I left so quickly
after meeting her? I saw the way she looked at me—but
the crush was on the Racing Sheikh.'

'So you knew that, too,' he jerked out.

Alim nodded. 'Of course I knew. Do you really think I'd have left you with all this responsibility three years ago if I didn't think you were going to be rewarded with your heart's desire? Leaving without a word to either of you would make her turn to you, because you were as hurt as she was by my disappearance.' By now they were both staring hard out the window, looking at the city view as if it held the answers to life's mysteries.

'Why?' Harun asked eventually. 'Didn't you know I'd rather have had you?'

'Not then, I didn't. I do now.' From the corner of his eye, he saw Alim shrug. 'I was the wrong man for her. I knew you'd step up, take the marriage and position I couldn't bear to. It was selfish, yes, and I wanted to run; but I couldn't stand the thought of taking someone so precious from you—again.'

Fadi. Oh, the guilt Alim carried on his shoulders…

Beyond an answer, Harun shook his head. Unable to stand any more emotion, he joked mildly, 'You always did have the gift of the gab. The only one of us who did.'

'It hasn't got me very far with Hana,' Alim muttered.

Harun resisted the urge to touch his brother's shoulder, and asked again, brother to brother. 'She won't marry you?'

This time Alim shook his head. 'She's running from all the stories. She thinks she isn't worthy to be my wife. I hoped when I met the family that they'd know her worth, but they agreed with her. Her father all but told me to forget her. I can't do that, I'll never do that! As if bloodlines matter when we're all descendants of the one man!'

Harun shrugged. 'There's a world of practical difference between the theory of being a fellow descendant of Abraham, and the reality of being royalty or a miner's daughter.'

'Not to me,' Alim growled. 'Would your ice princess have risked her life to save you—not once, but a half-dozen times?'

'I was only saying what she might be thinking,' Harun replied mildly. He knew when a man spoke from love and pain, and the foolishness of words regretted later, but unable to take back. 'I agree with you. Hana's a heroine, and she has a courage far more suited to the role you want her to take than any pampered princess—but it's what she thinks that counts.'

Mollified, Alim nodded. 'Sorry I jumped on you.'

'Forgiven—but I'd appreciate it if you'd never call Amber an ice princess again,' he added, gently frigid. 'She might not have saved any lives, but she's put up with quite a lot from the el-Kanar brothers, mostly without complaint, and with the kind of loyalty not one of us have earned from her. She forgave you not half an hour ago without even telling you about the very public embarrassment she suffered when you disappeared rather than marry her.'

Alim sobered once more. 'You're right. I apologise—and I think it's time you did, too. Go,' he said, half forceful, half laughing as Harun turned on his heel to stalk down his quarry.

It took him over an hour to find her—and in a night of surprises, she was sitting at a desk in the extensive library, her nose buried in a book on the archaeology of the Near East local area. She glanced up at his approach, but, with a flash of defiance in her eyes, she lowered her gaze to her book, and kept reading.

Fervently wishing for Alim's gift of the gab about

now, his ability to turn a phrase into something emotional and beautiful, Harun could only find his own words. 'I'm sorry. I know you were only trying to help.'

With careful precision, she turned a page, as if she was absorbed by the book. 'What is your plan?'

He didn't hesitate. 'I'm leaving tonight. I have a few leads—I have to find out who abducted us and why. Alim and the entire royal household cannot be safe until they have been brought to justice.'

Her gaze drifted a little further down the page. 'Goodbye, then. Enjoy your escape.'

'Amber, please understand. I have to do this.'

'And of course I'm far safer here, left alone in the place where I was kidnapped last time,' she remarked idly, turning another page. 'But then, I don't suppose my fears and wishes come into this. You're going, and leaving me here, no matter how I feel about it.'

The observation jolted him. 'I thought you of all people would understand. You said there wasn't anything you wouldn't do to save your family.'

'Hmm? What was that?' She ran her finger down a page before she looked up with a cloudy-eyed expression.

'Don't be childish,' he rebuked in an undertone.

Her brows lifted in a look of mild surprise. 'Sorry, I can hardly believe you're still here talking to me. You should be off saving your brother, your nation or anything else. After all, isn't he all you have? Isn't your duty to your brother and country above everything, especially me?'

That hit hard. 'I have to do this, Amber. If I don't disappear and hunt them down, they'll just take us again— or kill Alim to make me step up, now they know we're lovers.'

'We were lovers,' she replied, still in that indolent, I-don't-care voice. 'Rather hard to be anything when you're going undercover commando on me.'

Right now he wished she'd just say what she wanted, but she'd gone Ice Queen on him again, and it was taking all he had left after this long, very hard day not to respond in kind, or just walk away. 'When I'm done with this, I'm coming back for you.' He tried to smile. 'I want that honeymoon we agreed on.'

At that, she closed the book with a tiny snapping sound. 'Again, it's rather hard to believe that there will be a future at all when you're going to be outnumbered and if they find you, they'll probably kill you—' With a choking sound, she jumped up, wheeled around and ran from the room.

But not before he'd heard her gasp for breath on a sob, and seen her dash the tears from her eyes—and when he tried to find her, to make things right somehow, she'd retired to the section of the palace reserved only for women, where even Alim could not enter.

CHAPTER THIRTEEN

Four months later

'I UNEQUIVOCALLY refuse any position that belongs right-fully to my brother. I was never more than his care-taker while he healed. I have now handed over the full power to my brother Alim. I am leaving Abbas al-Din tonight, and will not be returning for a long time. I wish my beloved brother happiness in the life ordained for him by God, and fully approve of his choice of bride. Hana al-Sud is a fine, strong woman of faith, worthy of the highest position. Thank you and good evening.'

For the five hundredth time Amber felt the potent cocktail of hunger and fury as she watched the re-run of the security closed circuit TV. Harun stepped down from the podium at the ruling congress, refusing to an-swer any questions after reading his statement. A five-minute presentation before the people he suspected of abducting them, and then he'd disappeared. No one had heard from him since.

At least, she hadn't. She assumed Alim would tell her something if he knew, but he was very busy, taking the reins of power, planning his wedding—and since com-ing to the palace to accept Alim's proposal, Hana had a

terrible habit of dragging him into secret corners to kiss
and touch him whenever he had a minute to himself.

*Why didn't I think of doing that with Harun years
ago?*

*Because Hana's secure; she knows Alim loves her.
She's a blessed woman.*

With an angry snap she switched off the TV, resolv-
ing for the five hundredth time to never watch again,
but she knew she would. Again before bed tonight, leaving her to pace the floor until exhaustion drove her to
bed; again tomorrow when she'd finished the studies
she loved, but he did too—and before dinner, driving
her to eat next to nothing as she uttered polite inanities
with the family to prove to them that she was coping
with her isolated life, studying an archaeology course
in half the time, and living in the old women's quarters
with only one maid and guard for company.

Hana and Alim's wedding was to take place in two
days. She didn't even assume Harun would return for
that event. She'd made that mistake for their engagement party, dressing in her finest, making sure she
looked her best…and it was all for nothing.

Alim had no best man. He said if Harun didn't come
he didn't want anyone.

She knew exactly how Alim felt. Why, why couldn't
she just leave him behind, as he'd done with her? Why
didn't she just get on with her life?

'Because I have nowhere to go,' she muttered, leap-
ing to her feet and crossing the room rather than give in
to the temptation to throw something at the TV. Despite
her station, she had no personal fortune, or even a bank
account. Not one of the staff in the palace, even a foreign worker, would help her, at the risk of deporta-
tion; her face was too well known. Her father refused

to allow her to stay with them, or even send the jet for a week's visit.

Come when your husband returns to claim you, he'd said inflexibly.

And unless it was to family, the law of the land forbade her from leaving her husband unless she could prove ongoing physical abuse. She had no friends outside her family circle, nobody close that would offer her shelter, or believe her if she tried to claim abuse; they'd all loved Harun from the start.

No, she was a royal wife in a traditional land: just another possession left unwanted in the treasure room until her owner remembered her.

Instead of pacing the floor for the five hundredth time, she stared fiercely out of the window. What she wouldn't give to grow wings right now! She'd escaped once, but this time she was surrounded less by snipers than a thousand servants catering to her every need, and watching her every move. They were her protectors until her husband came back to take over the job. So until Harun chose to return from his wanderings and release her, she was caged as effectively as she'd been for her abductors.

Two days later

'So, *akh,* I hear you're one best man short.'

With an hour until the wedding Alim, standing alone in the sheikh's magnificent bedchamber and dressed in his groom's finery, whirled around to see Harun in the doorway, with a cheeky grin. Tired to the point of falling down, he was still ready to give his brother support during his day of days.

He threw Alim a mock salute. 'Your Highness.'

And found himself smothered in a hard embrace. *'Akh,* little *akh,* praise God you're alive.' Alim was trembling. 'I thought…feared…'

'I can hardly breathe here,' he complained with a laugh. 'I'm okay, *akh,* really—and when you come back from your honeymoon, I have good news to report.'

Alim pulled back, but hugged him again. 'I'll be grateful for that later. Right now, my little brother's back from the dead… It was so damn *hard* going through my transition and engagement alone. I wanted you with me, to share my happiness and hardships.'

Harun willed away the sense of irony in everything Alim had just said. Telling Alim he'd felt the same for years would only damage their fragile relationship; he understood, and that was enough. 'If it helps, I worked day and night the past few months to get here today.'

Alim peered at his face, and frowned. 'You do look like you're ready to fall down. Come, take some coffee. I can't have you falling asleep on me during the ceremony.' Alim led him inside, and poured him a cup of thick, syrupy black coffee. 'There's more. I've been drinking it all day.'

Harun chuckled and shook his head. 'No wonder you seem like one of those wind-up toys. Why are you so nervous? You know Hana loves you.'

Alim sobered. 'You know her first marriage was a sham. It's her first time tonight, as well as our first time. If I don't—'

Harun silenced him with a lifted hand, smiling. 'I was there a few months ago, *akh.* Take it from one who knows now. I've seen the way she looks at you in news reports, and heard how she drags you into cupboards.' Alim chuckled at that, as Harun intended. 'She loves you, Alim; she's ready. It will be everything she's dreamed of, because in her eyes, that's what you are.'

'That was—the perfect thing to say.' He was taken aback by Alim's hand cupping his cheek. 'I can't believe you came back for me.'

So much left unsaid, but it no longer needed to be said. 'Ah, you know me. I'm always hanging around just waiting to be useful.'

Alim grabbed the coffee cup from him and drew him into the stranglehold hug again, thumping him on the back. 'I don't deserve you, but I thank Allah every day for the gifts you've given me.'

'You found life's best gift all by yourself. You came home all by yourself, too. I had my bride and my life handed to me—by you, I should add.'

'You know what I mean. I can't believe we could have been friends all these years, but—'

Neither wanted to say it. Separated by those they'd loved and needed most, they could always have been allies. 'Nothing's stopping us now,' Harun said huskily.

'And nothing will again.' Another massive hug.

'You're choking me,' Harun mock complained, 'and crushing my best man's outfit.'

'Who was it that abducted you?' Alim asked abruptly, releasing him.

In answer, he handed Alim the file he'd dropped during the first hug. 'The entire group has been put out of action.'

'Hmm.' Alim scanned the first sheet rapidly. 'I wouldn't have thought it of the Jamal and Hamor clans, but yes, they are very conservative. With financial and armed backing from our more conservative neighbours, I guess they thought they could try. I think it's time we did something about our neighbours, too.'

'I did all that's needed, My Lord.' Harun bowed, laughing again. 'I told you I worked night and day. I found out who it was by word of mouth months ago— but proof had to be absolute. When it was, the perpetrators were easy to rout, especially after my public announcement. Now go, enjoy your wedding. It's time to go see your bride.'

And he pushed Alim out of the door. One relationship on track…but he had the feeling this lifelong breach would be the easier of the two to heal.

The wedding banquet was beautiful, filled with the daintiest dishes of the region. Sheikhs, presidents and first ladies sat at the tables, mingled and laughed, probably proposed or made new deals over a relaxing extended meal, while Alim and Hana ignored the world, feeding each other, giving small touches, their eyes locked on the other. So absorbed were they that when someone approached them, they jerked out of their own little world with obvious surprise that anyone else existed.

To think he could have had a similar wedding, if only he'd known Amber wanted him the way he'd wanted her…

But right now, even his memories of their two days of joy seemed false. Dressed in full, traditional clothing, covered from head to foot apart from her face, Amber sat at the royal table between two first ladies, speaking only with them. She was thinner, paler, wearing none of her soft make-up that made her face glow with life; her eyes were too calm, holding no emotion at all; her hands remained at the table instead of waving around as she talked.

She'd lost herself somewhere in the past few

months—or hours. She'd whitened when she'd seen him standing beside Alim, and looked away before he could move or even smile at her, and she'd avoided him ever since. He'd been trying to get her attention discreetly, but she wasn't responding. Any moment now, she'd excuse herself and retire to the women's quarters.

So he stalked over to her. 'I wish to speak to you, my wife.'

Amber's head snapped around to him, her lips parted in shock that he'd come right into the open; but trapped by law and convention, she could either cause a scene, or acquiesce.

The cheeks that had been pale were now rosy; her eyes were fiery with indignation. 'As you can no doubt see, I am fully occupied at present, my husband.' With the slightest sarcastic inflection on the title *husband,* she waved a hand at the important women sitting either side of her, who both immediately demurred, insisting that if her husband wished to speak with her, they'd be fine together.

Obviously fuming, she rose to her feet; but Harun, inwardly grinning—at least she was alive again—held out his hand, which again she had to take in seeming grace. He led her around the table, and out through the state banqueting rooms onto the back balcony of the palace, semi-private and with no public or press access.

Once there, she jerked her hand away, and folded her arms, waiting.

Instinct told him a joke wouldn't get him far this time. Neither would she reach out to him. This time, he had to be the one to give. Anything that would get her to talk to him, tell him what she was thinking and feeling, even if she hated him.

So he started there. 'Do you hate me for being away so long?'

She sighed, looking out into the night. 'Why don't you tell me what you want from me this time, so we can get on with our lives once you're gone again?'

The question confused him, but he felt it wasn't a topic to pursue, not yet. 'You look so thin,' he said softly. 'Are you feeling well?'

'I'm fine, thank you.' Cold words, with no compromise. She wasn't giving anything away, wasn't going to play his game. She wanted her question answered.

'You're my wife. I've come back for you, as I promised I would.'

'Like a dropped-off package, or a toy forgotten about until you want to play again?'

'No, like a wife I hoped would understand that what I was doing had to come first.'

Another sigh, harsh and rather bored, and she kept looking out into the night. 'Just tell me what you want.'

He shook his head. 'I don't understand. You're my wife. I've come back for you.'

'Your wife.' The words were flat, as was the laughter that followed. 'So says the imam that performed the service. Isn't that what you said?' Still she wouldn't look at him. 'What is a wife to you?'

She'd obviously had far too much time alone to think; every question she asked left him feeling more bewildered. 'I think you have ideas on what I think a wife is.' Soft, provocatively spoken, designed to break the wall of ice around her and get to the pain of abandonment hiding beneath.

She lifted her brows in open incredulity, but remained silent.

Feeling hunted and harried into a position he didn't

want to take, wishing fervently for the wife who'd
pushed and prodded her way into his bed and heart, he
snapped, 'Okay, Amber, I don't know what I think a
wife is, but I know what I want. I want those two days
we had. I want them again. I want a honeymoon with
you, to find the life we both want—'

Loud, almost manic laughter sliced his words off.
Amber was doubled over herself, laughing with a hard,
cynical edge that told him he'd better not join her. 'A
life we both want?' She gasped, and laughed over again.
'What do *I* want, Harun? Do you even know that much
about me? Do you know anything about me?'

Daylight began cracking apart the icy darkness she'd
wrapped herself in. 'I know you're brave and beautiful and loyal to me even when I don't deserve it,' he
said softly. 'I know you gave me chance after chance,
and forgave me time and again. I know you're the wife
I want, the woman I want to spend my life with. But
you're right, I don't know what you want. That's what
I'm here to find out. Doesn't that count for something?'

'Not right now, no.' Hands on hips, she seemed challenging, except she still refused to look at him, or make
a connection of any kind. If she'd heard how he felt
about her written between the lines he'd spoken she
wouldn't acknowledge it.

'All right, Amber, I understand.'

A little snort was her only answer.

'Oh, I do understand.' With swift, military precision, he whipped the burqa from her head, ignoring
her outraged gasp. 'You're hiding from me the way I
hid from you all those years. You're not going to make
it easy for me, and I don't deserve you to.' Grabbing
her and hauling her against him, he held her hard with
one hand, while he slowly played with a thick tress

of hair, unbound beneath the veil she'd worn. 'Have I missed anything?' he asked huskily, inhaling the rosemary scent in her hair.

'Ask yourself,' she retorted in a voice that shook just a little.

'Ah, thank you, *mee johara*. That means I did.' He grinned at her as her eyes smoked with fury. 'Ah, of course…you still want to know what I think a wife is?'

Her chin lifted.

'You,' he answered, trying to douse the flames in her heart. 'That's all. When I think of "a wife", I think of you. Just as you are.'

'Don't,' she snarled without warning. 'Don't worm your way in with pretty words and compliments. I thought you were dead—that—that they'd killed you. Or that you were never coming back. Why else would you not contact me once? What did I do to—to…?' She pulled at his hands until he released her. She'd startled him right out of his cocky assurance, and his belief that he'd win. She faced him, panting, her eyes shimmering with pain. 'I *loved* you. I loved you with all of me, I gave you everything I had, and you just left. You left me for the sake of the brother who'd abandoned and betrayed you. Do you have any idea what that did to me?'

Bewildered, he spoke from depths he hadn't known were in him. 'But he's my family, Amber. I had no choice. It was my duty.'

'What about me?' she cried. 'Was it your *duty* to seduce and then abandon me, to hurt me the way Alim hurt you? Do I have to run off like he did to make you see I'm alive and that I *hurt?*' She held up a hand when he would have spoken. 'I—I can't do this any more. I tried, Harun, I tried to make things work with you for three years. I tried to show you that love isn't manipula-

tion and emotional blackmail, but you won't see it. I'm
tired of hitting my head against a wall. Believe Fadi
and not me, and spend your life alone!'

She ran for the balcony doors.

*Love isn't manipulation and emotional blackmail...
believe Fadi...*

That was what Fadi had done to him since childhood, and he'd never known it until now. But she had.
She'd seen that he'd gained Fadi's love and approval
by doing anything asked of him, no matter what it cost
him personally. Fadi hadn't known any better, but followed the example set by their parents. Alim had found
a way to escape from it, and somehow, somewhere in
his worldwide travels, had learned how to love. But he,
Harun, had stayed like a whipped dog, always saying
yes, because he accepted the manipulation—because
he didn't know any better.

In three long years, Amber had asked only one thing
of him—and he hadn't even given her that, because she
didn't manipulate or blackmail him into it.

*If someone loves you, they ask the impossible over
and over...*and he'd believed it was normal, even right;
his duty.

Amber hadn't asked him to change, or to slay drag-
ons for her. So he'd never believed she loved him. Not
until now, when she'd stripped his lifelong beliefs in a
moment, left him bare and bleeding, and she was leaving him.

He couldn't stand it, couldn't take losing her. This
time would be for ever—

'I love you.' Three raw, desperate words. *God, let
them be enough, let her stay. Come back to me, Amber...*

Her hand on the door handle, she turned, and hope
soared—

She made a small, choking sound, the one she made when she was about to cry. 'I can't believe you'd be so cruel, after what they did to you. Don't ever use those words against me again.'

Then she was gone. Harun stood by the balcony rail, exposed to the bone, the world's greatest fool.

CHAPTER FOURTEEN

IT was 3 a.m. and Harun was pounding the road, gasping with each breath and pushing himself still harder. At least ten miles from the palace, his guards were running behind him and finding it hard to keep up. It had been hours since he'd seen Alim and Hana to their bridal chamber. He'd shepherded all of the guests downstairs, made sure the food and drink still overflowed for anyone who wanted it. He'd chatted amiably with heads of state he'd known for years, had quietly warned their friendlier neighbours against trusting certain people among the nations surrounding them, and in general played the perfect host.

The perfect host, the perfect brother, he thought now, with an inner wryness that never made it to his expression. *Why can't I be the perfect husband?*

He wished he knew how to be everything Amber wanted…

What does she want? an imp in his mind prodded. *All she ever wanted was you. But you pushed her away and abandoned her until it was too late. What does she want now—the freedom from you she'd asked for months ago?*

Her words replayed over and over in his brain. *I*

thought you were dead. Or that you were never coming back. Love isn't manipulation and emotional blackmail.

He was missing something. It wasn't in Amber's nature to hurt him without a reason; he knew that now. Everything she'd said taught him what love wasn't.

So what the hell *was* it, then? It seemed she had the secret, but he'd been deaf and blind the whole time she was trying to tell or show him.

He thought she'd *wanted* to hear he loved her. So what had gone so wrong?

At four a.m., he came to the inescapable conclusion: there was only one way to find out. He wheeled around and ran back for the palace, much to the relief of his stitching, gasping guards.

Five a.m.

'My Lord, it's written in the law! You cannot come into this place!'

'Unless you are the ruling sheikh—or the woman in question is your wife. I know the law. Is there any woman in here but my wife?'

'There is the maid, My Lord!'

'Then I suggest you send her out immediately. I will give you three minutes, then I am coming in no matter what—and I suggest you don't argue with me. I doubt you possess the skills to stop me.'

'Your wife is sleeping. Would you wake her?'

'No, she's not. She's behind the door, listening, as she has been since about a minute after I began yelling for her. I knew she'd be awake, or I wouldn't have come.'

The tone was more grim than amused. Even with her throat and eyes on fire, Amber smiled a bit. The door had no glass; he'd just known she'd be waiting for him.

'Let him in, Tahir,' she called, opening the door. 'I'll send Sabetha out.'

The maid, wakened by Harun's first roar for Amber, scuttled past her. Harun shouldered past the guard, snarling, 'No listening. If there's any gossip about this, you both lose your positions.'

'We love the lady Amber, My Lord,' little, delicate Sabetha said, with gentle dignity.

His face softened at that. 'I'm grateful for your loyalty to the lady Amber. I beg your pardon for insulting you.'

Sabetha smiled up at him, not with infatuation but instant affection. Tahir smiled also, but with a manly kind of understanding; he'd forgiven his lord.

Harun seemed to have the knack of making people care. She just wished he knew how to care in return.

In softer mode now, he walked into the room and closed the door. But instead of talking, he just looked at her until she wanted to squirm. 'Well?' she demanded, or tried to. It sounded breathless, hopeful.

Would she ever stop being a fool over this man?

'You are the most beautiful thing I've ever seen or will ever see,' he said, with a quiet sincerity that made her breath take up unmoving lodgings in her throat. 'I thought that the first time I saw you, and I still think it now.'

She lifted her chin, letting him see her devastated face clearly, her tangled hair and the salt tracks lining her cheeks. 'I've spent the past six hours crying and hating you, so it might be best if you use less practised lines. You have five minutes to give me a compelling reason to let you stay here any longer.'

'That you've cried over me only makes you more beautiful in my eyes.'

'That's nice.' Tapping her foot, she looked at her watch. 'Four minutes forty-five seconds.'

He closed his eyes. 'I don't know how to love any other way but through doing what I perceived as my duty. I thought it was all I had to give.' Taking her by the shoulders, he opened his eyes, looked at her as if she was his path to salvation and rushed the words out, as if he didn't say everything now, he never would. 'Those two days we were together, I felt like I was flying. Now it's gone, and the past few months I felt like I was starving to death. I'm suffocating under duty, lost and wandering and alone, and nothing works. I need you, Amber, by God I need you. Please, can you teach me how to make you happy—because without you, I never will be. I can't sleep, I can't eat, can't think about anything but touching you, being with you again.' He dragged her against him, and she didn't have the heart or will to pull away. 'Don't deny me, Amber, because I won't go, not tonight, not any night. Teach me the words you want to hear. I'll say whatever you need, do whatever it takes, because right now I need you more than my next breath. I can't let you keep shutting me out, not when you're everything to me.'

Ouch—it hurt to try to gulp with her mouth still open. How did he turn up just when she'd given up hope, and say the words she needed to hear more than life?

With a tiny noise, she buried her face in his neck. 'Me too, oh, me too, I need you so much,' she whispered as she cannoned into him, her fingers winding in his hair to pull him down to her. 'You just said everything I needed to know.'

'Except one thing,' he muttered hoarsely between kisses. 'I love you, Amber. I have from the day we met.

I just never knew how to say it, or how to believe you could ever love me in return.'

'Do you believe it now?' she whispered, pulling back a little. This was something she had to know now.

He smiled down at her. 'I knew it the day you yelled at Alim, my jewel. It's why I came back today so full of confidence. I'd hoped missing me would have softened you. But you taught me a valuable lesson tonight—that I have to trust in our love, and talk to you.' He nuzzled her lips. 'I'll never put you last again. From now on, you're my family, my first duty. My desire, my passion. My precious jewel.'

'I'm so happy,' she cried, kissing him. 'But though your words are wonderful, I want you to show me the desire and passion. I've missed you so much!'

He didn't need to be told twice. Devouring each other in desperate kisses, mumbling more words of desire and need, they staggered together back to the bed.

Later that morning

The sun was well up when Harun began to stir.

Amber was curled against him like a contented cat, her head on his chest, her body wound around his, one leg and arm holding him to her. He smiled, and kissed the top of her head. Her hair was splayed across his body; her breaths warmed his skin.

Unable to make the mat to give his morning prayer, he gave his thanks in silence, deep and heartfelt. *Thank you for helping me find the way back to her again.*

They'd made love twice, first in a frenzy and then slow and ecstatic. They'd said words of need and pleasure and love during the past four hours.

Now it was time for the next step.

'Amber.' He bent his head to kiss the top of her head. 'Love, we need to talk. No, I said *talk,* my jewel.' He laughed as she kissed his chest, slow and sensuous. 'I've made some arrangements for us I hope you'll like.'

'Mmm-hmm,' she mumbled through kisses. 'Tell me.'

'Are you listening?' He laughed again. She was peppering his torso with kisses and caresses, and he was getting distracted.

'Uh-huh, I always listen to you. Mmm…' More kisses. 'Hurry, *habibi,* it's been at least two hours since we made love. I need you.'

'I've secured us two part-time, unpaid places on a dig only half an hour's drive from the University of Araba Numara…and while I do my doctorate, you'll be finishing your course face to face.'

That stopped her. Completely. She gaped up at him. 'You know about my course?'

'Why do you think I applied for positions near that university? I've known everything you've been doing the past four months—and it made me so proud of you.'

'You—you don't mind?' she asked, half shyly. 'About being a woman and getting all high distinctions, I mean?'

'No, of course not—I've heard you've got lots of distinctions—I'm so proud of you. I've never felt threatened by your intelligence, Amber,' he said quietly. 'And I trust you completely. As I said, your success has made me so proud of you, *mee johara.* I married a woman of great intellect as well as good taste—in loving history and her husband.' He winked at her. 'Do my arrangements meet with your approval?'

'Approval? Oh, you have no idea! I love you, I love you!'

'We'll be living in the same tents as everyone else,

I warn you,' he put in with mock-sternness, but was turning to fire again at her touch. 'And it will mean no babies until you're done with your course.'

Again she looked up at him, almost in wonder. 'You don't mind waiting for children?'

'I've waited all this time for you,' he murmured, with the utmost tenderness. 'I can wait a little more for our family to start.'

'I love you,' she whispered again, with all the vivid intensity of her nature, and pulled him down on top of her.

Strange how falling down actually felt like flying...

EPILOGUE

Eight years later

'Iᴛ's a girl!'

In the sorting tent, deep in diagnosis of the siftings he'd just dug up, Harun frowned vaguely at his wife's excited voice coming from behind him. 'Hmm? What was that?'

'Harun, we have a new niece. Hana had a girl about an hour ago.'

'That's great. Look at this piece I found, *mee johara*. Is this beer jug belly Sumerian, do you think?'

'Harun, look at me.' Gently he was turned around. He knew, having finished her archaeology degree last year, as excited by the past as he could ever hope for, Amber wouldn't risk disturbing his findings. But, as she always said, *without families there wouldn't be history to discover.* 'Hana had a girl an hour ago. They named her Johara.'

The look in Amber's eyes warned him to return to the present. He blinked, focusing on what he'd only half-heard, and slowly grinned. 'That's wonderful! We have a niece at last. Kalila will be thrilled.'

Their five-year-old daughter always felt left out of her boy cousins' rowdy play. She was a girly-girl, and even though she was as enthusiastic as her parents on the digs, she somehow managed to stay clean. The only time she had someone as fastidious as her on the digs was when Naima stayed for the school breaks. Kalila adored her cousin, and followed her around like a puppy.

At not yet four, their son Tarif fitted in splendidly with his male cousins, rolling around as happily on the palace floors, indulging in masculine play with his father and uncle. But when on the dig, he confined his rougher antics to the hours Harun kept sacred for play with his son. He knew better than to disturb any promising-looking holes in the ground, though Harun swore their son was a genius from the day he'd inadvertently found the site of an ancient temple's foundations when he was trying to poke in a snake hole. 'Abi, Abi, pretty rocks over there,' he'd said, growing distressed until Harun followed his little son to the other side of the *tell,* where they hadn't yet sectioned off the ground to look.

Amber grinned. 'I've booked the jet for Monday. I can't fly after that, as you know—' the slight stress on *know* told him if he didn't remember she was twenty-seven weeks pregnant, he'd better catch up with real life and fast '—and I want to see my…well, my sort-of namesake.'

'Oh, of course she is.' Harun grinned again. 'I'm sure they named her for you, my jewel,' he assured her with mock-gravity.

Laughing, she swatted him with her fingers. 'You could at least pretend to believe it. You know I'm in a very delicate state right now.'

Both brows lifted with that one. 'Um, yes, very delicate,' he agreed. 'Remind me again how your delicate condition meant you had to crawl ahead of me five days ago into an unstable subterranean chamber?' Not to mention that, at night, she was the one to instigate loving as often as he did. They'd have at least six children by now, if they hadn't planned their family carefully around Amber's studies.

Finding no answer for his teasing, Amber put her nose in the air; then she looked at the small piece he'd found. 'Oh, I do concur, it is part of a beer jug, and it definitely looks the right period. It's a shame it isn't Amalekite. We're still not there,' she teased, backing off as he mock waved his fist at her. 'It's a very good piece. But you might want to call the family and congratulate them before you get lost in the Sumerian period again,' she suggested, turning his face back to her as her opinion distracted him. 'One more,' she murmured, kissing him again, deepening it to keep him in the here and now.

'One more kiss like that and I'll forget the Sumerian artefact as well as our new niece,' he mock threatened as his body awoke.

'Not you, my love,' she retorted, laughing. 'And anyway, there's always tonight.'

As if on cue, the baby kicked its father, squirming around as if to say, *Not again, you two!* It was a chant almost everyone on any dig said to them, sooner or later. Whether it was over their almost scary connection over their love of ancient history or their knowledge of ancient finds, or their touching and kissing so often when they were together, the protest was as loud as it was meant in fun. *I wish I could find what you two have,* was the lament of so many people on the digs, when another relationship failed with someone who could never understand the archaeologist's absorbing passion for the past.

'Okay, little one, okay,' he said softly, caressing Amber's

belly, leaning down to kiss his child. 'I think you're being told to rest, my jewel.'

'I think I am.' She smothered a yawn. 'Tarif will wake in about an hour, so I'd better get there.' She gave him one final kiss. 'But I want to hear all about the jug later—and don't think the other part of tonight's forgotten, either.'

'Never,' he assured her with a wink. 'Both have been duly noted.'

'And call Alim,' she reminded him a final time, at the tent flap. 'Don't forget to call Naima too. Tell her the car will pick her up the day we arrive, if Buhjah doesn't have anything else planned for her.'

Grinning, he waved in acceptance. Amber returned to their family tent where Tarif still slept in a partitioned-off section, and at the other end Kalila endured her long-suffering tutor's lessons on mathematics.

Harun, smiling as he always did when Amber had been with him or when he thought of his family, pulled out his phone to call his niece. Naima was thrilled she had a new girl cousin, and, after consulting with Buhjah, told him she could join in the family celebrations. He chatted with her for a few minutes longer, hearing all about her studies and her other family, the antics of her younger half-brothers at home, before hanging up with a smile.

Then he called the palace to congratulate Alim and Hana, and to hear about his new niece. The bubbling joy in his brother's voice when he spoke of their new 'little jewel' made Harun's cup run over.

He was a blessed man.

* * * * *

"What do I get if I find your nephew's team a coach?"

Lucy wondered if Ryland was serious or teasing her. His smile suggested the latter. "My undying gratitude?"

"That's a good start."

"More cookies?"

"Always appreciated—especially if they're chocolate chip, which happen to be my favorite," he said. "What else?"

His lighthearted and flirty tone sounded warning bells in her head. Ryland *was* teasing her, but Lucy no longer wanted to play along. His charm, pretty much everything about him, left her...unsettled.

"I'm not sure what else you might want."

He gave her the once-over, only this time his gaze lingered a second too long on her lips. "I can think of a couple things."

Dear Reader,

For the past eight years my fall and spring Dedication weekends have been full of soccer games. All three of my children have played and my husband has coached recreational teams for years.

Soccer isn't something I grew up with. I attended my first game in 1984, but wasn't really sure what was going on. Friends kept telling me how big soccer—they called it football—was outside the US, but I never realized how big until 26th June 1994, when I attended a match between Colombia and Switzerland at Stanford Stadium. Not even the two Super Bowls I'd gone to came close to matching the excitement and passion of these soccer fans.

Ever since then I've wanted to write a romance with soccer as the background, but it wasn't until my son started playing competitive soccer for an Oregon club in spring 2010 that the story ideas started flowing. After speaking with one of my son's coaches, who also played for the Portland Timbers, a professional soccer player named Ryland James came to life.

Having access to people who can help with research adds realism to a story. I was fortunate in the soccer assistance I received, but when it came to my heroine, Lucy, who'd had a liver transplant as a teen, I wasn't sure where to turn for help.

A friend had been a living donor for her daughter's successful liver transplant in 2007, but I happened to mention my work-in-progress to another mom during our kids' swimming practice. Turned out she was a two-time liver and kidney transplant recipient. Talking with her helped me understand and fill in Lucy's backstory of her having liver failure. It also made me understand the importance of organ donation and the lives being saved by transplants.

To all those who have signed up to be donors: thank you!

Melissa

IT STARTED
WITH A CRUSH...

BY
MELISSA McCLONE

MILLS &
BOON

First published in Great Britain 2012
by Mills & Boon, an imprint of Harlequin (UK) Limited,
Eton House, 18-24 Paradise Road, Richmond, Surrey TW9 1SR

© Melissa Martinez McClone 2012

ISBN: 978 0 263 89454 7
ebook ISBN: 978 1 408 97129 1

23-0812

Harlequin (UK) policy is to use papers that are natural, renewable and recyclable products and made from wood grown in sustainable forests. The logging and manufacturing processes conform to the legal environmental regulations of the country of origin.

Printed and bound in Spain
by Blackprint CPI, Barcelona

With a degree in mechanical engineering from Stanford University, the last thing **Melissa McClone** ever thought she would be doing was writing romance novels. But analyzing engines for a major US airline just couldn't compete with her "happily-ever-afters." When she isn't writing, caring for her three young children or doing laundry, Melissa loves to curl up on the couch with a cup of tea, her cats and a good book. She enjoys watching home decorating shows to get ideas for her house—a 1939 cottage that is *slowly* being renovated. Melissa lives in Lake Oswego, Oregon, with her own real-life hero husband, two daughters, a son, two loveable but oh-so-spoiled indoor cats and a no-longer-stray outdoor kitty that decided to call the garage home.

Melissa loves to hear from her readers. You can write to her at PO Box 63, Lake Oswego, OR 97034, USA, or contact her via her website, www.melissamcclone.com.

For all the people who generously volunteer their time to coach kids—especially those who have made such a difference in my children's lives. Thank you!

Special thanks to Josh Cameron, Brian Verrinder, Ian Burgess, Bernice Conrad and Terri Reed.

CHAPTER ONE

EVERY day for the past four weeks, Connor's school bus had arrived at the corner across the street no later than three-thirty. Every day, except today. Lucy Martin glanced at the clock hanging on the living-room wall.

3:47 p.m.

Anxiety knotted her stomach making her feel jittery. Her nephew should be home by now.

Was it time to call the school to find out where the bus might be or was she overreacting? This parenting—okay, surrogate parenting—thing was too new to know for certain.

She stared out the window, hoping the bus would appear. The street corner remained empty. That wasn't surprising. Only residents drove through this neighborhood on the outskirts of town.

What to do? She tapped her foot.

Most contingencies and emergencies had been listed in the three-ring binder Lucy called the survival guide. Her sister-in-law, Dana, had put it together before she left. But a late school bus hadn't been one of the scenarios. Lucy had checked. Twice.

No need to panic. Wicksburg was surrounded by farmland, a small town with a low crime rate and zero excitement except for harvests in the summer, Friday-night football games in the fall and basketball games in the winter. A number of things could have delayed the bus. A traffic jam due to slow-moving farm equipment, road construction, a car accident…

A chill shivered down Lucy's spine.

Don't freak out. Okay, she wasn't used to taking care of anyone but herself. This overwhelming need to see her nephew right this moment was brand-new to her. But she'd better get used to it. For the next year she wasn't only Connor's aunt, she was also his guardian while his parents, both army reservists, were deployed overseas. Her older brother, Aaron, was counting on Lucy to take care of his only child. If something happened to Connor on her watch…

Her muscles tensed.

"Meow."

The family's cat, an overweight Maine Coon with a tail that looked more like a raccoon's than a feline's, rubbed against the front door. His green-eyed gaze met Lucy's.

"I know, Manny." The cat's concern matched her own. "I want Connor home, too."

Something caught the corner of her eye. Something yellow. She stared out the window once again.

The school bus idled at the corner. Red lights flashed.

Relief flowed through her. "Thank goodness."

Lucy took a step toward the front door then stopped. Connor had asked her not to meet him at the bus stop. She understood the need to be independent and wanted to make him happy. But not even following his request these past two and a half weeks had erased the sadness from his eyes. She knew better than to take it personally. Smiles had become rare commodities around here since his parents deployed.

Peering through the slit in the curtains gave her a clear view of the bus and the short walk to the house. Connor could assert his independence while she made sure he was safe.

Lucy hated seeing him moping around like a lost puppy, but she understood. He missed his parents. She'd tried to make him feel better. Nothing, not even his favorite desserts, fast-food restaurants or video games, had made a difference. Now that his spring soccer team was without a coach, things had gone from bad to worse.

The door of the bus opened. The Bowman twins exited. The seven-year-old girls wore matching pink polka-dot dresses, white shoes and purple backpacks.

Connor stood on the bus's bottom step with a huge smile on his face. He leaped to the ground and skipped away.

Her heart swelled with excitement. Something good must have happened at school.

As her nephew approached the house, Lucy stepped away from the window. She wanted to make sure his smile remained. No matter what it took.

Manny rubbed against her leg. Birdlike chirping sounds came from his mouth. Strange, but not unexpected from a cat that barked when annoyed.

"Don't worry, Manny." She touched the cat's back. "Connor will be home in three…two…one…"

The front door flung open. Manny dashed for the outside, but Connor closed the door to stop his escape.

"Aunt Lucy." His blue eyes twinkled. So much like Aaron. Same eyes, same hair color, same freckles. "I found someone who can coach the Defeeters."

She should have known Connor's change of attitude had to do with soccer. Her nephew loved the sport. Aaron had coached his son's team, the Defeeters, since Connor started playing organized soccer when he was five. A dad had offered to coach in Aaron's place, but then had to back out after his work schedule changed. No other parent could do it for a variety of reasons. That left the team without a coach. Well, unless you counted her, which was pretty much like being coachless.

The thought of asking her ex-husband to help entered her

mind for about a nanosecond before she banished it into the far recesses of her brain where really bad ideas belonged. Being back in the same town as Jeff was hard enough with all the not-so-pleasant memories resurfacing. Lucy hadn't seen him yet nor did she want to.

"Fantastic," she said. "Who is it?"

Connor's grin widened, making him look as if he'd found a million-dollar bill or calorie-free chocolate. He shrugged off his backpack. "Ryland James."

Her heart plummeted to her feet. Splat! "*The* Ryland James?"

Connor nodded enthusiastically. "He's not only best player in the MLS, but my favorite. He'll be the perfect coach. He played on the same team with my dad. They won district and a bunch of tournaments. Ryland's a nice guy. My dad said so."

She had to tread carefully here. For Connor's sake.

Ryland *had* been a nice guy and one of her brother's closest friends. But she hadn't seen him since he left high school to attend the U.S. Soccer Residency Program in Florida. According to Aaron, Ryland had done well, playing overseas and now for the Phoenix Fuego, a Major League Soccer (MLS) team in the U.S. Coaching a recreational soccer team comprised of nine-year-olds probably wasn't on his bucket list.

Lucy bit the inside of her cheek, hoping to think of something—anything—that wouldn't make this blow up in her face and turn Connor's smile upside down.

"Wow," she said finally. "Ryland James would be an amazing coach, but don't you think he's getting ready to start training for his season?"

"MLS teams have been working out in Florida and Arizona since January. The season opener isn't until April." Connor spoke as if this was common knowledge she should know.

Given soccer had always been "the sport" in the Martin
household, she probably should. "But Ryland James got
hurt playing with the U.S. Men's Team in a friendly against
Mexico. He's out for a while."

Friendly meant an exhibition game. Lucy knew that much.
But the news surprised her. Aaron usually kept her up-to-
date on Ryland. Her brother would never let Lucy forget her
schoolgirl crush on the boy from the wrong side of town who
was now a famous soccer star. "Hurt as in injured?"

"He had surgery and can't play for a couple of months.
He's staying with his parents while he recovers." Connor's
eyes brightened more. "Isn't that great?"

"I wouldn't call having surgery and being injured great."

"Not him being hurt, but his being in town and able to
coach us." Connor made it sound like this was a done deal.
"I bet Ryland James will be almost as good a coach as my
dad."

"Did someone ask Ryland if he would coach the Defeeters?"

"No," Connor admitted, undaunted. "I came up with the
idea during recess after Luke told me Ryland James was at the
fire station's spaghetti feed signing autographs. But the whole
team thinks it's a good idea. If I'd been there last night…"

The annual Wicksburg Fire Department Spaghetti Feed
was one of the biggest events in town. She and Connor had
decided not to go to the fundraiser because Dana was calling home. "Don't forget, you got to talk to your mom."

"I know," Connor said. "But I'd like Ryland James's autograph. If he coaches us, he can sign my ball."

Signing a few balls, mugging for the camera and smiling
at soccer moms didn't come close to the time it would take
to coach a team of boys. The spring season was shorter and
more casual than fall league, but still…

She didn't want Connor to be disappointed. "It's a great
idea, but Ryland might not have time."

"Will you ask him if he'll coach us, Aunt Lucy? He might just say yes."

The sound of Connor's voice, full of excitement and anticipation, tugged at her heart. "Might" likely equaled "yes" in his young mind. She'd do anything for her nephew. She'd returned to the same town where her ex, now married to her former best friend, lived in order to care for Connor but going to see Ryland...

She blew out a puff of air. "He could say no."

The last time Lucy had seen him had been before her liver transplant. She'd been in eighth grade, jaundiced and bloated, carrying close to a hundred pounds of extra water weight. Not to mention totally exhausted and head over heels in love with the high-school soccer star. She'd spent much of her time alone in her room due to liver failure. Ryland James had fueled her adolescent fantasies. She'd dreamed about him letting her wear his jersey, asking her out to see a movie at the Liberty Theater and inviting her to be his date at prom.

Of course, none of those things had ever happened. She'd hated being known as the sick girl. She'd rarely been able to get up the nerve to say a word to Ryland. And then...

The high-school soccer team had put on two fundraisers—a summer camp for kids and a goal-a-thon—to help with Lucy's medical expenses. She remembered when Ryland handed her the large cardboard check. She'd tried to push her embarrassment and awkwardness aside by smiling at him and meeting his gaze. He'd surprised her by smiling back and sending her heart rate into overdrive. She'd never forgot his kindness or the flash of pity in his eyes. She'd been devastated.

Lucy's stomach churned at the memory. She wasn't that same girl. Still, she didn't want to see him again.

"Ryland is older than me." No one could ever imagine what she'd gone through and how she'd felt being so sick and tired all the time. Or how badly she'd wanted to be normal and healthy. "He was your dad's friend, not mine. I really didn't know him."

"But you've met him."

"He used to come to our house, but the chances of him remembering me…"

"Please, Aunt Lucy." Connor's eyes implored her. "We'll never know unless you ask."

Darn. He sounded like Aaron. Never willing to give up no matter what the odds. Her brother wouldn't let her give up, either. Not when she would have died without a liver transplant or when Jeff had trampled upon her heart.

Lucy's chest tightened. She should do this for Aaron as much Connor. But she had no idea how she could get close enough to someone as rich and famous as Ryland James.

Connor stared up at her with big, round eyes.

A lump formed in her throat. Whether she wanted to see Ryland James or could see him didn't matter. This wasn't about her. "Okay. I'll ask him."

Connor wrapped his arms around her. "I knew I could count on you."

Lucy hugged him tight. "You can always count on me, kiddo."

Even if she knew going into this things wouldn't work out the way her nephew wanted. But she could keep him smiling a little while longer. At least until Ryland said no.

Connor squirmed out of her arms. "Let's go see him now."

"Not so fast. This is something I'm doing on my own." She didn't want her nephew's image of his favorite soccer player destroyed in case Ryland was no longer a nice guy. Fame or fortune could change people. "And I can't show up empty-handed."

But what could she give to a man who could afford whatever he wanted? Flowers might be appropriate given his injury, but maybe a little too feminine. Chocolate, perhaps? Hershey Kisses might give him the wrong idea. Not that he'd ever known about her crush.

"Cookies," Connor suggested. "Everyone likes cookies."

"Yes, they do." Though Lucy doubted anything would convince Ryland to accept the coaching position. But what was the worst he could say besides no? "Does chocolate chip sound good?"

"Those are my favorite." Connor's smile faltered. "It's too bad my mom isn't here. She makes the best chocolate-chip cookies."

Lucy mussed his hair to keep him from getting too caught up in missing his mom. "It is too bad, but remember she's doing important stuff right now. Like your dad."

Connor nodded.

"How about we use your mom's recipe?" Lucy asked. "You can show me how she makes them."

His smile returned. "Okay."

Lucy wanted to believe everything would turn out okay, but she knew better. As with marriage, the chance of a happy ending here was extremely low. Best to prepare accordingly. She would make a double batch of cookies—one to give to Ryland and one for them to keep. She and Connor were going to need something to make them feel better after Ryland James said no.

The dog's whimpering almost drowned out the pulse-pounding rock music playing in his parents' home gym.

Ryland didn't glance at Cupcake. The dog could wait. He needed to finish his workout.

Lying on the weight machine's bench, he raised the bar overhead, doing the number of reps recommended by the team's trainer. He used free weights when he trained in

Phoenix, but his parents wanted him using the machine when he worked out alone.

Sweat beaded on his forehead. He'd ditched his T-shirt twenty minutes ago. His bare back stuck to the vinyl.

Ryland tightened his grip on the handles.

He wanted to return to the team in top form, to show them he still deserved the captaincy as well as their respect. He'd already lost one major endorsement deal due to his bad-boy behavior. For all he knew, he might not even have a spot on the Fuego roster come opening day. And that…sucked.

On the final rep, his muscles ached and his arms trembled. He clenched his jaw, pushing the weight overhead one last time.

"Yes!"

He'd increased the amount of weight this morning. His trainer would be pleased with the improvements in upper-body strength. That and his core were the only things he could work on.

Ryland sat up, breathing hard. Not good. He needed to keep up his endurance while he healed from the surgery.

Damn foot. He stared at his right leg encased in a black walking-cast boot.

His fault. Each of Ryland's muscles tensed in frustration. He should have known better than to be showboating during the friendly with Mexico. Now he was sidelined, unable to run or kick.

The media had accused him of being hungover or drunk when he hurt himself. They'd been wrong. Again. But dealing with the press was as much a part of his job as what happened for ninety minutes out on the pitch.

He'd appeared on camera, admitted the reason for his injury—goofing off for the fans and the cameras—and apologized to both fans and teammates. But the truth had made him look more like a bad boy than ever given his red cards during matches the last couple of seasons, the trouble he'd gotten into off the field and the endless "reports" on his dating habits.

The dog whined louder.

From soccer superstar to dog sitter. Ryland half laughed.

Cupcake barked, as if tired of being put off any longer.

"Come here," Ryland said.

His parents' small dog pranced across the padded gym floor, acting more like a pedigreed champion show dog than a full-blooded mutt. Ryland had wanted to buy his mom and dad a purebred, but they adopted a dog from the local animal shelter, instead.

Cupcake stared up at him with sad, pitiful brown eyes. She had mangy gray fur, short legs and a long, bushy tail. Only his parents could love an animal this ugly and pathetic.

"Come on, girl." Ryland scooped her up into his arms. "I know you miss Mom and Dad. I do, too. But you need to stop crying. They deserve a vacation without having to worry about you or me."

He'd given his parents a cruise for their thirty-second wedding anniversary. Even though he'd bought them this mansion on the opposite side of town, far away from the two-bedroom apartment where he'd grown up, and deposited money into a checking account for them each month, both continued to work in the same low-paying jobs they'd had for as long as their marriage. They also drove the same old vehicles even though newer ones, Christmas presents from him, were parked in the four-car garage.

His parents' sole indulgence was Cupcake. They spoiled the dog rotten. They hadn't wanted to leave her in a kennel or in the care of a stranger while away so after his injury they asked Ryland if he would dog sit. His parents never asked him for anything so he'd jumped at the opportunity to do this.

Ryland hated being back in Wicksburg. There were too

many bad memories from when he was a kid. Even small towns had bullies and not-so-nice cliques.

He missed the fun and excitement of a big city, but he needed time to get away to repair the damage he'd done to his foot and his reputation. No one was happy with him at the moment, especially himself. Until getting hurt, he hadn't realized he'd been so restless, unfocused, careless.

Cupcake pawed at his hands. Her sign she wanted rubs.

"Mom and Dad will be home before you know it." Ryland petted the top of her head. "Okay?"

The dog licked him.

He placed her on the floor then stood. "I'm getting some water. Then it's shower time. If I don't shave, I'm going to start looking mangy like you."

Cupcake barked.

His cell phone, sitting on the countertop next to his water bottle, rang. He read the name on the screen. Blake Cochrane. His agent.

Ryland glanced at the clock. Ten o'clock here meant seven o'clock in Los Angeles. "An early morning for you."

"I'm here by six to beat the traffic," Blake said. "According to Twitter, you made a public appearance the other night. I thought we agreed you were going to lay low."

"I was hungry. The fire station was having their annual spaghetti feed so I thought I could eat and support a good cause. They asked if I'd sign autographs and pose for pictures. I couldn't say no."

"Any press?"

"The local weekly paper." With the phone in one hand and a water bottle in the other, Ryland walked to the living room with Cupcake tagging alongside him. He tried hard not to favor his right foot. He'd only been off crutches a few days. "But I told them no interview because I wanted the focus to be on the event. The photographer took a few pictures of the crowd so I might be in one."

"Let's hope whatever is published is positive," Blake said.

"I was talking with people I grew up with." Some of the same people who'd treated him like garbage until he'd joined a soccer team. Most accepted him after he became a starter on the high-school varsity team as a freshman. He'd shown them all by becoming a professional athlete. "I was surrounded by a bunch of happy kids."

"That sounds safe enough," Blake admitted. "But be careful. Another endorsement deal fell through. They're nervous about your injury. The concerns over your image didn't help."

Ryland dragged his hand through his hair. "Let me guess. They want a clean-cut American, not a bad boy who thinks red cards are better than goals."

"You got it," Blake said. "I haven't heard anything official, but rumors are swirling that Mr. McElroy wants to loan you out to a Premier League team."

McElroy was the new owner of the Phoenix Fuego, who took more interest in players and team than any other head honcho in the MLS. He'd fired the coach/manager who'd wanted to run things his way and hired a new coach, Elliot Fritz, who didn't mind the owner being so hands-on. "Seriously?"

"I've heard it from more than one source."

Damn. As two teams were mentioned, Ryland plopped into his dad's easy chair. Cupcake jumped onto his lap.

"I took my eye off the ball," he said. "I made some mistakes. I apologized. I'm recovering and keeping my name out of the news. I don't see why we all can't move on."

"It's not that easy. You're one of the best soccer players in the world. Before your foot surgery, you were a first-team player who could have started for any team here or abroad. Not many American footballers can say that," Blake said.

"But McElroy believes your bad-boy image isn't a draw in the stands or with the kids. Merchandising is important these days."

"Yeah, I know. Being injured and getting older isn't helping my cause." As if twenty-nine made Ryland an old man. He remembered what the team owner had said in an interview. "McElroy called me an overpaid liability. But if that's the case, why would an overseas team want to take me on?"

"The transfer period doesn't start until June. None have said they want the loan yet."

Ouch. Ryland knew he had only himself to blame for the mess he found himself in.

"The good news is the MLS doesn't want to lose a home-grown player as talented as you. McElroy's feathers got ruffled," Blake continued. "He's asserting his authority and reminding you that he controls your contract."

"You mean, my future."

"That's how billionaires are."

"I'll stick to being a millionaire, then."

Blake sighed.

"Look, I get why McElroy's upset. Coach Fritz, too. I haven't done a good job handling stuff," Ryland admitted. "I'll be the first to admit I've never been an angel. But I'm not the devil, either. There's no way I could do everything the press says I do. The media exaggerates everything."

"True, but people's concerns are real. This time at your parents' house is critical. Watch yourself."

"I'm going to fix this. I want to play in the MLS." Ryland had already done an eleven-year stint in the U.K. "My folks are doing fine, but they're not getting any younger. I don't want to be an ocean away from them. If McElroy doesn't want me, see if the Indianapolis Rage or another club does."

"McElroy isn't going to let a franchise player like you go

to another MLS team," Blake said matter-of-factly. "If you want to play stateside, it'll be with Fuego."

Ryland petted Cupcake. "Then I'll have to keep laying low and polishing my image so it shines."

"Blind me, Ry."

"Will do." Everyone always wanted something from him. This was no different. But it sucked he had to prove himself all over again with Mr. McElroy and the Phoenix fans. "At least I can't get into trouble dog sitting. Wicksburg is the definition of boring."

"Women—"

"Not here," Ryland interrupted. "I know what's expected of me. I also know it's hard on my mom to read the gossip about me on the internet. She doesn't need to hear it firsthand from women in town."

"You should bring your mom back with you to Phoenix."

"Dude. Keeping it quiet and on the down low is fine while I'm here, but let's not go crazy," Ryland said. "In spite of the reports of me hooking up with every starlet in Hollywood, I've been more than discreet and discriminate with whom I see. But beautiful women coming on to me are one of the perks of the sport."

Blake sighed. "I remember when you were this scrappy, young kid who cared about nothing but soccer. It used to be all about the game for you."

"It's still about the game." Ryland was the small-town kid from the Midwest who hit the big-time overseas, playing with the best in the world. Football, as they called it everywhere but in the U.S., meant everything to him. Without it… "Soccer is my life. That's why I'm trying to get back on track."

A beat passed and another. "Just remember, actions speak louder than words."

After a quick goodbye, Blake disconnected from the call. Ryland stared at his phone. He'd signed with Blake when he was eighteen. The older Ryland got, the smarter his agent's advice sounded.

Actions speak louder than words.

Lately his actions hadn't been any more effective than his words. He looked at Cupcake. "I've put myself in the dog-house. Now I've got to get myself out of it."

The doorbell rang.

Cupcake jumped off his lap and ran to the front door bark-ing ferociously, as if she weighed ninety pounds, not nine-teen.

Who could that be? He wasn't expecting anyone.

The dog kept barking. He remained seated.

Let Cupcake deal with whomever was at the door. If he ignored them, maybe they would go away. The last thing Ryland wanted right now was company.

CHAPTER TWO

Lucy's hand hovered over the mansion's doorbell. She fought the urge to press the button a third time. She didn't want to annoy Mr. and Mrs. James. Yes, she wanted to get this fool's errand over with, but appearing overeager or worse, rude, wouldn't help her find coach for Connor's team.

"Come on," she muttered. "Open the door."

The constant high-pitch yapping of a dog suggested the doorbell worked. But that didn't explain why no one had answered yet. Maybe the house was so big it took them a long time to reach the front door. Lucy gripped the container of cookies with both hands.

The dog continued barking.

Maybe no one was home. She rose up on her tiptoes and peeked through the four-inch strip of small leaded-glass squares on the ornate wood door.

Lights shone inside.

Someone had to be home. Leaving the lights on when away wasted electricity. Her dad used to tell her that. Aaron said the same thing to Connor. But she supposed if a person could afford to live in an Architectural Digest–worthy home with its Georgian-inspired columns, circular drive and manicured lawn that looked like a green carpet, they probably didn't worry about paying the electricity bill.

Lucy didn't see anyone coming toward the door. She

couldn't see the dog, either. She lowered her heels to the welcome mat.

Darn it. She didn't want to come back later and try again. A chill shivered down her spine. She needed to calm down.

She imagined Connor with a smile on his face and soccer cleats on his feet. Her anxiety level dropped.

If no one answered, she would return. She would keep coming back until she spoke with Ryland James.

The dog's barking became more agitated.

A sign? Probably not, but she might as well ring the bell once more before calling it quits.

She pressed the doorbell. A symphony of chimes erupted into a Mozart tune. At least the song sounded like Mozart the third time hearing it.

The door opened slightly. A little gray dog darted out and sniffed her shoes. The pup placed its stubby front paws against her jean-covered calves.

"Off, Cupcake." The dog ran to the grass in the front yard. A man in navy athletic shorts with a black walking-cast on his right leg stood in the doorway. "She's harmless."

The dog might be, but not him.

Ryland James.

Hot. Sexy. Oh, my.

He looked like a total bad boy with his short, brown hair damp and mussed, as if he hadn't taken time to comb it after he crawled out of bed. Shaving didn't seem to be part of his morning routine, either. He used to be so clean-cut and all-American, but the dark stubble covering his chin and cheeks gave him an edge. His bare muscular chest glistened as if he'd just finished a workout. He had a tattoo on his right biceps and another on the backside of his left wrist. His tight, underwear model–worthy abs drew her gaze lower. Her mouth went dry.

Lucy forced her gaze up and stared into the hazel eyes

that had once fueled her teenage daydreams. His dark lashes seemed even thicker. How was that possible?

The years had been good, very good to him. The guy was more gorgeous than ever with his classically handsome features, ones that had become more defined, almost refined, with age. His nose, however, looked as if it had been broken at least once. Rather than detract from his looks, his nose gave him character, made him appear more…rugged. Manly. Dangerous.

Lucy's heart thudded against her ribs. "It's you."

"I'm me." His lips curved into a charming smile, sending her already-racing pulse into a mad sprint. "You're not what I expected to find on my doorstep, but my day's looking a whole lot better now."

Her turn. But Lucy found herself tongue-tied. The same way she'd been whenever he was over at her house years ago. Her gaze strayed once again to his amazing abs. Wowza.

"You okay?" he asked.

Remember Connor. She raised her chin. "I was expecting—"

"One of my parents."

She nodded.

"I was hoping you were here to see me," he said.

"I am." The words rushed from her lips like water from Connor's Super Soaker gun. She couldn't let nerves get the best of her now that she'd accomplished the first part of her mission and was standing face-to-face with Ryland. "But I thought one of them would answer the door since you're injured."

"They would have if they'd been home." His rich, deep voice, as smooth and warm as a mug of hot cocoa, flowed over her. "I'm Ryland James."

"I know."

"That puts me at a disadvantage because I don't know who you are."

"I meant, I know you. But it was a long time ago," she clarified.

His gaze raked over her. "I would remember meeting you."

Lucy was used to guys hitting on her. She hadn't expected that from Ryland, but she liked it. Other men's attention annoyed her. His flirting made her feel attractive and desired.

"Let me take a closer look to see if I can jog my memory," he said.

The approval in his eyes gave her goose bumps. The good kind, ones she hadn't felt in a while. She hadn't wanted to jump back into the dating scene after her divorce two years ago.

"I *have* seen that pretty smile of yours before," he continued. "Those sparkling blue eyes, too."

Oh, boy. Her knees felt wobbly. Tingles filled her stomach. *Stop.* She wasn't back in middle school.

Lucy straightened. The guy hadn't a clue who she was. Ryland James was a professional athlete. Knowing what to say to women was probably part of their training camp.

"I'm Lucy." For some odd reason, she sounded husky. She cleared her throat. "Lucy Martin."

"Lucy." Lines creased Ryland's forehead. "Aaron Martin's little sister?"

She nodded.

"Same smile and blue eyes, but everything else has changed." Ryland's gaze ran the length of her again. "Just look at you now."

She braced herself, waiting to hear how sick she'd been and how ugly she'd looked before her liver transplant.

He grinned. "Little Lucy is all grown up now."

Little Lucy? She stiffened. His words confused her. She hadn't been little. Okay, maybe when they first met back in elementary school. But she'd been huge, a bloated whale, and yellow due to jaundice the last time he'd seen her. "It's been what? Thirteen years since we last saw each other."

"Thirteen years too long," he said.

What was going on? Old crushes were supposed to get fat and lose their hair, not get even hotter and appear interested in you. He sounded interested. Unless her imagination was getting the best of her.

No, she knew better when it came to men. "It looks as if life is treating you well. Except for your leg—"

"Foot. Nothing serious."

"You had surgery."

"A minor inconvenience, that's all. Nothing like what you suffered through," he said. "The liver transplant seems to have done what Aaron hoped it would do. All he ever wanted was for you to be healthy."

"I am." She wondered why Aaron would have talked about her illness to Ryland. All they'd cared about were soccer and girls. Well, every other girl in Wicksburg except her. "I take medicine each day and have a monthly blood test, but otherwise I'm the same as everybody else."

"No, you're not." Ryland's gaze softened. "There's nothing ordinary about you. Never has been. It sucked that you were sick, but you were always so brave."

Heat stole up her neck toward her cheeks. Butterflies flapped in her tummy. Her heart...

Whoa-whoa-whoa. Don't get carried away by a few nice words from a good-looking guy, even if that guy happened to be the former man of her dreams. She'd been a naive kid back then. She'd learned the hard way that people said things they didn't mean. They lied, even after saying how much they loved you. Lucy squared her shoulders.

Time to get this over with. She handed Ryland the cookies. "These are for you."

He removed the container's lid. His brows furrowed. "Cookies?"

Ryland sounded surprised. She bit the inside of her mouth, hoping he liked them. "Chocolate chip."

"My favorite. Thanks."

He seemed pleased. Good. "Aaron's son, Connor, helped me make them. He's nine and loves soccer. That's why I'm here. To ask a favor."

Ryland looked at the cookies, then at her. "I appreciate your honesty. Not many people are so up-front when they want something. Let's talk inside."

She hesitated, unsure of the wisdom of going into the house. Once upon a time she'd believed in happily ever after and one true love. But life had taught her those things belonged only in fairy tales. Love and romance were overrated. But Ryland was making her feel things she tried hard not to think about too much—attraction, desire, hope.

But the other part of her, the part that tended to be impulsive and had gotten her into trouble more than once, was curious. She wanted to know if his parents' house was as nice on the inside as the exterior and front yard. Heaven knew she would never live in an exclusive neighborhood like this one. This might be her only chance to find out.

Ryland leaned against the doorway. The casual pose took weight off his right foot. He might need to sit down.

"Sure." She didn't want him hurting. "That would be nice."

He whistled for the dog.

Cupcake ran inside.

Lucy entered the house. The air was cooler than outside and smelled lemony. Wood floors gleamed. A giant chandelier hung from the twenty-foot ceiling in the foyer. She clamped her lips together so her mouth wouldn't gape. Original watercolor paintings in gilded frames decorated the textured walls. Tasteful and expensive.

She stepped through a wide-arched doorway into the living room. Talk about beautiful. The yellow and green décor was light, bright and inviting. The colors, fabrics and accessories coordinated perfectly. What she liked most was how comfortable the room looked, not at all like some of those unlivable magazine layouts or model homes.

Family pictures sat on the wooden fireplace mantle. A framed poster-size portrait of Ryland, wearing a U.S. National team uniform, hung on the wall. An open paperback novel rested cover-side up on an end table. "Your parents' house is lovely."

"Thanks."

He sounded proud, making her wonder about his part in his parents' house. She'd guess a big part, given his solid relationship with his mom and dad when he'd been a teen.

"My mom thought the house was too big, but I convinced her she deserved it after so many years of apartment living." Ryland motioned to a sofa. "Have a seat."

Lucy sat, sinking into the overstuffed cushions. More comfortable than the futon she'd sold before leaving Chicago. She'd gotten rid of her few pieces of furniture so she wouldn't have to pay for storage while living at Aaron and Dana's house.

Cupcake hopped up next to her.

"Is she allowed on the couch?" Lucy asked.

"The dog is allowed everywhere except the dining-room table and kitchen counters. She belongs to my parents. They've spoiled her rotten." Ryland sounded more amused than angry. He sat on a wingback chair to her right. "Mind if I have a cookie?"

"Please do."

He offered her the container. "Would you like one?"

The chocolate chips smelled good, but she would be eating cookies with Connor later. Better not overdo the sweets.

The trips to the ice-cream parlor and Rocket Burger with her nephew were already adding up. "No, thanks."

Ryland took one. "I can't remember the last time someone baked anything for me."

"What about your mom?"

"I don't spend as much time with my parents as I'd like due to soccer. Right now I'm dog sitting while they're away." Cupcake circled around as if chasing her own tail, then plopped against the cushion and placed her head on Lucy's thigh. "She likes you."

Lucy ran her fingers through the soft gray fur. She'd never had a dog. "She's sweet."

"When she wants to be." Ryland bit into the cookie. He took his time eating it. "Delicious."

The cookies were a hit. Lucy hoped they worked as a bribe. She mustered her courage. Not that she could back out now even if she wanted to. "So my nephew..."

"Does he want an autograph?" Ryland placed the cookie container on the coffee table. "Maybe a team jersey or ball?"

"Connor would love it if you signed his ball, but what he really wants is a coach for his spring under-9 rec. team." She didn't want to waste any more of Ryland's time. Or hers. "He wanted me to ask if you could coach his team, the Defeeters."

Ryland flinched. "Me? Coach?"

"I know that's a big request and likely impossible for you to do right now."

He looked at his injured foot. "Yeah, this isn't a good time. I hope to be back with my team in another month or so."

"I'm sure you will be. Aaron says you're one of the best players in the world."

"Thanks. It's just... I'm supposed to be laying low while I'm here. Staying out of the press. The media could turn my coaching your nephew's team into a circus." Ryland stared at the dog. "I'm really sorry I can't help you out."

"No worries. I told Connor you probably couldn't coach."
Lucy knew Ryland would never say yes. He'd left his small-
town roots behind and become famous, traveling all over the
U.S. and the world. The exotic lifestyle was as foreign to her
as the game of soccer itself. But maybe she could get him
to agree to something else that wouldn't take so much of his
time. "But if you happen to have an hour to spare sometime,
Connor and his teammates would be thrilled if you could give
them a pep talk."

Silence stretched between them. She'd put him on the spot
with that request, too. But she'd had no choice if she wanted
to help her nephew.

"I can do that," Ryland said finally.

Lucy released the breath she hadn't realized she was holding. "Thanks."

"I'm happy to talk to them, sign balls, pose for pictures,
whatever the boys want."

She hoped the visit would appease Connor. "That will be
great. Thanks."

Ryland's eyes darkened, more brown than hazel now. "Who
will you get to coach?"

"I don't know," she admitted. "Practices don't start until
next week so I still have a little time left to find someone. I
can always coach, if need be."

Surprise flashed across his face. "You play soccer?"

Lucy hadn't been allowed to do anything physical when
she was younger. Even though she no longer had any physical limitations, she preferred art to athletics. "No, but I've
been reading up on the game and watching video clips on the
internet, just in case."

His lips narrowed. "Aaron was great with those kids when
we put on that camp back in high school. Why doesn't he
coach the team?"

"Aaron's coached the Defeeters for years, but he's over-

seas right now with the army. Both he and his wife were deployed with their Reserve unit last month. I'm taking care of
Connor until they return next year."

"Aaron talked about using the military to pay for college,"
Ryland said thoughtfully. "But I lost track of him, of everyone, when I left Wicksburg."

"He joined the army right after high school." Lucy's medical expenses had drained their college funds, her parents'
saving account and the equity in their house. Sometimes it
felt as if she was still paying for the transplant years later.
Aaron, too. "That's where he met his wife, Dana. After they
completed their Active Duty, they joined the Reserves."

"A year away from home. Away from their son." Ryland
dragged his hand through his hair. "That has to be rough."

Lucy's chest tightened. "You do what you have to do."

"Still…"

"You left home to go to Florida and then England."

"To play soccer. Not protect my country," Ryland said. "I
had the time of my life. I doubt Aaron and his wife can say
the same thing right now."

Lucy remembered the tears glistening in Connor's eyes
as he told her his mom sounded like she was crying on the
phone. "You're right about that."

"I respect what Aaron and his wife, what all of the military, are doing. The sacrifices they make. True heroes. Every
one of them."

Ryland sounded earnest. She wanted to believe he was
sincere. Maybe he was still a small-town guy at heart. "They
are."

Cupcake rolled over on her back. She waved her front paws
in the air.

Lucy took the not-so-subtle hint and rubbed the dog's stomach.

"So you've stuck around Wicksburg," Ryland said.

"I left for a while. College. I also lived in Chicago." Aaron had accused her of running away when her marriage failed. Maybe he'd been right. But she'd had to do something when her life crumbled around her. "I moved back last month."

"To care for your nephew."

She nodded. "Saying no never entered into my mind. Not after everything Aaron has done for me."

"He was so protective of you."

"He still is."

"That doesn't surprise me." Ryland rubbed his thigh above the brace he wore. He rested his foot on an ottoman. "Did you leave your boyfriend behind in Chi-town or did he come with you?"

She drew back, surprised by the question. "I, uh, don't have a boyfriend."

He grinned wryly. "So you need a soccer coach and a boyfriend. I hope your brother told you the right qualities to look for in each."

Aaron always gave her advice, but she hadn't always listened to him. Lucy should have done so before eloping. She couldn't change the past. But she wouldn't make that same mistake again.

"A soccer coach is all I need." Lucy figured Ryland had to be teasing her, but this wasn't a joking matter. She needed a boyfriend as much as she needed another ex-husband. She shifted positions. "I have my hands full with Connor. He's my priority. A kid should be happy and carefree, not frowning and down all the time."

"Maybe we should get him together with Cupcake," Ryland said. "She goes from being happy to sad. I'm a poor substitute for my parents."

Lucy's insecurities rushed to the surface. She never thought she would have something in common with him. "That's how I feel with Connor. Nothing I do seems to be...enough."

Ryland leaned forward. His large hand engulfed hers. His touch was light. His skin was warm. "Hey. You're here to see me about his team. That says a lot. Aaron and his family, especially Connor, are lucky to have you."

Ryland's words wrapped around Lucy like a big hug. But his touch disturbed her more than it comforted. Heat emanated from the point of contact and spread up her arm. She tried not to think about it. "I'm the lucky one."

"Maybe some of that luck will rub off on me."

"Your injury?" she asked.

"Yeah, and a few other things."

His hand still rested upon hers. Lucy hadn't been touched by a man in over two years. It felt…good.

Better not get used to it. Reluctantly, she pulled her hand from beneath his and reached for her purse.

"If you need some luck, I've got just the thing for you." Lucy removed a penny from her change pocket and gave it to Ryland. "My grammy told me this is all a person needs to get lucky."

Wicked laughter lit his eyes. "Here I thought it took a killer opening line, oodles of charm and an expensive bottle of champagne."

Oh, no. Lucy realized what she'd said. Her cheeks burned. "I meant to change their luck."

He winked. "I know, but you gave me the opening. I had to take the shot."

At least he hadn't scored. Not yet, anyway. Lucy swallowed.

"Aaron would have done the same." She needed to be careful, though. Ryland was charming, but he wasn't her big brother. Being near him short-circuited her brain. She couldn't think straight. That was bad. The last time she allowed herself to be charmed by a man she'd ended up with a wedding ring on her finger.

"You said your nephew loves soccer," Ryland said.

She nodded, thankful for the change in subject. "Yes. Connor and Aaron are crazy about the sport. They wear matching jerseys. It's cute, though Dana says it's annoying when they get up at some crazy hour to watch a game in Europe. But I don't think she minds that much."

Lucy cringed at her rambling. Ryland didn't care about Aaron's family's infatuation with soccer. She needed to shut up. Now.

"That's great they're so into the game." A thoughtful expression crossed Ryland's face. "I haven't been back in town for a while, but I bet some of the same people are still involved in soccer. I'll ask around to see if there's someone who can coach your nephew's team."

Her mouth parted in surprise. She liked being self-reliant and hated asking for help, but in this case Ryland had offered. She'd be stupid to say no when this meant so much to Connor. "I'd appreciate that. If it's not too much trouble."

"No trouble. I'm happy to do it. Anything for…"

You, she thought.

"…Aaron."

Of course, this was for her brother. Ryland's childhood and high-school friend and teammate. She ignored the twinge of disappointment. "Thanks."

Ryland held the penny between the pads of his thumb and index finger. "You've made me cookies, given me a lucky penny. What do I get if I find a coach?"

Lucy wondered if he was serious or teasing her. His smile suggested the latter. "My undying gratitude?"

"That's a good start."

"More cookies?"

"Always appreciated, especially if they're chocolate chip," he said. "What else?"

His lighthearted and flirty tone sounded warning bells in

her head. Ryland *was* teasing her, but Lucy no longer wanted to play along. His charm, pretty much everything about him, unsettled her. "I'm not sure what else you might want."

He gave her the once-over, only this time his gaze lingered a second too long on her lips. "I can think of a couple things."

So could Lucy. The man was smokin' hot. His lips looked as if they could melt her insides with one kiss. Sex appeal oozed from him.

A good thing she'd sworn off men because she could tell the soccer pitch wasn't the only place where Ryland James played. Best not to even start that game. She'd only lose. Again.

Not. Going. To. Happen.

Time to steer this conversation back to where it needed to be so she could get out of here.

"How about you make a list?" Lucy kept a smile on her face and her tone light and friendly. After all, he was going to try to find Connor's team a coach. But if Ryland thought she was going to swoon at his feet in adoration and awe, he had another think coming. "If you find the team a coach, we'll go from there."

Ryland's smile crinkled the corners of his eyes, taking her breath away. "I always thought you were a cool kid, Lucy Martin, but I really like who you are now."

Okay, she was attracted to him. Any breathing female with a pulse would be. The guy was appealing with a capital *A*.

But Lucy wasn't stupid. She knew the type. His type.

Ryland James spelled T-R-O-U-B-L-E.

Once he visited the Defeeters, she never wanted to see him again. And she wouldn't.

It was so good to see Lucy Martin again.

Ryland sat in the living room waiting for her to return with Cupcake, who needed to go outside. Lucy had offered to take the dog to the backyard so he wouldn't have to get up. He'd agreed if only to keep her here a little while longer.

He couldn't get over the difference in her.

She'd been a shy, sweet girl with freckles, long braids and yellowish whites surrounding her huge blue eyes. Now she was a confident, sweet woman with a glowing complexion, strawberry-blond hair worn in a short and sassy style, and mesmerizing sky-blue eyes.

Ryland had been wrong about not wanting company this morning. Sure she'd shown up because she wanted something. But she'd brought him cookies—a bribe, no doubt—and been straightforward asking him for a favor.

He appreciated and respected that.

Some women were devious and played up to him to get what they wanted. Lucy hadn't even wanted something for herself, but for her nephew. That was…refreshing.

Cupcake ran into the living room and hopped onto the couch.

Lucy took her same spot next to the dog. "Sorry that took so long, the dog wanted to run around before she got down to business."

"Thanks for taking her out." Lucy had brightened Ryland's mood, making him smile and laugh. He wanted her to stick around. "You must be thirsty. I'll get you something to drink. Coffee? Water? A soda?"

Lucy shifted on the couch. "No, thanks."

Years ago, Aaron had told Ryland that his sister had a crush on him so to be nice to her. He had been. Now he was curious to know if any of her crush remained. "It's no trouble."

But he could get in trouble wondering if she were still interested in him. He was supposed to be avoiding women.

Not that he was pursuing her. Though he was…curious.

She grabbed her purse. "Thanks, but I should be going."

Lucy was different than other women he knew. Most would

kill for that kind of invitation from him, but she didn't seem impressed or want to hang out with him. She'd eagerly taken Cupcake outside while he stayed inside. Almost as if she'd wanted some distance from him.

Interesting. His charm and fame usually melted whatever feminine resistance he faced. Not with Lucy. He kind of liked the idea of a challenge. Not that it could go anywhere, he reminded himself. "I'd like to hear more about Aaron."

"Perhaps another time."

"You have somewhere to be?"

Her fingers curled around the leather strap. "I have work to do before Connor gets home from school."

Ryland would have liked it if she stayed longer, but he would see her again. No doubt about that. He rose. "I'll see you out."

She stood. Her purse swung like a pendulum. "That's not necessary. Stay off your foot. I know where the door is."

"My foot can handle it."

Lucy's gaze met his. "I can see myself out."

He found the unwavering strength in her eyes a big turn-on. "I know, but I want to show you out."

After what felt like forever, she looked away with a shrug. "It's your foot."

He bit back a smile. She would be a challenge all right. A fun one. "Yes, it is."

Ryland accompanied Lucy to her car, a practical looking white, four-door subcompact. "Thanks for coming by and bringing me cookies. I'll give you a call about a coach and talking to the team."

She removed something from an outside pocket of her purse and handed it to him. "My cell-phone number is on my business card. Aaron has a landline, but this is the best way to reach me."

He stared at the purple card with white and light blue

lettering and a swirly border. That looked more like Lucy. "Freelance graphic designer. So you're still into art."

"You remember that?"

She sounded incredulous, but the way her eyes danced told him she was also pleased.

"You'd be surprised what I remember."

Her lips parted once again.

He'd piqued her interest. Good, because she'd done the same to him. "But don't worry, it's all good."

A charming blush crept into Lucy's cheeks.

"We'll talk later." Ryland didn't want to make her uncomfortable, but flirting with her came so easily. "You have work to do now."

"Yes, I do." She dug around the inside of her purse. As she pulled out her keys, metal clanged against metal. "Thanks. I'm... I look forward to hearing from you."

"It won't be long." And it wouldn't. Ryland couldn't wait to talk to her again. "I promise."

CHAPTER THREE

THAT afternoon, the front door burst open with so much force Lucy thought a tornado had touched down in Wicksburg. She stood her ground in the living room, knowing this burst of energy wasn't due to Mother Nature—the warning siren hadn't gone off—but was man, er, boy-made.

Manny usually couldn't wait for Connor to get home and make another escape attempt, but the cat hightailed it into the kitchen. A ball of dark fur slid across the linoleum before disappearing from sight.

Connor flew into the house, strands of his strawberry-blond hair going every which way. He was lanky, the way his dad had been at that age, all limbs with not an ounce of fat on him. The set of his jaw and the steely determination in his eyes made him seem more superhero than a four-and-a-half-foot third grader. All he needed was a cape to wear over his jersey and jeans.

"Hey." Lucy knew he wanted to know about her visit to Ryland, but the sexy soccer player had been on her mind since she'd left him. Much to her dismay. She didn't want to start her time with Connor focused on the guy, too. "Did you have a good day at school? You had a spelling quiz, right?"

He slammed the front door closed. The entire house shook. His backpack hung precariously off one thin shoulder, but he didn't seem to care. "Did you talk to Ryland James?"

Connor had the same one-track mind as her brother. When Aaron had something he wanted to do, like joining the military, he defined tunnel vision.

Lucy might as well get this over with. "I went to Mr. and Mrs. James's house this morning. Ryland liked the cookies we baked."

The backpack thudded against the entryway's tile floor. Anticipation filled Connor's blue eyes. "Is he going to coach the Defeeters?"

This was the part she hadn't been looking forward to since leaving the Jameses' house. "No, but Ryland offered to see if he can find the team a coach. He's also going to come out and talk to the team."

Different emotions crossed Connor's face. Sadness, anger, surprise. A thoughtful expression settled on his features. "I guess he must be really busy."

"Ryland's trying to heal and stay in shape." Her temperature rose remembering how he looked in only a pair of shorts and gleam of sweat. "He doesn't plan on being in town long. Maybe a month or so. He wants to rejoin his team as soon as he can."

Manny peered around the doorway to the kitchen, saw Connor and ran to him.

Connor picked up the cat. "I guess I would want to do that, too."

Poor kid. He was trying to put on a brave face. She wished things could be different for him. "There's still time to find the Defeeters a coach."

He stared over the cat's head. "That's what you said last week. And the week before that."

"True, but now I have help looking for a coach." Lucy hoped Ryland had been serious about his offer and came through for…the boys. "A good thing, otherwise, you'll be stuck with me."

Connor nodded.

She ruffled his hair. "Gee, thanks."

"You're the one who said it." He flashed her a lopsided grin. "But no matter what happens, having you for a coach is better than not playing at all."

Lucy hoped he was right. "I'll do my best if it comes down to that."

"It won't." Connor sounded so confident.

"How do you know?"

"If Ryland James said he'd find us a coach, he will."

She'd been disappointed too many times to put that much faith into someone. Ryland had seemed sincere and enthusiastic. But so had others. Best not to raise Connor's hopes too high on the chance his favorite player didn't come through after all. "Ryland said he'd *try.* He's going to call me."

"Have you checked your voice mail yet?" Connor asked.

His eagerness made her smile. She'd been wondering when the call might come herself. They both needed to be realistic. "I just saw Ryland a couple hours ago."

"Hours? He could have found us five coaches by now."

She doubted that.

"All Ryland James has to do is snap his fingers and people will come running," Connor continued.

Lucy could imagine women running to the gorgeous Ryland. She wasn't so sure the same could be said about coaches. Not unless they were female.

"Check your cell phone," Connor encouraged.

The kid was relentless…like his dad. "Give Ryland time to snap his fingers. I mean, make calls. I know this is important to you, but a little patience here would be good."

"You could call him."

No, she couldn't. Wouldn't. "He said he'd call. Rushing him wouldn't be nice."

She also didn't want to give Ryland the wrong impression

so he might think she was interested in him. A guy like him meant one thing—heartbreak. She'd had enough of that to last a lifetime.

"Let's give him at least a day, maybe two, to call us, okay?" she suggested.

"Okay," Connor agreed reluctantly.

She bit back a laugh. "How about some cookies and milk while you tell me about school?"

Maybe that would get Ryland James out of Connor's thoughts. And hers, too.

"Sure." As he walked toward the kitchen, he looked back at her. "So does Ryland James have a soccer field in his back-yard?"

Lucy swallowed a sigh. And then maybe not.

After dinner, Ryland retreated with Cupcake into the media room aka his dad's man cave. He had all he needed—laptop, cell phone, chocolate-chip cookies, Lucy's business card and a seventy-inch LED television with ESPN playing. As soon as Ryland found Lucy a coach for her nephew's team, he would call her with the good news.

Forget the delicious cookies she'd made. The only dessert he wanted was to hear her sweet voice on the opposite end of the phone.

Ryland laughed. He must need some feminine attention if he felt this way.

But seeing Lucy again had made him feel good. She also had him thinking about the past. Many of his childhood memories living in Wicksburg were like bad dreams, ones he'd pushed to the far recesses of his mind and wanted to keep there. But a few others, like the ones he remembered now, brought a welcome smile to his face.

Cupcake lay on an Indianapolis Colts dog bed.

Even though Ryland played soccer, his dad preferred football, the American kind. But his dad had never once tried to change Ryland's mind about what sport to play. Instead, his father had done all he could so Ryland could succeed in the sport. He would be nowhere without his dad and his mom.

And youth soccer.

He'd learned the basic skills and the rules of the game playing in the same rec. league Aaron's son played in. When Ryland moved to a competitive club, playing up a year from his own age group, his dad's boss, Mr. Buckley, who owned a local farm, bought Ryland new cleats twice a year. Not cheap ones, but the good kind. Mr. Martin, Aaron and Lucy's dad, would drive Ryland to away games and tournaments when his parents had to work.

Lucy taking care of Aaron's son didn't surprise Ryland. The Martins had always been a loyal bunch.

In elementary school, other kids used to taunt him. Aaron stood up for Ryland even before they were teammates. Once they started playing on the same team, they became good friends. But Ryland had wanted to put Wicksburg behind him when he left.

And he had.

He'd focused all his effort and energy into being the best soccer player he could be.

Now that he was back in town, finding a soccer coach was the least he could do for his old friend Aaron. Ryland pressed the mute button on the television's remote then picked up his cell phone. This wouldn't take long.

Two hours later, he disconnected from yet another call. He couldn't believe it. No matter whom he'd spoken with, the answer was still the same—no. Only the reason for not being able to coach changed.

"Wish I could help you out, Ryland, but I'm already coaching two other teams."

"Gee, if I'd known sooner…"

"Try the high school. Maybe one of the students could do it as a class project or something."

Ryland placed his cell phone on the table. Even the suggestion to contact the high school had led to a dead end. No wonder Lucy had asked him to coach Connor's team.

Ryland looked at Cupcake. "What am I going to do?"

The dog kept her eyes closed.

"Go ahead. Pretend you don't hear me. That's what everyone else has done tonight."

Okay, not quite. His calling had resulted in four invitations to dinner and five requests to speak to soccer teams. Amazing how things and his status in town had changed. All his hard work had paid off. Though he was having to start over with Mr. McElroy and the Fuego.

"I need to find Lucy a coach."

Cupcake stretched.

Something flashed on the television screen. Highlights from a soccer match.

Yearning welled inside him. He missed the action on the field, the adrenaline pushing through him to run faster and the thrill of taking the ball toward the goal and scoring. Thinking about playing soccer was making him nostalgic for days when kids, a ball and some grass defined the game in its simplest and purest form.

Lucy's business card caught his eye.

Attraction flared to life. He wanted to talk to her. Now.

Ryland picked up his cell phone. He punched in the first three digits of her number then placed the phone back on the table.

Calling her tonight would be stupid. Saying he wanted to hear her voice might be true, but he didn't want to push too hard and scare her off. Other women might love a surprise phone call, but Lucy might not. She wasn't like the women he dated.

That, he realized, surprisingly appealed to him. Sitting in his parents' living room eating cookies and talking with a small-town girl had energized him in a way no visit to a top restaurant or trendy club with a date ever had.

Ryland stared at the cell phone. He wanted to talk to her, but if he called her he would have to admit his inability to find her a coach. That wouldn't go over well.

With him, he realized with a start. Lucy wouldn't be upset. She'd thank him for his efforts then take on the coaching role herself.

I can always coach, if need be.

You play soccer?

No, but I've been reading up on the game and watching coaching clips on the internet just in case.

He imagined her placing a whistle around her graceful neck and leading a team of boys at practice. Coaching would be nothing compared to what Lucy went through when she was sick. She would figure out the basics of what needed to be done and give the boys her all.

But she shouldn't *have* to do that. She was doing enough taking care of her nephew. The same as Aaron and his wife.

His gaze focused on Lucy's name on her business card. The script might be artistic and a touch whimsical, but it showed strength and ingenuity, too.

Ryland straightened. He couldn't let people saying no stop him. He was tougher than that. "I might have screwed up my career, but I'm not going to mess up this."

The dog stared at him.

"I'll find Lucy and those kids a coach."

No matter what he had to do.

Two days later, Lucy stood in the front yard kicking a soccer ball to Connor. The afternoon sun shone high in the sky, but the weather might as well be cloudy and gray due to the frown on her nephew's face. Practices began next week and the Defeeters still didn't have a coach. Ryland hadn't called back, either.

She tapped the ball with her left foot. It rolled too far to the left, out of Connor's reach and into the hedge separating the yard from the neighbor's. Lucy grimaced. "Sorry."

Connor didn't say a word but chased the ball. She knew what he was thinking because his expression matched her thoughts. The team needed someone who knew soccer better than she did, someone who could teach the kids the right skills and knew rules without having to resort to a book each time.

Her efforts to find a coach had failed. That left one person who could come to her—and the team's—rescue.

It won't be long. I promise.

Ryland's words returned to her in a rush. Pathetic, how quick she'd been to believe them. As if she hadn't learned anything based on her past experiences.

Okay, it had been only a couple of days. "Long" could mean a few days, a week, even a month. But "promise" was a seven-letter word that held zero weight with most of the people in this world.

Was Ryland one of them?

Time would tell, but for Connor's sake she hoped not. He kicked the ball back to her.

She stopped the ball with her right foot the way she'd seen someone do on a video then used the inside of her foot to kick the ball back. She had better control this time. "Your teacher liked your book report."

"I guess."

"You got an A."

Connor kicked the ball her way without stopping it first. "Are you sure he hasn't called?"

"He" equaled Ryland. Connor had been asking that question nonstop, including a call during lunchtime using a classmate's cell phone.

Lucy patted her jeans pocket. "My phone's right here."

"You checked your messages?"

"I did." And rechecked them. No messages from Ryland. From anyone for that matter. She hadn't made any close friends in Chicago. The ones who lived in Wicksburg had remained friends with her ex-husband after Lucy moved away. That made things uncomfortable now that she was back. The pity in their eyes reminded her of when she'd been sick. She wanted no part of that ever again. "But it's only been a couple of days."

"It feels like forever."

"I know." Each time her cell phone rang, thinking it might be Ryland filled her stomach with tingles of anticipation. She hated that. She didn't want to feel that way about any guy calling her, even if the reason was finding a coach for her nephew's soccer team. "But good things come to those who wait."

Connor rolled the ball back and forth along the bottom of his foot. "That's what Mom and Dad say. I'm trying to be patient, but it's hard."

"I know it's hard to wait, but we have to give Ryland time."

Connor nodded.

Please come through, Ryland. Lucy didn't want Connor's favorite player letting him down at the worst possible time. She didn't want her nephew to have to face the kind of betrayal and disappointment she'd suffered due to others. Not when he was only nine, separated from his parents by oceans and continents.

He kicked the ball to her. "Maybe Ryland forgot."

Lucy didn't want to go there. The ball rolled past her to-

ward the sidewalk. She chased after it. "Give him the benefit of the doubt."

Connor didn't say anything.

She needed him to stop focusing so much on Ryland. "Your
dad wants to see videotapes of your games. He can't wait to
see how the team does this spring."

She kicked the ball back. Connor touched the ball twice
with his foot before kicking it to her.

"Next time only one touch," she said.

Surprise filled his blue eyes. "That's what my dad says."

"It might come as a shock, but your aunt knows a few
things about the game of soccer." She'd found a book on
coaching on the living-room bookcase and attended a coaching clinic put on by the league last night while Connor had
dinner over at a friend's house. "How about we kick the ball
a few times more, then go to the pizza parlor for dinner? You
can play those video games you like so much."

"Okay."

Talk about an unenthused reaction.

An old beat-up, blue pickup truck pulled to the curb in
front of the house. The engine idled loudly, as if in need of
a tune-up. The engine sputtered off. The truck lurched forward a foot, maybe two.

The driver's door opened. Ryland.

Her heart thumped.

It won't be long. I promise.

Tingles filled her stomach. He hadn't let her down. He was
still the same nice guy he'd been in high school.

Ryland rounded the front of the truck. He wore a white
polo shirt with the Fuego logo on the left side, a pair of khaki
shorts and the boot on his right foot. He wore a tennis shoe
on his left. His hair was nicely styled. He'd shaved, remov-
ing the sexy stubble.

Even with his clean-cut look, she knew not to let her guard

down. The guy was still dangerous. The only reason she was happy to see him was Connor.

A little voice inside her head laughed at that. She ignored it.

"It's him." Awe filled Connor's voice. "Ryland James."

"Yes, it's him," she said.

Ryland crossed the sidewalk and stood near them on the lawn. "Hello."

Lucy fought the urge to step back and put some distance between them. "Hi."

He acknowledged her with a nod, but turned his attention to the kid with the stars in his eyes. "You must be Connor."

Her nephew nodded.

Lucy's heart melted. Ryland knew how important this moment must be for her nephew.

Connor wiped his right hand against his shorts then extended his arm. "It's nice to meet you, Mr. James."

As Ryland shook his hand, he grinned. "Call me Ryland."

Connor's eyes widened. He looked almost giddy with excitement. "Okay, Ryland."

He motioned to the soccer ball. "Looks like you've been practicing. It's good to get some touches on the ball every day."

Connor nodded. The kid was totally starstruck. Lucy didn't blame him for being wowed by Ryland. She was, too.

Better be careful.

Ryland used his left foot to push the ball toward Connor. "Let's see you juggle."

Connor swooped up the ball and bounced it off his bony knees. He used his legs and feet to keep the ball from touching the ground.

"You're doing great," Ryland encouraged.

Connor beamed and kept going.

Ryland glanced at her. "He reminds me of Aaron."

"Two peas in a pod," she agreed.

The ball bounced away. Connor ran after it. "I'll try it again."

"The more you practice, the better you'll get," Ryland said.

"That's what Aunt Lucy told me."

His gaze met hers. Lucy's pulse skittered at the flirtatious gleam in Ryland's hazel eyes.

"Your aunt is a smart woman," he said.

Lucy didn't feel so smart. She wasn't sure what to make of her reaction to Ryland being here. Okay, the guy was handsome. Gorgeous, really. But she knew better than to be bowled over by a man and sweet talk.

So why was she practically swooning over the sexy soccer star? Ryland showing up and the way he was interacting with Connor had to be the reason. Nothing else made sense.

She straightened. "I thought you were going to call."

"I decided to stop by, instead."

Warning bells rang in her head. "The address isn't on my business card. How did you find this place?"

"I went into the café for a cup of coffee and asked where Aaron lived," Ryland explained. "Three people offered directions."

"That's Wicksburg for you," she said. "Friendly to a fault."

"No kidding," he agreed. "I received a friendly reminder about the difference between a tornado watch versus a tornado warning. More than one person also suggested I drop my dad's old truck off at the salvage yard before he gets home from vacation. But it's a good thing he has it. The truck is the only vehicle that has enough room so I can drive with my left foot."

"You went to so much trouble. A phone call would've been fine."

He motioned to her nephew. "Not for him."

A big grin brightened Connor's face. The heartache of the

last few weeks seemed to have vanished. He looked happy and carefree, the way a nine-year-old boy should be.

Words didn't seem enough, but gratitude was all Lucy could afford to give Ryland. "Thank you."

"Watch this," Connor said.

"I'm watching," Ryland said, sounding amused.

Her nephew juggled the ball. His face, a portrait in concentration.

"Keep it going," Ryland encouraged.

"You're all he's talked about for the last two days," she said quietly. "I'm so happy you're here. I mean, Connor's happy. We're both happy."

"That makes three of us," Ryland said.

"Did you find a coach for the Defeeters?" Connor asked.

"Not a head coach, but someone who can help out for now."

"I knew it!" Connor screamed loud enough for the entire town to hear. The ball bounced into the hedge again.

Ryland had done his part, more than Lucy had expected. Warmth flowed through her. Not good. She shouldn't feel anything where he was concerned. She wanted him to give his talk to the team ASAP so she could say goodbye. "Thanks."

"So who's going to help coach us?" Connor asked eagerly.

Ryland smiled, a charming lopsided grin that made her remember the boy he used to be, the one she'd fallen head over heels for when she'd been a teenager.

"I am," he said.

CHAPTER FOUR

THE next week, on Monday afternoon, Ryland walked through the parking lot at Wicksburg Elementary School. Playing soccer here was one of the few good memories he had of the place.

He hoped today's soccer practice went well. He was looking forward to spending time with Lucy, and as for the boys… how hard could it be to coach a bunch of eight- and nine-year-olds?

Ryland adjusted the strap of the camp-chair bag resting on his left shoulder. He hated the idea of sitting during any portion of the practice, but standing for an entire hour wouldn't be good if his foot started hurting.

Healing was his number-one priority. He had to be smart about helping the Defeeters. Not only because of his foot. His agent and the Fuego's front office might not consider a pseudo coaching gig "laying low." He'd sent an email to all the boys' parents explaining the importance of keeping his presence with the team quiet.

A car door slammed.

He glanced in the direction of the sound. Lucy's head appeared above the roof of a car.

Ryland hoped she was happier to see him today. The uncertainty in her eyes when he'd said he would help with the

Defeeters had surprised him. When he explained no one else wanted to coach, so he'd decided to do it himself, a resigned smile settled on her lips. But she hadn't looked happy or relieved about the news.

He'd wanted a challenge. It appeared he'd gotten one.

She bent over, disappearing from his sight, then reappeared. Another door shut.

Her strawberry-blond curls bounced. His fingers itched to see if the strands felt as silky as they looked.

Lucy stepped out from between two cars with a bag of equipment in one hand and a binder in the other. She was alone.

He hoped her nephew wasn't sick. At least Lucy had shown up.

That made Ryland happy. So did the spring weather. He gave a quiet thanks for the warm temperature. Lucy had ditched the baggy hoodies she'd worn at his parents' house and at Aaron's. Her sweatshirts and pants had been hiding treasures.

Her outfit today showed off her figure to perfection. A green T-shirt stretched tight across her chest. Her breasts were round and high, in proportion and natural looking. Navy shorts accentuated the length of her legs. Firm and sexy. Ryland preferred the pale skin color to the orangey fake tan some women had.

Little Lucy Martin was a total hottie. Ryland grinned. Coaching the Defeeters was looking better and better.

Her gaze caught his. She pressed her lips together in a thin, tight line.

Busted. He'd been staring at her body. Practically leering. Guilt lodged in his throat.

A twinge of disappointment ran through him, too. Her reaction made one thing clear. She no longer had a crush on him.

He wasn't surprised. Crushes came and went. Over a decade had passed since they knew each other as kids. But Ryland didn't get why Lucy looked so unhappy to see him. If not for him, she would be on her own coaching the boys. He didn't expect her to fall at his feet, but a smile—even a hint of one—would have been nice.

She glanced toward the grass field.

He half expected her to walk away from him, but instead she headed toward him. Progress? He hoped so. "Hello."

"Hi," she said.

"Where's Connor?"

"He went home from school with a boy from the team. They should be here soon."

"A playdate and the first practice of spring. Connor is a lucky kid."

"I wanted to make today special for him."

"You have." Ryland liked how Lucy did so much for her nephew, but she seemed to give, give, give. He wondered if she ever did anything for herself. Maybe that was how he could get on her good side. "The first practice is always interesting. Getting to know a new coach. Sizing up who has improved over the break. Making friends with new teammates. At least that's how I remember it."

"All I know is Connor has been looking forward to this for weeks," she said. "He's been writing letters and sending emails to Aaron and Dana counting down the days to the start of practice, but they must be somewhere without computer access. They haven't replied the past couple of days."

That didn't sound good. "Worried?"

Lucy shrugged but couldn't hide the anxiousness in her eyes. "Aaron said this could happen. Connor just wants to hear what his dad thinks about you working with the team."

She hadn't answered Ryland's question about being worried, but he let it go. "I hope I live up to Connor's expectations."

"You really don't have to do this."

"I don't mind showing up early to practice."

"I was talking about coaching."

That wasn't what he'd expected her to say, but Lucy didn't seem to mince words. She also wore her heart on her sleeve. He didn't like seeing the tight lines around her mouth and narrowed eyes. He wanted to put her at ease. "It might be the last thing I expected to be doing while I'm in Wicksburg. But I want to do this for Aaron and his son."

For Lucy, too. But Ryland figured saying that would only upset her more.

"What if someone finds out?" she asked.

That thought had crossed his mind many times over the past few days. Someone outside the team would recognize him at some point and most likely wouldn't be able to keep quiet.

But he was a man who took chances.

Besides, how much trouble could he get into helping a bunch of kids? Community involvement was a good thing, surely? "I'll deal with that if it happens, but remember, I'm not coaching. I'm only helping."

A carefully laid out distinction that made a world of difference. At least he hoped so.

He waited for her to say something, to rattle off a list of reasons why his assisting the Defeeters was a bad idea or to tell him she'd found someone else to coach the team.

Instead, she raised the bag of equipment—balls and orange cones—in the air. "I picked up the practice gear. I also have a binder with emergency and player information."

Interesting. He'd expected her to put up more of a fight.

He'd kind of been looking forward to it. When Lucy got emotional, silvery sparks flashed in her irises. He liked her blue eyes. And the rest of her, too. "Thanks."

"So what do you want to do with the cones?" she asked. "I've never been to a soccer practice before."

This was why Ryland wanted—no, needed—to help. He wouldn't be working only with the kids. He would be teaching Lucy what to do so she'd be all set when fall season rolled around. He didn't want the Defeeters split up as a team in September because they didn't have a coach for fall league. That wouldn't be good for the boys or for Aaron when he returned home. Lucy might end up feeling bad, too. "I'll show you."

With Lucy at his side, Ryland stepped from the asphalt onto the field. The smell of fresh grass filled his nostrils, the scent as intoxicating as a woman's perfume. He inhaled to take another sniff. Anticipation zinged through him, bringing all his nerve endings to life.

Neither soccer nor women had been part of his life since his foot surgery. He shot a sideward glance at Lucy. At least one of them would be now. Well, sort of.

"It's good to be back," he said, meaning it.

"In town?" she asked.

"On this field." For the last eleven years, no matter what level he played, soccer had meant packed stadiums, cheering crowds and vuvuzelas being blown. Shirtless men with painted faces and chests stood in the stands. Women with tight, tiny tops wanted body parts autographed. Smiling, he motioned to the field in front of him. "It doesn't matter whether I'm at an elementary school for a practice or at a sold-out stadium for a World Cup game. This is…home."

A dreamy expression formed on Lucy's face.

He stared captivated wondering what she was thinking about.

"I felt that way about this loft in Chicago." The tone of her voice matched the wistfulness in her eyes. "They rented studio space by the hour. The place smelled like paint and thinner, but that made it even more perfect. I couldn't afford to rent time that often, but when I did, I'd stay until the last second."

All the tension disappeared from around her mouth and forehead. Joy lit up her pretty face.

Warmth flowed though his veins. This was how Lucy should always look.

"Do you have a place to work on your art here?" he asked, his voice thick.

"No. It's just something I pursue in my spare time. I don't have much of that right now between Connor and my graphic-design business."

He didn't like how she brushed aside her art when talking about the studio loft made her so happy. "If you enjoy it…"

"I enjoy spending time with Connor." She glanced at her watch. "We should get ready for the boys to arrive."

Ryland would have rather found out more about her art and her. But he still had time.

"So the cones?" she asked again.

Her practical, down-to-business attitude didn't surprise him, but he was amused. He couldn't wait to break through her hard shell. "How do you think they should be set up?"

She raised her chin slightly. "You tell me. You're the coach."

"Officially, you are." Lucy had listed herself as the head coach with the league, which kept Ryland's name off the coach's list and league website. Besides, he wouldn't be here for the whole season. "I'm your helper."

"I may be listed as the head coach," she said. "But unofficially, as long as you're here to help, my most important job is to put together the snack list."

"That job is almost as important as coaching. Snacks after the game were my favorite part of rec. soccer."

Though now that Ryland had seen her go-on-forever legs, he might have to rethink that. A mole on the inside of her calf just above her ankle drew his attention. He wondered what her skin would taste like.

"Ryland..."

Lucy's voice startled him. He forced his gaze onto her face.

Annoyance filled her blue eyes, but no silver sparks flashed. "The cones."

Damn. He'd been caught staring twice now, but all her skin showing kept taking him by surprise. He wondered how she'd look in a bikini or...naked. Pretty good, he imagined. Though thinking about Lucy without any clothes on wasn't a smart idea. He needed to focus on the practice. "Two vertical lines with a horizontal connecting them at the top. Five cones on each side."

She dropped the equipment bag on the grass. "While I do that, set up your chair and take the weight off your foot. You don't want anything to slow down your recovery."

And your departure from town. The words may not have been spoken, but they were clearly implied.

Before he could say anything, she walked away, hips swaying, curls bouncing.

Too bad she was out-of-bounds.

Ryland removed his chair from the bag and opened it up. But he didn't sit. His foot didn't hurt.

He ran over the practice in his mind. His injury would keep him from teaching by example. He needed someone with two working feet to show the boys what needed to be done. Someone like...

"Lucy."

"Just a minute." She placed the last cone on the grass. "What do you need?"

You. Too bad that wasn't possible. But a brilliant albeit somewhat naughty idea formed in his mind. "I'm going to need you to show the boys what to do during warm-ups and drills."

Her eyes widened. "I've never done anything like this before. I have no idea what you want me to do."

Ryland wanted her. It was as simple as that. Or would be if circumstances were different. "I'll show you."

"O-kay."

Her lack of enthusiasm made him smile. "It's soccer not a walk down death row."

"Maybe not from your point of view," she said. "Show me."

"I want the boys to do a dynamic warm-up," he explained. "They'll break up into two groups. One half will go on the outside of the cones, the other half on the inside. Each time around they'll do something different to warm up their muscles."

"That sounds complicated."

"It's easy."

"Maybe for a pro soccer star."

Star, huh? He was surprised she thought of him that way. But he liked it. "Easy for a nine-year-old, too."

She followed him to the cones.

"The first lap I want you to jog around the outside of the cones."

"The boys know how to do that."

"I want them to see how to do it the right way."

Ryland watched her jog gracefully around the cones.

"Now what?" she asked.

"Backward."

She walked over to the starting point and went around the cones backward.

Each time he told her what to do, whether skipping and jumping at each cone or reaching down to pull up the toe of her tennis shoe. A charming pink colored her cheeks from her efforts. Her breasts jiggled from the movement.

This had to be one of his best ideas ever. Ryland grinned wickedly, pleased with himself. "Face the cones and shuffle sideward."

She did something that looked like a step from the Electric Slide or some other line dance popular at wedding receptions.

"Let me help you." He walked over, kneeled on his good leg and touched her left calf. The muscles tightened beneath his palms. But her skin felt as soft as it looked. Smooth, too. "Relax. I'm not going to hurt you."

"That's what they all say," she muttered.

Ryland had no idea what she meant or who "they all" might be, but he wanted to find out.

"Bring your foot to the other one, instead of crossing the leg behind." He raised her boot off the ground and brought it over to the other foot. "Like this."

Her cheeks reddened more. "You could have just told me."

He stood. "Yeah, but this way is more fun."

"Depends on your definition of fun."

Lucy shuffled around the cones.

Ryland enjoyed watching her. This was as close as he'd gotten to a female, next to the housecleaner his mom had hired while she was away. Mrs. Henshaw was old enough to be his mother.

"Anything else?" Lucy asked when she'd finished.

There was more, but he didn't want to do too many new things at the first practice. Both for Lucy's and the boys' sakes.

"A few drills." The sound of boys' laughter drifted on the air. "I'll show you those when the time comes. The team is here."

"Nervous?"

"They're kids," Ryland said. "No reason to be nervous."

Lucy studied him. "Ever spend much time with eight- and nine-year-olds?"

Not unless you counted signing autographs, posing for photographs and walking into stadiums holding their hands. "No, but I was a kid once."

She raised an arched brow. "Once."

He winked.

Lucy smiled.

Something passed between them. Something unexpected and unwelcome. Uh-oh.

A loud burp erupted from behind them followed by laughter.

Whatever was happening with Lucy came to an abrupt end. Good, because whatever connection Ryland had felt with her wasn't something he wanted. Flirting was one thing, but this couldn't turn into a quick roll in the sheets. He couldn't afford to let that happen while he was here in Wicksburg. "The Defeeters have arrived."

Lucy looked toward the parking lot. "Aaron told me coaching this age is a lot like herding cats," Lucy explained. "Except that cats don't talk back."

Another burp sounded. More laughter followed.

"Or burp," Ryland said.

As she nodded, boys surrounded them. He'd played in big games in front of millions of people, but the expectant look in these kids' eyes disconcerted him, making him feel as if he was stepping onto the pitch for the very first time.

"Hey, boys. I'm Ryland." He focused on the eager faces

staring up at him, not wanting to disappoint them or Lucy. "I'm going to help out for a few games. You boys ready to play some football?"

Nine—or was it ten?—heads, ranging in size and hair color, nodded enthusiastically.

Great. Ryland grinned. This wouldn't be difficult at all.

A short kid with long blond hair scrunched his nose. "This isn't football."

"Everywhere else in the world soccer is called football," Ryland explained.

The kid didn't look impressed. "It's called soccer here."

"We'll talk more about that later." Soccer in America was nothing like soccer in other parts of the world. No sport in the U.S. could compare with the passion for the game elsewhere. "I want you to tell me your name and how long you've played."

Each boy did. Justin. Jacob. Dalton. Tyler. Marco. The names ran into each other. Ryland wasn't going to be able to remember them. No worries. Calling them dude, bud and kid would work for today. "Let's get working."

"Can you teach us how to dive?" a boy with beach-blond hair that hung over his eyes asked.

Some soccer players dived—throwing themselves on the field and pretending to be hurt—to draw a penalty during the game. "No," Ryland said firmly. "Never dive."

"What if it's the World Cup?" a kid with a crew cut asked.

"If you're playing in the World Cup, you'll know what to do." Ryland clapped his hands together. "Time to warm up."

The boys stood in place.

He knew the warm-up routine, and so did his Fuego team-mates, but based on these kids' puzzled looks, they hadn't a clue what he was talking about. "Get in a single-file line behind the first cone on the left side."

The boys shuffled into place, but it wasn't a straight line. Two kids elbowed each other as they jockeyed for the spot in front of Connor. A couple kids in the middle tried to trip each other. The boys in the back half didn't seem to understand the meaning of a line and spread out.

This wasn't working out the way he'd planned. Ryland dragged his hand through his hair.

"Meow," Lucy whispered.

"So where can I find a cat herder?" he asked.

Her coy smile sent his pulse racing. "Look in the mirror. Didn't you know cat herder is synonymous with coach?"

"That's what I was afraid you'd say."

The hour flew by. Lucy stood next to Ryland on a mini-field he'd had her set up using cones. She hadn't known what to expect with the boys' first practice, but she begrudgingly gave him credit. The guy could coach.

After a rocky start, he'd harnessed the boys' energy with warm-up exercises and drills. He never once raised his voice. He didn't have to. His excitement about the game mesmerized both the boys and Lucy. Out on the field, he seemed larger-than-life, sexier, despite the boot on his foot. Thank goodness practice was only sixty minutes, twice a week. That was more than enough time in his presence. Maybe even too much.

Ryland focused on the boys, but her gaze kept straying to him. The man was so hot. She tried hard to remain unaffected. But it wasn't easy, especially when she couldn't forget how it felt when he'd moved her leg earlier.

Talk about being a hands-on coach. His touch had surprised her. But his tenderness guiding her leg had made her want…more.

And when he'd stood behind her, his hard body pressed against her backside, helping her figure out the drills so she could show the boys…

Lucy swallowed. More wasn't possible, no matter how appealing it might sound at the moment. Being physically close to a man had felt good. She'd forgotten how good that could be. But getting involved with a guy wasn't on her list of things to do. Not when she had Connor to take care of.

"Great pass, Tyler." Ryland turned to her. "Do you know if Aaron uses set plays?"

"I have no idea," she admitted. "I have his coaching notebook if you want to look through it."

"I would. Thanks."

"I should be thanking you," she said. "The boys have learned so much from you today. More than I could have taught them over an entire season."

"I appreciate that, but you'll be ready to do this when the time comes."

She doubted that.

All but two of the boys surrounded the ball.

Ryland grimaced.

Lucy appreciated how seriously he took practice, because she needed to figure out what should be happening on the field. "Something went wrong, but I have no idea what."

He pointed to the cluster of boys. "See how the players are gathered together and focused only on the ball?"

She nodded.

"They need to spread out and play their position." He pointed to the fastest kid on the team—Dalton. "All that kid wants is the ball. Instead of playing in the center, where he should be, he's back on the left side chasing down the ball and playing defender. See how that black-haired kid, Mason—"

"Marco," she corrected.

"Yeah, Marco," Ryland said. "You've got Marco and Dalton and those other players all in the same area."

Ryland's knowledge of the game impressed her. Okay,

he was a professional soccer player. But he never stopped pointing things out to her and helping the boys improve. She should have brought a notebook and pen so she could write down everything he said. It was like being enrolled at Soccer University and this was Basic Ball Skills 101. She, however, didn't feel like she had the prerequisites to attend.

"So what do you do?" she asked.

Ryland raised the silver whistle around his neck. "This."

As he blew the whistle, she wondered what his lips would feel like against her skin. Probably as good as his hands. Maybe even better.

Stop thinking about it.

The boys froze.

"This isn't bunch ball," Ryland said. "Don't chase the ball. Spread out. Play your position. Try again."

The boys did.

Ryland directed them to keep them from bunching again. He clapped when they did something right and corrected them when they made mistakes.

As she watched Ryland coach, warmth pooled inside Lucy. She forced her gaze back on the boys.

The play on the field reminded her of an accordion. Sometimes the boys were spread out. Other times they came together around the ball.

"Will telling them fix the problem?" she asked.

"No. They're still very young. But they'll start realizing what they're supposed to do," he said. "Only practice and game time will make the lesson stick."

Lucy wondered if that was what it took to become a competent coach. She had a feeling she would be doing her best just to get by.

The energy on the field intensified. Connor passed the ball to Dalton who shot the ball over the goalie's head. Goal!

"Yes!" Ryland shouted. "That's how you do it."

The boys gave each other high fives.

"That score was made possible by Connor moving to a space. He has good instincts just like his dad." Ryland's smile crinkled the corners of his eyes.

Her pulse quickened. "Wish you could be out there playing?"

He shrugged. "I always want to play, but being here sure beats sitting on my dad's easy chair with a dog on my lap."

His comment about his dad made Lucy look toward the parking lot. A line of parents waited to pick up their boys. She glanced at her watch. Uh-oh. She'd lost track of the time. "Practice ended five minutes ago."

"That was fast." Ryland blew the whistle again. "I want everyone to jog around the field to cool down. Don't run, just a nice easy pace."

The boys took off, some faster than the others.

"The team did well," Ryland said to her.

"So did you."

He straightened. "This is different from what I'm used to."

"You rose to the occasion." Lucy couldn't have worked the boys like he had. She usually preferred doing things on her own. But she needed Ryland's help with the team. Thank goodness she'd listened to Connor and taken a chance by going to see Ryland. "I learned a lot. And the boys had fun."

"Soccer is all about having fun when you're eight and nine."

"What about when you're twenty-nine?" she asked, curious about his life back in Phoenix.

"There are some added pressures and demands, but no complaints," he said. "I'm living the dream."

"Not many can say that." She sure couldn't, but maybe someday. Nah, best not to get her hopes up only to be disappointed. "Aaron says you worked hard to get where you are."

"That's nice of him. But it's amazing what being motivated can do for a kid."

"You wanted to play professionally."

"I wanted to get out of Wicksburg," he admitted. "I didn't have good grades because I liked kicking a ball more than studying so that messed up any chance of getting a football scholarship."

Football? She was about to ask when she remembered what he'd said at the beginning of practice. Soccer was called football overseas. That was where he'd spent the majority of his career. "Small-town boy who made it big."

"That was the plan from the beginning."

His wide smile sent her heart beating triple time. Lucy didn't understand her response. "I'd say you succeeded splendidly."

Whereas she… Lucy didn't want to go there. But she knew someone successful like Ryland would never be satisfied living in a small, boring town like Wicksburg. He must be counting the weeks, maybe even the days, until he could escape back to the big city. While she would remain here as long as she was needed.

As the boys jogged toward them, Ryland gave each one a high five. "Nice work out there. Practice your juggling at home. Learning to control the ball will make you a better player. Now gather up the cones and balls so we can get out of here. I don't know about you, but I'm hungry."

The boys scattered in search of balls like mice looking for bits of cheese. They dribbled the balls back. Lucy placed them inside the mesh bag. The boys picked up their water bottles then walked off the field to their parents.

Connor's megawatt smile could light up half of Indiana. "That was so much fun."

"You played hard out there," Ryland said.

Her nephew shot her a quick glance. "All that running made me hungry, too."

"I've got dinner in the slow cooker," Lucy said.

"Want to eat with us, Ryland?" Connor asked. "Aunt Lucy always makes enough food so we can have leftovers."

Spending more time with Ryland seemed like a bad idea, but she was more concerned about Connor. She couldn't always shield him from disappointment, but with him adjusting to his parents being away, she wanted to limit it. "That's nice of you to think of Ryland. We have enough food to share, but I'm sure he has somewhere else to be tonight."

There, she'd given Ryland an easy out from the dinner invitation. No one's feelings would be hurt.

"I'm free tonight," he said to her dismay. "But I wouldn't want to intrude."

"You're not." Connor looked at Lucy for verification.

She was still stuck on Ryland being free tonight. She figured he would have a date, maybe two, lined up. Unless he had a girlfriend back in Phoenix.

"Tell him it's okay, Aunt Lucy." Her nephew was using his lost puppy-dog look to his full advantage. "Ryland's coaching the team. The least we can do is feed him."

"You sound like your mom." Lucy's resolve weakened. "She's always trying to feed everyone."

Connor nodded. "That's how we ended up with Manny. Mom kept putting tuna out for him. One day he came inside and never left."

Ryland smiled. "He sounds like a smart cat."

"We call him Manny, but his full name is Manchester," Connor said.

Amusement filled Ryland's eyes. "After the Red Devils."

Connor nodded. "Man U rules."

"If Manny was a girl, I'm guessing you wouldn't have named her Chelsea."

Connor looked aghast. "Never."

Ryland grinned. "At least I know where your loyalties lie."

"I have no idea what you're talking about," Lucy admitted.

"Manchester United and Chelsea are teams in the Premier League in England," Ryland explained.

"Rivals," Connor added. "Can Ryland come over, please?"

Lucy could rattle off ten reasons not to have him over, but she had a bigger reason to say yes—Connor.

"You're welcome to join us." If Lucy didn't agree, she would never hear the end of it from her nephew. Besides, she liked how he smiled whenever Ryland was around. It was one meal. No big deal. "We have plenty of food."

"Thanks," he said. "I'm getting tired of grilling."

Connor's eyes widened. "You cook?"

"If I don't cook, I don't eat," Ryland explained. "When I moved to England, I had to cook, clean and do my own laundry. Just like my mom made me do when I was growing up."

His words surprised Lucy. She would have expected a big-shot soccer star to have a personal chef or eat out all the time, not be self-sufficient around the house. Her Jeff, her ex-husband, did nothing when it came to domestic chores.

"I'll have to learn how to do those things," Connor said with a serious expression.

"You're on your way," Ryland encouraged. "You already make great chocolate-chip cookies."

Connor's thin chest puffed slightly. "Yeah, I do."

Lucy shook her head. "You're supposed to say thank you when someone compliments you."

"Even if it's true?" Connor asked.

Ryland's smiled widened. "Especially then."

Connor shrugged. "Okay. Thank you."

Having Ryland over was exactly what Connor needed. But a part of her wondered if it was what she needed, too.

Now that was silly.

Ryland was coming over for dinner because of her nephew. Just because she might like the idea of being around him a little longer didn't mean anything at all.

CHAPTER FIVE

IN THE kitchen, the smell of spices, vegetables and beef simmering in the slow cooker lingered in the air. The scents brought back fond memories of family dinners with Aaron and her parents. But other than the smell, tonight wasn't going to be as comfortable as any of those dinners growing up.

Lucy checked the oven. Almost preheated to the correct temperature.

Ryland had heated her up earlier. She couldn't stop thinking about how he'd touched her at practice. His large, warm hand against her skin. Leaning against the counter, she sighed.

The guy really was...

She bolted upright.

Lucy needed to stop fantasizing and finish making dinner. She was a divorced twenty-six-year-old, not a swooning teenager. She knew better than to be crushing on any man, let alone Ryland James. The guy could charm the pants off everybody. Well, everyone except for her.

She placed the uncooked biscuits on a cookie sheet.

The sounds of laser beams from a video game and laughter from all the fun drifted into the kitchen. Ryland's laugh was deep and rich, thick and smooth, like melted dark chocolate.

Lucy opened the oven door and slid the tray of biscuits onto the middle rack. Would he taste as good as he sounded?

The pan clattered against the back of the oven.

"Need help?" Ryland yelled from the living room.

Annoyed at herself for thinking about *him* that way when she knew better, she straightened the pan then closed the oven door. "Everything's fine."

Or would be when he was gone.

Okay, that wasn't fair. Connor was laughing and having fun. Her nephew needed Ryland, so did the team. That meant she needed him, too.

Watching a couple of videos and reading some books weren't the same as having Ryland show her what needed to be done at practice. The boys would have been the ones to suffer because of her cluelessness. Feeding Ryland dinner was the least she could do to repay him. It wasn't as if she'd had to go to any extra trouble preparing the meal.

Nor was it Ryland's fault he was gorgeous and seemed to press every single one of her buttons. Being around him reminded her that a few of the male species had redeeming qualities. Ones like killer smiles, sparkling eyes, enticing muscles, warm hands and a way with kids. But she knew better than to let herself get carried away.

"I'm going to win," Connor shouted with glee.

"Not so fast," Ryland countered. "I'm not dead yet."

"Just you wait."

The challenge in her nephew's voice loosened her tight shoulder muscles. Boys needed a male influence in their lives. Even if that influence filled her stomach with butterflies whenever he was nearby.

No worries, Lucy told herself. She hadn't been around men for a while. That had to be the reason for her reaction to Ryland.

She tossed the salad. The oven timer buzzed.

With the food on the table, she stood in the doorway to the kitchen with a container of milk in one hand and a pitcher of iced tea in the other. "Dinner's ready."

Connor took his normal seat. He pointed to a chair across, the one next to where Lucy had been sitting since she arrived a month ago. The "guest spots" at the table. "Sit there, Ryland. The other chairs are my mom's and dad's."

Ryland sat. The table seemed smaller with him there, even though it seated six.

Ignoring her unease, Lucy filled everyone's glasses. She sat, conscious of him next to her.

Her leg brushed his. Lucy stiffened. The butterflies in her stomach flapped furiously. She tucked her feet beneath her chair to keep from touching Ryland again. Next time…

There wouldn't be a next time.

Her nephew grabbed two biscuits off the plate. "These are my favorite."

Ryland took one. "Everything smells delicious."

The compliment made Lucy straighten. She hadn't cooked much after the divorce so felt out of practice. But Connor needed healthy meals so she was getting back in the habit. "Thanks."

As she dished up the stew, Ryland filled his salad plate using a pair of silver tongs. His arm brushed hers. Heat emanated from the spot of contact. "Excuse me."

"That's okay." But the tingles shooting up her arm weren't. Lucy hated the way her body reacted to even the slightest contact with him. She pressed her elbows against her sides. No more touching.

Flatware clinked against bowls and plates. Ryland and Connor discussed the upcoming MLS season. She recognized some of the team names, but nothing else.

"Who's your favorite team?" Ryland asked her.

She moved a carrot around with her fork. Stew was one of her favorite dishes, but she wasn't hungry. Her lack of appetite occurred at the same time as Ryland's arrival at the house. "The only soccer games I watch are Connor's."

"That was when you lived here with Uncle Jeff," Connor
said. "After you moved away you didn't come to any."

"That's true." Curiosity gleamed in Ryland's eyes, but she
ignored it. She didn't want to discuss her ex-husband over
dinner or in front of Connor. No matter how badly Jeff had
betrayed her and their marriage vows, he'd been a good uncle
and still sent Connor birthday and Christmas presents. "But
I'll get to see all your games now."

Lucy reached for the salt. Extra seasoning might make the
stew more appealing. She needed to eat something or she'd
find herself starving later. That had happened a lot when she
moved to Chicago. She didn't want a repeat performance here.

Ryland's hand covered hers around the saltshaker.

She stiffened.

He smiled. "Great minds think alike."

Too bad she couldn't think. Not with his large, warm hand
on top of hers.

Darn the man. Ryland must know he was hot stuff. But
he'd better think twice before he put any moves on her. She
pulled her hand away, leaving the salt for him.

Ryland handed the shaker to her. "You had it first."

Lucy added salt to her stew. "Thanks."

"I forgot to tell you, Aunt Lucy. Tyler got a puppy," Connor
said, animated. "His parents took him to the animal shelter,
and Tyler got to pick the dog out himself." Connor relayed the
entire story, including how the dog went potty on the floor
in the kitchen as soon as they arrived home. "I bet Manny
would like to have a dog. That way he'd never be lonely."

Oh, no. Lucy knew exactly where her nephew was going
with this. Connor had used a similar tactic to get her to buy
him a new video game. But buying an inanimate object was
different than a living, breathing puppy.

"Manny is rarely alone." She passed the saltshaker to
Ryland. "I work from home."

Connor's forehead wrinkled, as if he were surprised she hadn't said yes right away. "But you don't chase him around the house. When I'm at school he just lays around and sleeps."

Ryland feigned shock. "You don't chase Manny?"

Lucy wanted to chase Ryland out of here. She hated how aware she was of him. Her blood simmered. She drank some iced tea, but that didn't cool her down. "Cats lay around and sleep. That's what they like to do during the day. I don't think Manny is going to be too keen on being chased by a dog. He's not a kitten anymore."

"Don't forget. Dogs make big messes outside," Ryland said. "You're going to have to clean it all up with a shovel or rake."

Connor scrunched his face. "I'm going to have to scoop up the poop?"

Okay, maybe having Ryland here wasn't so bad. She appreciated how skillfully he'd added a dose of dog-care reality to the conversation. He might make her a little hot and bothered, but he'd saved her a lot of back and forth by bringing up the mess dogs left in the yard. A fair trade-off in the grand scheme of things. At least she hoped so.

"Yes, you would have to do that." No matter how badly Connor wanted a puppy she couldn't make that decision without Aaron and Dana. Getting a pet wasn't a commitment to make lightly. "A dog is something your parents have to decide on, not me. Owning a dog is a big responsibility."

"Huge," Ryland agreed, much to Lucy's relief. "I've been taking care of my parents' dog Cupcake. I never knew something so little would take so much work. She either wants food or attention or to go outside on a walk."

"I've never taken a dog on a walk," Connor said.

"Maybe you could take Cupcake for a walk for me," Ryland suggested.

Connor nodded enthusiastically. "If it's okay with Aunt Lucy."

The longing in his blue eyes tugged at her heart. She couldn't say no to this request, even if it meant seeing Ryland outside of soccer again. "I'm sure we can figure out a time to take Cupcake for a walk."

"You can get a glimpse of what having a dog is like," Ryland said. "It might also be a good idea to see what Manny thinks of Cupcake. Cats and dogs don't always get along."

His words were exactly what a nine-year-old dog-wannabe owner needed to hear. The guy was turning into a knight in a shining soccer jersey. She would owe him dozens of chocolate-chip cookies for all he was doing for Connor.

Ryland smiled at her.

A feeling of warmth traveled from the top of her head to the tips of her toes. She'd better be careful or she was going to turn into a pile of goo. That would not be good.

"Did you ever have a dog?" Connor asked her.

"No, but we had cats and a few other animals," she replied. "Fish, a bird and reptiles."

As Ryland set his iced tea on the table, she bit into a biscuit. "Has your aunt told you about Squiggy?"

Lucy choked on the bread. She coughed and swallowed. "You remember Squiggy?"

Mischief danced in his eyes. "It's a little hard to forget being asked to dig a grave and then rob it on the same day."

Connor's mouth formed a perfect O. "You robbed a grave?"

"Your dad and I did," Ryland said. "It was Squiggy's grave."

Connor leaned forward. "Who's Squiggy?"

Ryland winked at her.

Oh, no. He wouldn't tell... Who was she kidding? The mischievous gleam in his eyes was a dead giveaway he would spill every last detail. Might as well get it over with.

"Squiggy was my turtle. He was actually a tortoise," she explained. "But Squiggy was…"

"The best turtle in the galaxy," Ryland finished for her. "The fastest, too."

Lucy stared at him in disbelief. Those were the exact words she used to say to anyone who asked about her Squiggy. Other kids wanted dogs. She loved her hard-shelled, wrinkled reptile. "I can't believe you remember that."

"I told you I remembered a lot of stuff."

He had, but she thought Ryland was talking about when she'd been a teenager and sick. Not a seven-year-old girl who'd thought the sun rose and set on a beloved turtle.

"Your aunt doted on Squiggy," Ryland said. "Even painted his shell."

Lucy grinned. "Polka dots."

He nodded. "I recall pink and purple strips."

Memories rushed back like water over Cataract Falls on Mill Creek. "I'd forgotten about those."

"Your aunt used to hand-feed him lettuce. Took him on walks, too."

She nodded. "Squiggy might have been the fastest turtle around, but those walks still took forever."

"You never went very far," Ryland said.

"No, we didn't," she admitted. "Wait a minute. How did you know that?"

His smile softened. "Your mom had us watch you."

Her mother, make that her entire family, had always been so overprotective. Lucy had no idea they'd dragged Ryland into it, too. "And you guys accused me of following you around."

"You did follow us."

"Okay, I did, but that's what little sisters do."

Connor reached for his milk glass. "I wouldn't want a little sister."

"I never had a little sister," Ryland said. "But it felt like I had one with Lucy spying on us all the time."

She stuck her tongue out at him.

He did the same back to her.

Connor giggled.

Sitting here with Ryland brought back so many memories. When she was younger, she used to talk to him whenever he was over at the house with Aaron. Puberty and her crush had changed that. The awkward, horrible time of hormones and illness were all she'd remembered. Until now.

"Why did you have to rob Squiggy's grave?" Connor asked him.

Ryland stared into her eyes. His warm hazel gaze seemed to pierce through her. Breaking contact was the smart thing to do, but Lucy didn't want to look away.

For old times' sake, she told herself.

A voice inside her head laughed at the reasoning. A part of her didn't care. Looking was safe. It was all the other stuff that was…dangerous.

"Do you want to tell him or should I?" Ryland asked.

Emotion swirled inside her. Most of it had to do with the uncertainty she felt around him, not the story about her turtle. "Go ahead. I'm curious to hear your side of the story."

"I want to hear both sides," Connor announced.

"You will, if Ryland gets it wrong," she teased.

"I have a feeling you may be surprised," Ryland said.

She had a feeling he was right.

"Your aunt came to your dad and me with big crocodile tears streaming down her cheeks," Ryland explained. "She held a shoebox and said her beloved Squiggy had died. She wanted us to dig a hole so she could bury him."

"Before you go any further, I wanted to have a funeral, not just bury him. I would also like to remind Connor that I was only seven at the time."

Amusement gleamed in Ryland's eyes. "Age duly noted."

Connor inched forward on his chair. "What happened?"

"Your dad and I dug a hole. A grave for Squiggy's coffin."

"Shoebox," Lucy clarified.

Ryland nodded. "She placed the shoebox into the hole and tossed wilted dandelions on top of it. While your dad and I refilled the hole with dirt, your aunt Lucy played 'Taps' on a harmonica."

"Kazoo," she corrected. Still, she couldn't believe all he remembered after so many years.

"A few words were spoken."

"From my favorite book at the time, *Franklin in the Dark*," she said.

"Who is Franklin?" Connor asked.

"A turtle from a series of children's books," Lucy explained. "It was turned into a cartoon that was shown on television."

"Aaron said a brief prayer," Ryland said. "Then your aunt stuck a tombstone made of Popsicle sticks into the ground and sprinkled more dandelions over the mound of dirt."

Lucy nodded. "It was a lovely funeral."

"Yeah," Ryland said. "Until you told us that Squiggy wasn't actually dead, and we had to unbury him so he wouldn't die."

Connor stared at her as if she were a short, green extra-terrestrial with laser beams for eyes. "You think some video games are too violent and you buried a live turtle?"

She squirmed under his intense scrutiny. "Some games aren't appropriate for nine-year-olds. And nothing bad happened to Squiggy."

Fortunately. What had she been thinking? Maybe burying Barbie dolls had gotten too boring.

Ryland grinned. "But it was a race against time."

She had to laugh. "They dug so fast dirt flew everywhere."

"Aaron and I were sure we would be blamed if Squiggy died."

As her gaze collided with Ryland's again, something passed between them. A shared memory, she rationalized. That was all it could be. She looked at her untouched food. "But your dad and Ryland didn't get in trouble. They saved Squiggy."

Connor leaned over the table. "Squiggy didn't die under all that dirt?"

Ryland raised his glass. "Nope. Squiggy was alive and moving as slow as ever."

But that was the last time she'd thrown a funeral for anything living or inanimate. Her parents had made sure of that.

"So why did you bury him and have a funeral?" Connor asked.

Lucy knew this question would be coming once more of the story came out. "You know how some kids play house or restaurant?"

"Or army," Connor suggested.

She nodded. "One of the games I played was funeral."

"That's weird." Connor took another biscuit from the plate. "In school Mrs. Wilson told us turtles live longer than we do. Whatever happened to Squiggy?"

"He ran away," Lucy said. "Your dad and I grew up in a house that was near the park with that nice lake. We'd see turtles on tree trunks at the water's edge. Your dad told me Squiggy was lonely and ran away to live with the other turtles. I was sad and missed him so much, but your dad said I should be happy because Squiggy wanted to be in the park."

A beat passed. And another. Connor looked at Ryland. "So what really happened to Squiggy?"

Her mouth gaped.

A sheepish expression crossed Ryland's face.

Realization dawned. "Squiggy didn't run away."

Connor gasped. "Squiggy died!"

Ryland nodded once, but his gaze never left hers. "I thought you'd figured out what happened."

She'd been so quick to believe Aaron... Of course she'd wanted to believe it. "I never thought something bad might have happened to Squiggy."

"I'm sorry." The sincerity in Ryland's voice rang clear, but the knowledge still stung. "Aaron didn't want to put you through a real funeral because he knew how much Squiggy meant to you so we buried him one night in the park after you went to bed."

Lucy had imagined the adventures Squiggy had experienced at the pond. But the lie didn't surprise her. Few told her the truth once she'd gotten sick. It must have been the same way before she was so ill. "I should have figured that out."

"You were young," Ryland said. "There's nothing wrong with believing something if it makes us happy."

"Even if it's a lie?" she asked.

"A white lie so you wouldn't hurt so badly," he countered. "You know Aaron always watched out for you back then."

That much was true. Lucy nodded.

"My dad told me it's important to look out for others, especially girls." Connor scrunched his nose as if that last word smelled bad.

"He's right," Ryland said. "That's what your dad was doing with your aunt when Squiggy died. It's what he always did and probably still does with her and your mom."

Connor sat taller. "I'll have to do the same."

Ryland looked as proud of her nephew as she felt. "We all should," he said.

Her heart thudded. The guy was a charmer, but he sounded genuine.

But then so had Jeff, she reminded herself.

The harsh reality clarified the situation. She needed to rein in her emotions ASAP. Thinking of Ryland as anything other than the Defeeters' coaching assistant was not only dangerous but also stupid. She wasn't about to risk her heart with someone like that again.

She scooted back in her chair. "Who's ready for dessert?"

While Lucy tucked Connor back into bed, Ryland stared at the framed photographs sitting on the fireplace mantel. Each picture showed a different stage in Aaron's life—army, marriage, family, college graduation. Those things were as foreign to Ryland as a three-hundred-pound American football linebacker trying to tackle him as he ran toward the goal.

Footsteps sounded behind him. "I think Connor's down for the count this time," Lucy said.

Finally. The kid was cool and knew a lot about soccer, but he hadn't left them alone all evening. Twice now Connor had gotten out of bed after they'd said good-night. "Third time's the charm."

"I hope so."

Ryland did, too. A repeat performance of today's practice with some touching would be nice, especially if she touched back. Having a little fun wouldn't hurt anyone. No one, not Mr. McElroy or Blake or Ryland's mom, would have to know what went on here tonight.

She sat on the couch. "Looking at Aaron's pictures?"

"Yeah." Ryland ran his fingertip along the top of a black wood frame, containing a picture of Aaron and Connor fishing. That was something fathers and sons did in Wicksburg. "Aaron's looks haven't changed that much, but he seems like quite the family guy."

Many professional players had a wife, kids and pets. When Ryland first started playing overseas, he hadn't wanted to let anything get in the way of his new soccer career and making a name for himself. He'd been a young, hungry hotshot.

Wait a minute. He still was. Only maybe not quite so young…

"It's hard to believe Aaron's only thirty. He's done a lot for his age," Lucy said with a touch of envy in her voice. "You both have."

Ryland shrugged. "I'm a year younger and have four, maybe five, years left to play if I'm lucky."

"That's not long."

Teams used up and threw away players. But he wasn't ready for that to happen to him. He also didn't want to hang on past his time and be relegated to a few minutes of playing time or be on a team in a lower league. "That's why I want to make the most of the time I have left in the game."

"Soccer is your priority."

"It's my life." He stared at Aaron's wedding picture. Knowing someone was there to come home to must be nice, but he'd made the decision not to divide his focus. Soccer was it. Sometimes Ryland felt a sense of loneliness even when surrounded by people. But occasionally feeling lonely wasn't a reason to get involved in a serious relationship. "That's why I won't start thinking about settling down until my career is over with."

"Playing the field might be hard to give up," she commented.

"Is that the voice of experience talking?"

"Someone I knew," she said. "That's not my type of… game."

A picture of Aaron wearing fatigues and holding a big rifle caught Ryland's attention. His old friend might consider him a foe for putting the moves on Lucy. He nudged the frame so the photo of Aaron looking big, strong and armed didn't directly face the couch.

Ryland flashed her his most charming smile. "What kind of games do you play?"

"None."

He strode to the couch. "That doesn't sound like much fun."

She shrugged. "Fun is in the eye of the beholder."

Holding her would be fun. He sat next to her.

Lucy smelled like strawberries and sunshine. Appealing and intoxicating like sweet ambrosia. He wouldn't mind a taste. But she seemed a little tense. He wanted the lines creasing her forehead to disappear so they could get comfortable and cozy. "I see lots of family photographs. Is any of your artwork here?"

"Yes."

"Show me something."

Her eyes narrowed suspiciously. "Are you asking to see my etchings?"

"I was thinking more along the lines of sketches and paintings, but if you have etchings and they happened to be in your bedroom…" he half joked.

She glanced toward the hallway he assumed led to the bedrooms. Interest twinkled in her eyes. Her pursed lips seemed to be begging for kisses. Maybe Lucy was more game than she let on.

Anticipation buzzed through him. All he needed was a sign from her to make his move. Unless she took the initiative. Now that would be a real turn-on.

Her gaze met his. "Not tonight."

Bummer. He didn't think she was playing hard to get so he had to take her words at face value. "Another time, maybe."

"I'll…see."

Her response didn't sound promising. That…bugged him. Some women would be all over him, trying to get him to kiss, touch, undress them. Lucy wanted nothing to do with him. At least outside of soccer practice.

Calling it a night would be his best move. A challenge was

one thing, but there was no sense beating his head against the goalpost. He wasn't supposed to be flirting let alone wanting to kiss her. Too bad he didn't want to leave yet. "Anything I can do to help my cause?"

Her blue-eyed gaze watched him intently. "Not tonight."

Same answer as before. At least she was consistent.

Ryland stood. "It's getting late. Cupcake's been out in the dog run since before practice. She has a cushy doghouse, but she's going to be wondering where I've been. Thanks for dinner. A home-cooked meal was the last thing I was expecting tonight."

Lucy rose. "I wasn't expecting a dinner guest."

Ryland wished tonight could be ending differently, but he liked that she was honest and up-front. "We're even."

"I'd say your helping with the team outweighs my cooking dinner."

He wasn't quite ready to give up. "You could always invite me over for more meals."

Lucy raised an eyebrow. "Taking another shot?"

"Habit." A bad one under the circumstances. Not many would call him a gentleman, but Lucy deserved his respect. "Which means it's time for me to go. Practice is at five o'clock on Wednesday, right?"

She nodded.

He took a step toward the door. "See you then."

"Ryland…"

As he looked at her, she bit her lower lip. He would like to nibble on her lip. Yeah, right. He wanted to kiss her until she couldn't breathe and was begging for more.

Not tonight.

"Thanks," she said. "For coaching. I mean, helping out with the team. And being so nice to Connor."

Her warm eyes were as appealing as her mouth. "Your nephew is a great kid."

She nodded. "Having you here is just what we…he needed."

Ryland found her slip of the tongue interesting. Maybe she wasn't as disinterested as she claimed to be. He hoped she changed whatever opinion of him was holding her back. Earning her respect ranked right up there with tasting her kisses. "Anytime."

That was often a throwaway line, but he meant it with her.

Time to get the hell out of here before he said or did anything he might regret.

Lucy was the kind of woman you took home to meet your mother. The kind of woman who dreamed of a big wedding, a house with a white picket fence and a minivan full of kids. The kind of woman he normally avoided.

Best to leave before things got complicated. His life was far from perfect with all the demands and pressures on him, unwanted media attention and isolation, but his career was on the line. What was left of it, anyway. His reputation, too.

No woman was worth messing up his life for, not even the appealing, challenging and oh-so-enticing Lucy Martin.

CHAPTER SIX

On Wednesday afternoon, Lucy shaded an area on her sketch pad. The rapid movement of her pencil matched the way she felt. Agitated. Unnerved.

She'd filled half a sketch pad with drawings these past two days. An amazing feat considering she hadn't done any art since she'd left Chicago to return to Wicksburg. But she'd had to do something to take her mind off Ryland.

She took a closer look at the sketch. It was *him*. Again. If she wasn't thinking about Ryland, she was drawing him.

Lucy moved her pencil over the paper. She lengthened a few eyelashes. Women would kill for thick, luscious lashes like his. Heaven knew a tube of mascara couldn't come close to making her eyes look like that. So not fair.

Lucy shaded under his chin then raised her pencil.

Gorgeous.

Not the drawing, the man. The strength of his jaw, the flirtatious gleam in his eyes, his kissable lips.

Attraction heated her blood. What in the world was she doing drawing Ryland this way?

And then she realized...

She had another crush. But this felt different from when she'd been a teenager crushing on Ryland, stronger even than when she'd started dating her ex-husband.

Stupid.

Lucy closed the cover of her sketch pad, but every line, curve and shadow of Ryland's face was etched on her brain. She massaged her aching temples.

Connor ran from the hallway to the living room. "I'm ready for practice."

He wore his soccer clothes—blue shirt, shorts and socks with shin guards underneath. As the shoelaces from his cleats dragged on the ground, he bounced from foot to foot with excitement.

Soccer practice was the last place she wanted to go. The less time she spent with Ryland, the better. She was too old to be feeling this way about him. About any guy. But skipping out wasn't an option. She was the head coach, after all. "Let me get my purse."

On the drive, Lucy glanced in the rearview mirror. Connor sat in the backseat, his shoulders hunched, as he played a game on his DS console. He was allowed a certain amount of video-game time each day, and he liked playing in the car. At least that kept him from talking about Ryland. Connor had a serious case of hero worship.

But that didn't mean she had to have one, too. Ryland hadn't known about her crush before. He didn't need to know about this one.

She would stay focused on soccer practice. No staring, admiring or lusting. No allowing Connor to invite him over for dinner tonight, either.

With her resolve firmly in place, Lucy parked then removed the soccer gear from her trunk. As Connor ran ahead of her, she noticed Ryland, dressed in his usual attire of shorts and a T-shirt, talking with Dalton's mom, Cheryl.

Lucy did a double take. Cheryl wore a tight, short skirt and a camisole. The clothing clung to every curve, showing lots of tanned skin and leaving little to the imagination. Not that

Ryland would have to wait long to sample Cheryl's wares. She stood so close to him her large chest almost touched him.

Lucy gripped the ball bag in her hand.

Ryland didn't seem to mind. He stood his ground, not trying to put any distance between them.

Okay, maybe they weren't standing that close, but still…

Emotions swirled through her. She forced herself to look away.

No reason to be upset or jealous. She'd had her chance Monday night, but turned him down. Oh, she'd been tempted to have him stay and get comfy on the couch, but she was so thankful common sense had won over raging hormones. Especially now that he'd moved on to someone more…willing.

No worries. What two consenting adults did was none of her business. But like a moth drawn to a flame, she glanced over at them. She'd never considered herself masochistic, but she couldn't help herself.

Cheryl batted her mascara-laden eyelashes at him.

Ryland's grin widened. He'd used that same charming smile on Lucy after Connor had gone to bed.

Her stomach churned. Maybe she shouldn't have eaten the egg-salad sandwich for lunch. Maybe she needed to chill.

She quickened her pace. Not that either would notice her. They were too engrossed with each other.

No big deal. Ryland was a big boy, a professional athlete. He knew what he was getting into. He must deal with women hitting on him on a daily basis, ones who wouldn't think of telling him *not tonight.*

As she passed the two, Lucy focused on the boys. Seven of them stood in a circle and kicked the ball to one another while Marco ran around the center trying to steal the ball away.

Cheryl laughed, a nails-on-chalkboard sound that would

make Cupcake howl. Lucy grimaced. If Ryland wanted to be with that kind of woman, he'd never be satisfied with someone like her. Not that she wanted to be with him.

Stop thinking about it! About him!

But she couldn't. No doubt this was some lingering reaction to Jeff's cheating. She'd thought it was great how her husband and her best friend since junior high, Amelia, got along. Lucy hadn't even suspected the two had been having an affair.

Better off without him. Without any of them. Men and best friends.

"Lucy."

Gritting her teeth, she glanced over her shoulder. Ryland was walking toward her. She waited for him. Even with the boot on his injured right foot, he moved with the grace of a world-class athlete, but looked more like a model for a sportswear company.

She didn't want to be impressed, but she couldn't blame Cheryl for wanting to get to know Ryland better. The guy was hot.

Maybe if Lucy hadn't taken a hiatus—more like a sabbatical—from men…

No. Even if she decided to jump back into the dating scene, he wasn't the right man for her. He wasn't the kind of guy to settle down let alone stick around. A superstar like Ryland James had too many women who wanted to be with him and would do anything to get close to him. He'd admitted he wouldn't start thinking about settling down until his career was over with. Why should he? Ryland had no reason to tie himself to only one woman and fight temptation on a daily basis.

Or worse, give in to it as Jeff had.

Ryland was smart for staying single and enjoying the… benefits that came with being a professional athlete.

He stopped next to her. "You sped by so fast I thought we were late starting practice."

He'd noticed her? With sexy Cheryl right there? Lucy was so stunned she almost missed the little thrill shooting through her. "I like being punctual."

The words sounded stupid as soon as she'd spoken them. She did like being on time, but that wasn't the reason she'd rushed by him. Telling him she'd been jealous of Cheryl wasn't happening. Not in this lifetime. She didn't need to boost his ego and decimate hers in one breath.

Ryland pulled out his cell phone and checked the time. He glanced at the boys on the field. "Practice doesn't start for ten minutes. We're still missing players."

Lucy noticed he didn't wear a watch or jewelry. She liked that he didn't flaunt his wealth by wearing bling as some athletes she'd seen on television did.

Not that she cared what he wore.

Feeling flustered, she set the equipment bag on the grass. "That'll give me plenty of time to set up."

His assessing gaze made Lucy feel as if she were an abstract piece of art that he couldn't decide was valuable or not. She didn't like it. If he was looking for a list of her faults, she could give him one. Jeff had made it clear where she didn't stack up in the wife department.

She placed her hands on her hips. "What?"

"You okay?" Ryland asked.

"Fine." The word came out quick and sharp. "Just one of those days," she added.

Two more women, Suzy and Debbie, joined Cheryl. Both wore the typical soccer-mom uniform—black track pants and T-shirts. The women waved at Ryland. He nodded in their direction before turning his attention back to Lucy.

"Anything I can do to help?" he offered.

"You've done enough." She realized how that might sound.

She shouldn't be taking her feelings out on him. Like it or not, she needed his help if she was going to learn enough about soccer to be helpful to the boys. Not just for the spring season, but fall if no one else stepped up to coach. "I mean, you're doing enough with the team. And Connor."

"I'm happy to do more for the boys and for you."

She should be grateful, but his offer irritated Lucy. She liked being self-sufficient. Competent. Independent. Yet she was having to depend on Ryland to help with the team, to teach her about soccer and to keep a smile on Connor's face. She felt like a failure…again. No way could she have him do more. "Let's get set up so we can start on time."

As she removed the cones from the bag, she glanced up at him.

Ryland stood watching her. With the sun behind him, he looked almost angelic, except the look in his eyes made her feel as if he wanted to score with her, not the ball.

Lucy's heart lurched. Heat pooled within her. Common sense told her to ignore him and the hunger in his eyes. But she couldn't deny he made her feel sexy and desired. If only…

Stop. Now.

He was charming, handsome, and completely out of her league. An unexpected crush was one thing. It couldn't go any further than that.

"I can put them out," Ryland said.

No. Lucy didn't want any more help from him. She lowered her gaze to his mouth. His lips curved into a smile. Tingles filled her stomach.

And no matter how curious she might get or how flirtatious he might be, she didn't want any kisses from him, either. "Thanks, but I've got it."

A week later, Ryland gathered up the cones from the practice field. The sun had started setting a little later. Spring was his favorite time of year with the grass freshly cut, the air full of promise and the game fast and furious.

A satisfied feeling flowed through him. The boys were getting it. Slowly, but surely. And Lucy…

What was he going to do about her?

He'd had a tough time focusing during today's practice due to how cute she looked in her pink T-shirt and black shorts. Those sexy legs of hers seemed to have gotten longer. Her face glowed from running around.

Look, don't touch. Ryland had been reminding himself of that for the past hour. Okay, the last week and a half.

She held the equipment bag while he put the cones inside. Her sweet scent surrounded him. Man, she smelled good. Fresh and fruity. He took another sniff. Smelling wasn't touching.

"The boys had a good practice today," she said.

"We'll see how they put it to use in their first match."

"Connor said they've never beaten the Strikers." She tightened the pull string on the bag. "Will they be ready?"

"No, but soccer at this age is all about development."

"Scores aren't reported."

He was used to being surrounded by attractive women, but with Lucy her looks weren't her only appeal. He appreciated how she threw herself into learning about soccer, practicing the drills and studying the rules at home. "Maybe not, but the boys will know the score. And I'd be willing to bet so will the majority of the parents."

"Probably," she said, sounding rueful.

Empathy tugged at him. "You might have to deal with that. Especially toward the end of the season."

She nodded, resigned. "I can handle it."

Pride for her "can do" attitude swelled in his chest. "I know you can."

Lucy's unwavering smile during practices suggested she

might be falling in love with the game. Too bad she couldn't fall for him, too.

But that wasn't going to happen. She didn't look at him as anything other than her helper.

Many women wanted to go out with a professional athlete. Lucy wasn't impressed by what he did. He could pump gas at the corner filling station for all she cared. She never asked him anything about his "job" only how his foot was doing. Her indifference to him bristled, even if he knew it was less complicated that way.

She scanned the field. "Looks like we've got everything."

Without waiting for a reply, she headed toward the parking lot. He hobbled along behind her, watching her backside and biting his lip to keep from commenting on how sexy she looked in her gym shorts.

Flirting with her came so naturally, he'd tried hard during practices to keep the conversation focused on soccer. Maybe he should try to be more personable. She was back in town just like him. She could be...lonely.

Ryland fell into step next to Lucy. Maybe he was the one who was lonely. He'd had offers for company from one of the soccer moms and from several other women in town. None had interested him enough to say yes, but something about Lucy...

He knew all the reasons to keep away from her, but he couldn't stop thinking about her or wanting to spend time with her outside of practice.

Lines creased her forehead, the way they did when she was nervous or worried. "Uh-oh. Look how many parents stayed to watch practice today."

He'd been too busy with the boys and sneaking peeks at Lucy to notice the row of chairs along the edge of the grass. The different colors reminded him of a rainbow. Several dads sat alongside the moms who had come to the last two prac

ices. Some of the men were the same ones who had either
ignored or bullied him in elementary school. It wasn't until
he'd proven his worth on the pitch that he'd became a real
person in their eyes. Now they clamored to talk to him about
their sons. "I thought they were too busy or working to be at
practices."

"That's what they said when I asked if one of them could
coach."

"At least no one can use that excuse now."

Her eyes widened. "You're leaving already?"

Interesting. Lucy sounded upset. Maybe she wasn't as in-
different to him as she appeared to be. "Not yet. But when I
do you'll need a new assistant. Maybe two."

"Oh, okay," she said. "It's just the boys like having you
around, especially Connor."

"What about you?"

She flinched. "Me?"

Ryland had put her on the spot. He didn't care. The way
she reacted to his leaving suggested this wasn't only about the
team. If that were true, he wanted to know even if it wouldn't
change anything between them. Or change it that much. "Yes,
you."

"You're an excellent coach. I'm learning a lot."

"And…"

"A nice guy."

"And…"

The color on her cheeks deepened. "A great soccer player."

"Yes, but you haven't seen me play."

"Modest, huh?"

He shrugged.

"Aaron and Connor told me how good you are."

Ryland wouldn't mind showing her just how good he was
t a lot more than soccer.

Bad idea. Except…

He knew women. Lucy was more interested in him than she was letting on. His instincts couldn't be that off. Not with her. "You haven't answered my question."

She looked at the grass. "I appreciate you being here."

"Do you like having me around?"

"It doesn't suck," Lucy said finally.

Not a yes, but close enough. The ball had been passed to him. Time to take the shot.

"Bring Connor over tonight. He can walk Cupcake." Ryland might want to be alone with Lucy, but he knew that wasn't going to happen. A nine-year-old chaperone was a good idea, anyway. The last thing this could turn into was a date. "I'll have pizza delivered."

Her jaw tightened. "You don't have to do this."

"Do what?"

"Repay me for dinner."

"I'm not."

"So this is…"

"For Connor." That was all it could be. *For now,* a little voice whispered.

A beat passed. And another. "He'd like that."

Ryland would have preferred hearing she would like that too. "I'll order pizza, salad and breadsticks."

"I'll bring dessert."

If he told her not to bother, she'd bring something anyway. And this wasn't a date. "Sounds great."

"Ice-cream sundaes, okay?"

"Perfect."

He could think of lots of ways to use the extra whipped cream with Lucy. The cherries, too. Ryland grinned.

But not tonight. He pressed his lips together. Maybe not any night. And that, he realized, was a total bummer.

* * *

The Jameses' kitchen was four times the size of Aaron and Dana's and more "gourmet" with granite countertops, stainless-steel top-of-the-line appliances and hi-tech lighting. The luxurious setting seemed a stark contrast to the casual menu. But no one seemed to notice that except Lucy.

She felt as if she were standing on hot coals and hadn't been able to relax all evening. The same couldn't be said about Connor. A wide grin had been lighting her nephew's face since they'd left practice. He seemed completely at home, hanging on Ryland's every word and playing with Cupcake.

That pleased her since she'd accepted Ryland's invitation for Connor's sake. And *Starry Night* hadn't been painted from within the confines of an asylum, either.

Lucy grimaced. Okay, a part of her had wanted to come over, too.

Insane.

She had to be crazy to torture herself by agreeing to spend more time with Ryland outside of practice. Hanging out with him was working about as well as it had when she'd been in middle school. Her insides quivered, making her feel all jittery. She rinsed a dinner plate, needing the mundane task to steady her nerves.

It didn't help much.

Ryland entered the kitchen. The large space seemed smaller, more…intimate.

She squared her shoulders, not about to let him get to her.

"Connor is chasing Cupcake around the backyard," Ryland said. "It's lighted and fenced so you won't have to worry about him."

She loaded the plate into the dishwasher. As long as the conversation remained on Connor she should be fine. "What makes you think I worry?"

"Nothing, except you pay closer attention to your nephew than an armored car guard does to his cargo."

Lucy rinsed another plate. "I'm supposed to watch him."

"I'm kidding." Ryland placed the box with the leftover pizza slices into the refrigerator. "Aaron has nothing to worry about with you in charge."

She thought about her brother and sister-in-law so far away. "I hope you're right. Sometimes…"

"Sometimes?" he asked.

Lucy stared into the sink, wishing she hadn't said anything. Letting her guard down was too easy when Ryland was around. Strange since that was exactly the time she should keep it up.

"Tell me," he said.

Warm water ran over her hands, but did nothing to soothe her. "Until Aaron and Dana deployed, I had no idea what having someone totally rely on you meant. It's not as easy as I thought it would be. Sometimes I don't think I'm as focused on Connor as I should be."

Especially the past week and a half with Ryland on her mind so much.

"Any more focused and you'd be obsessing." He smiled. "Don't worry. Connor is happy. All smiles."

She placed the plate in the dishwasher. "That's because of you."

"Yeah, you're right about that."

Ryland's lighthearted tone told her that he was joking. She turned and flicked her hands at him. Droplets of water flew in his direction.

He jumped back. Amusement filled his gaze.

"Gee, thanks," she joked.

"Seriously, you're doing a great job," Ryland said. "Your kids will be the envy of all their friends."

Her kids? Heat exploded through Lucy like the grand finale of Fourth of July fireworks. Jeff had said she was too independent to be a decent wife. He'd told her that she would be a bad mother. Funny, how his liking a self-reliant girlfriend when they were dating turned out to be one-hundred-and-eighty percent different from his wanting a needy wife to stroke his fragile ego after they married.

"Thanks." She placed a plate in the rack next to the other. "I suppose being a surrogate parent now will help if I ever have a family of my own."

"If?"

She shrugged. "I've got too much going on with Connor to think about the future."

"Nothing wrong with focusing on the present," he said.

Yeah, she imagined that was what he did. But his situation was different from hers. He was doing something with his life. And she...

Lucy picked up the last plate and scrubbed. Hard.

A longing ached deep inside her. She wanted to do something, too. Be someone. To matter...

Uh-oh. She didn't want to end up throwing herself a pity-party. Not with Ryland here. Time to get things back on track.

She loaded the plate. "Connor has been writing his parents about soccer practices and telling them how well you coach."

"I bet Aaron sees right through that."

"Probably."

Ryland raised a brow. "Probably?"

"You said it," she teased.

He picked up the can of whipped cream with one hand and the red cap with his other. "You didn't have to agree."

"Well, Connor did say you're *almost* as good a coach as his dad."

"Almost, huh?" With a grin, Ryland walked toward her. "I thought we were on the same team, but since we're not..."

He pointed the can of whipped cream in her direction.

She stepped back. Her backside bumped into the granite counter. The lowered dishwasher door had her boxed in on the left. Ryland blocked the way on the right. Trapped. It didn't bother her as much as it should. "You wouldn't."

Challenge gleamed in his eyes. "Whipped cream would go well with your outfit."

His, too. They could have so much fun with the whipped cream. Anticipation made her smile.

What was she thinking? Forget about the whipped cream. Forget about him.

Self-preservation made her reach behind and pull the hand nozzle from the sink. She aimed it at him. The surprise in his eyes made her feel strong and competent. Her confidence surged. "I wonder how you'll look all wet."

A corner of his mouth curved and something shifted between them. The air crackled with tension, with heat. His gaze smoldered.

Heaven help her. She swallowed. Thank goodness for the counter's support or she'd be a puddle on the floor.

"I'm game if you are," he said.

For the first time in a long time, Lucy was tempted to... play. But nerves threatened to get the best of her. She knew better to play with fire.

Unsure of what to do or say next, she clutched the nozzle as if it could save her. From what, she wasn't sure.

Still Lucy wasn't ready to back down. Surrendering wasn't an option, either. "What if I'm out of practice and don't remember how to play?"

He took a step toward her. "I'm an excellent coach. I can show you."

She bet he could. She could imagine all kinds of things he could show her. Her cheeks burned. "What are the rules?"

He grinned wryly. "Play fair. Don't cheat."

A little pang hit her heart. "Those sound like good rules. I don't like cheaters."

"Neither do I."

His gaze captured hers. She didn't know how long they stood there with their weapons ready. It didn't matter. Nothing did except this moment with him.

Lucy wanted...a kiss. The realization ricocheted through her, a mix of shock and anticipation. No wonder she held a water nozzle in her hand ready to squirt him. She wanted Ryland to kiss her senseless. If only...

Not possible. She didn't want to get burned. Again.

Still her lips parted slightly. An invitation or a plea of desperation, she wasn't certain.

Desire flared in his eyes.

Please.

She wasn't brave enough to say the word aloud.

"How do I know this isn't a trap?" he asked with mock seriousness.

"I could say the same thing."

"We could put our weapons down on three."

"Fair play."

He stood right in front of her. "Exactly."

She nodded, still gripping the nozzle. "One, two..."

Ryland lowered his mouth to hers. The touch of his lips sent a shock through her. He tasted warm with a hint of chocolate from the hot-fudge topping.

His tender kiss caressed. She felt cherished and important. Ways she hadn't felt in years. Her toes curled. She gripped the nozzle.

This was what had been missing, what she needed.

Bells rang. Mozart. Boy, could Ryland kiss.

She wanted more. Oh-so-much-more.

A dog barked.

Lucy leaned into Ryland, into his kiss. She brought her right arm around him and her left...

Water squirted everywhere.

Ryland jumped back, his shirt wet.

She glanced down. Hers hadn't fared much better. Thank goodness she was wearing a camisole underneath her T-shirt.

Laughter lit his eyes. "At least you got the playing fair part. We're both wet."

Lucy attempted to laugh. She couldn't. She tried to speak. She couldn't do that, either. Not after being so expertly and thoroughly kissed. Ryland's kiss had left her confused, wanting more and on fire despite the water socking her shirt and dripping down her legs.

A crush was one thing. This felt like...

No, it was nothing but some hot kisses.

Lucy straightened. Letting him kiss her had been a momentary lapse in judgment. She should have ended the kiss as soon as his mouth touched hers. But she hadn't. She... couldn't. Worse, her lips wanted more kisses.

Stupid. The word needed to be tattooed across her forehead for the world to see. Correction, for her to see, a reminder of the mistakes she'd made when it came to men.

"Aunt Lucy." Connor ran into the kitchen with Cupcake at his heels. Her nephew stared at her and Ryland with wide eyes. "What happened?"

"An accident," Ryland answered.

Did he mean the kiss or the water? The question hammered at her. She wasn't sure she wanted to know the answer, either.

A sudden realization sent a shiver down Lucy's spine. For the few minutes she'd been kissing Ryland, she hadn't thought once about Connor. He'd been left unattended in a strange house. Okay, Cupcake had been with him and Lucy had only been in the kitchen, but still...

Ryland's kiss had made her forget everything, including her nephew. That could not happen again. She adjusted the

hem of her shirt, smoothed her hair and looked at her nephew.
"You okay?"

Connor nodded. "But there's a man at the front door. He
said his name is Blake. He's here to see Ryland."

CHAPTER SEVEN

STANDING in his parents' living room, Ryland dragged his hand through his hair. Uncomfortable didn't begin to describe the atmosphere. Blake's nostrils flared. A thoroughly kissed and embarrassed Lucy stared at Connor, who sat on the carpet playing with Cupcake, oblivious to what was going on.

Not that any of the adults had a clue.

At least Ryland didn't.

He was trying to figure out what had happened in the kitchen. He couldn't stop thinking about Lucy's kisses. About how silver sparks had flashed when she'd opened her eyes. About how right she felt in his arms.

Not good, since the last thing he needed was a woman in his life. Even one as sweet and delicious as Lucy Martin. But this wasn't the time to think about anything except damage control.

Blake hadn't seen them kissing, but Lucy's presence was going to be a problem. A big one.

"Let me introduce everyone," Ryland said.

Polite words were exchanged. Obligatory handshakes given.

Thick tension hung on the air, totally different from the sizzling heat in the kitchen a few minutes ago. That was where Ryland wished he could be now—in the kitchen kissing Lucy.

Whoa. He must have taken a header with a ball too hard

and not remembered. Ryland was in enough trouble with his agent. He needed to stop thinking about kisses. And her. Not even flings were in his playbook at the moment.

"What brings you to Wicksburg?" Lucy asked Blake.

Ryland wanted to know the answer to that question, too. Blake never dropped by unannounced. Something big must have happened with either Fuego or his sponsors.

Good news, Ryland hoped. But given the muscle flicking on Blake's jaw and the tense lines around his mouth, probably not.

"I was in Chicago for a meeting." That explained Blake's designer suit, silk tie and Italian-leather shoes. Not exactly comfortable traveling attire, but Blake always dressed well, even when he was straight out of law school and joining the ranks of sports agents. "I thought I'd swing by Indiana and see how Ryland was doing on his own."

Swing by? Yeah, right. No one swung by Wicksburg when the nearest airport was a two-hour drive away. Blake must have rented a car to get here. Something was up. The question was what.

The edges of Lucy's mouth curved upward in a forced smile. The pink flush that had crept up her neck after he'd kissed her hadn't disappeared yet. "That's nice of you."

Blake Cochrane and the word "nice" didn't belong in the same sentence. Of course Lucy wouldn't know that. He had the reputation of being a shark when it came to contract negotiations and pretty much anything else. His hard-nosed toughness made him a great agent. Blake eyed Lucy with suspicion. "I can see my concerns about Ryland being lonely are unfounded."

The agent's ice-blue eyes narrowed to slits. He focused first on Lucy then moved to Ryland.

The accusation in Blake's voice and gaze left no doubt what the agent thought was going on here. Ryland grimaced.

He didn't like Lucy being lumped in with other women he'd gone out with. He squared his shoulders. "I invited Lucy and Connor over to take Cupcake on a walk for me and have some pizza."

"And ice-cream sundaes," Connor added with a grin.

Blake's brow slanted. His gaze lingered on Lucy's damp shirt that clung to her breasts like a second skin. "A water fight, too, I see."

Ryland tried hard not to look at her chest. Tried and failed.

The color on Lucy's face deepened. She looked like she wanted to bolt.

His jaw tensed. He didn't like seeing her so uncomfortable. "Faucet malfunction."

"Hate when that happens," Blake said.

Damn him. Blake wasn't happy finding Lucy here, but he didn't have to be such a jerk about it. Ryland's hands balled. "Nothing that can't be fixed."

His harsh tone silenced the living room. Only Connor and the dog seemed at ease.

"Well, it's been nice meeting you, Blake. It's a school night so we have to get home," Lucy said. "Thanks for having us over for dinner, Ryland."

"Yeah, thanks. I had fun with Cupcake." Connor stood, stifling a yawn. "This is a cool house. The backyard is so big we could hold our practices here."

"You play soccer?" Blake asked.

Connor nodded.

Blake studied the kid, as if sizing up his potential. Scouts could recognize talent at a young age. In the United Kingdom, the top prospects signed with football clubs in their teens. "What position do you play?"

Connor raised his chin, a gesture both his dad and Lucy made. "Wherever I'm told to play."

Blake's sudden smile softened his rugged features. "With that kind of attitude you'll go far."

Connor beamed. "I want to be just like Ryland when I grow up."

The words touched Ryland. He mussed Connor's hair. Working with the boys reminded him of the early years of playing soccer, full of fun, friendship and laughter. "Thanks, bud."

Ryland turned his attention to Lucy. He wanted to kiss her good-night. Who was he kidding? He wanted to kiss her hello, goodbye and everything in between. She was sexy and sweet, a potent, addictive combo. He should have his head examined soon. There wasn't room in his life for a serious girlfriend, especially one who lived in Wicksburg. He couldn't afford to lose his edge now. "I'll see you out."

Lucy nodded.

That surprised him. He'd expected her to say it wasn't necessary, like the first time she'd visited.

"I'll stay here," Blake said.

Ryland accompanied them to the driveway where Lucy's car was parked. Lights on either side of the garage door illuminated the area. Cupcake ran around the car barking. She didn't seem to want Connor to go. Ryland felt the same way about Lucy.

That made zero sense. They weren't playing house. Being with her wasn't cozy. More like being on a bed of hot knives. She needed to leave before he got the urge to kiss her again.

Connor climbed into the backseat. Cupcake followed, but Ryland lifted the dog out of the car and held on to her. As soon as Connor fastened his seat belt, his eyelids closed.

"He's out," Ryland said.

She glanced back at the house. "You're in trouble."

The word "no" sat on the tip of his tongue and stayed there.

He didn't want to worry Lucy, but he also didn't want to lie. Blake's surprise visit concerned Ryland. "I don't know."

Lines creased Lucy's forehead. Her gaze, full of concern and compassion, met his. "Blake doesn't look happy."

Ryland was a lone wolf kind of guy. He wasn't used to people being concerned about him. It made him…uncomfortable.

Best not to think about that. Or her. "Blake's intense. No one would ever accuse him of being mild-mannered and laid-back."

"I wouldn't want to meet him in a dark alley. A good thing he's on your side."

"Blake's my biggest supporter after my folks." The agent had always been there for Ryland. One of the few people who had believed in him from the beginning. "He fights for his clients. I've been with him for eleven years. I was the second client to sign with him."

"You both must have been young then."

"Young and idealistic." Those had been the days before all the other stuff—the business stuff—became such a priority and a drag. "But we've grown up and been through a lot."

"You've probably made him a bunch of money over the years."

They were both rich men now. "Yeah."

But her words made Ryland think. Those closest to him, besides his parents, were people who made money off him. His agent, his PR spokesperson, his trainer, the list went on. His friends were plentiful when he was covering the tab at a club or throwing a party, but not so much now that he was stuck in the middle-of-nowhere Indiana. Bitterness coated his mouth.

Was that the reason Blake had dropped by? To make sure his income from "Ryland James" endorsements and licensing agreements wouldn't dry up?

Ryland hoped not. He wanted to think he was considered more than just a client after all the years.

The tip of her pink tongue darted out to moisten her lips.

He wouldn't mind another taste of her lips. He fought the urge to pull her against him and kiss her until the worry disappeared. "About what happened in the kitchen…"

The lines on her forehead deepened. She glanced at Connor who was asleep. "That shouldn't have happened. It was a… mistake."

Ryland studied her, trying to figure out what she was thinking. He couldn't. "It didn't feel like a mistake."

"I…"

He placed his finger against her lips, remembering how soft they'd felt against his own. They needed to talk, but this wasn't the time, and maybe the words needed to remain unsaid. "It's late."

"Blake's waiting for you."

"Don't let the suit and attitude fool you. He's not in charge here. I am," Ryland said. "Take Connor home. We'll talk soon."

She nodded.

"Blake's bag was in the entryway. He's staying the night." An ache formed deep in Ryland's gut. He wanted to kiss Lucy. More than he'd wanted anything in a long time. He didn't understand why he was feeling that way. Staying away from her was the smart thing to do. Though come to think of it, no one had ever accused him of being smart. "I'll call you tomorrow. Promise."

So much for playing it safe. But something about Lucy made him forget reason and make promises.

She started to speak then stopped herself. "Good luck with Blake."

"Thanks, but I've got all the luck I need thanks to your penny."

Her eyes widened. "You kept it?"

Bet she'd be surprised to know the penny had been sitting on his nightstand for the past two weeks. "Never know when I'll need it to get lucky."

The color on her cheeks deepened again. "That's my cue to say good-night."

Sweet and smart. It was a good thing Blake was going to be his houseguest tonight and not Lucy. Ryland opened the car door for her. "Drive safe."

After the taillights of Lucy's car faded from view, he went inside. He couldn't put off his conversation with Blake any longer.

His agent stood in the entryway. He'd changed into shorts, a T-shirt and running shoes.

"Tell me what you're really doing here," Ryland said.

"I've been on airplanes or stuck at conference tables for the last two days," Blake said. "Let's work out."

In the home gym, Ryland hopped on the stationary bike. His physical therapist had increased the number of things he could do as his foot healed. He liked being able to do more exercises, but working out was the furthest thing from his mind. Thoughts about Lucy and her hot kisses as well as his agent's purpose for coming here filled his brain.

Blake stepped on the treadmill. He adjusted the settings on the computerized control panel. "I knew you couldn't go that long without a woman."

Ryland's temper flared. But after receiving more red cards these past two seasons than all the seasons before, he'd learned not to react immediately. He accelerated his pedaling, instead. "You're checking up on me."

"Sponsors are nervous." Blake's fast pace didn't affect his speech or breathing. "They aren't the only ones."

So now his agent had added babysitter to his list of du-

ties. Great. Ryland's fingers tightened around the handle-
bars. "You."

"I don't get nervous." Blake accelerated his pace. "But I
am...concerned. You'll be thirty soon. We need to make the
most of the next few years whether you're playing with Fuego
or across the pond."

His agent had stressed the need for financial planning to
Ryland since he was eighteen years old. But he'd never set
out to amass a fortune, just be the best soccer player he could
be. "I'm set for life."

"You can never have too much money when your earning
potential will drastically diminish once you stop playing."

Ryland had more money than he could ever spend, but
dissatisfaction gnawed at him. He might be injured, but he
wasn't about to be put out to pasture just yet.

"Don't be concerned. I'm laying low," he said. "Tonight
is the first time I've had anyone over to the house other than
the housekeeper, who's old enough to be my mom. I made
sure Lucy and I had a chaperone."

"Nice kid," Blake said. "Is it his team you're coaching?"

Damn. Ryland slowed his pedaling. He reached for his
water bottle off the nearby counter then took a long swig.
The cool liquid rushing down his throat did little to refresh
him. "Where'd you hear that?"

"Someone tweeted you were coaching a local rec. team."
Blake kept a steady pace. "Tell me this was some sort of one-
off rah-rah-isn't-soccer-great pep talk."

"I'm helping Lucy with Connor's team." Ryland placed his
water bottle on the counter. "Her brother coaches the team,
but he's on deployment with his Reserve unit. No other parent stepped up so she took on the role as head coach even
though she knows nothing about soccer. I offered to help."

"Lucy's so hot she could get a man to do most anything,"
Blake said. "Those legs of hers go on forever."

The appreciative gleam in his agent's ice-blue eyes bugged Ryland. Women always swarmed around Blake. He didn't need to be checking out Lucy, too.

Ryland's jaw tensed. "I'm coaching for both her and the boys."

"Mostly Lucy, though." Blake grinned. "That's a good thing."

"It is?"

"Your coaching becomes a nonissue if you have a personal connection and aren't showing favoritism to one team."

"Favoritism?" Ryland didn't understand what Lucy had to do with this. "I'm helping the Defeeters, but I've also spoken to two other teams this week and will visit with three more next week."

"No need to get defensive," Blake said. "A guy helping out his girlfriend isn't showing favoritism."

Girlfriend? A knot formed in the pit of Ryland's stomach. Everything suddenly made sense. "So if Lucy and I aren't…"

He couldn't bring himself to say the word.

Blake nodded. "If you weren't dating Lucy, you wouldn't be able to coach the team."

Ryland's knuckles turned white. "What do you mean?"

As Blake moved from the treadmill to the stair-climber machine, he wiped the sweat from his face with a white towel. "You're public property. The face of the Phoenix Fuego. Showing favoritism to one team without a valid personal connection would be a big no-no for a player of your caliber. Especially one on shaky ground already."

Ryland gulped.

"But we don't need to worry about that," Blake added.

Emotion tightened Ryland's throat. His agent had always been overprotective. No doubt watching over his investment. Ryland understood that, but he wasn't going back on his word to help Lucy with the team. She needed him. "No worries."

If his agent believed a romance was going on between Ryland and Lucy, Blake wouldn't feel the need to play mother hen. No one would have to know the truth. Not the sponsors or the Fuego, not even Lucy…

Play fair. Don't cheat.

Not saying anything wasn't cheating, but it wasn't exactly fair, either.

"I must admit I'm a little surprised," Blake said. "Lucy's not your usual type."

Ryland wasn't sure he had a type, but the kind of women he met at clubs couldn't hold a candle to a certain fresh-faced woman with a warm smile, big heart and legs to her neck. Someone who didn't care how much he made or the club he played for or what car he drove. Someone whose kisses had rocked his world.

"I've known Lucy since she was in kindergarten," Ryland explained. "Her brother was one of my closest friends and teammates when I was growing up."

Blake's brows furrowed. "We might be able to use this to our advantage. McElroy is big on family. Childhood sweethearts reunited would make a catchy headline."

Whoa, so not going there. "Lucy was too young for me to date when we were in school. Don't try to milk this for something it's not. I'll be leaving town soon."

"The two of you seem cozy. Serious."

Ryland climbed off the bike. "I don't do serious."

"You haven't done serious. That doesn't mean you can't," Blake said. "Lucy could be a keeper."

Definitely.

The renegade thought stopped Ryland cold. Lucy might be a keeper, but not for him. Fame and adoring women hadn't always satisfied him, but things would improve now that he'd had a break. This time away was what he needed. He could concentrate on his career and get back on track with the same hunger and edge that had made him a star player.

Besides, Lucy needed a guy who would be around to help her with Connor. Someone who could make her a priority and give her the attention she deserved. He couldn't be that kind of guy, not when he played soccer all over the world, lived in Arizona and wasn't about to start thinking in the long-term until his career was over.

Ryland picked up his water bottle. "The only keeper I want in my life is a goalkeeper."

There wasn't room for any other kind. There just couldn't be.

While a tired Connor brushed his teeth, Lucy laid out his pajamas on his bed. She couldn't stop thinking about Ryland. About his kissing her. About what he might be saying to his agent right now.

Lucy wished she could turn back the clock. She would have turned down his offer to come over tonight. That way he wouldn't be in trouble and she wouldn't want more of his kisses.

Pathetic.

Crushing on Ryland didn't mean she should be kissing him. Crushes were supposed to be fun, not leave her with swollen lips and a confused heart.

Not her heart, she corrected herself. Her mind.

Her heart was fine. Safe. She planned on keeping it that way. Keeping her distance from Ryland would be her best plan of action. She wasn't supposed to see him again until the Defeeters' game on Saturday. Though he'd promised he would call tomorrow…

He'd used the word "promise" again. He hadn't let her down the first time. She hoped he wouldn't this time, but she had no idea. She didn't trust herself when it came to men.

Lucy's fingers twitched. Touching her tingling lips for the umpteenth time would not help matters. She needed to hold a pencil and sketchbook. She needed to draw.

As soon as Connor was in bed…

He was her priority. Not her art. Definitely not Ryland.

The phone rang.

Her heart leaped. Ryland. Oh, boy, she had it bad.

Connor darted out of the bathroom as if he'd gotten his second wind. He picked up the telephone receiver. "Hello, this is Connor, may I ask who's calling…Dad!"

The excitement in that one word brought a big smile to Lucy's face. Relief, too. Aaron must have returned to a base where phone calls could be made. Her brother was safe. For now.

"I'm so glad you got my emails." Connor leaned against the wall. "Yeah. Ryland knows a lot about soccer. He's cool. But no one is as good a coach as you…We had dinner at his house tonight…Pizza…No, just me and Aunt Lucy. I got to walk his parents' dog. Her name is Cupcake…Can we get a dog?…Ryland said they were a lot of work…" Connor nodded at whatever Aaron said to him. "Yeah, he's a nice guy just like you said…Okay…I love you, too." Connor handed Lucy the phone. "Dad wants to talk to you."

That was odd. Usually she emailed Aaron and Dana so they could spend their precious phone minutes speaking with Connor. She raised the phone to her ear. "Hey, Bro. Miss you."

"Ryland James?" Aaron asked.

Her brother's severe tone made her shoo Connor into his bedroom. "Ryland's helping with Connor's team."

"Dinner at his house has nothing to do with the *team*."

She walked down the hallway to put some distance between her and her nephew. "Connor likes spending time with him."

"And you're hanging with Ryland for the sake of Connor?"

"Yes. Connor's the reason I accepted the dinner invitation." She kept her voice low so her nephew wouldn't hear. "He misses you and Dana so much. But ever since Ryland started working with the team, Connor's been happy and all smiles."

"What about you?" Aaron asked. "You had a big crush on him."

"That was years ago," she said.

"Ryland James is a player, Luce. You don't follow soccer, but I do. The guy has a bad reputation when it comes to women. He'll break your heart if he gets the chance."

"I'll admit he's attractive," she said. "But after Jeff, I know better than to fall for a guy like Ryland James."

"I hope so."

Her brother sounded doubtful. "Don't worry. Ryland isn't going to be around much longer."

"Stay away from him."

"Hard to do when he's helping me with the team and teaching me what I need to coach."

"Limit your interaction to soccer. I hate to think he might hurt you," Aaron said. "Damn. Out of time. Love you. Be careful, Luce."

The line disconnected.

A lump of emotion formed in her throat. Aaron had tried to warn her about Jeff before she eloped, but Lucy hadn't listened. She couldn't make the same mistake again. Because she knew Aaron was right. Ryland James was dangerous. He could break her heart. Easily. She'd survived when that happened with Jeff. She wasn't sure she could survive that type of heartache again.

Lucy put away the phone receiver and made her way to Connor's bedroom. Aaron's words echoed through her head. She felt like an idiot. She'd questioned whether she could trust

Ryland, yet she'd kissed him tonight and still wanted more kisses.

So not good.

But she couldn't wallow or overanalyze. She'd done enough of that when her marriage had ended. She knew what to do now—start a new project. As soon as her nephew was tucked into bed, she would gather her art supplies.

Forget a pencil and sketchbook. Time to pull out the big guns—brushes, paints and canvas. Painting was the only thing that might clear her thoughts enough so she could forget about Ryland James and his kisses.

CHAPTER EIGHT

AFTER Connor left for school the next morning, Lucy worked. She enjoyed graphic design—creative, yet practical—but the painting she'd started last night called to her in a way her normal work never had. She emailed a proof to one client and uploaded changes to another's website. The rest of the items on her To Do list could wait until later.

Lucy stood in front of the painting. The strong, bright, vivid colors filled the canvas. The boldness surprised her.

She wasn't that into abstract art. She preferred subjects that captured a snapshot of life or told a story. But thanks to Ryland, her thoughts and emotions were a mismatched jumble. Geometric shapes, lines and arcs were about all she could manage at the moment.

Still the elements somehow worked. Not too surprising, Lucy supposed. She'd always found solace in art, when she was sick and after her marriage ended. The only difference was this time neither her health nor heart were involved.

She wouldn't allow her heart to be involved. That internal organ would only lead her astray.

Stop thinking. Just paint.

Time to lose herself in the work. Lucy dipped her brush into the paint.

She worked with almost a manic fervor. Joy and sorrow,

desire and heartache appeared beneath her brush in bold strokes, bright colors, swirls and slashes.

The doorbell rang.

The sound startled her. She dripped paint onto her hand.

A quick glance at the clock showed she'd been painting for the past two hours. She'd lost track of time. A good thing she'd been interrupted or she could have stayed here all day.

Using a nearby rag, she wiped her hands then headed to the front door. Most likely the UPS man. She'd ordered some paper samples for a client.

Lucy opened the door.

Ryland stood on the porch. Her breath caught and held in her chest. He wore warm-up pants and a matching jacket with a white T-shirt underneath. The casual attire looked stylish on him. His hair was styled, but he hadn't shaved the stubble from his face this morning. Dark circles ringed his eyes, as if he hadn't slept much last night.

Like her.

Though she doubted she'd played a role in his dreams the way he'd starred in hers.

He smiled. "Good morning."

Ryland was the last person she expected to see. He'd told her he would call, not show up in person. But a part of her was happy to see him standing here.

That bothered her. She blew out a breath. Remember what Aaron had said. Ryland was the last person she should want to spend any time with. Yet…

Her gaze slid from his hazel-green eyes to his mouth. Tingles filled her stomach. Her lips ached for another kiss.

Lucy clutched the doorknob. For support or ease in slamming shut the door, she wasn't certain. "What are you doing here?"

Her tone wasn't polite. She didn't care. His presence disturbed her.

His smile faltered a moment before widening. "Let's go for coffee."

"I'm not sure that's such a good idea."

Talk about a wimpy response. She knew going out would be a very bad idea.

"We need to talk about my coaching the Defeeters," he added.

He would bring up coaching and the Defeeters. She was torn. Seeing him over something soccer-related didn't make Ryland James any less dangerous. She glanced down at her paint-splattered shirt and sweatpants. "I'm not dressed to go out."

His gaze took in her clothes and her hands with splotches of purple on them. "You've been painting."

She didn't understand why he sounded so pleased. "Yes."

"We can stay here," he said. "I'd like to see what you're working on."

Lucy didn't feel comfortable sharing her work with Ryland. No way did she want to expose such an intimate part of herself. Not after kissing him had brought up all these feelings. Speaking of kissing him, being alone in the house wasn't a good idea at all. "We can go to the coffee shop. Let me wash up and get my purse."

A few minutes later, refreshed and ready, she locked the front door. "Do you want to meet there?"

"We can ride together."

That was what she was afraid he would say. "I'll drive."

"Your car is nicer than my dad's old truck."

"My car is closer." She motioned to her car parked on the driveway. "Less walking for you."

He headed to her car. "That's thoughtful."

More like self-preservation. She would also be in control. She could determine when they left, not him.

Lucy unlocked the car and opened the door for him. "Do you need help getting in?"

He drew his brows together. "Thanks, but I can handle it."

She walked around the front of the car, slid into her seat and turned on the engine. "Buckled in?"

Ryland patted the seat belt. "All set."

The tension in the air matched her tight jaw. She backed out of the driveway. "So what did you want to talk about?"

"Let's wait until we get to the coffee shop," Ryland said.

They were only five minutes away. She turned on the radio. A pop song with lyrics about going home played. The music was better than silence, but not by much. She tapped her thumbs on the steering wheel. "Does it have anything to do with Blake?"

Ryland nodded. "But no need to worry."

Easier said then done.

Lucy turned onto Main Street. Small shops and restaurants lined the almost-empty street. A quiet morning in Wicksburg. She parked on the street right in front of the Java Bean, a narrow coffee shop with three tables inside and two out front on the sidewalk.

A bell jangled when Ryland opened the door for her. She stepped inside. The place was empty. As they walked to the counter, he placed his hand at the small of her back. His gentle touch made her wish she were back in his arms again, even if that was the last place she should be.

Lucy ordered a cappuccino. He got a double espresso. She went to remove her wallet, but he was handing the barista a twenty-dollar bill.

"You can buy the next time," he said.

Going out to coffee with Ryland was not something she planned on doing again. She'd figure out another way to repay him.

Once their order was ready, she sat at a small, round table. Jazzy instrumental music played from hidden speakers.

Ryland sat across from her. His left foot brushed hers. "Excuse me."

"Sorry." Lucy placed her feet under her chair. The sooner they got this over with the better. She wrapped her hands around the warm mug. "So what's going on?"

Ryland took a sip of his coffee. "Somebody tweeted I was coaching a team of kids in Wicksburg."

"Blake saw the tweet?"

"A PR firm I use did."

She drank from her cup. "No wonder Blake looked so upset."

"He calmed down after you left," Ryland said. "Turns out helping my girlfriend coach a team is a perfectly acceptable thing for me to do."

Girlfriend? She stared at him confused. "Huh?"

"Blake thinks you and I are dating," Ryland explained.

Dating. The word echoed through her head. Even if the idea appealed to her a tiny, almost miniscule bit, she knew it would never happen. "How did he react when you told him we weren't dating?"

"I didn't tell him." Ryland wouldn't meet her gaze. "I didn't deny we were dating, but I didn't say we were a couple, either."

She stared in disbelief. "So Blake thinks we are—"

"I had no choice."

"There's always a choice." She knew that better than anyone. Sometimes the hard choice was the best option.

"I made my choice."

"You had to do what you thought was best for your career. I get that." He'd gotten into this mess with his agent for helping the Defeeters. She couldn't be angry. "I know how much soccer means to you."

His eyes narrowed. "It's not only about my career. If I'd told Blake we weren't dating, I wouldn't be able to help you and the team."

His words sunk in. Ryland hadn't been thinking of himself. He'd done this for her, Connor and the boys.

Her heart pounded so loudly she was sure the barista behind the counter could hear it.

"I wasn't sure if I should tell you," Ryland admitted.

"Why did you?" she asked.

"Fair play."

Play fair. Don't cheat. She remembered the rules he'd told her last night. Right before he'd kissed her senseless. "Thank you for being honest."

"If it's any consolation, I told Blake we weren't serious about each other."

She was glad they were on the same page about not getting involved, except she couldn't ignore a twinge of disappointment. Silly reaction given the circumstances. "Understatement of the year."

Amusement gleamed in his eyes. "True, but people will believe what they want if we don't deny it. And this way I can keep helping you and the team."

Her heart dropped. "You want us to pretend to be dating."

"It's not what I want, but what we have to do." Ryland's smile reached all the way to his eyes. "After those kisses last night, I'm not sure how much pretending is going to be involved."

Heat flooded her face. "We agreed kissing was a mistake."

"You said that. I didn't." His gaze held hers. "There's chemistry between us."

A highly combustible reaction, but she would never admit it. If she did, Ryland could use it to his advantage. She wouldn't stand a chance if he did.

"This is crazy." Lucy's voice sounded stronger than she

felt. She tightened her grip on the coffee-cup handle to keep her hand from shaking. "No more kissing. No pretend dating, either."

"Then you'd better find yourself a new assistant before the game on Saturday."

"Seriously?"

He nodded once.

Darn. Lucy watched steam rise from her coffee cup. She didn't know what to do. She needed to protect herself, but she also had to think about Connor.

Connor.

He was the reason she'd approached Ryland in the first place. Her nephew would be the one to suffer if he couldn't continue coaching the Defeeters. She couldn't allow that to happen.

She tried to push all the other stuff out of her mind, including her own worries, doubts and fears, and to focus on Connor. "What's important here is...the team."

"Especially Connor," Ryland said.

She nodded. What was best for Connor might not be the best thing for her, but so what? She had to put her nephew first even if it put her in an awkward position. "You're leaving soon. Until then I'm willing to do whatever it takes so you can keep coaching the team. I can't imagine it'll be that big a deal to pretend to date since your agent lives in California."

"The other coaches in the rec. league have to believe it, or there could be trouble," Ryland clarified. "The parents, too."

Maybe a bigger deal than she realized. But for her nephew she would do it. "Okay."

"Right now there's no press coverage, but that could change."

This had disaster written all over it. If Aaron found out... She couldn't think about him. Connor was her priority, not her brother.

No matter what life had thrown at Lucy, she'd proven she was capable and able to handle anything. She would do the same here. "It's only for a few weeks, right?"

Ryland nodded. "It'll be fun."

There was that word again. She doubted this would be fun. But as long as he was working with the team, keeping a smile on Connor's face and teaching her how to coach, it would be…doable.

Besides they were just pretending. What could go wrong?

Pretending to date wasn't turning out to be all that great. So far "dating" had amounted to several texts being exchanged about soccer and an impromptu dinner at the pizza parlor with the entire team. He'd have to step things up as soon as this game was over.

It couldn't end quickly enough for Ryland. He forced himself to stay seated on the bench. The Defeeters were outmatched and losing. He couldn't do a single thing about it, either.

"Great job, Defeeters!" Lucy stood along the sideline in a blue T-shirt with the name of the soccer league across the front and warm-up pants. She held a clipboard with a list of when players should be substituted to ensure equal playing time and waved it in the air when she got excited during the game. "You can do it!"

The way she cheered was cute. If only the team could pull off a victory, but that would take a miracle given their competition today.

Lucy glanced back at him with a big smile on her face. "The boys have improved over the past two weeks."

Ryland nodded. They had lots of work to do at the next practice.

Lucy checked the stopwatch she wore around her neck. "There can't be much time left."

He glanced at his cell phone. "Less than four minutes."

Connor stole the ball from a small, speedy forward. He passed the ball to Marco, who ran toward the field. He dribbled around a defender and another one.

Parents cheered. Lucy waved the clipboard. Ryland shook his head. Marco needed to pass before the ball got stolen.

The kid sped across the center line.

No way could he take the ball all the way to the goal alone. Not against a skilled team like the Strikers.

"Pass," Ryland called out.

Lucy pointed to Jacob, who stood down field with no defenders around him.

"Cross, Marco," Ryland yelled. "To Jacob."

Marco continued dribbling. A tall, blond-haired defender from the opposite team ran up, stole the ball and kicked it to a teammate. Goal.

The Defeeters parents sighed. The Striker parents cheered.

The referee blew the whistle.

Game over. The Defeeters had lost six–three. Not that the league kept score, but still...

Ryland would add some new drills and review the old ones. The boys needed to learn to pass the ball and talk to each other out on the field. This was a soccer match, not Sunday services at church.

Each of the teams shouted cheers. Great. The kids had found their voices now that the game was over.

The players lined up with the coaches at the end and shook hands with their opponents. Several of the Strikers grabbed their balls and asked Ryland to sign them. He happily obliged and posed for pictures.

By the time he finished, Lucy was seated on the grass with the boys. He walked their way, passing through a group of Defeeters parents.

Suzy, one of the moms, smiled at him. "They played well out there."

Cheryl nodded. "The last time they played the Strikers it was a shutout."

Marco's dad, Ewan, patted Ryland on the back. "This is the most competitive they've ever been. You've done a great job preparing them."

Interesting. Ryland would have thought the parents would be upset, but they sounded pleased. The boys were all smiles, too.

"Did you see?" Connor asked him. "We scored three goals."

Ryland had never seen so many happy faces after a loss. "Nice match, boys."

"Coach Lucy said if we could score one more goal than the last time we'd played the Strikers that would be a win in her book," Marco said.

Dalton pumped his fists in the air. "We needed one goal, but we scored three!"

Ryland had been so focused on winning he'd forgotten there was more to a game than the final score. Especially when skills development, not winning the game, was the goal. But Lucy, who might not have the technical knowledge, had known that.

She sat with a wide smile on her face and sun-kissed cheeks. Lovely.

A warm feeling settled over Ryland. They really needed to spend more time together.

"In the fall, we lost nine–zero," Connor explained.

Ouch. Ryland forced himself not to grimace. No wonder there was so much excitement over today's match. "You gave them a much better game today."

Dalton nodded. "We play them again at the end of the season."

"Let's not get ahead of ourselves. This is our first game," Lucy said. "We have lots to work on before that final match."

"I'll second that," Ryland agreed. "But that's what practice is for. All of you played so well today it's time for a celebration."

"Snacks!" the boys yelled in unison.

Suzy, the snack mom for today's game, passed out brown lunch bags filled with juice, string cheese, a package of trail mix and a bag of cookies. The boys attacked the food like piranhas.

Ryland walked over to Lucy, who jotted notes on her clipboard. "Snacks have improved since I played rec. soccer."

"Yes, but the game's still the same."

He didn't want things to stay the same between them.

Sitting behind her, he placed his hands on her shoulders. Her muscles tensed beneath his palms.

Ryland didn't care. They were supposed to be dating. Might as well start pretending now. Kisses might be off-limits, but she hadn't said anything about not touching. As he placed his mouth by her ear, her sweet scent enveloped him.

"I wanted to congratulate you," he whispered, noticing curious looks from parents and the other coaches. "Excellent job, Coach."

She turned her head toward him. Her lips were mere inches from his. It would be so easy to steal a kiss. But he wasn't going to push it. At least not yet.

Wariness filled her eyes, but she smiled at him. "Thanks, but I have the best assistant coach in the league. The boys wouldn't have scored any goals without his help."

Her warm breath against his skin raised his temperature twenty degrees. He could practically taste her. His mouth watered. Pretend kisses would probably feel just as nice as real ones.

"Though you're going to have to explain the offside rule to me again," she continued. "I still don't get it."

Ryland laughed. Here he was thinking about kisses, and she was still talking soccer. "I'll keep explaining until you understand it."

Waiting until Monday afternoon to see her again was unacceptable. He doubted she'd agree to a date, not even a pretend one. But she'd agreed to the pretending because of Connor. The kid would give Ryland the perfect reason to see Lucy before the next practice.

Not cheating, he thought. Perhaps not playing one hundred percent fair, but being able to spend some time with her was worth it. Once they were alone, she might even agree.

Ryland stood. "The way you boys played today deserves a special treat." He looked each boy in the eyes. "Who's up for a slushie?"

Sitting on a picnic bench outside Rocket Burgers, Lucy placed her mouth around the straw sticking out of her cup and sipped her blue-raspberry slushie. Suzy, Cheryl, Debbie and the other moms from the team sat with her.

Ryland and the dads sat with the boys on a grassy area near a play structure.

Suzy set her cup on the table. "Ryland is so nice to treat us all to slushies."

"I'm sure he can afford it. You are so lucky Lucy to spend so much time with him." Cheryl pouted. "I thought I had a chance, but it's better he chose you since I'm not divorced."

Suzy smiled at Lucy. "I thought you guys looked a little chummier at the pizza party, but I didn't realize you were dating until today."

"He is a total catch," Debbie said. "The two of you make a cute couple."

Happiness shot all the way to the tips of Lucy's hot-pink

painted toenails. Not for her, she countered. But for Connor. This charade was for him. She repositioned her straw. "Thanks."

Lucy was not going to confirm or deny anything about their "dating." The less she said, the less dishonest she would feel. She drank more of her slushie.

The men laughed. The boys, too. Through the cacophony of noise, the squeals and giggles, Lucy singled out Ryland's laughter. The rich sound curled around her heart and sent her temperature climbing. She sipped her slushie, but the icy drink did nothing to cool her down.

No biggie. She would be heading home soon and wouldn't have to see Ryland until Monday afternoon.

As the women talked about a family who'd moved to Iowa, Lucy glanced his way. Ryland sat with Connor on one side and Dalton on the other, the only two boys on the team without fathers here today.

While the other boys spoke with their fathers, Ryland talked to Connor and Dalton. The boys looked totally engaged in the conversation. Smiles lit up their faces. They laughed.

A soccer ball–size lump formed in her throat.

Ryland James might have a reputation as a womanizer, but she could tell someday he would be a great dad. The kind of dad she had. The kind of dad her brother was.

He flashed her a lopsided grin and winked.

Lucy had been caught staring. She should look away, but she didn't want to. She realized since they were pretending to date she didn't have to.

The fluttery sensations in her stomach reminded her of when she was thirteen and head over heels in love with Ryland. But she knew better than to fantasize about a happily ever after now with a guy like him. Besides, she knew happy endings were rare, almost nonexistent these days.

A dad named Chuck said something to Ryland. He looked at him, breaking the connection with her.

Lucy turned her attention to the table. The other women had gotten up except for Suzy.

"Well, this has been fun." Cheryl motioned to her son Dalton and gazed longingly at Ryland. "See you at practice on Monday."

"The boys will have their work cut out for them," he said.

Families said goodbye and headed to their cars. Several boys lagged behind, not wanting to leave their friends. Marco and Connor ran up to the picnic table. Ryland followed them.

"Can Connor spend the night?" Marco asked his mom.

"Sure. We have no plans other than to hang out and watch a DVD." Suzy glanced at Lucy. "Is it okay with you?"

Connor stared at her with an expectant look. "Please, Aunt Lucy?"

"He's had sleepovers at our house before," Suzy added.

Dana had provided Lucy with the names of acceptable sleepover and playdate friends. Marco had been at the top of the list. "Okay."

The boys gave each other high fives.

"But you're going to have to come home with me first. You need to shower and pack your things," she said.

"I have to run by the grocery store. We can pick him up on our way home," Suzy offered.

"Thanks." Lucy hugged her nephew. "This will be my first night alone since I've been back in Wicksburg. I don't know what I'll do."

Connor slipped out of her embrace. "Ryland can keep you company tonight."

She started to speak, but Ryland beat her to it.

"I have no plans tonight," he said. "I'd be happy to make sure your aunt doesn't miss you too much."

The mischievous look on Ryland's face made her wonder

if he'd planned this whole thing. She wouldn't put it past him. But a part of her was flattered he'd go to so much trouble to spend time with her.

Remember, it's pretend.

"Then we're all set." Suzy grinned. "See you in an hour or so."

As Marco and his parents headed to their SUV, Connor watched them go. "Tonight is going to be so much fun."

Maybe for him. Anxiety built inside Lucy. She had no idea if Ryland was serious about tonight. A part of her hoped he was serious about keeping her company. Not because she was going to be lonely, but because she wanted to see him.

Ridiculous. She blew out a puff of air.

"I'll see you at five," Ryland said.

Before she could say anything he walked off toward the old beat-up truck.

Okay, he was serious. But what exactly did he have in mind?

Connor bounced on his toes. "We'd better get home."

She wrapped her arm around his thin shoulders. "You have plenty of time to get ready for your sleepover."

"I'm not worried about me, but Dad says it takes Mom hours to get ready. You're going to need a lot of time."

His words and sage tone amused her. "What for?"

"Your date with Ryland."

Lucy flinched. She hadn't wanted to drag Connor into the ruse. "Date?"

"Ryland's taking you out to dinner." A smug smile settled on Connor's freckled face. "I told him Otto's was your favorite restaurant, and you liked the cheese fondue best. I also told him it was expensive and only for special occasions, but Ryland said he could probably afford it."

"He can." He could probably afford to buy the entire town.

"If you and Ryland got married, that would make him my new uncle, right?" Connor asked.

Oh, no. The last thing she needed was Connor mentioning marriage to Aaron. "Marriage is serious business. Ryland and I are just going out to eat."

"But it would be pretty cool, don't ya think?"

Maybe if she were nine she would think it was cool. But she was twenty-six and pretending to be dating a soccer star. Marriage was the last thing on her mind while she took care of Connor for the next year. She wasn't even sure if she wanted to get married again. Not after Jeff.

"When two people love each other, marriage can be very cool," Lucy said carefully. "But love is not something you can rush. It takes time."

"My dad knew the minute he saw my mom he was going to marry her," Connor said. "They didn't date very long."

"That's true, but what happened with your mom and dad doesn't happen to many people."

Definitely not her and Jeff.

"But it could happen with you and Ryland," Connor said optimistically.

She gave him a squeeze. "I suppose anything is possible."

But in her and Ryland's case, highly unlikely.

CHAPTER NINE

STANDING on Lucy's front doorstep on Saturday night, Ryland held the single iris behind his back. At the flower shop, he'd headed straight for the roses because that was what he usually bought women, but the purple flower caught his eyes. The vibrant color reminded him of Lucy, so full of life. He hoped she liked it.

Anticipation for his "date" buzzed through Ryland. He hadn't gone to this much trouble for a woman before. Not unless you counted what he did for his mom on Mother's Day, her birthday in July and Christmastime. But like his mother, Lucy was worth it. Even if this wasn't a "real" date.

He wanted her to see how much fun they could have together. And it would be a memory he could take with him when he left Wicksburg. One he hoped Lucy would look back on fondly herself. Smiling, he pressed the doorbell.

A moment later, the door opened.

Lucy stood in the doorway. Mascara lengthened her eyelashes. Pink gloss covered her lips. He couldn't tell if she was wearing any other makeup. Not that she needed any with her high cheekbones and wide-set eyes.

She never wore any jewelry other than a watch, but tonight dangling crystals hung from her earlobes. A matching necklace graced her long neck.

Her purple sleeveless dress hugged all the right curves and

fell just above her knees. Strappy high-heeled shoes accentuated her delicate ankles and sexy calves.

Beautiful.

Lucy was a small-town girl, but tonight she'd dressed for
the big city. Whether this was a real date or not, she'd put
some effort into getting ready. That pleased him.

"You look stunning."

She smiled softly. "I figured since we were going to
Otto's…"

"Connor told you."

"Nine-year-olds and magpies have a lot in common," she
explained. "So what did it cost you to enlist him and Marco
as your partners in crime?"

Manny lumbered over toward the door. Lucy blocked
his way so he couldn't get out of the house. The cat rubbed
against her bare leg. Ryland wished he could do the same.

"Twenty bucks," he said, unrepentant.

Her mouth gaped. If this were a real date, he would have
been tempted to take advantage of the moment and kiss her.
But it wasn't, so he didn't.

"You paid the boys that much?" she asked.

He shrugged. "They earned it."

"Paying someone to do your dirty work gets expensive."

But worth every dollar. "A man does what he has to do."

"Even for a pretend date?" she said.

"A date's a date."

"That explains your clothes." Lucy's assessing gaze traveled the length of him. The brown chinos and green button-
down shirt were the dressiest things he'd brought with him
to Wicksburg. Going out hadn't been on his list of things to
do here. "You clean up well."

He straightened, happy he'd pulled out all the stops tonight.
"You sound surprised."

A half smile formed on her lips. "Well, I've only seen you in soccer shorts, jerseys and T-shirts."

Ryland remembered the first day she'd shown up at his parents' house. He raised a brow. "And shirtless."

Her cheeks turned a charming shade of pink. "That, too."

He handed her the iris. The color matched her dress perfectly. "For you."

"Thank you." She took the flower and smelled it. "It's real."

"Not everything is pretend."

She smiled. "I've always liked irises better than roses."

Score. "It reminded me of you."

Her eyes widened. "You don't have to say stuff like that. No one is watching us."

He held his hands up, his palms facing her. "Just being honest."

She kept staring at the flower. "Let me put this in some water before we go."

With an unexpected bounce to his step, Ryland entered the house and closed the door behind him. He followed Lucy, enjoying the sway of her hips and the flow of her dress around her legs. Her heels clicked against the floor. Manny trotted along behind him.

In the kitchen, she filled a narrow glass vase with water. She studied the flower, turning it 360 degrees, then stuck the stem into the vase. "I want to paint this."

Satisfaction flowed through him. "I'd like to see your work."

"We need to get to Otto's."

"There's no rush," he said. "I called the restaurant. No reservations unless it's a party of six or more."

She tilted her chin. "You're going to a lot of trouble for a pretend date."

"Connor doesn't want you to be lonely tonight."

"Connor, huh?"

Ryland's gaze met hers. Such pretty blue eyes. "I don't, either."

And that was the truth. Which surprised him a little. Okay, a lot. This was supposed to be all make-believe, but the more time he spent with Lucy, the more he cared about her. He wanted to make her smile and laugh. He wanted to please her.

This had never happened to him with a woman before. He wasn't sure what to think or even if he liked it.

Silence stretched between them, but if anything, the quiet drew them closer together not apart.

The sounds of the house continued on. Ice cubes dropped inside the freezer. A motor on the refrigerator whirred. Manny drank water from his bowl.

Funny, but Ryland had never felt this comfortable around anyone except his parents. He needed to figure out what was going on here. "So your paintings…"

"I'm really hungry."

So was Ryland. But what he wanted wasn't on any menu. She was standing right next to him. "Then let's go."

As Ryland held open the door to Otto's, Lucy walked into the restaurant. The din of customers talking and laughing rose above the accordion music playing. She inhaled the tantalizing aromas of roasting pork and herbs lingering in the air.

Her stomach rumbled. She'd been too nervous about the soccer game to eat lunch. Big mistake because now she was starving.

For food and for…

She glanced over her shoulder at Ryland. The green shirt lightened his hazel eyes. He looked as comfortable in dressier clothes as casual ones. He'd gone out of his way to make tonight special. She appreciated that even if none of this was for real. "Thanks for taking me out tonight."

"Thanks for going out with me."

Otto's was packed. Not surprising given it was a Saturday night and the best place in town. The last time she'd been here was right before Aaron and Dana deployed—a going-away dinner for them.

Customers crammed into booths and tables. Servers carried heavy trays of German food and large steins full of beer. People waited to be seated. Some stood near the hostess stand. Others sat on benches.

Ryland approached the hostess, who was busy marking the seating chart. The woman in her early twenties looked up with a frown. But as soon as she saw him, a dazzling smile broke across her young, pretty face.

Lucy was beginning to realize wherever Ryland went female attention was sure to follow. But she saw he did nothing to make women come on to him. Well, except for being an extremely good-looking and all-around good guy. She stepped closer to him, feeling territorial. Silly considering this wasn't a real date.

"Hello. I'm Emily. Welcome to Otto's." She smoothed her hair. "How many in your party?"

"Two," he said.

She fluttered her eyelashes coquettishly. "Your name, please?"

"James."

The hostess wrote the information on her list. "You're looking at a thirty-minute wait, but I'll see what I can do."

Lucy was surprised the woman didn't ask for Ryland's phone number or hand him hers. More women, both staff and customers, stared at him.

He shot Lucy a sideward glance. "Half hour okay?"

"The cheese fondue is worth the wait."

Ryland raised a brow. "Even when you're hungry?"

"Especially then."

Other customers made their way out of the restaurant while

more entered. He moved closer to her to make room in the small, crowded lobby area. "Connor told me how much you love the cheese fondue here."

"It's my favorite."

"Not chocolate?"

"Chocolate, cheese. I'm not that particular as long as it's warm and…"

"Gooey."

"Lucy?" a familiar male voice asked.

No. No. No. Every muscle in her body tensed. She squeezed her eyes shut in hopes she was dreaming, but when she opened them she was still standing in Otto's. Her ex-husband, Jeff Swanson, and his wife, Amelia, weaved through the crowd toward her. Jeff's receding hairline had gotten worse. And Amelia. She looked different…

Lucy narrowed her gaze for a better look.

Pregnant.

Pain gripped her chest. Life wasn't fair. She sighed.

Ryland stiffened. "You okay?"

"No." Not unless aliens were about to beam her up to the mother ship would she be okay. Being probed and prodded by extraterrestrials would be better than having to speak with the two people who had hurt her most. "But I'll survive."

At least she hoped so.

Jeff crowded in next to them. "I almost didn't recognize you."

The smell of his aftershave brought a rush of memories she'd rather forget. The bad times had overshadowed any good ones that might have existed at the beginning. "It's me."

"I see that now." Jeff's gaze raked over her. "But you cut your hair short. And you must have lost what? Twenty-five pounds or more?"

Stress had made eating difficult after the divorce. Going out solo or fixing a meal for one wasn't much fun, either.

She'd also discovered Zumba classes at a nearby gym when she moved to Chicago. "Fifteen."

"Good for you," Amelia said. "It seems like we never stopped dieting when we were in high school. Remember that soup diet? I still can't stand the sight or smell of cabbage."

Until finding out about the affair, Lucy had been thankful to have Amelia for a best friend. Lucy had always felt inadequate, an ugly duckling compared to pretty Amelia with her jade-green eyes and shoulder-length blond hair. Amelia's hair now fell to her mid-back. Jeff liked long hair. That was why Lucy had chopped hers off.

Jeff extended his arm to shake hands. "Ryland James. I'm surprised to see you back in town."

His jaw tensed. "My parents still live here."

"Amelia, do you remember Ryland?" Jeff asked. "Soccer player extraordinaire."

"Of course." Amelia smiled sweetly. "Lucy had the biggest crush on you when we were in middle school."

"I know," Ryland said.

Lucy's heart went splat against the restaurant's hardwood floor. "You did?"

He nodded.

Aaron must have told Ryland. But why would her brother have done that? Her crush was supposed to be a secret.

"I didn't know," Jeff announced.

"Husbands." Amelia shook her head. "I mean, ex-husbands are always the last to know."

Ignore her. Ignore her. Ignore her.

Lucy repeated the mantra in her head so she didn't say anything aloud. The words wanting to come out of her mouth were neither ladylike nor appropriate for a public setting.

So what if she would have rather told Ryland about her failed marriage? Amelia was not worth causing a scene over.

Ryland put his arm around Lucy and pulled her against him. He toyed with her hair, wrapping a curl around his finger.

Her heart swelled with gratitude. She hated needing anyone. She'd been so weak when she'd been younger she wanted to be strong now that she was healthy. But she needed him at this moment.

She sunk against Ryland, soaking up his warmth and his strength, feeling his heart beat. The constant rhythm, the sound of life, comforted her.

Lucy smiled up at him.

He smiled back.

Both Jeff and Amelia stared with dumbfounded expressions on their faces.

Ryland had been right. Words weren't always necessary. People believed what they wanted, even if their assumptions might be incorrect.

Amelia's eyes darkened. She pressed her lips into a thin line.

Jeff's gaze bounced between Lucy and Ryland. "The two of you are…together?"

Lucy understood the disbelief in his voice. She and Ryland made an unlikely pair, but still she nodded. She didn't like dishonesty after all the lies people had told her, but this didn't bother her so much. They were having dinner together tonight. Not the "together" Jeff had been talking about, but "together" nonetheless.

"I'd heard you were back in town taking care of Connor, but I had no idea about the two of you," Jeff said, not sounding pleased at all.

Good. Let him stew in his own cheating, miserable, arrogant juices.

Biting back a cutting retort, she glanced up at Ryland.

He kept playing with her hair with one hand while the other

kept a possessive hold around her. His gaze held Lucy's for a long moment, the kind that elicited envious sighs from movie audiences. She'd owe him big-time for pretending like this, but she would gladly pay up.

"Soccer isn't that big in the U.S.," Ryland said. "But I played in the U.K. where the media coverage is insane so I try to keep a low profile with my personal life."

Amelia's face scrunched so much it looked painful. "But you're not staying here, are you? I thought you played on the West Coast somewhere."

"Phoenix." Ryland's gaze never wavered from Lucy's, making her insides feel all warm and gooey. "Though I wouldn't mind playing for Indianapolis so I could be closer to Wicksburg."

A thrill rushed through her. That was only a couple of hours away.

"We're having a baby," Amelia blurted as if no one had noticed her protruding belly. "It's a boy."

"Congratulations," both Lucy and Ryland said at the same time.

"I know how badly you wanted children when you were with Jeff," Amelia said to her. "Maybe something happened because of your liver. All those medicines you took and the transplant. But adoption is always an option."

After two years of trying to conceive, she hadn't been able to get pregnant. The doctors said there was no medical reason why she shouldn't be able to have a baby. Amelia knew that. So did Jeff. And it wasn't as if the two of them had gotten pregnant right away. Still feelings of inadequacy pummeled Lucy. Her shoulders slumped.

Ryland cuddled her close, making her feel accepted and special. "Kids aren't easy to handle. But you should see how great Lucy is with Connor."

Amelia patted her stomach. "Jeff and my best friend,

Madison, are throwing me a baby shower. They've been planning it for weeks. I can't wait."

The words reminded Lucy of something she'd buried in the far recesses of her mind. Pain sliced through her, sharp and unyielding, at the betrayal of trust by Jeff and Amelia.

"I remember when the two of you spent all that time planning my birthday party." The words tasted bitter on Lucy's tongue. "That's when your affair started, right?"

Amelia gasped. She glared at a contrite-looking Jeff then stormed out of the restaurant.

"Damn." Jeff ran after her calling, "It's not what you think."

Lucy looked toward the door. "I almost feel sorry for her."

"Don't. She knew who and what she was marrying. Swanson is a complete moron." Ryland kept his arm around her. Lucy felt safe and secure in his embrace. His presence took the sting out of the past. "Any guy who would choose that woman over you doesn't have a brain cell in his head."

"Thanks," she said, grateful for his support in the face of her bad judgment. "But the truth is, I should have never married a guy like him."

"Why did you?" Ryland asked.

At a small table for two in the corner of the restaurant, candlelight glowed from a glass votive holder, creating a dancing circle against the white linen tablecloth. Ryland sat across from Lucy, their knees brushing against each other. A bowl of cheese fondue, a basket of bread cubes and a plate with two Bavarian Pretzels were between them.

As Lucy talked about Jeff Swanson, Ryland wished he could change the past and erase the pain she'd experienced from her disastrous marriage.

"People warned me about Jeff." Lucy kept her chin up, her gaze forward, not downcast. But the hurt in her voice was unmistakable. "Told me to break up with him while we were dating. Aaron. Even Amelia. But I thought I knew better than all of them. I thought I could trust Jeff, but he had me so fooled."

"I doubt you're the only one he fooled."

She nodded. "After we eloped, I discovered Jeff hadn't been honest with me. He didn't like how independent and self-reliant I'd been while we were dating. He expected me to turn into his needy little wife. One who stayed home, cooked, cleaned and doted upon him. I admit I was far from the ideal spouse he expected. Amelia is more the doting type he wanted." Lucy stabbed her fork into a piece of bread. "But that didn't give him a reason to cheat."

"Jeff treated girls badly in high school, but they still wanted to go out with him."

She poked the bread again. "I don't think he knew I existed in high school. But when we bumped into each other in college, he laid on the charm. He knew what girls wanted to hear. At least what this girl needed to hear."

Her piece of bread had been stabbed so many times it was falling apart. He didn't think Lucy realized what she was doing with her appetizer fork. "There's not much left of that piece of bread. You might want to try another cube."

"Sorry." She stuck her fork into another piece and dipped the bread into the cheese. It fell into the pot. "I know I played a part in the breakup. It takes two people to make a marriage. But I wish Jeff had been more up-front and honest about what he wanted from me."

Ryland respected how she took responsibility, not laying all the blame on a cheating spouse. "If you could do it over..."

"I wouldn't," she said firmly. "I'm better off without him, but I'll admit it's hard being back in town. So many people know what happened. I'm sure they're pitying me the way they did when I was sick and talking behind my back."

"What people say doesn't matter." He wanted to see her smile, not look so sad. "Forget about them. Don't let it get to you. You're strong enough to do that."

"Strong?" Her voice cracked. "I'm a wimp."

"You came back to Wicksburg."

"Only because Aaron asked me," she admitted. "I couldn't have taken this leap on my own."

Damn Jeff Swanson. He'd not only destroyed Lucy's trust in others, but also in herself. "Give it time. Go slow."

She winced. "I'm trying. It's just when we were dating, Jeff made me feel…"

Ryland didn't want to push, but curiosity got the best of him. "What?"

Her gaze met his. The depth of betrayal in her eyes slammed into him, as if he'd run headfirst into the left goalpost. He reached across the table and laced his fingers with hers.

She took a deep breath and exhaled slowly. "You know about my liver transplant."

Ryland nodded.

"Someone died so I could live." Her tone stressed the awfulness of the situation and made him wondered if she somehow felt guilty. "I always wondered—I still wonder—whether that person's family would think I was living up to their expectations. I mean, their child's death is what enabled me to have the transplant. Given that ultimate sacrifice, would they be disappointed with what I've done with my life? What I'm doing or not doing now?"

Ryland's heart ached for her. That was a heavy load for anyone to carry. Especially someone as sensitive and sweet as Lucy. He squeezed her hand.

"Jeff's real appeal, I think, was that he made me believe we could achieve something big, something important together. With his help, I could prove I deserved a second chance with a new liver." Her mouth turned down at the corner. Angst clouded her eyes. "But we didn't. It was all talk. He no longer cared about that once we were married."

The sorrow in her voice squeezed Ryland's heart like a vice grip.

"I wanted to make a difference because of the gift I was given." Her mouth twisted with regret. "But I didn't do that when I was married to Jeff. I haven't done anything on my own, either. I doubt I ever will."

Her disappointment clawed at Ryland. "You're making a huge difference for Connor. For Aaron and his wife, too."

She shrugged. "But it's not something big, world changing."

"For your family it is." Did Lucy not know how special she was? "Look at yourself. You graduated college. You run your own business. That's a lot for someone your age."

"I'm twenty-six," she said with wry sarcasm. "Divorced. In debt with college loans and a car payment. I'm living at my brother's house, and all my possessions fit inside my car."

"You beat liver disease," Ryland countered. "Your being here—alive—is more than enough."

She stared at him as if she was trying to figure him out. A soft smile teased the corners of her mouth. "Where have you been all my life? Well, these past two years?"

Ryland was wondering the same thing. The realization should bother him more than it did.

"Thank you." Gratitude filled her eyes. Her appreciation wasn't superficial or calculated, but from her heart and made him feel valued. She squeezed his hand. "For tonight. For listening to me."

He stroked Lucy's hand with his thumb. "Thanks aren't necessary. I asked you to tell me. I've also been there myself."

Oops. Ryland hadn't meant to say that. He pulled his hand away and took a sip from his water glass.

She pinned him with a questioning gaze. "You?"

He tightened his grip on the glass, wanting to backpedal. "It's not the same. Not even close."

"I've spilled my guts," Lucy said. "It's your turn."

Ryland never opened up the way she had with him. People only valued him for what he could give them. If they knew him, the real him, they would think he wasn't worth much off the pitch. He took another sip of water then placed the glass on the table.

The tilt of her chin told him she wasn't going to let this drop. Of all the people in his life, Lucy didn't care about his fortune or fame. She had never asked him for anything for herself. She was always thinking of others. That included him. If he could tell anyone the truth, it was Lucy.

He swallowed around the emotion clogging his throat. "When I was in elementary school, I was bullied."

"Verbally?"

He nodded. "Sometimes...a lot of times...physically."

Lucy gasped. She placed her hand on top of his, the way he'd done with hers only moments before. "Oh, Ryland. I'm so sorry. That had to be horrible."

"Some days I felt invisible. As if kids were looking right through me." He'd never told anyone about this. Not even his parents. He thought telling Lucy would be hard, but the compassion in her eyes kept him going. "Those were the good days. Otherwise I would get pushed around, even beat up."

He'd felt like such a loser, a nobody, but he'd soon realized bullies were the real losers. Bullies like Jeff Swanson. Ryland would never tell Lucy her ex-husband had been one of the kids who terrorized students like him at Wicksburg Elementary School. That would only upset her more.

Concern knotted her brow. "I had no idea that went on."

"You were a little girl." He remembered her with ponytails and freckles playing hopscotch or swinging at recess.

Seemingly without a care in the world. He hadn't known until later that she was so sick. "Some older kids like Aaron knew, but if they stood up to the bullies, they got beat up, too."

Her mouth formed a perfect O. "The time Aaron said he'd fallen off the monkey bars and gotten a black eye."

"One kid couldn't do much. Even a cool guy like your brother." Ryland remembered telling Aaron not to interfere but the guy wouldn't listen. "I hated going to school so much. I hated most everything back then. Except football. Soccer."

Lucy's smile filled him with warmth, a way he'd never felt when thinking about this part of his past. "You found your passion at a young age."

"I liked being part of a team," he admitted. "It didn't matter that I lived in a dumpy apartment on the wrong side of town or was poor or got beat up all the time. When I put on that jersey, I fit in."

She squeezed his hand. "Thank goodness for soccer."

"It was my escape. My salvation." He took a sip of water. "With my teammates alongside me, the bullies had to leave me alone."

She smiled softly. "Your teammates took care of their star player."

He nodded. "Football gave me hope. A way out of Wicksburg so I could make something of myself. Be someone other than the scrawny kid who people picked on."

Kindness and affection reflected in her eyes. "You've done that. You've accomplished so much."

His chest tightened. She was one of a kind. "So have you."

Her hand still rested on his, making everything feel comfortable and natural. Right.

Ryland was in no hurry to have her stop touching him. He had no idea what was going on between them. Pretend, real... He didn't care.

Slowly, almost reluctantly, Lucy pulled her hand away. "Wicksburg holds some bad memories for both of us."

He missed her softness and her warmth. "Some good ones, too."

Like the memories they were creating right now.

She tried to pull the lost bread cube out of the fondue bowl. "At first I wasn't sure about us pretending to date. I don't like being dishonest. But after seeing Jeff and Amelia, I'm thankful you were with me tonight. I know this is what's best for Connor. And the only way for you to help the team."

"And help you."

"And me."

"We're not being that dishonest," he said. "If you think about it, what we're doing is kind of like the funeral."

Her eyes widened. "Funeral?"

Lucy reminded him of Connor. "Playacting at Squiggy's funeral."

She laughed. "You mean his first funeral. Not the top-secret one I wasn't supposed to know about."

Ryland smiled at her lighthearted tone. "Now this is more like it. No more being upset over an idiot like Jeff. It's time for laughter and fun."

"That's exactly what I need."

She raised the piece of fondue-covered bread to her mouth. Her lips closed around it.

So sexy. Ryland's temperature soared. He took another sip of water. Too bad she also didn't need some kisses.

A drop of cheese remained at the corner of her mouth. Ryland wished he could lick it off. "You have a little cheese on your mouth."

She wiped with a napkin, but missed the spot.

Reaching across the table, he used his thumb to remove the cheese, ignoring how soft her lips looked or how badly he wanted to taste their sweetness again. "It's gone."

Her eyes twinkled with silver sparks. "Thanks."

Lucy wouldn't be thanking him if she knew what he was thinking. "You're welcome."

The server arrived with their main courses. Sauerbraten, spatzle noodles and braised red cabbage for Lucy. Jagerschnitzel with mashed potatoes for him. The food smelled mouthwateringly delicious.

As they ate, Ryland couldn't stop thinking about what would happen after dinner and dessert were finished. When it was the two of them back at her house. Alone. This might be a pretend date, but he wanted to kiss her good-night.

For real.

CHAPTER TEN

RIDING in the old, blue truck, Lucy glanced at Ryland, who sat next to her on the bench seat. With his chiseled good looks, his handsome profile looked as if it had been sculpted, especially with the random headlights casting shadows on his face. But there was nothing hard and cold about the man. He was generous, caring and funny. He might be portrayed as being a bad boy in the press, but she'd glimpsed the man underneath the façade and liked what she saw.

He turned onto the street where she lived.

After spilling secrets, she and Ryland had spent the rest of dinner laughing over jokes, stories and memories. Too bad the evening had to end.

"I can't believe we ate that entire apple strudel after all the fondue and dinner," she said.

"We," he teased. "I only had two bites."

"More like twenty-two."

He parked at the curb and set the gear. "Math's never been a strong point. Which is why soccer is the perfect sport for me. Scores rarely reach two digits."

She grinned. "That's why they invented calculators. For all us right-brained people who can't tell the difference between Algebra and Calculus."

"What about addition and subtraction?" With a wink, he removed the key from the ignition. "Stay there. I'll get the door for you."

His manners impressed Lucy. Okay, she may have assumed athletes had more in common with Neanderthals than gentlemen, but Ryland was proving her wrong. About many things tonight.

The passenger door opened. He extended his arm. "Milady?"

Lucy didn't need Ryland's help, but accepted it anyway. He wasn't offering because she was incapable or unhealthy. He was doing this to be polite. She would gladly play along. "Thank you, kind sir."

The touch of her fingers against his skin caused a spark. Static electricity from the truck's carpet? Whatever it was, heat traveled through her, igniting a fire she hadn't felt in a long time and wasn't sure what to do with.

As soon as she was out of the truck and standing on the sidewalk, Ryland let go of her. A relief, given her reaction, but she missed his touch.

"You must be cold," he said.

Even with the cool night air and her sleeveless dress, she wasn't chilly. Not with Ryland next to her.

"I'm fine." Thousands of stars twinkled overhead. She'd forgotten what the night sky looked like in the country compared to that in a city. "It's a beautiful night."

"Very beautiful."

She glanced his way.

He was looking at her, not the sky. Her body buzzed with awareness. She could stand out here with him all night.

His smile crinkled the corners of his eyes and did funny things to her heart rate.

Tearing her gaze away, Lucy headed up the paved walkway toward the front porch. Ryland followed her, his steps sounding against the concrete.

Uncertainty coursed through Lucy. Ryland made her feel so special tonight, listening in a way Jeff never had and sharing a part of himself with her.

This wasn't a real date. Except at some point this evening, she hadn't been pretending. Ryland hadn't seemed to be, either. That…worried her.

Lucy didn't trust herself when it came to men, especially Ryland. Best to say a quick good-night and make a hasty retreat inside. Alone. So she could figure this out.

On the porch, she reached into her purse with a shaking hand and pulled out her keys. "I had a great time. Thanks."

"The night's still young."

Anticipation revved her blood. She wanted to invite him in. Who was she kidding? She wanted to throw herself into his arms and kiss him until they ran out of air. Or the sun came up.

Lucy couldn't deny the flush of desire, but if they started something would she be able to stop? Would she want to stop? To go too far would be disastrous. "I'm thinking we should call it a night."

He ran his finger along her jawline. "You think?"

Lucy gulped. "I'm not ready for taking any big leaps."

"What about a small one?"

His lips beckoned. Hers ached. Maybe just a little kiss…

She lifted her chin and kissed him on the mouth. Hard.

Ryland pressed his mouth against Lucy's with a hunger that matched her own. He wrapped his arms around her, pulling her closer. She went eagerly, arching against him. This was what she wanted…needed.

The keys dropped from her fingers and clattered on the step. She placed her hands on his shoulders, feeling the ridges of his muscles beneath her fingertips.

His lips moved over hers. She parted her lips, allowing their tongues to explore and dance.

Pleasurable sensations shot through her. She clung to him and his kiss. Longing pooled low in her belly. A moan escaped her lips.

Ryland drew the kiss to an end. "Wow."

That pretty much summed it up. She took a breath and another. It didn't help. Her breathing was still ragged. And her throbbing lips...

She fought the urge to touch them to see that what she'd experienced hadn't been a dream. "I've been trying to curb my impulsive side. Looks like I failed."

"I'd give you an A+ and recommend letting yourself be more impulsive." Wicked laughter lit his eyes. He kept his arms around her. "We could go inside and see where our impulses take us."

Most likely straight into the bedroom. Lucy's heart slammed against her chest.

A sudden fear dampened her desire. She'd been hurt too badly, didn't trust her judgment or the feelings coursing through her right now. Especially with a man who had more opportunity to cheat than her ex-husband ever had.

Ryland James is a player, Luce. He'll break your heart if he gets the chance.

Aaron's words echoed through her head. "We can't. I mean, I can't."

Ryland combed his fingers through her hair. "If you think I'm pretending, I'm not."

"Me, either." Her resolve weakened. "But I have to think of Connor."

"He's spending the night with Marco."

Her mouth went dry with the possibilities. "You're leaving town soon."

"True, but we can make the most of the time I have left,"

Ryland said, his voice husky and oh-so tempting. "You said you didn't want a boyfriend. I'm not looking for a girlfriend."

"Not a real one at least."

"Touché."

"This has nowhere to go. I'm not up for a fling. Aaron thinks if we get involved, you'll break my heart."

Ryland stiffened. "Your brother said that?"

"The other night when he called."

His mouth quirked. "So let's just keep doing what we've been doing."

"Pretending."

"We'll date, but keep it light," he said. "No promises. No guarantees."

"No sex."

"You've made that clear." He sounded amused, not upset. "Except how do you feel about pretend sex?"

"Huh?"

"Never mind," he said. "We'll just have fun and enjoy each other's company until it's time for me to go back to Phoenix."

Lucy wasn't one to play with fire. She'd done everything in her power these past two years to keep from getting burned again. But this was different. She knew where she stood with Ryland. He'd been honest with her. They could make this work. But she would keep a fire extinguisher handy in case the flames got out of control. Getting burned was one thing. She didn't want to wind up a pile of ash. "Okay. We can keep doing what we've been doing."

On Sunday afternoon, Ryland knocked on Lucy's front door. He'd done the same thing less than twenty-four hours ago. But he felt more anticipation today.

She'd been on his mind since last night. Her kisses had fueled his fantasies, making him want more.

But she wasn't ready to give more. At least not the more he wanted.

I don't sleep around.

I'm not up for a fling.

No sex.

She hadn't said anything about no kisses. He'd settle for those. Maybe Lucy would change her mind about the physical part of their...not relationship...hanging out.

The front door opened. Connor smiled up at him with a toothy grin. "Fuego plays in an hour."

This was the second game of the season for his team. They were in L.A. to play against the Galaxy. Ryland had missed not being at the season opener earlier this week when the team lost to the Portland Timbers. He'd felt like he was letting down his teammates and fans down being unable to play. He looked at his foot.

The orthopedist had told Ryland he might get the boot off in another week or two. That meant he would be able to return to the team, but in order to do that he would have to leave Wicksburg.

Wait a minute. Leaving town would be a good thing. Nothing was holding him here. Well, except his parents who would be returning home this week.

And Lucy. But he couldn't let himself go there. When he could play again, soccer would have to be his total focus. He couldn't afford any distractions. She would be a big one.

"Aunt Lucy told me to cheer loudly." Connor grabbed Manny who was darting between his legs, trying get out of the house. "I have to finish my math homework first. Aunt Lucy said so."

"Better get to it, bud." Ryland entered the house. He closed the door behind him. "I don't want to watch the game without you."

Connor ran off to his bedroom to finish his homework. Ryland walked to the kitchen.

The scents of cheese and bacon filled the air. His mouth watered, as much for whatever was baking as the woman unloading the dishwasher. Lucy wore a pair of jean shorts. Her T-shirt inched up in the back showing him a flash of ivory skin in the back as she bent over to grab silverware. Her lime V-neck T-shirt gaped revealing the edge of her white-lace bra.

Beautiful.

He stepped behind and wrapped his arms around Lucy. Her soft-in-all-the-right-places body fit perfectly against his. Knowing they were alone while Connor did his math, Ryland showered kisses along her jawline.

She faced him. Silver sparks flashed in her eyes. "Is this how you normally say hello?"

"No, I prefer this way."

He lowered his mouth to hers. His lips soaked in her warmth and sweetness. His heart rate tripled. The blood rushed from his head.

She arched against him, taking the kiss deeper. He followed her lead, relieved she was as into kissing as he was. He liked kissing Lucy. He wanted to keep on kissing her.

Forever.

Ryland jerked back.

He didn't do forever.

She stared up at him with flushed cheeks and swollen lips. The passion in her eyes matched the desire rushing through his veins. Definitely a keeper. If he was looking for one…

Lucy grinned. "I like how you say hello."

He liked it, too. Especially with her.

But he had to remember to keep things light. No thoughts

about forever. They had two weeks, if they were lucky. No reason to get carried away.

And he wouldn't. That wouldn't be fair to Lucy. Or her brother.

He owed Aaron that much, even if his old friend was wrong about Ryland breaking Lucy's heart. He wouldn't do that to her.

He inhaled. "Whatever you're cooking smells delicious."

"Macaroni and cheese." She turned on the oven light so he could see the casserole dish baking inside. "Dana marked her cookbooks with Connor's favorite recipes."

"I smell bacon."

Lucy smiled coyly. "That's one of the secret ingredients."

"I didn't know you were allowed to divulge secret ingredients."

She shrugged. "We shared our secrets last night so I figured why not."

The vase containing the iris he'd given her sat on the counter. Paintbrushes dried alongside it. "If we have nothing left to hide, show me your paintings."

Her lips quirked. "You really want to see them?"

She sounded surprised by his interest in her art. "I do, or I wouldn't keep asking."

"I—I don't show my work to a lot of people."

"It's just me."

Uncertainty flickered in her eyes. "Exactly."

Ryland didn't understand what she meant. "Show me one."

She raised a brow. "That'll be enough to appease your curiosity?"

He wasn't sure of anything when it came to Lucy. But he would take what he could get. "Yes. I'll leave it up to you if you want to show me more."

She glanced at the oven timer. "I suppose we have time now."

Not the most enthusiastic response, but better than a no. "Great."

Lucy led him down a hallway covered with framed photographs. One picture showed a large recreational vehicle that looked more like a bus.

"Is that your parents' RV?" he asked.

"Yes," she said. "How did you know about that?"

"Connor told me his grandparents were living in a camper and traveling all over the country."

"Yes, that's how they dreamed of spending their retirement. They finally managed to do it three months ago." She peeked in on Connor, who sat at his desk doing his homework. "They're in New Mexico right now."

Ryland wondered what Lucy dreamed of doing. He considered asking, but any of her dreams would be on hold until Aaron and his wife returned. Ryland admired Lucy's sacrifice. He'd thought watching Cupcake had been a big deal. Not even close. He followed her through another doorway.

The bedroom was spotless with nothing out of place. The queen-size bed, covered with a flower-print comforter and matching pillow shams, drew his attention. This was where Lucy slept. Alone, but the bed was big enough for two.

Don't even think about it. He looked away.

She went to the closet.

Ryland knew what to expect from a typical twenty-something woman's closet—overflowing with clothing, shoes and purses.

Lucy opened the door.

Only a few clothing items hung on the rack. A sheet of plastic covered the closet floor. Five pairs of shoes sat on top. Not a handbag in sight. Instead, the backsides of different-size canvases and boxes of art supplies filled the space.

Not typical at all.

Given this was Lucy he shouldn't have been surprised.

"This is something I painted when I was living in Chicago."

As she reached for the closest painting, her hand trembled. Ryland touched her shoulder. He wanted to see her work, but he didn't want to make her uncomfortable. Her bare skin felt soft and warm beneath his palm. "We can do this another time."

"Now is fine." She glanced back at him. "It's just a little hard…"

"To show this side of yourself."

She nodded.

The vulnerability in her eyes squeezed his heart. Her affect on him unnerved Ryland. He lowered his arm from her shoulder. "If it's any consolation, I know nothing about art. I'm about as far removed from an art critic as you can get."

"So if you like it, I'll remember not to get too excited."

He smiled.

She smiled back.

His heart stumbled over itself. His breath rushed from his lungs as if he'd played ninety minutes without a break at halftime.

What was going on?

All she'd done was smile. Something she'd done a hundred times before. But he could hardly breathe.

She pulled out the canvas. "Ready?"

No. Feeling unsteady, he sat on the bed.

"Sure." He forced the word from his tight throat.

Lucy turned the canvas around.

Ryland stared openmouthed and in awe. He'd expected to see a bowl of fruit or a bouquet of flowers. Not a vibrant, colorful portrait full of people having fun. The painting depicted a park with people picnicking, riding bicycles, pushing baby strollers and flying kites.

A good thing he was sitting or he would have fallen flat on his butt. The painting was incredible. Amazing. He felt transported, as if he were in the park seeing what she'd seen, feeling what she'd felt. Surreal.

He took a closer look. "Is that guy eating a hot dog?"

She nodded. "What's a day in the park without a hot dog from a vendor?"

Drops of yellow mustard dripped onto the guy's chin and shirt. The amount of detail amazed Ryland. He noticed a turtle painted next to the pond. An homage to Squiggy? "You're so talented."

"You know nothing about art," she reminded him.

"True, but I know quality when I see it," he said. "This is a thousand times better than any of the junk hanging on my walls in Phoenix."

She raised a brow. "I doubt those artists would consider their work junk."

He waved a hand. "You know what I mean."

"Thank you."

"No, thank you." This painting told him so much about Lucy. He could see her in each stroke, each character, each detail. Life exploded from the canvas. The importance of community, too. "I know a couple of people who own art galleries."

Her lips pursed. "Thanks, but I'm not ready to do that."

"You're ready," he encouraged. "Trust yourself. Your talent."

"I don't think I should do anything until Aaron and Dana get home."

Ryland hated to see Lucy holding back like this. "Think about it."

"I will. Would you like to see another one?" she asked to his surprise. "Not all of them are so cheery as this one. I went through a dark stage."

"Please." Looking at her work was like taking a peek inside her heart and her soul. He wanted to see more, as many paintings as she allowed him to see. "Show me."

Lucy would have never thought the best date ever would include mac and cheese, her nine-year-old nephew and a televised soccer game, but it had tonight. At first she'd been so nervous about showing Ryland her work, afraid of exposing herself like that and what he might think. He not only liked her paintings, but also understood them. Catching details most people overlooked.

She stood at the doorway to her nephew's bedroom while Ryland, by request, tucked Connor into bed.

The two talked about the game. Even though Fuego lost 0–1 to the Galaxy, both agreed it was a good game.

"They would have won if you'd been there," Connor said.

Ryland ruffled Connor's hair. "We'll never know."

"I can't wait to see you play."

As the soccer talk continued, Lucy leaned against the hallway wall.

Thanks to Ryland, her nephew was a happy kid again. Connor still missed his parents, but a certain professional soccer player had made a big difference. At least for now.

Lucy wondered if Connor realized when Ryland could play again he wouldn't be coaching. But if the Fuego played the Indianapolis Rage, maybe they could get tickets. She would have to check the match schedule.

Seeing Ryland play in person might be just the ticket to keep a smile on her nephew's face. Lucy had to admit she would like that, too.

"Good night, Connor." Ryland turned off the light in the bedroom. "I'll see you at practice tomorrow."

"'Night."

In the hallway, he laced his fingers with hers and led her into the living room. "I finally have you all to myself."

"We don't have to watch the post-match commentary?" she teased.

"I set the DVR so I wouldn't have to subject you to that." He pulled her against him. "But I will subject you to this."

Ryland's lips pressed against hers. His kiss was soft. Tender. Warm.

She leaned against him, only to find herself swept up in his arms. But his lips didn't leave hers.

He carried her to the couch and sat with her on his lap. Lucy wrapped her arms around him. Her breasts pressed against his hard chest.

As she ran her hands along his muscular shoulders and wove her fingers through his hair, she parted her lips. She wanted more of his kisses, more of him.

The pressure of his mouth against hers increased, full of hunger and heat. Her insides felt as if they were melting.

Ryland might be a world-class soccer player, but he was a world-class kisser, too.

Pleasurable sensations shot through her. Tingles exploded. If she'd been confused about the definition of chemistry, she understood it now.

Thank goodness he had his arms around her or she'd be falling to the floor, a mass of gooey warmth. Not that she was complaining. She clung to him, wanting even more of his kisses.

Slowly Ryland loosened his hold on her and drew the kiss to an end. "Told you this would be fun."

"You did." A good thing he wasn't going to be around long enough or this could become habit forming. Her chest tightened.

Lucy couldn't afford for anything about Ryland to become habit. She couldn't allow herself to get attached.

Neither of them was in a place to pursue a relationship. Neither of them could commit to anything long-term.

This was about spending time together in the short-term and having fun. And sharing some very hot kisses.

That had to be enough. Even if a part of her was wishing there could be...more.

CHAPTER ELEVEN

As THE days passed, the temperature warmed. The sun stayed out longer. The Defeeters won more games than they lost. But Lucy wasn't looking forward to the end of spring. She didn't want Ryland to leave.

Being with him was exciting. Wicksburg no longer seemed like a boring, small town as they made the most of their time together. Practice twice a week. Dinner with Connor. Lunch when her work schedule or his physical therapy allowed. When she was alone, her painting flourished with heightened senses and overflowing creativity.

After Mr. and Mrs. James returned from their vacation, they became fixtures at games and invited everyone to dinner following a practice.

That Monday evening, a bird chirped in a nearby cherry tree in the Jameses' backyard. The cheery tune fit perfectly with the jubilant mood. The boys kicked a soccer ball on the grass while Cupcake chased after them barking.

Standing on the patio, Lucy watched the boys play.

"Connor reminds me of his father," Mrs. James said. She wore her salt-and-pepper hair in a ponytail, a pair of jeans and a button-down blouse. "Though he's a little taller than Aaron was at this age."

"Connor's mom is tall." Lucy glanced at Mrs. James. "Thank you for having us over tonight."

"Our pleasure. It's so nice to have children here." She stared at the boys running around. "I've been telling Ryland to settle down so I can have grandchildren to spoil, but that boy has only one thing on his mind."

"Soccer," Lucy said at the same time as his mother.

Mrs. James eyed her curiously. "You know him well."

Lucy shifted her weight between her feet. "He's been helping me with the team."

"And going out with you." Mrs. James smiled. "Hard to keep things secret in a town Wicksburg's size."

They hadn't tried hiding anything. The more people who knew they were going out, the better. Lucy wanted nothing more than to enjoy her time with Ryland, but she felt as if she was trying to hold on to the wind. He would be blowing out of her life much too soon.

"It's so nice Ryland is with someone who knew him before he became famous," Mrs. James said.

"He was always a star player around here."

Ryland shouted something to the boys. Laughter filled the air.

"Yes, but he thinks of himself as a footballer, nothing else," Mrs. James explained. "Ryland needs to realize that there's a life for him off the pitch, too. I hope being here and getting reacquainted with you and others will help him see that."

"Soccer is his only priority." Lucy had been reminding herself that for days now. All the smiles, laughter and kisses they shared would be coming to an end. But she didn't want to turn into a sighing lump because he was leaving. "He's not interested in anything else."

"I wonder if soccer would be as important to him if he thought there was somewhere else he belonged."

I liked being part of a team. It didn't matter that I lived in a dumpy apartment on the wrong side of town or was poor or got beat up all the time. When I put on that jersey, I fit in.

Lucy remembered what he'd told her. "Belonging is important to him, but Ryland doesn't think he belongs in Wicksburg."

Mrs. James's eyes widened. "You've talked about this?"

Lucy hoped she wasn't opening a can of worms for Ryland, but his mother seemed genuinely concerned. "A little."

"That's a start." Mrs. James's green eyes twinkled with pleasure. "It's going to take Ryland time to realize where he belongs, and that he's more than he thinks he is."

"Maybe when he gets back to Phoenix." Lucy's chest tightened. "He doesn't have much time left here."

"He can always come back."

Lucy nodded. She hoped Ryland would return after the MLS season ended, but that was months away.

"Well, I'd better finish getting the taco bar ready," Mrs. James said. "The boys must be starving."

"What can I do to help?" Lucy asked.

"Enjoy yourself."

As Mrs. James walked away, Cheryl came up. She held an iPad. "Getting on the mother's good side is smart. I should have done that with my mother-in-law."

"It's not too late," Lucy said.

"Well, the divorce papers haven't been filed yet. But I don't want to talk about my sorry situation." Cheryl showed Lucy an article from a U.K. tabloid's website. "Guess this is what happens when you're with one of the hottest footballers around."

Lucy stared at the iPad screen full of pictures of her and Ryland. "Why would they do this?"

Cheryl sighed. "Because it's so romantic."

Romantic, perhaps. But not…real. The photos made it appear as if Lucy and Ryland were falling for each other. Falling hard.

The top photograph was from the Defeeters' first game

when Ryland kneeled behind her and whispered in her ear, but it looked as if he were kissing her neck. The second showed them in a booth at the pizza parlor sitting close together and gazing into each other's eyes. The last one captured their quick congratulatory peck after the team's first win, but the photograph made it seem like a long, tongue shoved down each other's throats full-on make-out session. Okay, they'd had a couple of those, but not where anyone could see them let alone take a picture.

As Lucy read the article, the blood rushed from her head. The world spun. The pictures didn't imply a serious relationship. The words suggested an imminent engagement.

Oh, no. This was bad. "I can't believe this."

"I didn't realize things were so serious."

"Me, neither." Ryland wasn't going to like this. Lucy re-read a paragraph. "They call me a WAG. Is that a British euphemism for hag or something?"

Cheryl laughed. "WAG stands for Wives and Girlfriends. Many women aspire to be one."

The acronym wasn't accurate. Surprisingly the thought of being Ryland's girlfriend didn't sound so bad. Unease slithered down Lucy's spine. She knew better to think that way. Dating Ryland didn't include being his girlfriend. Except everyone reading the article... "I hope people don't believe all this."

"You and Ryland care about each other. That's all that matters."

Care.

Yes, Lucy cared about Ryland. She cared...a lot.

As she stared at one of the photographs, a deeper attraction and affection for Ryland surfaced, accompanied by a sinking feeling in her stomach.

Oh, no. She'd been ignoring and pretending certain feelings didn't exist, but the article was bringing all that emotion out. She couldn't deny the truth any longer.

Lucy didn't just care about Ryland.

I love him.

The truth hit her like a gallon of paint dropped on her head. She'd fallen in love with Ryland James. Even though she'd known all the reasons why she shouldn't.

Stupid, stupid, stupid.

"You look pale," Cheryl said. "Are you okay?"

"I don't know," Lucy admitted. "I really don't know."

Ryland had pursued her. She'd pretended she couldn't be caught, but she'd been swept up by his charm and heart the minute he'd turned them on her.

Lucy wanted people to be honest with her, but she'd lied to herself about how safe it was to date Ryland, to hang out with him, to kiss him.

"Don't let a gossip column bother you. Talk to Ryland about it," Cheryl suggested. "I'm sure he's dealt with this before."

Gossip, yes. But Lucy wasn't sure how many women had fallen in love with him. She couldn't imagine being the first, but she wasn't sure she wanted to know the number of women who had gone down this same path.

Talk to Ryland about it.

She'd experienced a change of heart about wanting a relationship. Maybe he'd had one, too. And if not...

No. This wasn't a crush. Her feelings weren't one-sided. His kisses were proof of that as was his wanting to spend time with her. He had feelings for her. She knew he did.

Lucy had shared her secrets and art with him. How hard could it be to tell him she'd lost her heart to him, too?

She would talk to Ryland and see where their feelings took them.

* * *

After dinner, Ryland carried in the leftovers from the taco bar while a soccer match between kids and adults was being fought to determine bragging rights.

In the kitchen, he set the pan of ground beef on the counter. "That's the last of it."

His mother handed him a plastic container. "I like Lucy."

"So do I."

"Good, because it's about time you got serious with a woman."

Ryland flinched. He stared at his mom in disbelief. "Who said anything about getting serious?"

"Your father and I aren't getting any younger. We'd like grandkids while we can still get around and play with them. You and Lucy would have cute babies."

"Whoa, Mom." Ryland held up his hands, as if that could stop a runaway train like his mom. "I like Lucy. That's a long way from having babies with her. I need to focus on my career."

His mom shrugged. "A soccer ball won't provide much comfort after you retire."

He spooned the meat into the container. "I'll settle down once I stop playing."

"That's years away."

Ryland covered the ground beef with a lid. "I hope so."

"That's not what your mother wants to hear."

"It's the truth," he admitted. "If I put down any kind of roots, I'm not going to be able to finish out my career the way I want to."

"A woman like Lucy won't wait around forever. She won't have to in a town like Wicksburg." His mom filled a plastic Ziploc baggie with the leftover shredded cheese. "While you're off playing football and partying with WAG wannabes, another man will sweep Lucy off her feet. She'll have a ring on her finger before Christmastime."

Ryland clenched his hands. Wait a minute. His mom had no idea what she was saying. "Lucy doesn't want a ring. Not from me or anyone else."

"You sound confident."

"I am," he admitted. "We talked about it."

"It?"

"Relationships. Lucy and I are on the same page." He wished his mom wasn't sticking her nose into his business. He kept his social life private so she wouldn't know what was going on. "I can't be thinking about a relationship right now because of soccer. Lucy doesn't want to be entangled by any guy while she's taking care of Connor."

His mom studied him. "So when you go back to Phoenix..."

"It's over."

"And when you come back?"

"You and Dad can visit me," Ryland said. "I've worked too hard to get out of Wicksburg."

"You ran away."

"I left to play soccer."

His mother took a deep breath then exhaled slowly. "You're an adult and capable of making your own decisions, but please, honey, think about what you may be giving up if you leave town, leave Lucy, and never look back."

He picked up the container of meat and placed it in the refrigerator. "You're way off base here, Mom."

"Maybe I am, but one of these days you're going to realize soccer isn't the only thing in the world. I'd like for you to have a life outside the game in place when that happens."

"You just want me back in Wicksburg raising a bunch of kids."

"I want you to be happy."

"I am happy." So what if a lot of his happiness right now had to do with Lucy? Their dating was only for the short-term. They both agreed. His mother was wrong. This was for the best. "I know what I'm doing. I know what I want."

And that didn't include Wicksburg or...Lucy.

Later that evening, after everyone had left, Lucy sat with Ryland on his parents' patio. Mr. James was showing Connor his big-screen TV while Mrs. James gave Cupcake a bath after the dog jumped into a garbage can.

Ryland leaned back in his chair. "The boys enjoyed themselves."

"Their parents, too." Lucy had thrown herself into playing soccer. A way to put a game face on, perhaps?

"Cheryl showed me an article from a U.K. tabloid tonight." Lucy held up the display screen of her smartphone. "It's about...us."

Heaven help her, but she liked saying the word "us." Ryland had to see how good they were together.

He took the phone and used his finger to scroll through the words. "This happens all the time. Don't let it bother you."

He sounded so nonchalant about the whole thing. "You don't mind that total strangers halfway across the globe are reading about us?"

"It's not about minding." As Ryland laced his fingers with hers, tingles shot up her arm. "Football is almost like a religion in other countries. Fans follow their favorite players' every move. If someone tweets that a star player is at the supermarket buying groceries, hundreds of people might show up in minutes. This article is no different than others they've published about me and other players."

"But you don't play over there anymore."

"I did," he said. "I could go back someday."

So far away. Lucy felt a pang in her heart. She didn't want him to leave. Not to Phoenix. Not anywhere.

She took a deep breath to calm her nerves. "The article

makes it read like we're seriously dating, practically engaged."

"But we're not."

Ryland sounded so certain. No hesitation. No regret.

Lucy searched his face for a sign that he'd had a change of heart like her, but she saw nothing. Absolutely nothing to suggest he felt or wanted…more.

That frustrated her. She wanted him to be her boyfriend. The guy should want her to be his girlfriend.

Ryland put his arm around her. "This can be hard to deal with when you're not used to it. But it's how the game is played. You have to ignore it."

Lucy didn't want to ignore it. She wanted the article to be true. She wanted to be a WAG. Ryland's WAG. Not only his girlfriend, she realized with a start. But his…wife.

Mrs. Ryland James.

Lucy suppressed a groan. This was bad. Horrible. Tragic. *No promises. No guarantees. No sex.*

"Hey, don't be sad." Ryland caressed her face with his hand. "It's just a stupid article full of gossip and lies. Nothing to worry about."

His words were like jabs with a pitchfork to Lucy's heart. The more he downplayed the article, the more it bothered her. And hurt.

Irritation burned. At Ryland. At herself.

Forget about telling him how she felt. She wasn't going to give him the satisfaction of knowing how much she cared about him when he didn't or wouldn't admit how he felt about her.

Annoyed at the situation and at him, she raised her chin. "I'm not worried. I just wanted to make sure this wouldn't damage the Ryland James brand."

* * *

The next day, Ryland took Cupcake on a walk around the neighborhood without the boot, per his doctor's orders. He'd chosen this time because he knew Lucy had a call with a client and wouldn't see him.

He didn't know what was going on with her. She'd given off mixed signals last night. Her good-night kiss suggested she was into him. But her attitude about the tabloid article made him think she might be getting tired of him and unsettled by that side of his fame.

Ryland didn't know what her reaction to his getting the boot off would be.

The little gray dog ran ahead, pulling against the leash.

"Are you ready for me to go back to Phoenix, Cupcake?"

The dog ignored him and sniffed a bush.

"I'm not." He had to leave, but what he and Lucy had together was going to be hard to give up. More time with Lucy would be nice. More than nice. Too bad he couldn't go there or anywhere on the other side of nice. "But I'm not going to have a choice."

His cell phone rang. He pulled it from his pocket and glanced at the touch screen. Blake. About time. Ryland had left him a message last night.

"Did you plant the story about me and Lucy?" he asked.

"Hello to you, too." Blake sounded amused. "Yes, I'm doing well. Thanks for asking."

Ryland watched Cupcake sniff a patch of yellow and pink flowers. "Was it you?"

"No," Blake admitted. "That's not to say I didn't have a suggestion for the person who did."

Ryland knew it. The PR firm had to be involved. But Blake would never give him firm details. At least he hadn't in the past when something like this occurred. "Why?"

"Your future with Fuego isn't a sure thing," he said. "A serious girlfriend will help your image. Bad Boy Ryland James getting serious with a hometown girl. It sends the message you're maturing and getting out of the party scene."

Ryland pulled Cupcake away from a rose bush with thorns. "You're reaching for something that isn't there."

"I spoke with both your coach and Fuego's owner," Blake said. "Settling down is the best thing you can do right now."

"You're sounding a lot like my mom."

"Your mom's a smart woman."

Ryland looked around to see if anyone was on the street. Empty. "Lucy and I aren't serious."

"A big, sparkling diamond engagement ring from Tiffany & Co. will change all that."

He felt a flash of something, almost a little thrill at the thought of proposing to Lucy. Must be a new form of nausea. "Yeah, right. I'll catch a flight to Chicago tonight and go buy one."

"Indianapolis is closer," Blake said. "They have a store there according to their website."

"You're joking, right? Otherwise you've lost your mind."

"You said you wanted to play in the MLS," he said. "I'm making that happen for you."

"By lying."

"It's called stretching the truth," Blake said. "Let people see you buy an engagement ring. They can make their own assumptions."

"Lucy would never go for something like this."

"She'll be thrilled. Anyone who looks at those photographs can tell she's as crazy about you as you are about her."

"Crazy, maybe. But not in…" Ryland couldn't bring himself to say the word. "I like her." A lot. More than he'd ever thought possible. "But that doesn't mean I'm ready to get… serious."

Okay, so he'd thought about summer break and time off

when he could be with Lucy and Connor. And Manny, the fat cat, too.

But Ryland had realized doing anything more than thinking about the future was stupid. He needed to focus, to prove himself, to play...

"Her life is in Wicksburg. At least as long as she's taking care of Connor," Ryland said. "My life is in Phoenix."

"You don't sound so excited about that anymore."

"I am." Wasn't he? Of course, he was. All this was messing with his head. "But Lucy can't spend the next year or so with us traveling back and forth between here and there, to see each other."

"You can afford it."

"Blake."

"Just playing devil's advocate."

"Be my advocate. That's what I pay you for."

"What do you want?"

Lucy. No, that wasn't possible. "I want to play again. Not the way I played last season with the Fuego, but the way I played over in the Premier League. When it...mattered to me. Working with the kids and Lucy reminded me how much I love the game. And how much I miss it."

"You don't sound the same as you did a month ago." Emotion filled Blake's voice. "For the first time in two years it sounds like the real Ryland James is back."

"Damn straight, I am." But he couldn't get too excited. Thinking about leaving Lucy left a football-size hole in his chest.

But what could Ryland do? He had a team to play for, a job to do. His goal had always been to escape Wicksburg, not move back and marry a hometown girl.

Whoa. Where had that come from? Marriage had always been a four-letter word to him.

"The team's training staff is itching to work with you,"

Blake said. "They've been concerned about your training and conditioning."

"They'll be pleasantly surprised."

"Exactly what I hoped you'd say." Blake sounded like he was smiling. "My assistant can make your travel arrangements to Phoenix when you're ready."

Ryland's stomach knotted. He should be ready to leave now after weeks in Wicksburg, but Phoenix didn't hold the same appeal for some reason. "I see the orthopedist this afternoon."

"I hope we hear good news."

We. The only "we" that had come to matter to Ryland was him and Lucy. Uh, Lucy and the Defeeters, that is. They were a package. Emotion tightened his throat. "I'll let you know."

Face it. What could he do? No matter how wonderful Lucy might be, Ryland wasn't picket-fence material, even if he could now understand the appeal of a committed, monogamous relationship. Marriage wasn't a goal of his. He had a career to salvage. The longer he stuck around playing at having a relationship, the deeper things would get and he might end up hurting Lucy.

Ryland knew what he had to do. Get the hell out of Wicksburg. And get out fast before he did any more damage than he'd already done.

CHAPTER TWELVE

OUT on the field Wednesday afternoon, Lucy glanced at her watch. Fifteen minutes until the end of today's practice. Strange. Ryland had yet to show up or call. She glanced at the parking lot, but didn't see his father's blue truck.

Even though he'd annoyed her on Monday night, she still wanted to see him. She hoped nothing was wrong. He'd bowed out of dinner last night. After Connor went to bed, she'd used the time to paint.

Marco passed the ball to Tyler. Connor, playing defense, stole the ball and kicked it out of bounds.

Lucy blew the whistle. "Push-ups for the entire team if the ball goes out again."

The boys groaned.

She scooped up the ball and tossed it onto the field. Play continued.

"You're doing great, coach."

Her toes curled at the sound of Ryland's voice. She glanced over her shoulder. He walked toward her in a T-shirt and shorts and…

She stared in shock at the tennis shoe on his right foot. "Your boot. It's gone."

"I no longer need it."

"That's great." And then she realized what that meant. With his foot healed, he would return to Phoenix. Her heart sank, but she kept a smile on her face. Pride kept her from showing how much he'd gotten to her. "I'm happy for you."

"Thanks." He stared at her with a strange look in his eyes. "I want to talk to the boys."

Her muscles tensed. Lucy had a feeling this might not be his usual end-of-practice pep talk. She blew the whistle.

The boys stopped playing and looked her way. Smiles erupted on their faces when they saw Ryland.

He motioned to them. "Everyone gather around."

The boys sat on the grass in front of Ryland. So did Lucy.

"Sorry I was late for practice, but I like what I saw out there," Ryland said. "Keep talking to each other, passing the ball and listening to your coach."

He winked at Lucy.

Her tight shoulder muscles relaxed a little.

"I appreciate how hard you're working. I know the drills we do can be boring, but they work. If you do them enough times at practice, you won't have to think about doing the moves in a game. It'll just happen."

"I can't wait until Saturday's match," Connor said.

"Me, either," Jacob agreed.

The other boys nodded.

Ryland dragged his hand through his hair. "I know you guys are going to play hard on Saturday. But I won't be there. My foot's better. It's time for me to return to my team."

Frowns met his words. Sighs, too. The disappointment on the boys' faces was clear. The kids talked over one another. A few were visibly shaken by the news.

Tears stung Lucy's eyes. She blinked them away. She needed to be strong for Connor and the team. "Let Ryland finish."

The boys quieted.

"I'm sorry I won't be able to be with you during those last two games," he said. "But Coach Lucy will do a great job."

She cleared her dry throat. "Why don't we thank Ryland for all his help with the team?"

The boys shouted the Defeeters' cheer, but the words lacked the same enthusiasm shown on game day. Their hearts weren't in it.

Lucy didn't blame them. Her heart was having a tough time, too. She couldn't believe Ryland hadn't told her about leaving before he'd told the boys. He could have called if he hadn't had time. Even sent a text. But then she remembered the all-too-familiar words.

No promises. No guarantees.

Lucy couldn't be angry with him. Disappointed, yes. But Ryland hadn't played her. He hadn't lied. She'd known all along he was leaving. So did the boys and their parents. She just wasn't ready for the reality of it.

But this couldn't be goodbye. Even if he wasn't willing to admit it, they'd had too much fun, gotten to know each other too well for their dating to simply end. Of that, she was certain. They would stay in contact and see each other...somehow.

While Ryland said goodbye to each boy personally, she gathered up the equipment. As they finished, the boys ran off the field toward their parents.

Finally it was Connor's turn. He threw himself against Ryland and held on tight.

Her nephew's distress clogged Lucy's throat with emotion. She hoped this didn't put him back into a funk. He'd been handling his parents' deployment much better recently. Ryland might have been part of their lives for only a short time, but Connor had already gotten attached.

As Ryland spoke to her nephew, Connor wiped his eyes. This was one more difficult goodbye for the nine-year-old. But it wouldn't be a forever kind of goodbye. Ryland wouldn't do that to the kid, to his bud.

Someone touched Lucy's arm.

"Marco is in the car pouting. He told me Ryland is leaving," Suzy said. "I take it you didn't know."

"I knew he would be leaving. I just didn't know when," Lucy admitted.

"Cheryl showed me that article. His leaving won't change anything between you. You'll see each other. Every chance you can get."

Lucy nodded, hoping that was true.

"I'm going to take Marco to the pizza parlor for dinner. I'll take Connor with us," Suzy said. "You need some alone time with Ryland."

Yes, Lucy did. "I'll meet you there."

"If not, you can pick Connor up at my house."

She appreciated Suzy's thoughtfulness. "Thanks so much."

Suzy winked. "Don't do anything I wouldn't do."

Lucy could imagine what Suzy would want to do. If only she were that brave...

All Lucy could think about was how much she would miss Ryland, his company and his kisses. The memories would have to suffice until they saw each other again.

Ryland finished talking with Connor and sent him over to Lucy. She hugged her nephew and explained the plans for the evening.

Connor nodded, but the sadness in his eyes made her think he was simply going through the motions. Still, he hadn't said no. Being with Marco and having pizza, soda and video games might help Connor feel better.

Lucy watched Suzy walk off the field with an arm around Connor.

"He's upset," Ryland said, sounding almost surprised.

"He's had to say goodbye to his parents and now you," Lucy explained. "That's a lot for a nine-year-old boy to deal with."

"He'll rally."

Eventually. "So when are you leaving?"

"Tonight."

The air whooshed from her lungs. "That soon?"

"You knew I'd be leaving."

"Yes, I did." She kept her voice steady. Even though she was trembling inside, getting emotional would be bad. "But I thought I'd find out before everyone else."

She expected an apology or to hear him say this wasn't really goodbye because they would see each other soon.

"I have to go."

No apology. Okay. "You want to go."

A muscle twitched at his jaw. "Yeah, I do. I'm a soccer player. I want to play."

"I was thinking Connor and I could come and watch you play against the Rage when you come to Indianapolis."

"That would be—" Ryland dragged his hand through his hair "—not a good idea."

His words startled her. "Connor wants to see you play. So do I."

"I'm going to be busy."

"Too busy to say hello to us?"

"I need to focus on my career," Ryland said, his voice void of emotion. "I don't want a long-distance relationship or a girlfriend. I thought we were clear—"

"You can't tell me the time we spent together didn't mean anything to you." Hurt, raw and jagged, may have been ripping through her, but anger sounded in her voice. Lucy didn't care. She'd fallen in love with Ryland. She believed with her whole heart that he had feelings for her, too. "Or all those kisses."

"You know I like you," he said.

"Like." A far cry from love.

"Nothing more is possible."

Lucy stared down her nose. "Maybe not for you."

His gaze narrowed. "You said you weren't ready for a relationship or a boyfriend."

"I wasn't, but you showed me how good things could be. You opened me up to the possibility."

"I…" He stared at the grass. "I'm sorry, but I don't think something more between us would work out."

"It would." Her eyes didn't waver even though he wasn't looking at her. "I think you know it, too."

His gaze jerked up.

"You've admitted we're good together," she added.

"Chemistry."

"It's not just physical."

"We were never that physical."

"Sex is the easy part. Everything else is a lot harder."

"If we can't even manage the sex part, then we're not going to be able to handle anything else."

Ryland might like her. He might even care for her. But he would downplay whatever he felt because it would be too hard for him to deal with. Distancing himself rather than admitting how he felt would be much easier. He liked being a famous footballer. Soccer was safe. What he'd found here in Wicksburg with her wasn't.

Lucy took a deep breath. "You're scared."

"I'm not scared of you," he denied.

"You're scared of yourself and your feelings because there might be something more important in your life than soccer."

"That's crazy."

"No, it's not." Sympathy washed over her. "I've felt the same way myself. Not wanting to take any risks so I wouldn't get hurt."

He shook his head. "Did you take some headers with the boys during practice?"

Lucy wasn't about to be distracted. She pursed her lips. "I

know you. Better than you realize. I'm not deluding myself. I'm finally being honest with you. But it's too late."

"I know you're upset. I have time before my flight. I can drive you home."

"No." The force of the word stunned her as much as Ryland. She almost backed down, but realized she couldn't. Dragging this out any longer wouldn't be good for either one of them. It was obvious he was pushing her away. Ryland wasn't ready to step onto the pitch and take the kickoff from her. She'd thought he was different, but he wasn't. Not really.

If he couldn't be honest with himself, how could he ever be honest with her? Bottom line, he couldn't. Even though her heart was splintering into tiny pieces, she needed to let him go.

"It's time we said goodbye." She would make this easy on him. Lucy took a deep breath. "Thank you your help with the team and Connor. You've taught me a lot. More than I expected to learn. Good luck. I hope you have a great career and a very nice life."

His nostrils flared. "That's it?"

That was all he wanted to hear from her. He wasn't about to say what she needed to hear. That he…cared. And even though she was positive he did, he couldn't say it.

Her heart pounded in her throat. Her lower lip quivered.

Hold it together. She didn't want him to see her break down. "Yeah, that's it."

Time to get out of here. Lucy gripped the equipment bag. She forced her feet to move across the field, but it wasn't easy. Her tennis shoes felt more like cement blocks. Each step took concentration. She wasn't sure she would make it all the way to her car.

Her insides trembled. Her hands shook. She thought nothing could match the heartache and betrayal of her husband and best friend. But the way she felt about Ryland…

I really do love him.

A sob wracked through her. Tears blurred her vision. She gripped the equipment bag until her knuckles turned white and her fingernails dug into her palms.

"Lucy," he called after her.

She forced her feet to keep walking.

Even though Lucy was tempted, she didn't look back. She couldn't. Not with the tears streaming down her face. And not when Ryland wasn't ready to admit the truth.

Saturday evening in Phoenix, Ryland stood next to the wall of floor-to-ceiling windows in his condominium. He rested his arm against the glass and stared at the city lights.

What a day.

He'd gotten an assist as an eighty-fourth-minute substitute. He hadn't expected any playing time his first game back, but was happy contributing to the 2–1 win. Mr. McElroy had greeted Ryland with a handshake when he came off the pitch. Coach Fritz had said to expect more playing time during a friendly scheduled for Wednesday and next Saturday's game.

Ryland James was back in a big way. Blake agreed. His teammates, however, were more subdued about Ryland's return. A few handshakes, some glares.

He didn't blame them. He was captain of the team and had missed the start of the season because he'd goofed off and injured himself. Really bad form. Irresponsible. Like much of his behavior last season and the one before that. At practice, he'd apologized, but it would take time to build that sense of camaraderie. He was okay with that.

On the coffee table behind him, his cell phone beeped and vibrated with each voice message and text that arrived. People, including the bevy of beauties he'd left behind, were more than happy to welcome him home with invitations to

join them tonight at various clubs and parties, but he didn't
feel like going out and being social. Not when that scene
meant nothing to him now.

He kept thinking about Lucy and Connor and the rest of
the boys. The Defeeters had played a match today. Ryland
wondered how they did. He hoped they'd played well.

A part of him was tempted to call and find out. But ap-
peasing his curiosity might only hurt Lucy more. She'd been
angry with him. Hurting her hadn't been his intent, but he'd
done it anyway and felt like a jerk.

Ryland missed Lucy, longed to see her, hear her voice,
touch her, kiss her. But he needed to leave her alone. He
needed to respect her decision to say goodbye the way she
had. Respect her.

Aaron had warned her not to see him. Rightfully so. She
deserved more than Ryland could give her. Not that he'd offered her anything. But he'd thought she was okay with that.
Instead, she'd gotten upset at him. Told him he was scared.

Yeah, right.

All he'd tried to do was be honest with her. That had
worked out real well.

Regret poked at Ryland. Maybe he could have done things
better. Told her about his leaving differently. Said more... He
shook it off.

What was he supposed to do? Give Lucy an engagement
ring as Blake had suggested? Pretend he felt more for her
than he did? She deserved better than that.

His cell phone rang. The ringtone told him it was his
mother. "Hey, Mom. Did you watch the game?"

"No, we lost power."

Her voice sounded shaky. His shoulders tensed. "Is everything okay?"

"A tornado touched down near the elementary school. Your
father and I are okay, so is the house, but we don't know the

extent of the damage elsewhere," she said, her voice tight. "A tornado watch is still in effect. We're in the basement with Cupcake."

"Stay there. Keep me posted." Concern over Lucy and Connor overshadowed Ryland's relief at his parents being safe. A ball-size knot formed in his gut. "I love you, but I need to make a call right now."

"Lucy?"

"Yes."

"Let us know if she needs anything or a place to stay."

A potent mix of adrenaline and fear pulsed through him. He hit Lucy's cell-phone number on his contact list. Aaron's house was nowhere near the elementary school, but Ryland couldn't stop worrying. The Wicksburg soccer league played homes games at the elementary and middle schools. If the tornado touched down during match time…

There would have been sirens. No one would have been out at that point. Still he paced in front of the windows.

The phone rang.

Tornado warnings were all too common in the Midwest, especially in springtime. More than once he'd found himself in the bathroom of their apartment building in the tub with a mattress over him. But the twisters had always touched down on farmland, never in town.

On the fourth ring, Lucy's voice mail picked up. "I can't talk right now, but leave a message and I'll call you back."

The sound of her sweet voice twisted his insides. His chest hurt so badly he could barely breathe. He should be in Wicksburg, not here in Phoenix.

"Beep."

Ryland opened his mouth to speak, but no words came out. Not that he had a clue what he wanted to say if he could talk. He disconnected from the call.

Maybe she didn't have her cell phone with her. If she were at home...

He called the landline at Aaron's house. The phone rang. Again and again.

Ryland's frustration built; so did his fear. He clenched his hand. Why wasn't she answering? Where could she be?

"Hello?" a young voice answered.

He clutched the back of the couch. His fingers dug into the buttery leather. "Connor?"

"Ryland." The relief in the boy's voice reached across the distance and squeezed Ryland's heart like a vise grip. "I knew you wouldn't forget about us."

"Never." The word came from somewhere deep inside him, spoken with a voice he didn't recognize. "My mom called me about the tornado."

"Aunt Lucy and I got inside the closet in the basement with pillows, a couple flashlights and the phone. It's one of those old dial ones." His voice trembled. "I have my DS, too."

"Extra playing time for you," Ryland teased, but his words fell flat. "Can I talk to your aunt?"

"She's looking for Manny."

The fat cat always tried to escape whenever the door opened. But if he'd gotten out today... "Where is he?"

"I don't know. Aunt Lucy moved the car into the garage and thinks he could have slipped out because she was in a hurry," Connor said. "We couldn't find him after the warning sounded. The siren might have scared him."

Sounded like Manny wasn't the only one frightened by the noise. Poor kid. "Your aunt will find him."

The alternative, for both Lucy and Manny, was unacceptable. Ryland glanced at the clock. If he caught a red-eye to Chicago and drove... But he had a team meeting tomorrow. And would Lucy want him to show up uninvited in the morning?

"Aunt Lucy said she would be back soon," Connor said finally. "She waited until the siren stopped to go outside. She didn't want to leave me alone if it wasn't safe."

Lucy would never put her nephew at risk, but Ryland didn't like the thought of her outside in that kind of weather with a tornado watch still in effect.

Silence filled the line.

"You hanging in there, bud?" he asked.

"Yeah," Connor said. "But the flashlight died. It's kind of dark."

Ryland grimaced. "See if your DS gives off some light."

"That helps a little."

Being thousands of miles away sucked. "I wish I were there."

"Me, too. But even if you were, you still wouldn't get to see our last game next Saturday," Connor said.

"Why not?"

"The field was destroyed so the season is over with. No more soccer until fall. If then."

"Because of the tornado?" Ryland asked.

"Yeah. Marco's mom called earlier," Connor explained. "My school is gone. The fields. The middle school. Some of the houses around there, too."

Gone. Stunned, Ryland tried to picture it. He couldn't. "Are Marco and his family, okay?"

"Yeah, but a tree landed on their car. Marco's dad is mad."

"Cars can be replaced." People couldn't.

Lucy.

Ryland wanted her in the basement with Connor, not out looking for Manny.

Damn. He hated not being able to do anything to help. Not that Lucy would want *his* help. Still… He gripped the phone.

Images of his weeks in Wicksburg flashed through his mind like a slideshow. Lucy handing him a container of cookies, teaching her how to do the warm-up routine and drills, watching her coach during the first match, drinking slushies with the team after games, kissing her.

You said you weren't ready for a relationship or a boy-friend.

I wasn't, but you showed me how good things could be.

Things had been good. Great. If he could go back and do over his last day in Wicksburg...

But soccer had been the only thing on his mind. That and getting the hell out of town, running away as his mom had accused him of doing before.

A lump formed in his throat and burned like a flame.

"It's probably a good thing we can't play the last game." Connor's voice forced Ryland to focus on the present. "We got beat six–nothing today. Aunt Lucy said we were going through the motions and our hearts weren't in the game."

That was how Ryland had spent the last two years. He'd gotten tired of having to prove himself over and over again. He'd lost his hunger, his drive and his edge. He'd acted out without realizing it or the reasons behind his actions—anger, unhappiness and pressure. But he hadn't figured out how self-destructive his behavior had become until he'd returned to Wicksburg. Lucy and the boys had been his inspiration and let him rediscover the joy of the game. He'd connected with them in a way he hadn't since leaving town as a teenager.

And Lucy...

She showed him it wasn't about proving things to others, but to himself.

"The Strikers would have killed us anyway," Connor continued, talking about the game that wouldn't be. He sounded more like himself, less scared. "Ten–nothing or worse."

Ryland may have gotten his soccer career back on track here, but he still had things to take care of in Wicksburg. He wasn't about to drop the ball again. "No way. The entire team has improved since that first match. The Strikers won by three goals. You need to play that game if only to prove you can challenge them."

"There's no field to play on."

"Come on." Ryland couldn't let those boys down after all they'd given him. He pictured each of their faces. In a short time, he'd learned their strengths and discovered their weaknesses. Secrets were hard to keep when you were nine and ten. He'd watched their skills improve, but also saw other changes like limbs lengthening and faces thinning. "That's not the Defeeter attitude."

"It was a big tornado."

And a big loss with the game today. Ryland took responsibility for that. The way he'd left, as if he could ride into town and then just leave again without anyone noticing or being affected was selfish and stupid. "No worries, bud. I'll figure something out."

"Really?"

"Really." Ryland didn't hesitate. He would find the team a place to play next Saturday. "Is your aunt back?"

"No, but I don't know how to use call-waiting. I should get off the phone in case she needs to talk to me."

"Smart thinking. Tell your aunt to call me when she finds Manny." Ryland checked the time again. "I'll let you know where you're going to play against the Strikers."

"I wish you could be there if we get to play."

"So do I." A weight pressed down on Ryland. "There's no place I'd rather be than with you and the team and your aunt Lucy."

But it wasn't possible. Ryland had an away match next Saturday. He was supposed to get playing time. But he needed to be in Wicksburg with Lucy and the boys.

Just remember, actions speak louder than words.

Blake's words echoed through Ryland's mind. He straightened. He'd been so blind. What he wanted—needed—was right there in front of him. Not here in Phoenix, but in Wicksburg. He just hadn't wanted to see it.

But now...

Time to stop talking about what he wanted and make it happen.

For the boys.

And most importantly, with Lucy.

CHAPTER THIRTEEN

LUCY's arms, scratched and sore after digging through tree limbs and debris to reach a howling Manny, struggled to carry the squirming, wet cat with a flashlight in her hand down to the basement. The warning siren remained silent, but they would sleep downstairs to be on the safe side. "You need to go on a diet, cat."

"Aunt Lucy?" Connor called from the closet. "Did you find Manny?"

"I found him." She opened the door, happy to see her nephew safe, dry and warm. "Why is it so dark in there?"

"The flashlight stopped working."

Yet Connor had stayed, as she asked, even in the pitch-black when he had to be scared. Her heart swelled with pride and love for her nephew. Aaron and Dana were raising a great kid. "Sorry about that. The batteries must have been low."

"It's okay." He held up his glowing DS console. "I had a little light."

Manny pawed trying to get away from her. The cat looked like a drowned rat with his wet fur plastered against his body. "I think someone wants to see you."

Connor reached for the cat. "Where was he?"

"In the bushes across the street. I have a feeling he's had quite an adventure." Enough to last eight lives given the winds and flying debris the cat must have experienced. "I doubt he'll be so quick to dash outside again."

Connor cuddled Manny, who settled against her nephew's chest as if that were his rightful and only place of rest. At least until a better spot came along. "Oh, Ryland called."

Lucy's heart jolted. She hadn't expected to hear from him again. "When?"

"A little while ago." Connor rubbed his chin against the cat. Manny purred like a V-8 engine. "He wants you to call him back. He was worried about you finding Manny."

Lucy whipped out her cell phone. Service had been spotty due to the storm, but three bars appeared. She went to press Ryland's number.

Wait. Her finger hovered over the screen. Calling him back would be stupid. Okay, it was nice he was concerned enough to call and want to know about Manny. But this went beyond what was happening in Wicksburg today.

Lucy had been thinking about him constantly since he left town. She missed him terribly. She needed to get him off her mind and out of her heart. But she wouldn't ignore his request completely. That would be rude.

Lucy typed in a text message and hit Send. Now she could go back to trying to forget about him.

Early Monday morning, Ryland stood in the reception area of the Phoenix Fuego headquarters. He'd spent much of yesterday trying to figure how to help those affected by the tornado in Wicksburg. Money was easy to donate. But he wanted to do something for the team and Lucy.

Waiting, he reread the text she'd sent him.

Manny wet & hungry but fine.

Ryland had wanted to hear her voice to know she was okay. He'd received a six-word text, instead. Probably more than he deserved.

The attractive, young personal assistant, who was always cheering on the team during games, motioned to the door to her right. "Mr. McElroy will see you now."

"Thanks." Ryland entered the owner's office. The plush furnishings didn't surprise him. All the photos of children everywhere did. "I appreciate you seeing me on such short notice."

Mr. McElroy shook his hand. "You said it was important."

"Yes."

He pointed to a leather chair. "Have a seat."

Ryland sat. "A tornado rolled through my hometown on Saturday night."

"I heard about that on the news. No casualties."

"No, but homes, two schools and several soccer fields in town were destroyed," Ryland said. "The Defeeters, a U-9 Boys rec. team I worked with while I was home, has their final game of the season this Saturday, but nowhere to play. I want to find them, and all the teams affected by the tornado, fields so they can finish out their spring season. I'd also like to be on the sideline with the Defeeters when they play."

Mr. McElroy studied him. "This sounds important to you."

"Yes," Ryland said. "I'm who I am today because of the start I got in that soccer league. I owe them and the Defeeters."

Not to mention Lucy. He wanted a second chance with her. A do-over like young players sometimes received from refs when they made a bad throw-in or didn't quite get the ball over the line during kickoffs.

"That's thoughtful, but haven't you forgotten about the match against the Rage on Saturday night?"

Mr. McElroy's words echoed Blake's, but Ryland continued undeterred. "The Rage plays in Indianapolis. The stadium is a couple hours from Wicksburg. I know a way I can be at both games, but I'm going to need some help to pull it off. Your help, Mr. McElroy, and the owner of the Rage."

A tense silence enveloped the office. Ryland sat patiently waiting for the opportunity to say more.

"You've been nothing but a thorn in my side since I bought this team." Mr. McElroy leaned forward and rested his elbows on the desk. "Why should I help you?"

"Because it's the right thing to do."

"Right for the kids affected by the tornado?"

"And for us. Those kids are the future of soccer, both players and fans." Ryland spoke from his heart. The way Lucy would have wanted him to. "I know you don't want me on the team. I wasn't okay with that before. I am now. I don't care what team I'm on as long as I can play. But until the transfer window opens so you can loan me out across the pond, you need me as much as I need you."

Mr. McElroy's eyes widened. No doubt the truth had surprised him. "What kind of help are you talking about?"

Ryland explained his plan. "This is not only good for the players and the local soccer league, but it's also a smart PR move for the Fuego and Rage."

"Not smart. Brilliant. You can't buy that kind of publicity." Mr. McElroy studied him. "You're not the same player who left the club in March. What happened while you were away?"

"That U-9 team of boys taught me a few things about soccer I'd forgotten, and I met a girl who made me realize I'm more than just a footballer."

Smiling, Mr. McElroy leaned back in his chair. "You have my full support. I'll call the owner of the Rage this morning. Tell my assistant what you need to pull this off."

Satisfaction and relief loosened the knot in Ryland's gut. He stood. "Thank you, sir."

"I hope it all works out the way you planned," Mr. McElroy said.

"So do I."

Ryland had no doubt the soccer part would work, but he wasn't as confident about his plans for Lucy. He couldn't imagine his life without her.

She'd been right. Ryland had been scared. He still was. He just hoped it wasn't too late.

On Saturday, Lucy entered the training facility of the Indianapolis Rage. The MLS team had offered the use of their outdoor field for the final game of the Defeeters' spring soccer season against the Strikers.

Parents and players from both teams looked around in awe. The training field resembled a ministadium complete with lights, two benches and bleachers.

Lucy couldn't believe they were here.

When the soccer league president had offered the Defeeters an all-expenses-paid trip to Indianapolis to play their final game of the season, she thought Ryland was behind it because Fuego was playing the Rage that same day. But then she learned all youth soccer teams without fields to finish the spring season had been invited.

She hadn't known whether to feel relieved or disappointed.

Pathetic. No matter how hard she tried to push Ryland out of her mind and heart, he was still there. She wondered how long he would remain there—days, weeks, months…

Stop thinking about him.

Connor ran onto the field, his feet encased in bright yellow soccer shoes. The other kids followed, jumping and laughing, as if the damage back home was nothing more than a bad dream.

"This is just what we all needed after the tornado." Suzy took a picture of the boys standing on the center mark of the field. "A weekend getaway and a chance to end the soccer season in style."

"The hotel is so nice." Cheryl's house had been damaged

by the tornado. They were staying with Dalton's father, who had traveled with them for today's game. Maybe something good would come from all of this and they could work out their differences before the separation led to a divorce. "I can't wait for tonight. I've never been to a professional soccer game before."

Tickets to the Rage vs. Fuego match had been provided to each family. Much to the delight of the boys, who couldn't wait to see Ryland play. Connor was beside himself with excitement, positive his favorite player would be in the game for the entire ninety minutes.

Lucy hoped not. Watching Ryland play for only few minutes would be difficult, let alone the entire match. Hearing his name mentioned hurt. Connor talked constantly about Ryland. That made it hard to forget him.

Thing would get better. Eventually. She'd been in this same place before with Jeff. Except with Ryland the hurt cut deeper. Her marriage had never been a true partnership, but she'd felt that way with Ryland, in spite of the short time they'd been together.

She shook off the thought. The match will be a nice way to cap off the day.

The boys screamed, the noise deafening. Only one thing— one person—could elicit that kind of response.

Her throat tightened.

Ryland was here.

Emotions churned inside her.

"That man gets hotter each time I see him." Cheryl whistled. "But who are all his buddies?"

"Yowza," Suzy said. "If it gets any hotter in here, I think I'm going to need to fan myself."

"Am I a bad mom if I'm jealous of a bunch of eight- and nine-year-olds?" Debbie asked.

"I hope not, because I feel the same way," Cheryl replied.

Lucy kept her back turned so she wouldn't be tempted
o look at Ryland. But the women had piqued her curiosity.
"What are you talking about?"

"Turn around." Cheryl winked. "Trust me, you won't be
lisappointed."

Reluctantly, Lucy turned. She stared in disbelief. Nearly a
lozen professional soccer players with killer bodies and smil-
ng faces worked with the Defeeters and the Strikers, helping
he boys warm up and giving them pointers.

One Fuego player, however, stood out from all the others.
Ryland.

His dark hair was neatly combed, his face clean shaven.
He looked handsome in his Fuego uniform—blue, orange
nd white with red flames. But it was the man, not the ath-
ete, who had stolen her heart. A weight pressed down on her
chest, squeezing out what air remained in her lungs.

Suzy sent her a sympathetic smile. "This is a dream come
rue for the boys."

Cheryl nodded. "I think I've died and gone to heaven my-
elf."

Lucy had gone straight to hell. Hurt splintered her already-
ching heart. She struggled to breathe. She didn't even at-
empt to speak.

Everyone around her smiled and laughed. She wanted to
ry. If only he could see how good the two of them would be
ogether...

"Look at all the photographers and news crews," Suzy
aid.

Cheryl combed through her hair and pinched her cheeks.
"No wonder the league had us sign those photo releases."

The media descended on the field, but their presence didn't
listract the professional players from the kids. The boys, how-
ver, mugged for the cameras.

As the warm-up period drew to an end, the referee called

over the Strikers. That was Lucy's cue to get ready. She had player cards to show the ref and her clipboard with the starting lineup and substitution schedule so each boy would play an equal amount of time.

"We're taping the game." Debbie motioned to the bleachers where her husband adjusted a tripod. "For Aaron and Dana."

"Thanks," Lucy said.

The referee called the Defeeters over.

Nerves threatened to get the best of Lucy. But in spite of all the hoopla and media, this was still a rec. soccer game. She had no reason to interact with Ryland and wouldn't.

With her resolve in place, Lucy lined up the boys for the ref. Ryland stood near the Defeeters' bench.

Her heart rate careened out of control.

Oh, no. He was planning to be there during the match.

The ref excused the Defeeters. As she walked to the bench she looked everywhere, but at Ryland. Maybe if she didn't catch his eye or say—

"It's good to see you, Lucy," he said.

Darn. She cleared her dry throat. "The boys are so happy you're here."

"This is the only place I want to be."

The referee blew his whistle, saving her from having to speak with him.

The game was fast-paced with lots of action and scoring. At halftime with the score Defeeters two and Strikers three, Ryland talked to the boys about the game. With two minutes remaining in regulation time, Connor stole the ball from a defender and broke away up the left sideline. He crossed the ball in front of the goal. Dalton kicked the ball into the corner of the net.

Tie score!

The parents screamed. The boys gave each other high fives.

The Strikers pulled their goalie. A risky move, but they

wanted an extra player in the game. The offense hit hard after the kickoff, took a shot on goal, but missed.

Defeeters' turn. Marco took the ball. His pass to Dalton was stolen. The Strikers' forward headed down the field, but Connor sprinted to steal the ball. He kicked the ball down the line to Dalton, who passed it to Marco. The goal was right in front of him. All he had to do was shoot at the empty goal.

"Shoot," Ryland yelled. So did everyone else.

The referee blew his whistle. The game was over.

The Defeeters had tied the Strikers.

"Great job, coach," Ryland said to her. "You've come a long way.

But she had so much further to go, especially when it came to getting over him. She didn't smile or look at him. "Thanks."

"You boys played a great game," Ryland said to the excited boys gathered around him. "The best all season."

Lucy knew they would rather hear from him than her. She didn't mind that one bit.

Connor beamed. "You said we could challenge them. We did."

Ryland messed up the kid's hair. "You did more than that, bud."

The two teams lined up with the coaches at the end, followed by the professional players, and shook hands. Ryland and the other players passed out T-shirts to both teams, posed for pictures and signed autographs. Talk about a dream come true. And there was still the match to attend tonight.

She gathered up the balls and equipment. "Come on, Connor. We can go back to the hotel for a swim before the game."

Connor looked at Ryland then back at her.

Lucy's heart lodged in her throat. She knew that conspiratorial look of his.

"I'm riding back to the hotel with Marco and his family," Connor said.

"I told the boys we could stop for an after-game treat on the way back to the hotel," Suzy said.

"Slushies, slushies," the boys chanted.

Those had become the new Defeeter tradition. Thanks to Ryland. But he wasn't offering to take the team out today.

Lucy remembered. He had to prepare for the match against the Rage tonight.

She thought about offering to drive the boys herself, but from the look on Connor's face, he had his heart set on going with Marco. She couldn't ruin this magical day for him on the off chance Ryland might try to talk to her.

Time to act like an adult rather than a brokenhearted teenager. She raised her chin. "Sounds like fun. I'll meet you back at the hotel."

As the boys headed out, she followed them, eager to escape before Ryland—

"Lucy."

She kept walking, eyeing the exit.

"Please wait," Ryland said.

She stopped. Not because she wanted to talk to him, but because he'd helped her with the team. Five minutes. That was all the time he could have.

Ryland caught up to her. "You've been working hard with the boys."

"It's them, not me." She glanced back at the field. "I don't know what your part in making this happen was, but thank you. It meant a lot to the boys on both teams." She tried to sound nonchalant, but wasn't sure she was succeeding.

"I didn't do this only for them."

Her pulse accelerated.

"I'm sorry." His words came out in a rush. "The way I left was selfish. I was only thinking about myself. Not the boys.

Definitely not you. I never meant to hurt anyone, but I did. I hope you can forgive me."

The sincerity in his eyes and voice tugged at her heart. She had to keep her heart immune. She had to get away from him. "You're forgiven."

His relief was palpable. "Thank you. You don't know what that means to me."

She didn't want to know. Just being this close to him was enough to make her want to bolt. The scent of him surrounded her. She wanted to bottle some up to take home with her. *Not a good idea.* "I need to get back to the hotel. Connor…"

Ryland took a step closer to her. "He's stopping for a snack on the way back."

Lucy stepped back. "I still should—"

"Stay."

The one word was a plea and a promise, full of anxiety and anticipation. She tried not to let that matter, but it wasn't easy. "Why?"

"There's more I want to say to you."

She glanced around the stadium. Everyone seemed to have left. "Make it quick."

He took a deep breath. "Soccer has been the only thing in my life for so long. I defined myself as a footballer. Playing made me feel worthy. But I lost the love for the game. The past couple of years, I made some bad decisions. I had no idea why I was acting out so badly until I got to Wicksburg. I realized how unhappy I'd been trying to keep proving my-self with a new league, team and fans. Nothing satisfied me anymore. Working with the boys helped me discover what was missing. Soccer isn't only about scoring goals. I'd forgotten the value of teamwork. You made me realize I don't want soccer to be the only thing in my life. I want—I need—more than that. I need you, Lucy."

The wind whooshed from her lungs. She couldn't believe what he was saying.

"I know how important honesty is to you," he continued. "When I got to Phoenix, I realized you were right. I was scared. A coward. I wasn't being honest about my feelings. Not to you or myself. You mean so much to me. I'm finally able to admit it."

"I'm…touched. Really. But even if you're serious—"

"I am serious, Lucy." He took her hand in his. "More serious than I've ever been in my entire life. I was trapped by the expectations of others, the pressure, but you set me free. I'm more than just a soccer player. I don't want to lose you."

They way he looked at her, his gaze caressing her skin like a touch, brought tears to her eyes. She blinked them away. She couldn't lose sight of the truth.

Lucy took a deep breath. "We live in different worlds, different states. It would never work."

"I want to make it work."

"You know what happened with Jeff."

He nodded.

"Look at you," she said. "You're hot, wealthy, a superstar. Women want you. They fantasize about you. That's hard for me to handle."

"I know you've had some tough times in your life. We can't wash away everything that's happened before, but we can't dwell on it, either," he said. "Trust doesn't just happen. I can tell you all the right words you want to hear. That I'm not like Jeff. That I won't cheat. But what it really takes is a leap of faith. Are you willing to take that leap with me?"

Her heart screamed the answer it wanted her to say. Could she leap when her heart had been broken after spending only a few weeks with him? How could she not when Ryland was everything she'd dreamed about?

"When I was sick, people lied to me. The doctors, my parents, even Aaron. Maybe not outright lies, but untruths about the treatments, how I would feel and what I could do. I hated having to rely on people who couldn't be honest with me."

"So that's where your independent streak came from."

She nodded. "And then Jeff came along. He was honest with me, sometimes brutally so, but I liked that better than the alternative. I fell hard and fast only to find out he was nothing more than a lying, cheating jerk." She took a deep breath so she could keep going. "You've taught me so much and not only about soccer. Because of you I've learned I can accept help without feeling like a burden to someone. I've also learned I can forgive and trust again. I would love to take that leap with you. But I'm not sure I'm ready yet."

"I don't care how long it takes," he said. "I'll wait until you're ready."

"You're serious."

"Very." He kissed each of her fingers, sending pleasurable shivers up her arm. "I love you."

The air rushed from her lungs. She tried to speak, to question him, but couldn't.

Sincerity shone in his eyes. "I tried to pretend I didn't love you, but I'm no good at pretending when it comes to you."

Joy exploded inside her. She could tell they weren't just words. He meant them. Maybe taking the leap wouldn't be so hard. "I love you, too."

"That's the first step to taking the leap."

"Maybe the first two steps." Lucy kissed Ryland, a kiss full of hope and love and possibility. None of her dreams had come true so far, but maybe some…could.

Ryland pulled her against him. She went willingly, wrapping her arms around him. Her hand hit something tucked into the waistband of his shorts. It fell to the ground. She backed away.

A small blue box tied with a white ribbon lay on its side.

She recognized the packaging from ads and the movies. The box was from Tiffany & Co.

Her mouth gaped. She closed it. He really was serious.

His cheeks reddened. "If I told you that's where I keep my lucky penny, I'm guessing you won't believe me."

Shock rendered her speechless.

"It's nothing." He took a breath. "Okay, I'll be honest. It's something, but it can wait. You're not ready right now."

She placed her hand on his. "Maybe I'm more ready than I realized."

As he handed her the box, hope filled his eyes. "This is for you. Today. A year from now. Whenever you're ready."

Lucy untied the ribbon and removed the top of the box. Inside was a midnight blue, almost black, suede ring box. Her hand trembled so much she couldn't get the smaller box out. She looked up at him.

"Allow me." Ryland pulled out the ring box and opened it. A Tiffany-cut diamond engagement ring sparkled against the dark navy fabric. The words Tiffany & Co. were embossed in gold foil on the lid. "Nothing matters except being with you. I love you. I want to marry you, Lucy, if you'll have me."

She couldn't believe this was happening. She forced herself to breathe. All her girlhood fantasies didn't compare to the reality of this moment. Ryland James had asked her to marry him. He'd been honest to himself and to her. He was fully committed to making it work. Lucy's heart and her mind agreed on the answer. Make the leap? She had no doubt at all. "Yes."

He placed the ring on her finger. A perfect fit, the way they were a perfect fit together. "There's no rush."

"No, there isn't." The love shining in his eyes matched her own. "Aaron and Dana won't be home until next year."

"It might take me that long to convince your brother I'm good enough for you."

"Probably," Lucy teased. "But with Connor in your corner, it might take only six months."

"Very funny."

She stared at the ring. A feeling of peace coursed through her. "So this officially makes me a WAG."

Ryland brushed his lips across hers. "A *G* who will eventually become a *W*. But you're already an *M*."

"An *M*?" Lucy asked.

"Mine."

"I'll always be your *M*. As long as you're mine, too."

"Always," he said. "I think I may have always been yours without even realizing it."

"If you're trying to score…"

"No need. I already won." Ryland pulled her against him and kissed her again. "I love you, Lucy."

A warm glow flowed through her, making her heart sigh. "I love you."

* * * * *

So you think you can write?

Mills & Boon® and Harlequin® have joined forces in a global search for new authors.

It's our biggest contest yet—with the prize of being published by the world's leader in romance fiction.

Look for more information on our website:
www.soyouthinkyoucanwrite.com

So you think you can write?
Show us!

MILLS & BOON Book Club

2 Free Books!

Get your free books now at
www.millsandboon.co.uk/freebookoffer

Or fill in the form below and post it back to us

THE MILLS & BOON® BOOK CLUB™—HERE'S HOW IT WORKS: Accepting your free books places you under no obligation to buy anything. You may keep the books and return the despatch note marked 'Cancel'. If we do not hear from you, about a month later we'll send you 5 brand-new stories from the Cherish™ series, including two 2-in-1 books priced at £5.49 each, and a single book priced at £3.49*. There is no extra charge for post and packaging. You may cancel at any time, otherwise we will send you 5 stories a month which you may purchase or return to us—the choice is yours. *Terms and prices subject to change without notice. Offer valid in UK only. Applicants must be 18 or over. Offer expires 31st January 2013. **For full terms and conditions, please go to www.millsandboon.co.uk/freebookoffer**

Mrs/Miss/Ms/Mr (please circle) _____

First Name _____

Surname _____

Address _____

_____

_____ Postcode _____

E-mail _____

Send this completed page to: Mills & Boon Book Club, Free Book Offer, FREEPOST NAT 10298, Richmond, Surrey, TW9 1BR

Find out more at
www.millsandboon.co.uk/freebookoffer

Visit us Online

0712/S2YEA